PRAISE FOR
THE NIGHT THE RIVER WEPT

"*The Night the River Wept* is a pag[e]
town secrets and the far-reaching
wisdom, Lo Patrick weaves an un[...]
love, and second chances—and proves herself as a compelling new
voice in Southern fiction."

—Kristy Woodson Harvey, *New York Times*
bestselling author of *The Summer of Songbirds*

"In *The Night the River Wept*, Arlene is a frustrated, lonely housewife
until she finds a job at the local police station bagging evidence. There
she immerses herself in a decades-old murder, determined to solve
the crime. Lo Patrick writes an original and moving tale brimming
with mystery, heartache, and wit. Sure to be a Southern fiction favorite, Arlene's journey pulls the reader in and doesn't let go."

—Rochelle Weinstein, *USA Today* bestselling author
of *This Is Not How It Ends* and *What You Do to Me*

"Lo Patrick introduces us to vivid characters populating an authen-
tic small Georgia town, their lives tangled like kudzu vines. *The
Night the River Wept* is an intriguing mystery that will have you
turning pages until the wee hours of the morning."

—Beth Duke, bestselling author of *It All Comes Back
to You*, *Tapestry*, and *Dark Enough to See the Stars*

"Haunting and unputdownable, *The Night The River Wept* is a gritty rendering of small-town tragedy and the far-reaching shadows it casts. Lo Patrick writes a stubbornly resilient heroine determined to untangle the secrets of a forgotten past and skillfully leads the reader along a twisty path to an unexpected yet satisfying ending!"

—Laura Barrow, author of *Call the Canaries Home*

"Lo Patrick's sophomore novel, set in a small Southern town, explores what drives us to murder and how solving the mysteries of the past can captivate and even unite strangers. The tragic killing of three boys has repercussions that resonate through the town of Faber and in the heart of Arlene. On a journey of personal growth and redemption that pulls the reader along, Arlene becomes obsessed with solving the long cold case and with her neighbors and coworkers who still live with the trauma of it. This is a gripping portrayal of a small town where everyone has their secrets and the lines between guilty and innocent blur."

—Quinn Connor, author of *Cicadas Sing of Summer Graves*

"Smart, sassy, and utterly heartbreaking, this seductive Southern novel has to be my favorite mystery of the year. I rooted for Arlene as, struggling with her own loss, she becomes obsessed with the Broderick boys and their story. *The Night the River Wept* is a brave book that explores how difficult it can be to escape the past."

—Emily Critchley, author of *One Puzzling Afternoon*

ALSO BY LO PATRICK

The Floating Girls

the
night
the river
wept

a novel

LO PATRICK

sourcebooks
landmark

Published by Sourcebooks Landmark, an imprint of Sourcebooks
P.O. Box 4410, Naperville, Illinois 60567-4410
(630) 961-3900
sourcebooks.com

Cataloging-in-Publication Data is on file with the Library of Congress.

Printed and bound in the United States of America.

LSC 10 9 8 7 6 5 4 3 2 1

A CONDEMNED MAN

I HAD DREAMS ABOUT KILLING them since the day I met her. I couldn't look at 'em without thinking about it. They were always with her, always; all of 'em looked alike too—same hair, same noses, same blank look on their faces like they were ready to be filled up. She didn't want them around anyway. She was always trying to figure out how to get rid of them. She didn't care what happened to those kids; she just didn't want to be the one to do it.

She didn't even cry. I didn't feel bad about it, because she wasn't even crying. I don't think I woulda felt bad even if she did, but I had a mind to think I did her a favor.

I've always known where to circle. I figure I'm a bit like a buzzard. The day I met her I could already smell them dead.

1

We ended up buying a place on Lake Patton. It wasn't how I would have had it, but I'm only one half of the equation. It's a stucco number with a large backyard. I've never felt right in it, kind of too small or too directionless in its massive rooms with their molding and plush cream-colored carpets. It's a fine house; I'm not complaining, but it tells no story, certainly not the story of me and Tommy. The split-level had my mark on it, but we took off out of there a while back. The stucco house had more room for the kids—not ours, but the ones we took in. In that way, the house had a good feeling. It welcomed us, them, everyone.

I get a chance to reflect now. I don't see any of those people anymore, and that's okay. It makes the thinking clearer. It's a lot to explain, even to myself some days, but now I have time to contemplate life's rich pageant, so stuffed full of events that it would take ten lifetimes to fully experience a single one of them. And I do think about it. Especially the boys.

The Brodericks. The cold ground ate them like a snack. It was casual for the earth, like tearing a small package of ketchup, dotting a pile of fries, and tossing the rubbish in the bin. One does have to wonder how the earth is able to absorb so much of our trash, and that which we treat like it, with nary a flicker of resentment. Or maybe we're coming on to that now; the resentment is steaming.

I wasn't one to have an affinity for the destitute or downtrodden. Kind of a shallow person, I was usually worried about my outfits or the color of my lipstick on any given day. The Brodericks changed all of that—and Mitchell Wright too. I hadn't had the occasion to pity someone so close to me, to feel sorry for something my neighbor had done. I'd had my heartstrings tugged at by visions of swollen bellies on other continents, war-torn villages and fleeing people with satchels and small children under their arms in places with languages I don't understand, but I hadn't considered the silent tragedy of neglect and apathy. The tragedy that was behind me, tapping away, pulling at the tips of my overdone hair.

They were left on the side of the river—the bank. Deck River was home to few, home to none now—not even shit flows right there. The sewer pipes were laid wrong, so a person couldn't take a piss without fear of retribution. After a while, everyone left for lack of a good flush, and it's now the land that time forgot. It wasn't long after those kids were murdered there that we forgot about it.

I was never even told about the Brodericks. That's the real shame; it wasn't seen as a threat to anyone else. No one thought it would happen to their child, because their child wasn't like the Broderick kids. A waste—both before and after.

They weren't dressed right for a cold November evening; they were hardly clothed at all. It was barely dark and not the cryptic time of night that invites mania. It was dinnertime. They didn't appear to struggle or run; they were lying, all three of them, right next to one another, like they'd been expecting this for all of their short lives. Ten, seven, and six, a combined age of not even thirty years. The weight of their small frames is still pressing on that wet dirt though they've been long removed. It can't be said that no one cared, but they didn't care enough, because it remained a closeted mystery for nearly two decades after it happened. Mitchell Wright was blamed, then dead too. And I really had no part in this at all. I was a child when it happened; it escaped both my awareness and recollection. I was only involved later, when there was nothing I could really do to help. I reminded myself of my Uncle Steve, who only offered to help tidy up dinner when most of the work was already done. It was a running joke with my parents that he'd saunter in with the dishrag when everything had been wiped down and put away. I was the Uncle Steve of a murder investigation, only I did get the last bit off the pan.

It was because of me that we got the confessions, and I've read every word of them. It was because of me that no one got away with it. Finally, no one got away with it.

It's because of those boys that I'll never be able to lie on my back beneath a tree again—a real issue living in a place so densely populated with timber. I see what they saw when I look up through the leaf-dotted awning that covers this part of the world, the only place I've ever called home. When I gaze up from under a branch canopy, I feel that final bit of life slipping away from them, as they realized this was the last thing they would ever take in. And I do think they realized it. That's what bothers me the most, this awareness. This profound understanding of a chance evaporating, a chance that never really was.

2

It didn't start with the murders or any memory of them; it started with my miscarriage. This sudden loss was like a rock inserted into my shoe, forcing discomfort with every step. I frowned while traversing and stood awkwardly even while still. Because I couldn't get rid of this irritating pebble of unhappiness simply by being unhappy, I drove to the police department and told the lady sitting at the front desk that I wanted to be a detective. She had a perm and pink nails. She said I could fill out an application. I did and wrote in the "notes" section that I had already worked on a murder investigation. "My baby died," I told her when I handed over the clipboard with the application attached. I was twenty-four.

"That's such a shame," she replied. "My name's Ronna."

"It's nice to meet you, Ronna." She assured me that the powers that be would review my application "forthwith." I left the building, wishing I'd worn something other than gym shorts and a T-shirt that said "Hot Tamale!"

"You what?" Tommy, my husband, asked me when I got home that evening. He had arrived first, which never happened. I was always there to greet him cheerfully, even if he already smelled like a bar after a long night.

"I've decided I want to be a cop," I said. "I've always wanted to be a cop in a small town. Arlene Ridell, Esquire."

"Well, Faber's growing; the upward trajectory is undeniable," he began. Being somewhat of a bigwig in the field of commercial real estate, Tommy had a sales pitch that not even I was immune from. He told me on a weekly basis that Faber was set to outnumber Augusta in due time and that the opportunity here matched that of Atlanta, which was a bunch of bull, considering Faber was a small town in the foothills without a single building over three stories high. "But I don't think cops are esquires."

"Then there will be more crime for me to investigate," I said, choosing to ignore that I might have accidentally called myself a lawyer. "Forthwith."

"What? Arlene, don't get me wrong," Tommy began, "but you've been a little off your rocker since we lost little Tommy, and I know your heart is all over the place, but we've got to make a good life even without him. You can't be runnin' all over hell's half acre trying to arrest local folks. Number one—it's dangerous, and two—you're not right right now. Not a good time to make a hasty decision like that. Plus if you arrest people, it could be bad for business. I can't sign leases with people in jail." He laughed as if any of this was funny.

Because I was a bit trigger-happy, I did not worry about arresting Tommy's real estate clients, but instead imagined myself crushing his skull with a bowling ball—I had one in the trunk of my car for Tuesday night league—such was my instant and irreconcilable fury. I was surprised that I got so mad. I'd never reacted like that; I figured extremely-pissed-off-and-bitterly-angry was a near-perfect disposition for a hard-nosed detective in a practically crimeless small town on the edge of nowhere, Georgia. Police work was in my blood even if I'd only just recently discovered it.

Instead of assaulting Tommy or telling him that I'd had a vision of assaulting him, I said I was tired and went to bed. He mumbled something about his dinner, but I didn't answer.

———————

The next day, Captain Larson Gamble called me from the Faber Police Department and said he'd looked over my application. Having woken up calm and feeling rather lovingly toward Tommy, I told Larson Gamble I'd changed my mind about working in law enforcement. "I don't think it's the right career for me," I said. "I'm not as angry as I thought I was. It just comes in spurts."

"Well, I was going to offer you a job," he told me. "It's only part-time, in the mornings. And you don't necessarily need to be angry."

I was quiet for a moment. "Will I have to carry a gun?" I asked.

"No, ma'am. We need someone to tag evidence."

It didn't sound like my style but I didn't immediately say no. "Can I think about it?" I asked. "I don't really even know what you're talking about, but I'd like to think it over, because I don't have a job or a kid, and my mind is like a chain saw on top of my head. It would be good to focus on something. Crime is really what I'd like to focus on. We watch a lot of crime TV and I do think it's a calling." I had no idea what I was talking about. I'd never considered a career in law enforcement before, not even while watching *Law and Order*.

"Well, there's not too much of that in Faber, something we're grateful for, which is why we don't have need for a full-time evidence tech, but I appreciate you coming in and taking the initiative, and I think your timing was good, so let's see if we can't work it out, okay?"

We hung up, and I immediately called Tommy's sister, Lacey, to tell her that I was considering a job. "Offered it to me right there on the phone. Thinks I'd be good at it," I said.

Lacey and I were close, tight like a good knot. I'd known Lacey as long as I'd known Tommy and, in some ways, could talk to her easier. She was older than Tommy and me by a year and a half but looked younger—not fond of the bottle the way Tommy was, she held on to her youthful glow. She always told me to tell him to quit drinking.

"Tell him yourself" was usually how I answered.

"So what would you be doing at the police?" she asked, not without genuine interest.

"Evidence."

"Hmmm…" She told me she was baking when she answered the phone. She sounded distracted. I could hear the rattle of kitchen items and burned with the urge to make a large meal. Lacey liked to bake, but I was one for pots, pans, knives, cutting boards, and a hot stove.

Lacey had two small children, twins, Margo and Michael. It was a damn shame, but I never really warmed up to either of them; sometimes I thought it was because I didn't have small children of my own. Jealousy has always given me a bit of a mean streak.

"What does Tommy think?" she asked.

"He thinks I'm having a crisis because of the baby, which I am, but maybe something good will come out of it, so I'm trying."

"Good from bad," Lacey said. "Common theme. I just finished…" As soon as I heard those words, I tuned her out. Lacey was a big reader and liked to brag about it. There's nothing less interesting than hearing someone talk about the book they just read, except maybe listening to someone talk about their fitness routines. Lacey liked to brag about her exercise regimen too—and her religious zeal. She needed a lot of affirmation; I suppose that comes with the territory if you're home with little kids all day. All I ever wanted was to be home with little kids all day; I'm not sure I would have needed anyone to give me compliments about it.

Eventually Lacey came back around to the conversation and said the job sounded good. "I support your decision. You could always devote your life to fitness, reading, and religion like me, but if you want to be around lawbreakers and perverts all day, that sounds great!" I think I imagined that last part, but she did tell me it sounded "cool."

I went to the police station the following morning, unannounced. I'd gotten my job at Schroder's Restaurant by showing up with my hair in a bun; I figured this would be much the same. Ronna was at the front desk, looking like a blueberry muffin in a heavily starched navy dress with large plastic buttons down the front and basking in her authoritative glory. I greeted her sternly, believing life in law enforcement would require me to toughen my exterior a bit. "Hello, Ronna," I said.

"Arlene," she answered. We shared a knowing stare and a small nod. I could tell she was a woman I could trust. She wore her hair high on her head, and by high I mean it had a lot of volume and stood off her scalp like a flag flying. She used a lot of eye shadow and appeared to prefer wide, rectangular dresses worn over her stout frame. I too liked the freedom of sack-like clothing but was afraid of looking like a pastry. Ronna clearly overcame any concern she might have had about drowning in her garments. I can't say I wasn't impressed.

"I'm here for my interview," I told her.

"Oh," she said, looking down at her day planner. "With Mr. Gamble? Did we have that scheduled?"

"No," I said. "I just thought…well…" Now I was embarrassed. "He called me," I told her. "He called my house."

"He's here," she said. "Let me check to see if he's got time. The position needs to be filled." She lifted a finger and picked up the phone. "No time like the present," she said both to me and the receiver. "Chief Gamble, it's Ronna. Arlene Ridell is here. She's ready to be interviewed. Yes, well, she knows that, but she was in the area. I understand, but she's chomping at the bit, ready to work… Good work ethic is hard to find, and it would be helpful for our image to have another woman at the precinct. You know that incident with Fisher Donohue didn't sit well with a lot of folks. Yessir." Ronna put down the phone. "He'll see you shortly," she said. We looked at one another again and I could almost feel the connection—womb-like. We had different mothers, but that was beside the point where Ronna Rhodes and I were concerned.

Police Captain Larson Gamble assured me several times during the interview that the job was not difficult and it would not require special training, nor would I be granted special privileges like a badge or a firearm. "You put on your application that you'd worked a murder investigation. I'm not sure…"

"Dead baby," I said, interrupting him. "I know who did it."

"I'm sorry, Ms. Ridell, but what do you mean…?"

I jumped in again. "Some people can't have babies, and I fear I'm one of those people. My husband drinks a lot, and my mother always said that a woman who marries a drunk is married to his sorrow, so I believe now that I'm to have a life of sorrow. Most people have never seen a dead body or had the unfortunate situation to know that they couldn't keep a child alive, and I have. I think that qualifies me for the most difficult of homicide investigations. I won't faint. I've seen worse."

Larson Gamble looked at his desk and then back at me. "My deepest sympathies," he said and then said no more. I was glad. People talked too much, especially when they were sad to hear your life wasn't going as planned. It was like they were trying to make excuses for you. I didn't need the excuses. I needed a distraction.

"I was a waitress at Schroder's," I said to fill the silence. "I only quit because my husband, Tommy, is nothing but a moneybags bigwig nowadays, and we just don't need the cash. But I'm finding that in my depressive state, sitting around the house or getting my hair done with my girlfriend, Maureen, just isn't filling the space the way it once did."

"Well, I am prepared to offer you the job. It pays nine dollars an hour. You'll work from eight to twelve Monday through Friday. Sometimes there will be a whole heap of evidence to bag and tag, and other times, I suggest you bring a book."

"That sounds interesting," I said, lying through my teeth. I was second-guessing my need for work in a popping economy with Tommy out every day hustling and making friends, playing golf, and signing contracts. I could do whatever I wanted. This strange desire to sit in the basement of a lime-green building for four hours every morning had me wondering. "I'll take it," I replied, like Captain Gamble had offered me a piece of gum.

"Welcome to the team." Gamble smiled as he shook my hand.

3

I told Tommy I needed a new wardrobe for my job in police work. We were eating dinner. Tommy was sloshed, which was a blessing. The food was terrible, overcooked and oversalted. I'd forgotten cumin in the chicken chili (one of my specialties that wasn't so special without the cumin), and the lima beans were supposed to be pintos. I'd been distracted and went for the wrong bag. I didn't even notice halfway through the soak.

"They wear uniforms," he replied. "Are you sure you won't be wearing a uniform?"

I wasn't sure, so I kept my mouth shut about the clothes and put a spoonful of limas on my plate and told him to pass the butter instead. "I start next week."

"I don't know, Arlene. A high-powered real estate magnate's wife working for minimum wage at the local lockup?"

"Oh give me a break, Tommy, you just sold a strip mall lot to a tire store. You're not a Rockefeller, for Pete's sake." I waited. "And it's more than minimum wage," I said not unproudly.

"Who's Pete?" And there it was. We both giggled. "It isn't necessary though, Arlene. But I don't want to stop you. I know you're all messed up about little Tommy." He frowned. He was messed up over it too, but he drank so much, he most of the time didn't know which way was up. He didn't have a lot of opportunity to take inventory of his feelings with a clear head the way us people who stayed sober for at least the first five hours of the day did.

"I feel like I've let this slide long enough," I said. "But we were never going to name the baby Tommy. We didn't even know it was a boy until he died. You can keep saying that if it makes you feel better, but I can't say I condone you naming the child after its passing. I just can't."

"Well, you're telling people the baby was murdered," he argued.

"It was," I said. "He was."

"By who?"

"Me, I guess. I was the one carrying him." I rose from the table and went to our bedroom, where I locked the door and cried into my pillow. I knew nothing would be the same. I remembered that my cousin, Danielle, who was a lot older than I was, lost a child when I was in middle school. His name was Xavier, and he got hit by a car. She turned purple and moved to a cabin somewhere in Blairsville. At first with her husband, but he was eventually asked to leave. She's still there. No matter how long she held her breath,

Xavier never came back. I looked in the mirror sometimes to see if I'd turned purple. I was still the color of a wet peppermint.

I hadn't yet gone back to the doctor to see if the problem was permanent. I didn't know if I was able to have babies. All I knew is that I'd killed the last one.

———

The summer of the pregnancy had been hotter than the devil's fingernail. I went around half-naked but was still sweating from head to toe all hours of the day. I was in such a state I had to quit waitressing at Schroder's. I didn't care. I'd seen enough greasy omelets and day-old pie to last a lifetime, and we didn't need the money anymore. Tommy was already making a killing.

At the twenty-three-week mark, the baby decided it did not want to live with us after all and died. I asked the doctor if it was because of me. He was a kindly gentleman with gray hair and a red, bulbous nose. He said, "No, Arlene. You've had a miscarriage. It's not because of anything you've done." I cried for a month. Tommy tried to comfort me by making a lot of money and working late. He said he wasn't sure he wanted children anyway. I asked him if he killed the baby, which we discovered was a boy; he said no and told me to get a grip.

It was my mother who said it was Tommy's drinking that did it. "His juice was bad...made of whiskey. What did you expect?"

4

The job is dull as hell," I admitted to Tommy over dinner after my first day working at the precinct. "I was so bored at one point I counted how many times I could mouth the word 'donut' in a minute."

"How many?" Tommy asked, leaning over his dinner plate. I made goulash like a Hungarian, and we ate it often.

"Seventy-eight. But I guess one cool thing is that I get to read about the old cases when there's nothing else to do."

"How's that? Seems that would be some sort of violation." Tommy was on his fifth beer. The more he drank, the more lucid he tried to sound. He would start using fancier words, trying to come across as very smart and knowledgeable just to slow his roll a little.

Normally I didn't count his drinks, but he seemed extra self-conscious and I'd had a call from Max Payton the week before.

Max thought he was Tommy's best friend, although I'm not sure Tommy agreed. Max had told me he was seeing Tommy sloshed all over town and that I might want to talk to him. "I mean—it's like noon on a Tuesday and I can't make out what he's saying. I ran into him at The Delfry. He was all over the place." I'd practically hung up on Max. He called to tell on Tommy quite a bit; he always did have that hall monitor-type of personality that I really can't stand.

"No," I said. "The case files are kept in the same room. This is Faber, for Pete's sake. There's not a lot in there," I said about the old cases.

"Who's Pete?"

"So anyway, I've been reading about this messy divorce and then some older stuff about people who used to live on Deck River that's pretty interesting—back when people used to live on Deck River."

Tommy was at the refrigerator again, not uninterested in what I was saying, but otherwise occupied by the presence of another cold one inside.

"Don't make me worry about you," I said, nodding to the beer he'd just pulled from the fridge. He looked at me and shut the door. "I don't want to worry."

"I always liked Deck River," Tommy said, ignoring my comments. "Shame that place kinda went to the dogs."

"I think it was always with the dogs." I stood up and started to clear the table.

Tommy walked upstairs after telling me he was going to take a shower. Our house was a split-level. Everyone on our street had a different version of the same house. I liked it fine, and it was a nice home, mostly made of brick, well painted, and Tommy did a commendable job with the yard. We had flowering azalea bushes in the front, roses by the mailbox, and a variety of trees: few sweet gums, a smattering of pines in the back, a crape myrtle in front of the kitchen window, and my favorite—a southern magnolia right smack-dab in the middle of our property next to a Bradford pear that bloomed white in the spring like a cloud. The two of them competed for the sun, so neither got very big. The magnolia dropped a whole heap of leaves and bark and other mess on the ground and attracted its fair share of beetles, but I loved it and refused to tame it in any way. Tommy said it threw off too much shade and killed all of our grass. I said I didn't care.

"My mama killed the grass after Bobby died," I reminded him. "We gonna get rid of her too?"

When he was eighteen years old, my brother Bobby Black drove his car off the road in Bingham County and was killed instantly. He got going too fast around a turn on the 890, and we never saw him again. Robert was his Christian name, anyway—my brother.

I was seven when it happened and the only one of four kids left at home. I'd been a little on my own before that, and then even more on my own after. Both of my parents moved into a silent house with their grief and didn't want roommates. I lived with them anyway and got used to the quiet, but it was a lot like living alone.

My mama said she knew she'd never see Bobby again the day he left. She said she could feel it when she pressed her face to his—the last touch of his cheek right there in the driveway before he drove away. She'd always poured what was left of her coffee, the part she couldn't finish, in the yard next to the driveway—in almost that exact same spot where she said goodbye to Bobby for the last time. Every morning she went out there—rain or shine—to dump her mug and look at our street. She stopped doing that the day Bobby died. I don't know where the coffee went after that, but all the grass died. I guess it had liked the coffee.

I think it was this small loneliness as a child that made Tommy Ridell look world class to me. When I met him, I figured if I could keep him around, then I would never be lonely again. I was right, but I had to share Tommy with the bottle. A smarter woman would have known what that meant before she agreed to it.

I heard the shower start and felt a little guilty for giving Tommy grief about his one true love. My mother told me I'd never be able to change him when I told her we were getting married. "Don't even try," she'd said. "All that effort'll change you—not him."

But I hadn't changed. Kids were still the only thing I really wanted. Tommy and I had been married for three years now, and I still didn't have anyone to cook for but him.

5

Ronna kept an eye on me at work. We didn't smile or joke or talk about our families. We nodded in understanding. Ronna's hair said more about her than her mouth ever could. I appreciated that in a person. Still do.

On most days, there was hardly any evidence to tag, so I began reading more and more case files in the basement. Most of the evidence I was being asked to tag as a part of my job related to tree limbs falling on people's property—a pine cone was bagged in evidence once. But the cases in the dilapidated boxes on the back shelves and side table were altogether different. I could get a real tickle in my toes when I got into a file from way back. It had gnarled people and twisted stories a plenty, and all of this had happened right down the street. The proximity really got me buzzing.

I had only one gnarled and twisted story of my own, only one bad deed on my résumé that I do think was to blame for losing the baby, even if I never told anyone that's what I thought.

Tommy proposed marriage during a long weekend of swimming and fishing at Lake Belfrey, and he only did it because I told him I was pregnant. I wasn't.

"You're just asking me so you won't have to tell your sister you got me knocked up without making me your bride first," I said to him instead of yes. "She's a real holy roller these days." I cast my line and took a sip of my whiskey sour. We'd made a pitcher and put it in a canteen with a lot of ice. "But yes. Yes, I will marry you."

"You supposed to be drinking whiskey with a baby on the way?" He pointed at my stomach. He was smiling funny with an eyebrow raised.

I put my cup down real fast and went back to watching my line. "Yea, I gotta ask the doctor about that," I said. "Feel it kicking," I said, unaware that that part didn't start 'til a lot later in the process. Tommy smiled proudly. Two bigger idiots a person couldn't find with a telescope.

We were married in April. I wore a short white dress with my hair in a braided twist and stood proudly inside Faber Presbyterian while the cherry blossoms surfed the spring breeze outside. Their petals rode waves of sliding air down to the ground where they'd be trampled by shoes and indifference, much like my dreams of being married by the ocean and having three kids by the age of twenty-five. I should have known my lie about being pregnant was going to become my truth. I never could get away with anything.

But Tommy already knew I'd spun a yarn, and he still wanted to make it legal. About two weeks before the wedding, Tommy asked me what happened to the baby.

"Fell out," I told him.

"You do have a big vagina," he said like he was giving me a compliment.

"That's a fine thing to say to your betrothed!"

"Oh please, Arlene. All you had to do was say you wanted to get married."

We never mentioned that "pregnancy" again, but I did always think I cursed myself by lying like that, even if Tommy didn't seem to care.

We honeymooned in Jekyll Island on the Georgia coast and ate crab legs dipped in butter with plastic bibs tied around our necks. Tommy drank too much most nights, and when I couldn't keep up with him, I shuttled him around under my arm and made excuses for his stumbling and slurred speech. I'd been living with my parents up to this point, who were go-to-bed-at-eight-up-with-the-crows kind of people, so rolling Tommy over so he could pass out on his stomach at eleven each night felt exotic and exciting to me.

We went back to Jekyll for our anniversary a year later. The trip was much the same as our first time there, and it was then that I really did get pregnant.

"Well, don't let it fall out this time," Tommy said upon hearing the news. "Wear underwear, for God's sake." He winked at me, and we both shared a giggle. He went out and bought me a pack of Hanes Her Way and told me to squeeze like hell. It didn't matter that we were joking around and that we both knew a baby couldn't fall out like that. I liked the idea of holding something in for a long time and squeezed anyway. The baby didn't last; turns out all that squeezing had no effect.

———

Now, instead of squeezing, I was sitting all by my lonesome in the basement of the police station without a thing to do. It wasn't like me to be idle. The less my hands had to do, the more my brain got to working. I didn't make my best decisions with an overactive mind on the loose, but I kept my chin up thinking that I might just be able to do some good as a public employee. I wouldn't lay an eye on the Broderick file for another few weeks, but I had already decided that I wasn't in that basement to use a Sharpie, I was there to find the truth—I was on a mission.

Ronna had told me that she organized the evidence room herself. I squinted in approval of her efforts. "It's fine work," I told her. "It's very organized." We were both nodding subtly at the time. She never moved from behind the front desk. I had actually wondered if she kept a camping toilet back there so she wouldn't have to leave her post to use the ladies.

"I have an eye for alphabetization," she said.

"It's a worthy skill," I replied.

"You're gosh darn right." She closed her eyes in solidarity. I did too.

Boxes lined several shelves along the walls in the basement of the station. They had the tattered, abandoned look of cartons of high school trophies and blue ribbons for science fairs. I didn't think I was doing anything wrong, and when I was caught with one of the old case files on my desk, about a house fire on Deck River— I'd been through it four times and had no reason to be looking at it whatsoever—I didn't try to explain but rather waited for a glowing review of my initiative.

Captain Gamble came down to check on me, which he sometimes did. "Reading?" he asked, pointing to the file. "I know it can get boring."

"Yes," I said. "This happened in Deck River. We used to fish over there—me and Tommy." I knew I was blushing and blinking too much. I swallowed to keep my color down

"Oh man, Deck River," he said. "Not much over there anymore. Kind of a sad place."

"No," I said. "Hardly anybody lives there now. So sad about the plumbing—and all the abandoned houses and all'a that. Tommy and I used to fish there all the time...before...like I said. Now the river just cries it's so lonesome. Anyway. That's what Tommy says— about the crying." I was rambling to keep from getting in trouble for reading other people's life stories in private police files. "Had some time to kill today. I like Deck River," I said stupidly. "Sorta."

"The worst cases were always from Deck River." He looked away. "Bad deal."

"This one?" I asked, holding up the file I'd been reading.

"Oh no." He shook his head. "That was before my time. I remember it, but I wasn't a cop then, and they got all that figured out. The dad shot the mom and took all the money, and then the other guy burned their house down. Awful. No, the other thing—more recent, kind of, was the Broderick kids. That's the worst thing that's ever happened around here. Ever. Anyway—I'll leave you to it. I think some stuff is coming in this afternoon, so there'll be something for you to do in the morning. If you even want anything to do."

"I'll be sure and drink my coffee," I said pertly. "So it's okay if I look at the old files?"

"Yeah." Gamble nodded. "Everything down here is ancient history. No harm in it." He paused. "No, the Brodericks were a real bad business," he said more to himself. "I almost left the force. Still bothers me. Them and the Wrights—Mitchell." He shook his head and turned to go. "Never felt good about how that turned out." I watched him closely as he left the room, trodding up the steps with heavy feet, his hand on the rail.

Ronna and I usually ate our lunch together in companionable silence. We met almost every day at the picnic tables outside the station. She had a forty-minute lunch break, and I was just off work, but we sat together nonetheless and ate bagged lunches we brought from home. Ronna wore large sunglasses and reapplied lipstick immediately after eating, even though I knew she went to brush her teeth in the hall bathroom. I'd seen her toothbrush. It had a handle that looked like it had been painted red, the remnants of her Maybelline.

She always brought a juice box like she was a little kid, and upon punching the small foil circle with the small bending straw, she would point to the carton and say, "Vitamin C." She did it every day and with the same amount of authority. The only days we didn't share lunch together were the days it rained. Then, Ronna would go to McDonald's with her book, and I would go home and eat in front of the television. I'd only, so far, worked during the months with agreeable weather. I didn't know what we were going to do come winter when we couldn't sit outside. I figured I'd look to Ronna for guidance.

"Ever heard of the Brodericks?" I asked Ronna over lunch that day. "Captain Gamble was telling me about them and the Wrights. Do you remember them?"

"I'm done with my juice," she said sharply.

"Yeah, that's good." I played with the edges of the brown paper sack in which I'd packed my lunch. "Gamble was just telling me—"

Ronna stood up with the rest of her half-finished lunch in hand. "I'm hot," she said. "I'm going to finish my lunch at my desk."

"Okay, then," I said. I'd been a little uncomfortable too, and my tuna sandwich had lost its appeal after a couple of bites. I thought I could make myself something else when I got home.

––––––––

I had decided I was rather pleased with my situation at the Faber PD—feeling useful instead of like a servant. Schroder's had been a little like manual labor what with all the walking and tray carrying and people barking orders at me. I felt at ease in more cerebral work, using Post-it notes and putting check marks on printed logs. I was happy but bored stiff a good ninety percent of the time. A woman of my word, however, I did not consider quitting. Even after Tommy said we could move into a house on Lake Patton, I never considered relinquishing my credentials—Evidence Tech. If you had money in Faber, you lived on Lake Patton. I imagine I would be the first evidence tech to live on Lake Patton. Tommy was certainly the first evidence tech's husband to go house hunting there.

A CONDEMNED MAN

I MET HER AT RAM'S. I didn't know she was in high school. She didn't act like she was that young. I heard of her anyway—Claire Broderick. She was getting around a long time before me, like old boots wore all over. She had that way about her like girls who want something real bad. She was trashy, but all girls from over there are. They can't help it.

I took her around a few times, picked her up from school. She always needed money, so I'd give it to her. She said it was for the kids or her dad. I really didn't care what she did with it. It wasn't anything serious. She looked good, but she had all those kids with her all the time. I'd take her away from 'em, and she liked that. We left 'em on the side of the road a few times and told 'em to walk back to their dad's house. She kept the little one close but the others she didn't care about. She always got this fog over her when we was trying to get rid of 'em. Her eyes just wouldn't meet anything anymore, like she was trying to figure out how to disappear. I guess I thought it was kind of mysterious or something, but I got a charge out of ditching those boys without shoes and shit. They never cried or ever really said anything. They just walked on. I think they wanted to get away from me too—as bad as I wanted to get rid of them—not like scared, just they didn't think it was fun to ride around in the back of the truck listening to her complain about 'em. And she wouldn't touch me when they were around. The little one was okay though. He'd fall asleep in my truck and didn't know what was going on. She'd do anything in front of him.

I still saw the kids all over the place though—when I'd go to Deck River. They were out all hours of the day, just wandering around. I talked to 'em all the time. They weren't scared of me. They didn't like me, but they weren't scared none.

When she got pregnant and moved in with her boyfriend, that's what ended it for me. I wouldn't mess around with a pregnant girl. And I can't get a girl pregnant. No matter what I do the devil swallows the seed back up in me. I don't even have to worry about it. I knew it wasn't mine as soon as her belly popped. God won't let me add to anything. I can only take away.

6

ell, rather than buying a new house, I think I want to try and have another baby," I said to Tommy's suggestion that a five-thousand-square-foot place on Patton's best side was our destiny. We were eating on the back deck of the split-level, a place I felt most at home, fulfilled, and satisfied. I didn't need Lake Patton or any of the people who lived there.

"Destiny!" he shouted. His eyes were disconnected and wired from the Tom Collins. I might have been dismayed but he was like this all the time, and it never led to me being buried alive or us joining a cult.

"I wouldn't get too excited. Those people who perished in Oklahoma City thought it was their destiny too—you know, to be in that building in Oklahoma." I frowned. It was beneath me to make jokes about the dead. I'd been spending too much time in the basement evidence locker. Anyway, I liked the split-level and was much more focused on getting knocked up than I was on Lake Patton.

"Are you drunk?" Tommy asked sincerely. He certainly was. It was 7:48. He was three cocktails in and raring to go.

"No. I'm keeping my body as a sanctuary for a baby…a baby that doesn't like gin."

"Don't you think it's too soon?" Tommy said.

"For gin?" I nodded at his glass. "No—I mean who am I to judge?"

"No." He shook his head. "Too soon to have another kid."

"No time like the present to just get on with things. When won't it be too soon?"

"When it happens without us trying." Tommy seemed certain. I thought sometimes that Tommy felt some contemptible responsibility to take care of me like a person who adopted a cat and then realized they hated cats. "You know you don't have to work," he said, like maybe I was hanging out in the basement of the Faber Police Department because I thought I had to.

"What does that have to do with having a baby?" I said.

"I just mean if you want to play tennis or something…"

"I want to solve a crime," I said defiantly. "And I have bad knees. I can't play tennis—you know that."

"Are you drunk?" he asked again.

"Never." I grit my teeth. "Does it embarrass you that I work for the police?" I asked.

"No, but it just seems like you're trying to stay busy. You don't have to stay busy there." He looked a little incredulous. I could tell he'd actually given this a good deal of thought.

"I want to have a purpose," I said honestly. "I don't want to play tennis."

"I just don't want you to end up working at the pancake factory or plugging tires or something."

"What's the pancake factory?" I asked. He didn't answer. He was far away again. It was common for him to drift off like a feather on a stream. I never worried, however, that I was the one more caught on him than him on me. In our relationship, I was the line and he was the flopping fish, slowly dying for lack of air and only liquor to drink—no water. Every man with that distance in him latches on to someone. They're like leeches.

"I want to have a baby," I said again. "I was born to do it."

"I thought you were going to solve a mystery," he said like he was genuinely trying to understand my state of mind, not continually contradict me. "But either's fine with me."

I dipped my chin, glad to have his approval but annoyed that he thought I was asking for it. "I can do both," I said. I really didn't know what had gotten into me. I wasn't myself since...since any of it.

We went with a real estate agent to look at a house on Lake Patton the following week. "Seems they'd rename this place after that guy turned out to be crazy," the agent said as we pulled up to a Tudor-style home on a large lot with a dock and a small boat house. "He was knee-deep in sin and debt when he died. Fool still got a lake named after him. I guess you never can tell."

I didn't follow and looked to Tommy for counsel. He was staring out the window—distracted. We were sitting in the back seat of Melba's car. She'd been recommended by Lacey who said, "Melba's the best thing since sliced bread!" Tommy made a joke about Melba toast that made me grimace. He was not improving with age.

The house was immaculate but empty. "It was the Pendleys' place, but she passed, and he couldn't keep up with it anymore. He's over at the Hidden Meadows Retirement Home now, biding his time 'til the good Lord calls him home. Duke Pendley. He was chief of police for a spell," Melba told us. She wore glasses on a small chain around her neck. She had to have been in her late seventies and walked very slowly and deliberately. Her fingers and toenails were painted turquoise, and she had a high-pitched voice that sounded like a fire alarm just about out of batteries.

We looked around, and all I could think about was our current house. "I don't know..." I kept saying. "What's a Tudor house anyway? Is it because it's brown? It's two different shades of brown." I wasn't sure how I meant this, but two shades of brown was really something.

"It's the style," Melba said, dismissing me. She knew who would be securing the financing. "Duke Pendley was a real fine detective," she said proudly, as if she herself had something to do with his lofty calling.

"At the Faber PD?" I said. I looked around, a little more closely. "Detectives nowadays must have taken a real pay cut." I was commenting on how, as far as I could tell, no one at the station could afford a place like this, but Tommy misunderstood.

"No, Arlene—he died. That's why they're selling the place."

"No," Melba interrupted. "His wife died some years ago. He's selling the place, because of his arthritis."

"I just mean this is an awful nice place for someone who worked for the police department."

"I really don't know," Melba said like I'd insulted her. "Duke Pendley is a wonderful man—a real class act."

"I'm sure he is!" Tommy bellowed enthusiastically. I couldn't help but roll my eyes.

I was silent on the car ride home and barely responded to Melba asking for our opinions on the place. "So?" she said over and over. She had her seat so close to the steering wheel, she appeared dangerously trapped there.

"I like our house," I finally said rather decisively. "I don't want to move."

Tommy looked at me and smiled. He gripped my hand, grateful that I wasn't the kind of gal who wanted a Tudor house. The next day, Tommy bought me a two-seater Mercedes convertible. I was excited and put several scarves for tying my hair back in the glove box before realizing that there was no place for a car seat. I removed the scarves from the car and walked back inside.

"It has to have a back seat...for the baby," I said to Tommy, who'd been smiling at my enthusiasm from the front window. His broad frame eclipsed my view from the doorway of the formal living room with its peach carpet and watermelon rind-colored sofa. He frowned but almost immediately drove back to the dealership that afternoon and came home with a sedan model instead—this one in cherry red. I put the scarves in the glove box of the new car and assured Tommy I would always drive with the windows down.

7

Do you remember the Brodericks?" I asked that evening over dinner. Tommy was feeling very pleased with himself after a day of remaining mostly sober and being so in tune with my needs—and with being able to exchange expensive cars seemingly in the blink of an eye. He was a good man who wanted to make me happy, wanted to understand me, didn't want to let me down, but I was becoming more and more of a labyrinth.

"Who? Is that who owns the pancake factory?"

"What?" I said, putting down my fork. "What is with you and the pancake factory?"

"Who are you talking about?"

I took a gulp of my sweet tea. "Captain Gamble said there was some awful case in Deck River. The Broderick boys."

"Those kids who died over there? Yeah, I remember that. It was a pretty long time ago, when you and me were little."

"You and I."

"Yeah." Tommy nodded.

"What happened?"

"I don't know," he said. "Little kids got killed. That's when people used to live there."

"Right."

"Were they little kids?"

"Who?"

"The Broderick boys who died."

"Yeah, pretty little, I guess."

"That's so sad."

"You want a beer?"

"No, thank you. Was that Pendley guy on the force when it happened?"

"What pencil guy?"

"Pendley—the house we saw today."

"No, he died. His wife has arthritis."

"Never mind." I went and got myself a beer, figuring it was my only hope in this house.

————

"I saw the Pendley place yesterday," I told Captain Gamble when I walked into the station the following morning. It seemed to me he was waiting for me by Ronna's desk.

"Oh hello, Arlene!" he said loudly. "You look lovely today."

"Thank you." I swallowed forcefully.

"Mmmhmmmph," Ronna said, focusing on the keyboard of her computer. "Mmmhmmm," she hummed a little more quietly.

"The Pendley place?" Captain Gamble said distractedly. "Duke Pendley?"

"Yes. We're house hunting." Ronna rolled her eyes. I couldn't figure out why. "Did he work here? Chief Pendley?"

"Yeah, but…" Gamble shook his head a little.

"Was a real nice place. He must have been some detective," I said. "I didn't know detectives were rich like that."

"Oh, well…" Gamble raised his shoulders to his ears. "I don't really know about any of that."

Ronna dipped her chin. "That right?" She tapped the keys on her computer loudly, indicating she was done with us standing by her desk.

"I love that new car," Gamble said. "I saw you out in it yesterday." He turned to Ronna. "Arlene got a Mercedes."

"Of course she did. Excuse me." She turned in her chair and rolled herself to the file cabinet behind her.

"You look great in it." Gamble smiled dreamily.

"Oh." I was surprised and uncomfortable. "Yes, a gift from my husband."

"He's a lucky guy."

I widened my eyes and glanced at Ronna, whose face was

puckered incredulously. The phone rang, which gave me and Gamble cause to scatter so Ronna could answer the call.

I thought to ask Tommy why he'd gotten me a red car; it was so conspicuous. Everyone in town would see me coming. It was true I dressed to the nines for my police job. A person could hear the drop of my designer heels on the precinct basement stairs from a mile away, but I meant it to be professional, not so I could get attention.

I was keeping a well-tended calendar with my periods and the times I thought I would be ovulating. I didn't tell Tommy how focused I was, but Ronna figured it out during one of our silent, but comfortable lunches.

"You want a baby," she said.

"I had a baby," I told her, putting a potato stick in my mouth. Part of my connection with Ronna was that I wanted to be just like her; it was her confidence that had me so smitten. Ronna liked meatloaf and always had a fried potato item in her lunch—like sticks or chips, and once an actual deep-fried potato, whole and covered in salt. I asked her how she was going to eat it, to which she replied, "With ketchup." She emptied several packets on the aluminum foil in which the potato had been packed and dipped away.

"My baby was real as that fork there. I want one that makes it past the threshold."

"Babies like meatloaf," she said.

I wondered how many nights a week Ronna and her husband, Platt, ate meatloaf. I prepared it for Tommy one evening in Ronna's honor and brought a container the following day—two slices. She looked pleased.

"Leftovers," I said.

"You can put that in the blender for the baby."

It gave me a good feeling to be so connected to someone. I'd brought a small bag of Lay's that day as well. I turned the open end toward her.

"Don't mind if I do." She took a handful of chips, leaving only a smattering of crumbs at the bottom of the bag.

I wore a long green wrap dress to work one day with crocodile-skin shoes and dangling gold earrings. I'd applied new lipstick and had my hair tied back in a fashionable twist that somewhat mimicked the waist of my dress. Ronna raised an eyebrow, and I knew I'd crossed the line. The next day I donned oversized khaki pants and a mauve turtleneck.

Tommy had seen me leave that morning and asked, "What the hell happened?"

"I need to tone it down," I had said. "Ronna might be getting the wrong idea."

"About what?"

"I can just tell she likes things understated. She says her and Platt are humble people." I could tell Tommy was unimpressed—he didn't want a lick of humble to go with his fancy new self.

I'd actually never met Ronna's husband, Platt. I did, however, see the photo album from their trip to Lake Erie, where her uncle had a house. Ronna wore the same pale green ankle-length sundress the entire time they were there, and her face went one shade closer to ripe raspberry with each passing day. She was without makeup in all of the photos and sweating profusely. Platt also had huge sweat circles under his armpits in every single picture, even the ones where he wasn't wearing a shirt, when the circles were visible in trickles of moisture cascading down the side of his bulging torso. There was one picture of Ronna standing on a ladder in the shallow water of the lake that led up to her uncle's property. I tried to make sense of the ladder out there in the lake and then flipped to the next picture, which was of Platt careening off it with one leg in the air and his arms flailing behind him, a look of terror on his face.

"Why the ladder?" I'd asked Ronna.

"Wanted to see farther," she said, applying a little more powder to the sides of her nose. She used a CoverGirl compact.

"I thought Ohio was cold," I remarked after looking at the last picture where she and Platt were literally soaking wet with what must have been sweat and not lake water. They were standing on shore, fully clothed and wearing socks and shoes, their faces dripping with perspiration, especially Platt's upper lip and Ronna's sideburns. Their hair was bone-dry except at the edges, where it met their flush faces.

"It was summer," Ronna told me before snatching the photo album back. "We had a wonderful time."

"Where else do you like to go for vacation?" I asked. I'd never thought of vacationing in Ohio. I was curious what other tricks Ronna had up her sleeve.

"Platt's brother's house in North Carolina," she said. "To see the leaves."

I asked Ronna what was special about the leaves in North Carolina, and she gave me a blank stare before saying, "They're the same as the ones here, but he has a cabin in the mountains, so you can see more of them." I knew that Ronna and Platt were interested in seeing more of whatever it was there was to see. I decided Tommy and I needed to see more too. If Ronna had that much imagination, then we could have some as well.

When I got home from work that day, I told Tommy I wanted to go to North Carolina to see the leaves.

"We have leaves here," he told me.

"I also want to go on more vacations," I added. "No moving but more movement." I was quite pleased with how clever this sounded.

"We could fish," Tommy said. He was drinking a Moscow mule. He'd asked me to get him ginger beer in order to make it. I didn't know what ginger beer was and just got Schweppes instead.

"We could go to Moscow," I said.

"Right." He looked confused. We were eating meatloaf for the fourth time that month. It was only the twelfth of September.

———

Things at the station were slow enough to sometimes make me wonder if I should quit just to save the town some money. Tommy complained about taxes all the time; I figured I was part of the problem. I was too used to sitting at my desk, looking at catalogs and writing checks for new belts and rouge, that I was almost angry when a big pile of evidence showed up. I did bring a book most days, that or the catalogs, to pass the time, but it was a waste.

The real problem was that I hadn't been able to locate the Broderick file, and I was damn near frothy to read it. I hated to be so preoccupied with the macabre; Gamble had said he almost quit it was so bad, but I was dying to get my hands on it. Even though he was the one who brought it up, I wasn't sure I should ask Gamble where it was since either it might make him relive terrible memories or because he would know that I had literally nothing to do and would be given cause to fire me—and Ronna always changed the subject when I mentioned the Brodericks, so she was of no use.

I did my own digging around, but a lot of what I could find

was either depressing, boring, or crude. I'd read the house fire file about six times and couldn't say I was all that riveted anymore. There were enough domestic violence reports, small-time drug busts, and vicious bar fights to last a lifetime, but nothing that buzzed my antenna. As far as I could tell, there was no Broderick file in the basement, period. I'd all but given up.

As if summoned by my boredom, Captain Gamble came down to say hello and check on things, and also to tell me to use smaller print on the evidence bags. He was authoritative and concentrating on my cleavage. "You're doing a great job, Arlene. I'm happy to have you here." I was almost certain he winked. I nodded and stared straight ahead, trying to look serious and wise—and flat-chested. It didn't seem an opportune moment to bring up the Brodericks.

When he came down to the basement again the next day, I was nervous there was another complaint…or worse, more embarrassing flattery. He stopped and stood awkwardly in front of my desk and cleared his throat a few times before speaking in a squeaky, cautious way. "Ummm," he began. "We've picked Tommy up for drunk driving."

"It's ten thirty in the morning," I said, like it was Larson Gamble's fault that it wasn't a more appropriate drinking hour.

"I know," he said, and then nothing more. He stood waiting for me to make us both feel better.

"Well, he drinks too much," I said. "He does. It's his way to dream. Can't dream without it. Otherwise he's just here…stuck here, selling garages and places where people can use staplers, and he doesn't have a way to deal with that." I didn't talk about Tommy's drinking with anyone. I didn't know I really had anything to say about it until I started talking. "He's always drank too much. He's got the gene."

"I just wanted to let you know. They're running his paperwork now. Of course you can go get him out later. We'll release him to you. Let him off with a warning or whatever."

"I don't know if that's necessary," I said. "I mean, don't do that on my account. If he's in trouble, then he's in trouble."

"He is in trouble," Larson said. "But he can be out of trouble real quick. We'll just put the fear of God in him."

"He doesn't fear God," I said. "The only way he can find God is at the bottom of a bottle." My hands were shaking. I felt small and weak, helpless even. I didn't need things to be perfect, but I didn't want them like this.

"I just wanted to let you know," Larson said. "In case you wanted to go pick him up. The car's been impounded, so you'll have to pay to get that out. Sorry about that part."

"Don't be sorry. I sure am mortified." I thought I might cry. "I'll go get him when my shift's over."

"Okay, then." Larson walked back to the stairs. He paused and took a breath like he was about to speak. I was frightened of what else I was going to have to answer for this Wednesday morning, but he didn't say anything more about Tommy. "There's a whole other section of unsolved cases over there," he said, pointing at a table that I'd mostly ignored. It was covered in boxes, with stacks of smaller file boxes underneath. "I know you liked reading about that house fire, or at least I've noticed you with that file a few times. There's a lot more like that but just ones we didn't solve. Deck River was like *Something Wicked this Way Comes* for a while…did you read that book?"

I blushed and pushed my copy of *People* magazine under some papers on my desk. "Oh. No, I haven't yet. It's on the list."

"Oh…well, sure. It's okay." He shrugged and began to exit. "You can read whatever you want down here. It's all public, but the worst cases—you know, all the really bad unsolved stuff—is over there. The Brodericks and all that." He pointed at the table. "Let me know when you leave to get Tommy."

"Maybe next month," I said. I wasn't sure if I was joking, but Larson Gamble laughed heartily and walked up the stairs.

I was piping-hot mad and had to pull at my turtleneck. I'd worn the same mauve one again this day. It seemed to get a favorable response from Ronna.

I tried to calm down and not think about killing Tommy. I'd heard a woman say, what she thought was under her breath, the other afternoon that "Tommy Riddell's wife is becoming an embarrassment…he's got more money than Croesus, and there she is working at the police place in her snakeskin boots." I was at the butcher shop on Feldt Avenue and had my back turned. The first thing I thought was that I didn't own any snakeskin boots, but before I could put more thought into that, the other woman replied, "No kids…that's what happens." I was still like a stick of overdone bacon and so mad I thought I'd be sick. I felt similarly this morning as I contemplated how long to leave Tommy in the clink before springing him.

The next hour and a half passed without incident, and I did nothing during it but stare at the cinder block wall in front of my desk with a perfect scowl.

I ate lunch with Ronna per usual and then, only after I'd wiped my mouth and the crumbs from my turkey sandwich off the picnic table, I went to the jail and said I would pay Tommy's bail. Luther, who was the gatekeeper of the Faber County Jail, said that we didn't need to pay anything, but I insisted. It was twelve hundred dollars, for which I wrote a check. Tommy was sitting in a small cell, alone, with his shoes off. He was in his gray suit with his red tie loosened and his top button undone. "How much did you have to drink at eight o'clock in the morning?" I asked as I walked back to where he sat. A young fella named Wendell was opening the cell but didn't say a word to me or to Tommy. I was pretty sure he'd been told to be nice and discreet.

Tommy looked up at me but didn't speak. He was pensive with hands clasped. "I'm sorry I embarrassed you," he muttered finally.

"Me?" I asked. "You embarrass yourself. Why the hell were you drunk before noon? I know you're drunk after lunch…everyone knows that, but at ten a.m.? Did you pour bourbon in your cereal? Have we really come to that?"

"No." He was emphatic. "I had Bloody Marys with Chuck at the club. One too many."

"Sounds like five too many. Chuck who? Register? Why are you hanging out at the golf club with Chuck Register? I thought you were working."

"I am. I was. Chuck wants to lease that building on Sprawl Street."

"I don't care. I don't even care," I said. "I really don't. Let's go." We'd been having our conversation in the jail cell with onlookers and policemen present who were trying not to pay attention or at least look like they weren't. Tommy got up and walked with me. He might have been my new puppy. We drove home in silence after I refused to take him to the impound lot to retrieve his car. "You can walk back," I said. I knew he'd call a friend, probably Chuck Register, a bad influence, if you asked me.

Upon arriving home Tommy went upstairs to our room and closed the door. I could hear him talking on the phone. I wondered if this meant he would be fired. I picked up a Spiegel catalog and threw it in the trash just in case. "Might have to tighten our belts," I said to the kitchen table.

I wiped down the kitchen counters and stacked some papers on my desk in the sitting room. There was nothing else to do. Not even the coffee table needed dusting, so I picked up the phone and called Celeste McMichael, who lived down the street. She answered immediately and asked me to come over. "I made iced tea," she said. I grabbed a package of shortbread cookies and headed to the door. I did not tell Tommy I was leaving or where I was going. As I walked, I thought I might start crying, so I slowed down. Celeste wouldn't understand if I told her Tommy was arrested that morning. I couldn't imagine understanding that myself. I didn't understand it, and he was my husband.

8

Tommy put the "incident" as we were calling it behind him quickly. Chuck and Paula Register came over to take him to his car. Apparently, Paula had been with them at the club before Tommy got pulled over for swerving. I flashed with jealousy when Tommy said it had been her idea to have Bloody Marys. I wondered why I wasn't invited even though I don't really like Chuck or Paula and like Bloody Marys even less. It made me wonder if I was becoming too much of a dud, spending all of my time with Ronna and sitting in the basement at the precinct. Even Celeste hadn't seemed to know what to say to me when I came by her house with my cookies and my bad morning trailing behind me. We sat stiffly for a prison-sentence-like hour during which I remarked about her curtains, "not new," and her porch swing, "came with the house...you know that." Celeste had two small children named Zoe and Robert. I looked at them with remorse and then walked home feeling stuffed and dissatisfied.

I decided to throw caution to the wind and told Tommy I wanted to have a party. I needed to prove my zest. I thought about the baby every day and then again every time my period came. The only person who appeared to want to spend time with me was Ronna.

"I want to have a dinner party," I said while we got ready for work together in our bathroom. Tommy was tying his tie and looked agreeable to the idea.

I was quite handy at lamb chops and a crown roast. I decided I would do two types of potatoes, a salad, and fresh green beans along with a tomato tart and homemade creamed corn. "I can do mint jelly for the lamb, and you can make mint juleps…keeping with the theme," I said. "I'll make a strawberry pie with the pretzel crust and chocolate cupcakes, and maybe some meringues." Tommy's face was expressionless. "We can invite ten couples," I told him. "And I want to invite Ronna and Platt and Larson Gamble and his wife."

"Okay, Arlene," Tommy said.

"I've been a bit of a dud," I admitted. "Time to have some fun. You should call Chuck and Paula. I haven't seen them in so long…"

"You never want to hang out with them," he said a little defensively.

"She's just a little pushy, but I can handle them on my turf." I applied a thin layer of eye shadow in pale pink. Tommy was in the closet, running his hands through his hair. He loosened the one tie and found another. I was excited to go to work so that I could invite Ronna and Larson Gamble over. I wore a black sweater and black pants and thought I looked both professional and elegant. My hair was longer than it had been in some time. I applied mascara and a lanyard-style necklace.

"You look nice," Tommy said.

"Thank you." I was chipper, bordering on manic. It might have been an act, but I read in one of my women's magazines that attitude was everything and could actually change circumstance. I was willing to give it a go.

Ronna looked fearful when I mentioned the party. "O…kay…" she said, scanning me with her skeptical brown eyes. "I'll talk to Platt. We're picky eaters, so we don't usually go out for dinner," she said.

"I'll make you anything you want," I said brightly. She pursed her lips and again assured me that she would speak to her husband.

Larson Gamble was a little more amenable and said he and his wife, Laura, would try to make it. I'd set the date for two Saturdays away. After the initial excitement about having something to say to the people at work wore off, I found myself once again in the basement, staring at the small, rectangular windows. Tommy's run-in with the law had not been mentioned again—at least at the station, and I was grateful. They'd given Tommy the bail money back when he got his car, and he took it. I thought that was a trashy thing to do, but I was tired of being mad, so I let it slide.

There had been seven pieces of evidence to tag and put away on my desk that morning. It took me fourteen minutes in total and then I had the remaining three hours and forty-six minutes to fill. The Broderick files turned out to be easy to find once I knew where to look—there were dozens of them, filling several boxes, and sitting on the table in the corner. The promise of getting to dive into this is what had gotten me to the station on Monday. I was in full party-prep mode and had considered calling in sick to work. It dawned on me that I was only there for something to do. If I had something else to do—anything—then I would probably dump the job.

Inside the most overstuffed folder that sat on top of one of the boxes were two pictures stapled to the folder itself. Written under a photo of a girl with raven hair and blue eyes—not a speck of color on her face, and a stark expression like the settlers or kids going to get shot in the Civil War—was the name Claire Rebecca Broderick. The other was of a young man who looked to be about Claire's age, maybe a little older. He was sandy haired, also with light eyes, but he had an angrier expression with pursed lips and a sneer. Mitchell Wayne Wright, the black writing said. Both names were like sweaters I'd once owned. I remembered them but couldn't recall what I'd done with them. The dates under the photos meant that Claire and Mitchell were a little more than ten years older than Tommy and me. I considered that my brother Bobby, or better yet my brother Lou, who was eleven years older than I was, probably knew

Mitchell. When Bobby died, my mother never really forgave the rest of us who didn't. Being that Lou sensed her anger at his continued existence, he didn't come around much. I thought I could call him later and ask him if he knew Mitchell and Claire. I had a little bee in my bonnet after seeing their pictures; this could prove to be interesting. They were younger and more regular looking than a lot of the people in the files. So far, I'd mostly seen hobo types or drug addicts covered in tattoos and track marks with skinny mustaches and that broken look of a person who's lost all sense of where they are and why. These two were different. They hadn't yet been destroyed before this happened.

Claire Broderick had four brothers, all younger than her. Cedar, Colton, Chase, and Carter. There was a lot of talk in the file about the youngest boy, whose birth brought about Claire's mother's passing at Faber Memorial Hospital. Becky Massey Broderick died of massive blood loss from a uterine tear during labor. Cecil Broderick was the father and Becky's husband. Becky Broderick was only thirty-one when she died. I did the math, and that meant she had Claire when she was fifteen years old. I knew that sort of thing happened in Faber and especially Deck River, where the Brodericks lived, but it had been a while since I'd heard anything about country marriages that made people blush, and babies being born to babies.

Chase Broderick, the youngest of the three older boys, would have been about my age, but I didn't know him. If he didn't go to school with us, then chances were good that we'd never crossed paths. I knew some kids from way out of town didn't go to school so they could work or hustle or because no one cared what they did. I'd only met a handful of these people over the years. They were the backwoods types that my mama wanted me to stay away from, and I did for the most part. Carter Broderick had been in diapers when all of this went down. I definitely didn't know him or either of the older boys who were ten and seven at the time.

The gist of the Broderick case was, as I discovered after reading about ten pages on these people living out in the woods with no mother, that the eldest three of the boys—Cedar, Colton, and Chase—died near Deck River one evening. It didn't say how or why in this particular stack of documents, but the case was considered a triple homicide.

Claire Broderick and her boyfriend, Mitchell Wright, were charged with murder over the incident, but I hadn't seen why yet. I knew people drowned in lakes and rivers all the time in Faber and of course in Deck River with its angry current and rising waterline, hurling itself up the sides of the bank without notice or polite caution. People were warned not to swim there. I knew that; everyone knew that. There were even signs in the one parking lot, cautioning people to steer clear when the water was high. Either way, Claire and Mitchell were charged with murder, but the case was still considered unsolved. I also couldn't make sense of that.

It appeared to me that quite a big stink had been made of the murders, but I'd be damned if I remembered it at all. I was a little kid then—probably too young to have been paying attention. It seemed a funny thing to stop talking about—ever. That happened in places like Faber—people wanted either to stop talking about it right away or to never ever let it go. There was no in-between with bad times.

There were several more pictures of Claire and Mitchell in the file and then of course the victims before they died. Claire was a young seventeen when the boys were killed. Mitchell was eighteen. The baby, Lucille, was a newborn—only a few months old. There were a couple of pictures of her being held by a cheerful Claire and a pensive Mitchell, who looked like a person accused of a crime— and he was a person accused of a crime, in the end.

I found that I'd been reading for almost two hours when I heard noise from above. The door to the basement opened with a thud, and Larson Gamble came down the stairs quickly. I automatically thought that I was about to be told that Tommy had been arrested again.

"Hi, Arlene," Captain Gamble said. "I have some more stuff. Won't take you long, but anyway…" He put a few items on the desk. Everything was already in a bag, as it always was, but not the larger, labeled bag. That was my job, and then of course to put all of the correct information on the outside and triple check it, then put it back in the box to be appropriately stored.

"Ah, there they are—the Brodericks," Gamble said. "Don't say I didn't warn you. It's pretty dark stuff."

"Oh yes. Incredibly disturbing. Incredibly." I was standing. I always stood when Captain Gamble came down the stairs, even though he'd assured me it wasn't necessary.

"It's a good read though. Have you gotten to the part about Mitchell yet?"

"No, I mean…yes, he's in here. What happened to Mitchell?"

"Well, what didn't happen is more like it." Gamble paused, moving the four bags he'd just put on my desk while staring embarrassedly at my crotch. "We never really knew what happened—to any of them. We kind of ran out of leads or information. The whole thing faded a little; it was the kind of thing people wanted to fade. Claire's family had a bad reputation, bottom-feeder types, you know. I don't want to say anyone was glad that happened, but it was a little bit like the worst thing happening to the worst people. It was hard to get good information on a Broderick anyway, even Claire and the other kids. They lived on Deck River back before everybody left. The dad was a mess and couldn't take care of any of them. I'm not really sure what happened there, but Claire, who was really just a kid herself, had to raise all the boys on her own—she was the oldest. And then she went and got pregnant by Mitchell Wright, and they were a really good family, the Wrights. The dad owned the pool place. Anyway, she got pregnant, and they were living over in some shack by Deck River in squalor. There were all sorts of rumors about her and him and the kids, and none of them having enough to eat, and the school's complaining because the older boys came to class without underwear and filthy from their knees to their elbows, and then there were rumors that they were swimming down by Deck River alone at night, and then they ended up dead. Not even really hidden, just dead on the bank. A lady..." He paused. "Sorry, am I rambling?"

"No," I lied emphatically. "Please go on."

"So...someone was driving by and saw them. Just lying there. They originally thought it was the boys' father who did it, because he just wasn't right. That's—" Gamble shook his head in dismay. "That's another thing...just awful that any of those kids were left with him in the first place. You know the system is broken. Real broken, and when something like this happens, you start to see it loud and clear.

"I was only an officer then. I hadn't made detective yet—it was Duke Pendley—well, you know. You said you saw his house or something. He was on homicide, and I mean, he had almost zero experience investigating murders. Most of the time, he helped out on drug busts and runaway kids and all that. There were maybe two homicides a year in Faber or anywhere near it, and usually it was a bar fight thing, not like...a real murder. Duke's only suspects were Claire and Mitchell. They were really young and totally overrun, and the kids were living with them, and of course there were lots of stories about Claire and the way she treated the kids, and then some people were saying the youngest boy, Carter, was actually her baby, which was preposterous, because the doctor delivered

Carter at the hospital, and Becky Massey—that was the Brodericks' mother—died, and that was that, but you know how people talk. Claire just got stuck raising him. Anyway, it was a whole sad mess. Just a mess. I did a lot of the interviews—helped Duke out. Those two never really said anything though—Claire and Mitchell, and then you know—" Gamble nodded. "Anyway, the sister—Mitchell's sister, Natalie, gave him an alibi, and she stuck to it. So even though Pendley was sure it was him—at least at first, there was nothing anybody could do."

I thought I'd never heard anything so interesting in my life, especially after seeing their photos and knowing they'd lived just down the road and that all this happened when I was a little kid. It was like I was watching a movie while Gamble talked. He moved his head and chin around along with his eyes; it was clear he was trying to get a glimpse of my bottom now that my crotch had been thoroughly examined. I stayed facing forward.

"What about Mitchell?" I said. "What happened to him? And how did the kids die? It doesn't really say. Did they drown?"

"No. No, they didn't drown. No." Gamble stopped talking.

"Is it okay to ask?" I said. "Sorry."

"No, no—of course it's okay, it's just… Anyway, at first we didn't know what happened, but it wasn't drowning. I mean— we've had a few drowning deaths over there, but those boys didn't drown." He moved toward the stairs, an indication that he needed to go, but stopped. He put his fist over his mouth. "There were a lot of stories," he said calmly. "People said Claire was taking the boys down there right when the dam broke every night, hoping they'd die. Someone said she tried to get them to cramp, so they'd go under. Mitchell and Claire were really desperate for money— his parents stopped helping them out. And I know Claire was going over to Ram's bar—you know, that hole-in-the-wall place that used to be over on the river—late at night. People said she was hanging out trying to sell herself to the patrons. I don't know about any of that, but other people—more upstanding people who didn't want to admit they were hanging out at Ram's but came forward after we put out a press release that anyone who knew anything and who didn't come forward was asking for trouble— they said she was working at Ram's, serving drinks in a tight skirt, but that was it. The kids lived out in the woods half the time. It's a wonder something bad didn't happen to them sooner than it did. Anyway, sad business. But they didn't drown." He pointed at me like he'd tried to make me understand this information a half dozen times already. He hadn't answered me about Mitchell; that gave me a bit of a drop in my stomach. "It had nothing to do with the river," he added.

"How'd they die, then?" I asked.

"Suffocated. They had rags shoved down their throats." He turned again to go.

"Who found them?" I said. "It doesn't say who found them."

"Oh," he frowned. "I don't really remember about that." He

patted the wall next to the stairs with his right hand and started to head up.

"What about Mitchell?" I called after him. He was out of sight and moving at a clip.

"He killed himself." I could tell he'd stopped on the landing. "'Bout two weeks after they found the kids."

August 21, 1982

The power went out for a solid hour. Mitchell let me drink a margarita at Huey's with him. We took off there when the air-conditioning went out with the lights. It was too hot to sit at the house. My dad called before we lost power and said he was in the Piggly Wiggly, waiting it out. The worst of the storm blew over, so Mom stayed at the house. She said she didn't care if it was hot. She went out on the porch like she always does.

Margaritas have a ton of salt on them. I love pretzels, but I didn't like just plain salt on a glass like that. Mitchell had two! He's not old enough to drink—only eighteen. I'm fifteen, nearly sixteen. My birthday is next March. I've had this journal for a couple of years. I guess you could call it a diary, but I think maybe I'm too old for that. I'm going to start writing every day now. My grandpa has always kept a journal. He even writes down if he goes to the grocery store or the driving range. He says it's nice to remember your life. A person can only keep track of so much in their head. Everything in here before is just different ways to write my name and love letters to my favorite horses. I ride all the time—that's my sport. I don't really like any of the sports at school, but I go train with the horses a few days a week. I don't have a horse of my own—yet. When I get older and have a job, I'm going to have two horses that I ride every day.

Mitchell played basketball his whole life, but he didn't make the varsity team this year. I think that's why he was having a margarita, to drown his sorrows. Aunt Alaina says there's nothing a good drink can't fix. My mom hates when she says stuff like that, because it might make us alcoholics. Mitchell did seem a lot happier after he got all that salt down the hatch though. He's played basketball every year—since he was six—but the coach cut him the last day of tryouts. My dad was so mad he kicked the door to the garage. I never saw Mitchell cry before—at least not since we were little kids. He cried a lot over that.

And anyway, Aunt Alaina isn't my aunt really. She's my mom's best friend. They're like sisters, so much so that it makes my dad jealous. Aunt Alaina needs people though. Her husband, Stanton, ran around on her after he got disbarred—which means he can't be a lawyer anymore. He stole some people's money and used it for illegal purposes. He didn't have to go to jail, but he had a couple of affairs because of the strains of community service and being made such an example of. Alaina said it was the stress that made him stray. Alaina comes over all the time to sit with my mother. She acts like my mother needs the company, but it's definitely Alaina who can't stand to be alone. They dress exactly alike and decorate their houses the same. It's like the chicken and the egg though—I can never tell who did what first.

My dad is Dan Wright. He owns Fischer Pool Service. We don't have a pool, but he knows everything about them. He used to run the place before Dill Fischer got too old to handle anything anymore. He sold it to my dad. My mom stays home with me and Mitchell...and Alaina. Stanton covers Alaina in jewels and buys her fancy cars to make up for everything. I think my mom is jealous about that part—the cars and necklaces, not the reason for them.

That's all for now.

P.S. I know it's bad to drink alcohol when you're a kid, but I just wanted to try it. You're the only one I'm telling, journal. If anybody from Youth Group found out, I'd be in trouble or maybe kicked out. When Janice Forrest smoked cigarettes last year at retreat, she wasn't allowed to go to chapel for a month. I don't want that to be me.

9

I was dumbstruck when Gamble left the room. "Suffocated," I said to myself. "And suicide. God, what is this country coming to?" I shook my head in heavy dismay. Surely nothing like this had happened before my generation got the keys to the car. I heard the door at the top of the stairs close heavily and wondered if Gamble had heard me talking to myself.

Because I was feeling guilty about the way the country was going down the toilet what with all these horrible things happening in my backyard and then being hushed up because they happened to the poverty-stricken and destitute, I thought to call my mother when I got home. She enjoyed a good discourse on how awful things were now that all the good politicians were dead or in jail.

My mother and I only talked about once a week, less since the baby went away. My mother would probably remember the

Brodericks. She remembered everyone. It was one of her main interests in life—to know about other people's tragedies.

I rushed through my lunch with Ronna, who was standoffish, more than normal, acting strangely angry that I'd invited her to my house for dinner. "Well, see you tomorrow," I said, hurrying to my car.

"Yes. Here. You'll see me here," Ronna said. She wiped her mouth.

I called my mother the second I got home. "Hello." She sounded like she'd been sleeping.

"Do you remember Claire Broderick?" I asked.

"Who? No. What time is it?" Now she sounded tired and confused.

"It's one in the afternoon," I told my mother, as if this alone would change her demeanor. "Do you remember Claire Broderick?"

"No. I mean I remember the Brodericks. That name is familiar, but I don't know anyone called Claire."

"Cecil Broderick?" I asked.

"Yes, maybe. I really don't know. Here, ask your father."

I heard the phone being passed off, and my mother saying something about exhaustion, which was, in addition to the weather, an all-too-frequent topic of conversation. Sales at the grocery store, fatigue, and whether it was this hot or cold or wet or dry the previous year were the exclusive content of their discourse. With me, she liked to blame the younger generations too.

"Hello?" my father said. He always answered the phone like he was shocked that someone was calling.

"It's Arlene. Do you remember the Broderick family? They lived over on Deck River."

"Well…vaguely. I remember a Broderick. Older fella with two kids. I don't know what happened to them. It's been a long time. How do you know the Brodericks?"

"I don't! Anyway—" I sighed, regretting the call. "I'm having a party next weekend. I'm really excited about it. I'd love if you and Mom could come. We'll be having mint juleps."

"Oh, well, we don't really do parties anymore. You know we go to bed so early, and your mother gets headaches from wine, so…"

"Well, I'm making a ton of food. It's not going to be some raucous thing with people hanging from the ceiling. It's an adult party."

"I'll let your mother decide. Aren't mint juleps a summer drink?" my dad said while handing over the phone.

"They're for horses," my mother said before letting me know, rather finally, that she was tired and needed to lie down. She suggested we talk about the party later. I might as well have asked them if they wanted to count acorns in the backyard; their disinterest would have been similar.

Tommy's sister, Lacey, came for dinner that night. I regaled her with the story about the Broderick kids and Claire and Mitchell and everything in between. "Interesting," she said before putting some more asparagus on her plate.

"It's more than interesting," I told her, but her and Tommy's faces were blank and staring.

"Arlene here missed her calling. She should have been a detective," Tommy said, bright-eyed. His hair was too long in back, and he'd spit a small bit when he spoke because he was talking with his mouth full. If it weren't his own sister at our house, I would have been embarrassed for him looking like such a simpleton. He was even holding his fork incorrectly and had both elbows on the table.

"Tommy, really," I said, but I don't think either of them knew what I was talking about. Lacey grew up with him; I couldn't expect her to want him to change as much as I did. "I don't know if I should have been a detective," I said, "but I think this is a fascinating case. I just wish someone I knew remembered them. Can you get your elbows off the table? Did we lose our manners?"

"I never had any! Ha!" Tommy laughed uproariously.

"I'd like to have manners," I said.

"Good luck," Lacey said, shaking her head with attitude. "But yeah, I remember all of that," Lacey added, more to herself than to me. I perked up, about to ask her what she knew. Being that she was so much older than us, she probably went to school with at least one of these people for a while.

"Hell, I remember the Brodericks," Tommy sprayed across the table. I considered that I'd put entirely too much butter on the vegetables the way he was having such trouble keeping Lacey's and my faces dry while eating. "I do," he went on after wiping his mouth.

I noticed Lacey wipe her mouth too and look down. She was in closest proximity. "One of them was named after a tree or something," she said to me sincerely, as if she knew the way they weren't taking this very seriously was hurting my feelings.

"Cedar," I told her.

"What's for dessert?" Tommy asked. "Did you make cookies? I thought I smelled something when I came in…"

I was annoyed. Here I was, introducing pertinent, if not riveting, investigative information to an otherwise-dull dinner, and all Tommy could think about was cookies. "Yes, but two per customer limit," I told him. "I don't think you need to go losing your hand in the cookie jar the way those trousers are fitting lately." Tommy's face was blank, then red. Lacey dropped her fork and cleared her throat. "Sorry," I muttered. I didn't talk to Tommy or anyone else like that. I wasn't the kind of woman who belittled her husband. "Sorry," I said again, ashamed.

"I think the story sounds really interesting," Lacey said like she was trying to figure how to continue. "And I do remember them. If you want to talk about it, I'd like to help. Or…I don't know, are you—"

Tommy interrupted. "We did hear about it, but they were poor white trash and nobody cared. Sad state of affairs, but it's true. Everyone sort of thought they had it coming the way they lived. If I show you a picture of the one kid our age, you'll remember, Arlene." He rose from the table and walked over to where I'd set the plate of cookies. He took exactly two and opened the refrigerator.

"Would anyone like some milk?" he asked loudly. He couldn't have been more vulnerable to my judgment at that moment than if he'd been asking for money in his underwear.

"Yes, I'll have some milk," I said. Tommy reached for the Kahlúa too from where it had been resting on top of the refrigerator.

We sat down on the couches in the formal living room after dinner with the idea to chat, but no one seemed to have the energy. My mind was singularly on the Brodericks. I did want to talk to Lacey about it, but Tommy was like a bull in a china shop, smashing through every conversation with food flying out of his mouth. Lacey was saying something about a sale on fabric at Joann's, and I talked over her after a moment of silent, distracted contemplation. "What about Mitchell Wright?" I asked. "Did you know Mitchell Wright?"

Lacey looked at me and then at Tommy, who now appeared to be sleeping with his eyes open. I knew he was waiting for Lacey to leave so he could really enjoy himself, a game on the television and a drink in his hand. Lacey reported all of Tommy's behavior— good or bad—to his mother and his other sister, Liv, who in turn told his brother, Mark. Mark lived in Oregon with his distant wife. They were like foreigners when they came home, scoffing at the local customs and lifestyle, bewildered that anyone would choose to live here, like this.

"That was who Claire Broderick was married to," I said. "Mitchell Wright. Did you know the Wrights?" I asked Lacey.

"No." She shook her head. "No, I don't know any of these people, but I remember them. I'm sure there are a lot of Wrights in Faber anyway. That's kind of a common name. Well," she said, standing. "I better get going." Clearly Tommy and I were not the consummate hosts I'd thought we were; we were boring even Lacey, who liked to talk about jogging, Psalms, Oprah's Book Club, and quilts—although this was the first I'd heard of this hobby. I thought long and hard about my upcoming party. It seemed I was going to need to invent a new personality for the evening.

I had a little trouble falling asleep. I was worried about what had become of me, a person who used to be so carefree and buoyant, Tommy and I both. Now I preferred Ronna and her meatloaf for company and actually got a charge from reading about dead people in the basement of the police station, and there Tommy was—in jail half the time with a leaky mouth. I got so worked up thinking that I was all dried up and uninteresting at the ripe old age of twenty-four and found that I was crying. I couldn't stop and knew I was making a racket.

Tommy came up the stairs to check on me, his bourbon still in his hand. "What's a matter?" he asked.

"Are we sticks-in-the-mud?" I asked through my tears. I didn't want to mention his table manners again.

"I don't know," he said, shrugging. He looked at his drink, put it on the bedside table, and sat down. "I don't know that I even care. I don't feel like a stick-in-the-mud."

"We're awful young to be sitting around talking about cloth and pancake factories with your mouth open drooling on the couch..." I said, again sounding like I was criticizing him.

Tommy flinched. "Who was talking about cloth?"

"Your sister. It doesn't matter...it just seems like I'm in a bad mood all the time now, and there's nothing interesting to talk about, and I used to think I had all this in front of me—you know, excitement—and we were gonna do so much, but I don't feel like doing anything, and I'm tired, and I just..." I'd stopped actually crying and was now just sniffling and frowning.

"Gosh," Tommy said. "I thought you were real hyped up about your party. You know, all that cooking and cleaning and stuff that makes you so happy."

"Don't gosh me," I said. "We can't have a party if we can't think of anything to say! And I don't like cleaning. Whoever told you I liked cleaning? Am I so dull that you think I like cleaning? There were crows circling over our house the other day—big, ugly ones. They thought we were about to die, we're so boring in here. And you got arrested and there's no baby, and it doesn't look like there is ever going to be one. I really have zero personality most of the time. I was over at Celeste's house the other day, and we had absolutely nothing to say to each other. She asked me if I watched *America's Most Wanted.*"

"Maybe because you work at the police station." Tommy was hopeful. I noticed the damp bourbon glass dropping condensation on our cherry furniture but chose to stay mum for fear of being a self-fulfilling prophecy. Only a seriously dull person would interrupt the only good conversation she'd had in a month with her husband to complain about a stain on furniture from Sears.

"I can't lie…" I shook my head. "I'm real fascinated by these dead people from Deck River. Maybe a little too fascinated." I looked at him for reassurance.

Tommy looked back but didn't say anything. I wondered for the first time—in all my mental tossing and turning—if he was happy. I'd always felt so lucky to have snagged him, but I was having my doubts. He suddenly seemed weak and simple. I put the thought out of my head. He smelled like liquor, and I didn't want to see him whatever way it was I was trying not to see him.

"Everybody thinks those murder cases are interesting," he assured me.

"Right, but I want to be happy." It didn't make sense, but I was having a difficult time wrangling my thoughts.

"I guess I think happy comes and goes," he finally said to my blotchy stare. "I don't know how I feel all the time, and I think that's a big difference between us. When I do notice how I'm doing, I'm usually happy though." He shrugged. "I don't like to let you down," he said like he was asking a question.

"No one is letting me down," I said. "I don't know…" I shook my head. "I had my heart set on that baby, and I don't know where it went. It's like it's still inside me."

"No, I don't think so," Tommy began. "There's something inside you, maybe. Like loss." He drew his brows together and stood up. "I'll leave you alone." I knew that was code for him needing another drink. I could hear my wind chimes clanging from their hook on the back porch. It sounded like a call on an ancient telephone. The house creaked a little from a powerful gust. I heard the leaves— crisp and dying—clatter like potato chips dropped on a kitchen floor. I had a chill from how unsettled it all made me feel. The onset of a mountain fall was always a little lonesome. All we have up here in the hills are our leaves. When they go, it can be hard to keep your head up.

I rolled to my side and thought about Mitchell Wright's face, stark and distant in his mug shot. He didn't have a dinner party or a Spiegel catalog to consider, especially not when they arrested him for killing those kids. I sure had dippy concerns. It really was sad that I was so worked up over how boring I'd become and whether it was proper to serve a mint julep in early October.

I heard the distant call of a crow, and for the briefest moment a vision of Claire walking up on her brothers' bodies on the banks of Deck River on a rainy November day filled me with the most overwhelming sense of dread. The crow cawed again. I've always hated crows.

Mitchell's gone and done it. He told my dad he's not going to college. They had a huge fight. There's this change that's come over Mitchell this year. I think it's because of basketball. He won't even go to the games, and that used to be his life. He stays home by himself and ignores his friends. I think he's been hanging out with Claire Broderick some. She's my grade but looks a lot older. A lot of people call her white trash and a whore and all that. It's kind of sad. She's gone to my school forever, but we've never been friends. When we were little she was always dirty, and nobody could understand her. Her parents never came to any of the stuff at the school, so she had to sit by herself. My mom said her clothes were too small and for boys and that Claire got free lunch. She's different now; she grew up to be kind of pretty and mature looking. The really sad thing is that her mom died in childbirth a couple of years ago and she's got all these little brothers—like four of them. They live in Deck River. It's kind of the wrong side of the tracks if you know what I mean. My dad says he's never worked on a pool in Deck River. Those people are lucky to have furniture much less a pool. It's on the other side of downtown Faber. There's something wrong with the water there. I think it's the pipes, so that's why no one really lives there much anymore. Well—except the Brodericks. Claire wears a lot of makeup and has big boobs. The boys all look at her and talk about how many slices of tomatoes her boobs are. I have only a seed and one small slice from the end. At least that's what I think; the boys don't talk about me. I hang out with the church crowd. We all have matching bracelets and want to be good people like not having sex before marriage and not drinking even though I did that once, but I know it's wrong. Mitchell used to come to Youth Group all the time, but he sort of quit that too. People ask me about him, but I don't really know what to say. He's not very interested in anything lately. That's why I think maybe he's hot and heavy with Claire. He's never had a real girlfriend before this. He dated Callie Francis from our church, but they broke up last year. My parents don't really know about Claire yet. Mitchell has his own car, so he can come and go as he pleases. Sometimes I think Mitchell got too hurt when Callie broke up with him, and then he didn't make the basketball team. I think he's trying to be a different person now. He thinks his old self is a failure or something. Callie and Claire kind of sound alike too. It might be that.

Anyway, he's not going to University of Georgia. He told my

parents he sent the paperwork back. He got early acceptance, but that means he had to agree to go there right away. It was the only school he applied to. My dad called him a loser, and I could tell my mom was crying even though she tried to hide it. She went into their bedroom and called Alaina, which is what she always does when she's really upset. Mitchell and my dad had it out, but then Mitchell left. My dad said he wouldn't support him anymore, but I don't think Mitchell cares. He has a job at Flannigan's Sporting Goods. I don't know where he went when he left. He didn't come home until way after nine, which isn't allowed on a school night. He's supposed to be home by eight.

I also found a condom in his backpack the other day. I was only snooping because I saw him leaning up into Claire by the cafeteria at school. He told me they were hanging out, but it looked like more than that. She always has her nails painted and her boobs out of her clothes. She's been sent home to change a couple of times. Once she just safety pinned a piece of paper over her V-neck. She looks like a cherry—all round—with dark hair on top. Her face is very sweet, almost angel-like, but the way she talks and moves around is more like Eve than Mary. I'm sure Mitchell's just in it for the goods. We talk about that at Youth Group a lot…getting pulled into sin by good feelings and bodily pleasures. I was going to say something to Mitchell about it, but he doesn't seem very interested in Youth Group anymore. I've never seen Claire at church, period.

A CONDEMNED MAN

I'VE ALWAYS CONSIDERED MYSELF A condemned man, so it's no surprise. I don't have the good nature my mother tried to give me. She didn't have it either. She was dumb as a skunk and living on welfare her whole life, but she hoped I'd be different. She wanted me to be a good man. That's how she talked about my dad, such a good man. He died before I could argue with her about it. It was me, my sister, Chrissy, and mama, who was just like me. That's why she was so worried—she could see it on me too.

They were mean to me when I's a kid. There were brothers up the road—the Charleys. That's what I called 'em, because I only knew the one's name, Charley. He spelled it funny—with a y. The others were his brothers or cousins or something.

They messed with me bad. I try to forget about it, but it creeps in. It wasn't like sex stuff, they were just mean. They were mean to my sister too, real mean. She ran away cause of 'em. I shoulda done the same, but my mama was so set on me being a good boy. She's the one who took me over to the barn all the time. She wanted me to have a job, so she drove me over and told me to be good. "Be sweet," she'd say. "Be sweet." She'd dig her hand into the base of my back when she said it—where all the bones are, like she was trying to find a handle there, something she could turn. I didn't get turned. "Be sweet." The bones didn't move.

The Charleys followed me there a few times and tried to shove shit up my ass when I was out mending the fences. They'd find me out there and spit on me and stuff. Once, and I don't even know why, I left the pasture with them, and we went over to these girls' house that lived off Cove Street. I didn't want to do nothing sexy to 'em, but Charley did. He had this thing about people's assholes. I don't really know what happened, because he and his brother had those girls back behind their house. They were screaming something serious. At first I was just standing out by the road, but then when the screaming got too loud, I went back there and just lit 'em up. The one girl's nose slid halfway 'cross her face I swear. They stopped screaming, and it was like a good feeling to have shut 'em up. Charley didn't mess with me so much after that. Those girls moved away too. Their dad had some trouble with money, and I guess he didn't want 'em gettin' tore up no more.

I really only had one friend in my life. The Charleys weren't my friends. Jorge—he could saddle a bull, I swear to God. I really admired him, and he was a good man—the kind my mama dreamt about. He had a wife and kids he took care of. He was real religious and used to say I had a bad mark on me. Like he could see it. He'd put his hand on me and say he hoped I could find Jesus.

Jorge was around for a while but then he got a better deal somewhere down south. I never thought I could miss somebody, but I did miss him. He was the best man I met in my whole life. He was always worried about me because of his religion. He thought I needed to get right with God or I was gonna end up in the fiery furnace.

Jorge told me about the bad mark I had on myself, and it just seemed like I better have it here and not some other place. Faber seemed as good a place as any to have a bad mark on you. Jorge said it was like a line down the front of me that split me in half. He said one side was good and the other bad. He said my mama had it too, but she killed her bad side. He was always praying for me. It didn't work though. I guess God didn't owe Jorge any favors, and I couldn't kill one-half myself like my mama. I think about Jorge all the time. I still do. He'd be real disappointed to know what I did. I did other stuff too, but he'd be real down to hear about me now. I think he'd know Jesus didn't find me. Or I didn't find him, however it works.

10

I'd slept very restlessly. I wanted to say it was party prep and Tommy's table manners keeping me up, but the Brodericks were everywhere in my mind. When I thought about Tommy spraying his food across the table, I wondered if Mitchell Wright did that when he ate. I wondered if Claire ever cooked meatloaf or had dreams of owning a lodge.

There was a recurring character in the case file that I'd been ignoring a little. Alaina Watson. She was a detective it seemed, but not until the end. In the beginning she'd been the Wright family's friend. She seemed pushy and insistent. I didn't like reading her interviews and avoided her and Mitchell's sister, Natalie, as much as I could—Natalie because she was boring and clearly didn't know anything. She was barely sixteen when all of this happened. She sounded like a goody-two-shoes to me, not someone Mitchell would have shared anything important with.

It was because she was his alibi; that was it. She was the linchpin. How disappointing for the case to have counted on her; she had braces, for God's sake.

With the Brodericks and my increasingly bland personality ever on my mind, I spent the entire weekend preparing for the party. It was nice to be busy on a Saturday for a change. Tommy and I had used to go fishing on the weekends, but he wasn't as keen on that anymore. He'd also lost interest in camping, which had been one of his favorite pastimes up until the dough started rolling in. I thought maybe the money ruined us, but here I was spending it like a drunken sailor. I was part of our problem.

I bought almost four-hundred-dollars' worth of food at both the big grocery store and then a few of the specialty shops around town that carried niche things liked spiced cashews and cheese that no one really liked but wanted to eat in order to seem worldly. The weather was brisk and windy. My hair flipped about my head like a broken umbrella turned inside out every time I got out of the car. I'd made list after list of exactly what and when I would prepare and set about cleaning the house from top to bottom when I got home from my six-store jaunt, even employing a toothbrush for the nooks and crannies. Tommy stayed out of my way and said encouraging things about the "shiny" floors and "damn that smells good." I'd set out the meringues, which had no smell at all.

Tommy claimed he'd been read the riot act at work for his arrest but if he did get in trouble, they welcomed him back into the fold with open arms almost immediately. He told me he made it by the skin of his teeth and was now on the straight and narrow. No more two-martini lunches or treks to the golf club before ten. He acted like I'd asked this of him, but I hadn't. I wasn't even sure anyone at work had. Tommy was cut from the same cloth as most of his buddies at Hall Street. I had a hard time imagining any of them really caring about his slap on the wrist.

"Meringues don't smell," I said to Tommy a little while later, like I'd just decided I was annoyed he'd said that. I leaned over the plate. There was a slight scent of orange, but I wasn't going to admit it. "They're not going to last out like this," I said more to myself. I walked to the cabinet for some Tupperware.

"I'll eat 'em mushy," Tommy said enthusiastically. He was so intent on pleasing me these days. It was a little irritating.

Celeste, who'd I'd obviously invited to the party because I considered her one of my closest friends even if I couldn't figure out what to say to her half the time anymore, grew mint in her backyard and offered me several handfuls of it for our juleps. It was the end of the growing season, and she needed to get rid of it.

I'd made a big fuss out of having mint juleps in silver cups, which is how they're supposed to be served. After boxing the meringues and thinking forlornly about Tommy for a while, I walked over to take Celeste up on her offer. She answered the door with a plastic baggie already in hand, filled to the brim with mint leaves. Shrugging off the sensation that she didn't want me to stay, I thanked her and turned to go. She made some comment about not being sure she could come to the party after all.

"Oh. Why?" I asked, instantly hurt.

"We don't have a babysitter," she said. "Wes says we can leave the kids here asleep and take turns running back to check on them, but I'm not comfortable with that."

"Oh." These were problems I didn't have. No matter how I tried to relate to the concerns and responsibilities of caring for children, I couldn't. "I don't know of any babysitters," I said finally. "I wish I did." I went home with the mint clutched a little too tightly in my fist.

The street between ours and Celeste's felt wide and uninspiring, not even her mums—planted neatly by the mailbox—could warm my mood. A gust of wind dipped and blew up the back of my neck. Errant, brittle leaves on the driveway twirled in a circle, like a small tornado with a lazy eye. The swirl calmed and the leaves tossed themselves back on the cement in defeat. Once off the limb, there's really nothing left for a leaf. Dust to dust. The Broderick boys and Mitchell had returned to the earth already. And Bobby. I swallowed my discomfort at having to think about these people every time my mind was the least bit unoccupied. My mind was like the best parking spot at the store; it wouldn't stay empty for long.

We had twelve confirmed guests, which, according to Tommy, wasn't a very large crowd. He told me I was acting like I was preparing for the Normandy invasion. I told him he could help or shut up. I'd come to talking to him like that, and I wasn't proud.

When I had my mini-outbursts, I thought of him in his old beat-up Toyota truck with the American flag sticker on the back that he drove when we first met and into the first years of our marriage. I couldn't be mean to the guy in that truck if I could just find him again, or maybe it wasn't him I was looking for but the girl who fell in love with him.

The Bumper: that's what we'd called the truck. I never used to let go of Tommy's hand, not even when he was trying to steer. If I did have to release my grasp, then I put my hand on his shoulder, his thigh, or I just scooted over and nuzzled into his armpit. I was certain—for the longest time—that I was born to ride in that truck with him. I'd never considered that anything would change. In the summer the trees grew over the road, so thick and grasping, they'd create a tunnel through which we'd skate like a busted wagon. I called it the Tunnel of Love, but it was more like a birth canal. I went through and came out a different person—first attached to my mother, and then attached to Tommy. I was the kind of gal who keeps a chord wrapped around her own neck.

February 26, 1983

I was at the stables today, and Tina Callahan told me Claire was pregnant. I was combing Feather—my mare (she's not really mine, but I ride her all the time). She boards at Starling Hollow where I ride. I love her. If I could have any horse in the world, it would be Feather. She's only about three with a mane the color of butter. Right now, it's a little shaggy because she's still got her winter coat, but she is such a good girl. I've been riding for six years. It's my first love (besides Jesus and my family). Anyway—sorry, sidetracked. Tina Callahan who works at the stables said Claire Broderick is pregnant. She said she knows, because Claire told her. Tina's way older than us. She went to Faber High School but that was a long time ago. She used to be considered the most beautiful girl in Faber; all the boys loved her; they still talk about her sometimes, but she's older now. She still tries to dress like she's a teenager, even though she's not. Tina has a boyfriend who works at the stables too, but I kind of stay away from him. He gives me the creeps. He wears his hat pulled real low and a lot of the girls say he tries to get with them when Tina's not looking.

Tina just came up to me out of the blue and said Claire was pregnant and I better ask Mitchell about it. Claire is definitely Mitchell's girlfriend even if Mitchell never really said that. She comes over to the house all the time. She has to bring her little brothers with her everywhere, because her dad is an unfit parent, and she doesn't have a mom. There are four of them—the little one is Carter. Claire's mom died when he was born. All the kids have C names. I can't keep them straight. They embarrass me so much. They're filthy and eat my parents out of house and home whenever they come—which is literally almost every day. Most of the time they aren't even wearing underwear; I can tell. They're gross kids, and I know the dad gets in trouble all the time for how he doesn't take care of them. Claire can drive— she's already sixteen, so she takes them around with her after school. Wherever she goes, they go. They aren't allowed to be at the house alone.

Mitchell acts like he doesn't care, but those kids drive me crazy. I can't understand a word they say, and they are so LOUD. My mom tries not to complain about the mess they make and how they're always going through the pantry and the fridge, but I do complain. I said something to Alaina last time she was over. She said we have to be charitable. I told her my mom is about to lose it, and she said no, she isn't. Alaina says my mom is a good woman and will do the right thing no matter what.

We had Claire and her dad over for dinner once right after my parents finally admitted that Mitchell and Claire were boyfriend and girlfriend. They left the other kids in the car. My mom didn't know until we were almost done eating. One of them—the oldest one—came to the door and said he had to poop. My mom was so confused. She let him in and asked where he'd been. He said in the car with the rest of them—even the baby. Carter's only two years old, and he was sitting out in the car in his diaper. He is definitely Claire's favorite though. She usually holds him and gives him her food.

My mom says she's concerned because those kids always have colds. They are snot factories. It's all over their faces half the time, dried and crusty. They're always hungry too. Claire complains that they don't have enough fruits and vegetables at home. She always talks about it when my mom is nearby. I saw my mom give her some oranges and cans of green beans once. I know she's given her more than that. The boys immediately ask for food as soon as they show up. They even asked my mom to take them to Wendy's once! She did. She took all of us. They got giant burgers and drank their Frosties so fast they had stomachaches. One of them kept burping and screaming that he had brain freeze, not that I can understand what any of them are saying half the time. Mitchell just acts like this has always been the way things are. Our family is nothing like Claire's, but for some reason Mitchell acts like he wants to be the same as them.

Anyway, so Tina Callahan said Claire is pregnant. She said it like she was mad at me about it. I'm going to ask Mitchell when I get the nerve. Part of me thinks it's gossip and that I'm being a bad Christian if I believe it rather than talking to my brother. But I also just plain want to know.

11

I think the harried pace of my party preparations reminded Tommy of when I found out I was pregnant after our anniversary trip. We had nursery furniture before my first doctor's appointment. I didn't tell a lot of people that. My mother knew and Celeste too, because she'd popped by and seen the boxes in the hall. Tommy did something with the furniture—I didn't know what, but one day it wasn't there anymore. I hoped he didn't throw it away, but then again I hoped he did. I didn't want to stumble upon it in the basement or attic, hidden behind a stack of suitcases, still waiting to be assembled.

Ronna told me rather formally when I got to work on Monday that she and Platt would be "attending" the dinner party and that she planned to have her hair done before. I told her that wouldn't be necessary. She looked disappointed.

"I'm so glad you'll be able to attend," I said. I thought to ask her one more time about the Brodericks and Mitchell Wright—who'd narrowly escaped my hawk-like focus by the end of the weekend.

"I pass calls, stamp reports, and get it out of my workspace," Ronna always said if I tried to gossip while at the station. That or she completely ignored me. I wanted to know about the guy who got caught with his pants down, the janitor who stole from the vending machine, and the old-timer, Sam Long, who was retiring so he could sail a boat down the Mississippi River. (Apparently it can't be done. He was, however, righteously determined.) "I just pass the calls, stamp reports, and get it out of my workspace," she answered time and time again, nodding gruffly.

I made my way down to the basement quarters and was strangely happy to be in my little hole. I'd become accustomed to the privacy and the solitude. I felt like that at home lately, all Tommy could do was talk a mile a minute about domestic duties that he somehow thought I relished in. Just the other day he asked me how often I ironed the curtains. When I said never, he was shocked. "That seems like something you'd really enjoy!" I just shook my head. He had no idea who I was, is what I really thought. I barely knew myself.

I could hear footsteps and voices above me for the four hours I was there, but I was rarely visited. I continued to dress nicely for work, but not too nicely on account of Ronna's judgment—and Captain Gamble's wandering eyes. As if summoning him by getting comfortable in my chair with a stack of as-of-yet unread files open on my desk, Gamble came barreling down the stairs.

"Hello, Mrs. Ridell," he said all too cheerfully as he got to the bottom and did a little skip step to the left as if trying to prove his agility and balance even at sixty. He was still making up for the other day when they had to take my husband in. I smiled back. "I'm afraid Laura and I won't be able to make the dinner party. It's our weekend to see our grandkids, and we can't cancel. My daughter made plans, so we're stuck with them, and anyway, we like to be stuck...so..." He was sheepish. "The Brodericks have their hold on you, don't they?" He pointed at the file.

"I don't think I've ever heard anything like it," I said. "I mean, I have but not around here." I was disappointed he wasn't coming. If I had to put up with these awkward visits at the station, then I expected him to make an effort to be awkward at my home too.

"No." Gamble shook his head. "No, there's nothing like it."

"Where are all of these people now?" I asked.

"Well, the boys are dead, as you know. Mitchell too, of course. The rest...I really can't say. Claire left. Cecil is long dead. He was gone before we even closed the file on it. He had a lot of substance issues."

"My brother died," I said. "Bobby Black. He died, crashed his car over in Bingham."

"That's a real shame, Arlene. I may even remember that..." he trailed off absently.

"My mother'll never be the same." It was the excuse I'd been making for her for most of my life.

"I'm not sure any of us are ever the same from day to day." He dipped his head in reverence to his own wisdom.

"I'd like you to let me open this case," I said, very surprised to hear myself make this suggestion.

Gamble was quiet at first, then almost appeared to be chuckling. "I guess I don't know what you mean." He put his hands in his pockets uncomfortably. I could tell they weren't good pants for hands—not even room for a stick of gum.

"I want to solve this case," I told him. "It's all I can think about day and night. I'm bored as hell and I can't have a baby, and the only reason I'm having this stupid party is because Tommy and I don't have fun anymore. All we used to do was laugh and carry on. In every memory, we're laughing ourselves silly and just bein' fools and fishing, and now it's all serious in our house. He works and is drunk all the time, and I can't seem to get my act together anymore. I love to cook, but now I only want to cook serious food. I want to be serious about everything. I even want to be serious about having fun. You should see how worked up I am about having ten people over. It's embarrassing! I need something to do with myself. I want serious endeavors too. I never wanted endeavors before, but here I am. It's not enough for me to sit around and spend someone else's money like an empty-headed fool. I need a purpose. I can't promise I won't change my tune if I find out I'm expecting, but it's been over a year now, and there's no fruit of my labors to speak of. Let me track these people down. Let me figure it out. I want to crack the case. I really don't have anything else to do." I was fully aware how unstable I sounded, but these were things that just needed to be said—even if I had to say them to Larson Gamble and his tight pants.

"Natalie Wright is who you'll want to talk to. If she'll talk to you," Gamble said pensively. "She was a kid then, but...well...let me think about it. Her and Alaina. Alaina Watson. She used to work here for a spell. She was a little like you in a way. I guess. I know you're interested. I don't even really know what I can do. You're not a police officer, so I can't... I'm not sure I can let you..."

I couldn't believe he was actually considering it. I must have seemed on the verge of a real breakdown for him to extend himself this way—it was that or overwhelming guilt at declining my party invitation right after arresting my husband.

"Okay," I said. I felt a little bad about completely ignoring Natalie Wright. If she was the key to the investigation, I was going to have to find her more interesting.

"I'll get my license," I said loudly. My tinny voice echoed off the metal staircase.

"I don't think that's going to be necessary. You are an employee of the police department. I'm not sure if you mean private detective's license, or...but either way I don't think you're going to need to do that." He paused. "It's really heavy stuff, Arlene. I don't know, if you're feeling a little…well, I don't… It wasn't all that long ago anyway. Only about seventeen years, and I know that sounds like a long time, but bad stuff takes a lot longer than that to clear. The air is still sick with this…even if it happened when you were a kid."

"I already solved the worst mystery of my life about who killed my baby. I solved that one," I told him with a stern look.

"Right, but…"

"Me," I said. "That's who. It was my fault."

"You shouldn't think that way, Arlene," Gamble told me seriously. "God is a busy man, but he's not too busy to hear you say that, and it isn't right. You shouldn't say that."

"It's the truth."

Claire's showing something serious. My mom said it's unusual for a girl to show like that for her first baby. She tells Alaina stuff about Claire, and Mitchell hears her. It's that kind of talk that's going to turn him against my mom too and not just my dad.

Anyway, he doesn't think he needs my parents anymore. Mitchell's been calling himself a man lately. He said as soon as school's out, he's getting a place for him and Claire, like a man. They're going to get married. He's going to be a "man" about it. He keeps saying that.

My dad's so pissed about how everything is going, he can hardly look at Mitchell anymore. They had a big banquet for the basketball team, because they made it to the state championships even though they didn't win. My dad went to the banquet! He went all by himself and sat in the back. My mom tried to get him not to go, but he said he was going. He wore a suit. Mitchell kicked the kitchen cabinet when my dad left the house. They won't speak to each other half the time anyway. I don't know why my dad wants to make things worse. Even if Mitchell wasn't marrying Claire, he still wouldn't have gone to the basketball banquet. He's not even on the team anymore.

It was when my dad came home from the banquet that Mitchell said he was moving out with Claire as soon as school was over. My dad threw a glass against the wall. He's never done anything like that, not in my entire life. My mom was crying and trying to keep the peace, just telling everyone to calm down. Mitchell wasn't really riled up; he said everything calmly. He said he'd made up his mind and that was it. I'm not really talking to him all that much anymore either. He doesn't act mad at me the way he acts toward my dad. He just acts like I'm too young to understand anything. My mom's the only one who seems to be able to get through to him. They still talk all the time. Mitchell goes out on the porch with her and sits. If I go join them, Mitchell acts like I'm interrupting and changes the subject.

He told me he's excited to be a dad and get a full-time job, but my dad says Mitchell will be working minimum wage for the rest of his life and living in places like Deck River. Mitchell told me Dad is a snob who's always hated Georgia. My dad is from Pennsylvania originally. We used to go see my grandparents all the time before they moved into a nursing home. I don't really like where my dad's from. It's too cold in the winter and real rough.

Sometimes when my dad and Mitchell fight, they get really loud. Mitchell starts saying mean stuff about my parents—my mom even. He says she'd rather be married to Aunt Alaina than to my dad. Alaina's not really my aunt. I'm not sure if I mentioned that. She's my mom's best friend. Mitchell says my dad hates his life and wishes he was anything but a pool salesman. Then he says my mom's depressed. She hears him say this stuff but doesn't argue. She just tries to get him to calm down. He hurts my feelings all the time now. He never used to. The only times we'd ever fight before was when we were stuck in the back of the car on the way to Pennsylvania or something. Now when he gets mad, he says I'm naive and a Jesus freak who believes everything everyone tells me. I guess I'm a little like my mom, because I never know what to say. Once I slammed my door and cried in my bedroom, but normally I just stand there. If I'm a Jesus freak, then Mitchell used to be one too. My mom asked him if he and Claire were going to go to church, but he didn't answer. That's what he does when he doesn't want to say no to her.

School's out in a couple of months. A lot of the kids are planning graduation parties and getting ready for college. Mitchell says he doesn't care. He has a baby on the way. That's his answer to everything I ask him and now they're going to get married. He's going to be a husband and a father.

12

The dinner party was like a sore on my foot, caused by shoes I forced myself to wear because I spent so much money on them. I'd invested too much in the event to cancel it even though I really wanted to—especially when I started to think about what all of those people were going to say to each other standing around my chafing dishes. But I stuck with my commitment. What would we do with all of that food if I bailed? Tommy said he didn't care one way or another.

"What if it's no fun?" I asked him over breakfast that very day.

"I always have fun," he told me like a cheerleader. He held up his glass in salute to good times—orange juice and vodka. I exhaled sharply with my lips pressed together. "Oh, sorry," he said. He put the glass down.

"I don't always have fun." It was a painful confession.

"I always have fun with you," Tommy said. I rested my head

on his shoulder. I didn't want to mention the booze at breakfast. I thought I'd be having a good time too if I couldn't remember most of my day.

We always sat close to one another at the table—me and Tommy. When we went out for dinner, we got a booth and squeezed in side by side. I often wondered where we'd put the kids—if they ever came. There had to be room for at least an infant between us at Chili's. I had time to figure it out; I'd just had my period. Twenty-eight more days of not having to worry about where to put a baby at Chili's.

People were set to arrive at six, and on the button, Lacey showed up alone. "No Raynold?" I asked immediately. I was thinking about the head count.

"No. He had a migraine," she said.

"Well, we're down to nine people. Eleven including Tommy and me, so that's not much of party." I thought I might cry, and I couldn't figure out where all of this emotion was coming from. I'd made too much roast. It didn't keep well. "We'll have to throw some meringues out," I told her quickly. "There's no way nine people can eat all of those meringues." One might have thought Raynold was the key to any celebration's success.

"Okay." Lacey shrugged. "I need a drink. You're making me want a drink." She pushed past me brusquely. She smelled a little of sweat, like she always did.

A few other people showed up, and as far as I could tell, the evening was off to a lame start. Everyone was standing around with their thumbs up their asses and nothing to talk about. I told Tommy to put some music on. Instead he walked to the television and turned on the Braves game. All of the men ended up in front of the TV after that and were talking loudly and in their throats about sports and fishing and general male pursuits. I grew irritated. "Can you mingle, please?" I asked him as he mimicked throwing a pitch and nearly hit me in the face.

Ronna and Platt were not yet there, which I found very strange. Ronna was not one minute late to work, ever. I looked around for her several times, but being that there weren't that many people in the house as it was, it was clear that she had not arrived. I calculated in my head. If only seven people came, then it was hardly a party at all, and the food would be embarrassing, because it would look like I'd been stood up by a whole heap of friends. I planned for a way to not bring everything out. I thought if I had extra plates in the kitchen, I could quickly dump some of the servings on those plates and cover them with plastic, then tell Tommy to hurry them down to our extra refrigerator. I was almost sweaty with planning and calculating when the doorbell rang. I was so relieved that I ran to the front door and slid on the rug there before regaining my footing and reaching for the handle. It was not Ronna and Platt but Larson and Laura Gamble. "Oh," I said, surprised. Now I was wondering if we had enough food if Ronna and Platt did show up, and then I had the thought that Larson would feel strange that he'd been invited to such a small gathering. Clearly I didn't have any friends and was desperate for company and that was the reason I invited my boss. I regretted inviting him and wondered why he said he couldn't come and then showed up.

"Hi, Arlene," Larson said as I opened the door. "I'm so sorry to show up unannounced like this, but we tried to call when my daughter cancelled. She has the flu, so we were home and thought if you'd still have us. We took a chance." He was staring at me very intensely.

"Oh of course," I said. "Come in! Ronna's not here yet. They're late, so..." I moved hurriedly. "Can I take your coat?"

"Ronna from the station?" Laura said almost with disgust.

"We're not wearing coats," Gamble said—motioning at his short-sleeve shirt. His wife was in a sundress. It had been unseasonably warm all day.

"Yea, Ronna Rhodes."

"I didn't know she was invited," Gamble said, reaching for his wife's hand.

"It's an assorted guest list," I replied quietly. I was glad I hadn't emptied any food off the platters, but Ronna and Platt still needed to show up to get the portions and presentation just right.

At eight, Tommy told me we needed to eat. "People are starving," he said. "They're getting that hungry breath. There was something in the dip, I think...something with raw onion."

"Well, Ronna and Platt aren't here," I hissed. I was near hostile.

"Who?" he asked.

"My coworker. Ronna Rhodes."

"Well, she's late, and we shouldn't be punished for it."

"No one is punishing you," I said. It was like I could barely see him, I was so wound up from thinking about the serving platters. "Oh shit!" I cried out like I'd just realized somebody's cat was in the oven set to four-hundred degrees. "Larson said they tried to call, but I can't hear the phone in here, you've got the baseball game so goddamned loud." I ran into the kitchen to check the answering machine but saw that we only had one message. I played it, pressing my ear next to the speaker, but it was only Gamble's message telling me they were coming. "Where the hell is Ronna?" I asked the machine.

I heard Tommy announcing that dinner was served, and I imagined him in the oven with the cat and me turning the heat up fifty more degrees. "Everybody!" he called out, banging a metal coaster against his beer's neck. "Everybody, we're going to eat now. Let's all get to the kitchen, buffet style."

"No, it is not a buffet!" I yelled. "We are eating in the dining room. Proper style." I continued hollering while I marched to where Tommy was standing in front of the TV. "There were supposed to be eleven of you plus myself and Tommy, no twelve, but Lacey's husband didn't come, so there will be more elbow room. But it's not buffet style, Tommy. It's not a buffet!" I was now at a screeching roar.

"Okay, Arlene!" Tommy yelled back in an attempt to provide comic relief. "Okay!" he called out louder.

"Can you turn down the fucking baseball game?" I hissed under my breath.

I felt my hands shaking and wondered if I would faint. I kept thinking no one was talking to one another and that the rooms of our home were riddled with uncomfortable silences. I began laying the food out on the table when Tommy walked over to me with a glass of red wine in his hand. "Oh God," I said. "I hate when you drink wine. You get so weird. Can you please not drink wine tonight?"

"It's for you," he said, handing me the glass. "Please drink wine tonight. Please. You're going to have a nervous breakdown over having...like...five people in the house." He was slurring a little; I wasn't sure he realized he'd just insulted me.

"Where the fuck is Ronna?" I asked Tommy furiously. "I don't even know if we should put chairs at the table for them or not. Seriously. I really don't know."

Tommy's face was confused. "Are you okay?" he asked me. "I mean...really. Are you okay?"

13

onna and Platt never showed up. I got a message the following morning in which she explained that she didn't feel well and that Platt didn't think he had anything nice enough to wear to our house being that my husband was a real estate "mogul." I hated that word. I didn't call her back—she didn't request that I do so—and figured I would give her a little cool breeze on Monday. I didn't like last-minute cancelers.

I felt sick all day Sunday and laid around on the couch, thinking of nothing but failure and anxiety. Tommy told me he'd had a "great!" time at our party. "You really are a great housewife!" he said in a hopeful, scripted way that made me think he assumed that was just what I wanted to hear and had been waiting for the perfect time to say it. He then took his car in to get it washed and was conspicuously gone for two hours. When he got back, he smelled a little of booze, but I figured it was left over from the night before—that or I didn't want to bother with asking.

I had all of the Broderick case files at the house. I'd been cleared to take them home with me, because of the age of the case and the fact that there was no active investigation going on with respect to any of the people involved. And anyway, this was Faber. There was no telling if anyone really knew the rules.

Gamble had briefly mentioned my new "assignment," as he was calling it, the night before at the party. Lacey said something stupid like "oh that again?" but Tommy—who was beside her, both of them next to the olive bowl—didn't appear to have any idea what we were talking about. I'd mentioned to Tommy a couple of days earlier that Captain Gamble was allowing me to look into the Broderick deaths.

"You know? What we talked about the other night?" I said impatiently to Tommy's blank face.

"Yea, I know," he said just as impatiently. "I know. I guess I just don't know what you mean by you're going to investigate it. Sounds cool though." He smiled and grabbed a kalamata. I felt completely alone.

Then I really was alone—with the Broderick files—while Tommy was at the car wash. I was once again overcome with a sinking feeling when I started looking at the pictures. I couldn't shake this pulsing sense of foreboding. Up until this point, I hadn't seen any photos of the three Broderick boys other than their school pictures, attached with a paper clip to the back of one of the folders. Their blank, innocent faces staring into the lens looked just like any other small child growing up around Faber. The oldest of the three, Cedar, had a harder edge to him, probably due to more time in his family's situation, but even he was a bit cherubic and adorable. Like Claire, they all had a sprinkle of freckles over their noses and dark hair that stood up all over their scalps that looked like it had been trimmed using a butter knife and not combed in weeks. Their lips were all chapped, bright pink and puckered on their faces. There was a warmth to the kids that I did not see in the photos of Claire and Mitchell. Their innocence still clung. They didn't know how the rest of the world saw them, the pity it took while trying to look away. Of course these photos had been taken before they were murdered. Claire's and Mitchell's pictures were from after their arrest.

In the next folder there were several photos of the dead bodies lined up on dark leaves at the edge of Deck River. I could see the water in the background, gray and dipping in a hectic current. Cedar, Colton, and Chase Broderick died in November of 1983. The ground was wet as was their hair—pressed into deep leaf cover—and their little bodies, left exposed with flecks of dirt and grit around their ankles and back edges of their legs and torsos. According to the notes it had been cold the night they died—in the upper thirties. They were wearing only shorts and T-shirts, lying on their backs with their arms by their sides. Their faces were blue. No one's hands were tied; the only bruises were typical of a little boy—on shins and knees, maybe an elbow. The photos had a colorless, black-and-white quality—as did Deck River in early winter, but these were modern photographs. I could see that one of the boys' shorts were red and that there was a distant burnt-mustard-colored leaf in the corner of the shot.

"May God strike you down," I said to whoever did this. I had to cover the photos after a few minutes of their vacant faces staring up at me, empty like doll eyes. They had tags on their toes. I tried not to notice that their toenails needed a trim.

There were notes from an initial interview with Claire that seemed out of order. There had been very little, so far, on how she found them. She claimed she went to her father's house, thinking they were with him, and discovered the house empty. She then said she went out looking for them "in the woods." Pendley pressed her hard here, over and over he kept asking how she ended up where the bodies were—which was not near the home she shared with Mitchell nor near Cecil Broderick's house. This Pendley was a real jerk is all I could think. The poor girl just found three of her brothers dead back in a ditch, and he's asking her how many steps she took in each direction before she saw their corpses lying there. I found it hard to read transcripts of conversations, but even with the formal way everything sounds when it's typed out, I could feel Claire's unease. She didn't seem able to give a straight answer. Everything I'd read of Mitchell so far had him spouting off "yes's" and "no's" with ease. Claire meandered her way around the point and ended up somewhere else.

I was alone. She said over and over. *Wasn't with nobody.*

I came home from work and fell asleep on the couch. I never saw them that day.

My daddy thought they were with me.

I just figured they run off. It wasn't dark out yet, just rainy.

Sometimes. I don't know. That's what she said when Pendley asked her if they ran off a lot. *I don't know. I was by myself. I told you. I was asleep. Mitchell wasn't home. He wasn't there.*

As if the pictures of the Broderick boys on the edge of Deck River weren't bad enough, I finally got to the part about Mitchell Wright. He'd been all over the files—public enemy number one as far as I could tell. About halfway through the eighth folder on the case, there was a note in bold type at the bottom of a report that Mitchell Wright was deceased. He hanged himself. It was about two weeks after the boys were found dead. The police—at least Duke Pendley—assumed he did it because he was guilty over killing the kids. There was really very little on it, just this casual mention that guilt can kill. And it did. He died at approximately four o'clock in the afternoon.

It was after this that Alaina Watson was sworn in to assist Duke Pendley. I'd seen her a few times already in the paperwork. She was as thick as thieves with the Wright family, but then—all of a sudden—she was a cop. I really did love living in a small town—it was all I'd ever known—but sometimes the way our dealings looked on paper could make me a little embarrassed. It was like the time they did a fundraiser at the car wash for an assisted-living home, and the money got stolen from the lunch box where it had been hidden until there could be an official ceremony to dedicate the funds. Everyone kept asking why they would keep all that cash in a lunch box, but that was just the way it was. This was the kind of place where people kept their valuables in lunch boxes and angry family friends could become cops whenever they wanted.

I fell asleep looking at the contents of box two and woke to the sound of Tommy talking too loudly on the phone and a sharp crick in my neck from the angle I'd been bent over. He had to be on with his boss; I could tell by the more formal way Tommy was speaking and by how enthusiastic he was trying to sound. "Well, you know how hard I work, Peck!" He laughed uproariously. "You know it!" I rolled my eyes as he went on. "I'm justa' natural-born hustler! Ha-HAAA!" He seemed to be getting louder with each passing syllable.

"Tommy, can you keep it down?" I said from my drool-marked spot at the dining room table. I'd started cleaning up the remnants of the party but didn't finish on account of the files. When Tommy hung up the phone, he came around the corner from the kitchen where he'd been yelling.

"You sleeping?" he said.

"Yeah, I guess." I wiped my mouth.

"Place is a wreck."

"So clean it up. You were here too, no?"

"I put away all the leftovers," he said like this was all that could possibly be required. I sat up straighter, rubbing my lower back and pressing my shoulder blades together. My spine gave a little pop. "Was last night fun?" I asked.

"I thought so!" He sounded like he was talking to his boss again.

"I'm not so sure. No one was talking."

"Oh, Arlene," Tommy said. "They were all talking. That one fella even danced a little. The police boss guy."

"Oh, Captain Gamble?" I said. "I must have missed that part." I frowned at the thought of Captain Gamble dancing in my living room. "Anyway, do you know the Wrights?" I leaned my head on my hand.

"No. Those the people who all got killed?" He nodded to the stack of papers.

It was fiercely bright outside. I could tell I'd been asleep for quite a while by the way the light was coming in through the kitchen window.

"No, they didn't all die. Just the brother. Or the son. Or the dad. Whatever you want to call him. But yes, he's dead."

"I don't know that name. You really gonna be an investigator?" Tommy asked.

"I wouldn't be the first. There's this woman, Alaina Watson… or she's not that now, but she was—got divorced, now it's

Hopewell apparently. She became a police officer when all this went down. She wanted to solve the case. She was good friends with the Wrights."

"Wait—Alaina Watson?" Tommy said. He leaned his weight on the doorframe   that caught his balance. I could tell a bender at noon when I saw one.

"Yeah," I said. "Do you know her?"

"I know Stan. He just washed my car! I mean—he didn't, but he owns Watson's."

"Oh," I said. I hadn't made the connection. Watson's was the big car detailer in town. They'd come to your office, your house, or you could go there and act too big for your britches with all the other big shots who paid forty bucks a pop for a rubdown. "That's her ex-husband then."

"Yeah!" Tommy was clearly ecstatic over this news.

"I gotta get in touch with her," I said.

NATALIE WRIGHT'S JOURNAL
June 23, 1983

My dad got me a truck for my sixteenth birthday in March. It's a Ford and the color of a cherry. I was actually pretty upset about it at first. I definitely didn't want a truck, especially not an old red one, and by red, I mean BRIGHT red. My mother said he was so excited about it though. Soooooooooo excited. She told me to be grateful. It was like she was begging me. She doesn't want anyone else to let my dad down. His heart is broken about Mitchell. I guess I don't totally understand. It's not like Mitchell's in jail or a drug dealer or something. He's just marrying his girlfriend and having a baby with her.

Mitchell and Claire got a place over in Deck River. It's a house. I thought for a second they already got married and didn't invite us, but Mitchell says Claire wants to wait until after the baby is born, because she's so big. She wants to wear a wedding dress. She told my mom her own mother didn't have a wedding. Claire's dad had to go to jail for a while, and when he got out there wasn't time for a wedding. They just had to get busy. Claire said she wants to have a wedding in a church. My mother said she thought that was strange. The Brodericks don't even go to church anywhere. Mitchell just laughed when Claire said this. It's like he doesn't even believe in God anymore. He used to be one of the leaders in Youth Group. I really don't understand him now.

He also started smoking cigarettes. He's been smelling like it a lot lately. My mom said something to him about Claire smoking. He said Claire didn't smoke, because of the baby. My dad saw a box of Camels in his car and threw them out. Mitchell went looking for them and got into it with my dad—again. My dad pushed him up against the wall in the kitchen. My dad has never ever done anything like that. Mitchell left right after and didn't come back until the following morning to get his work clothes. He's delivering pizzas now. My dad said that Mitchell would have to give his car back if he kept smoking, but my mom calmed everyone down and said that Mitchell needed the car. She's arguing with my dad all the time now too, but it's always this weird, quiet arguing with her whispering and pressing her hands down in the air just to get him to stop being so mad.

Claire told me that Carter is going to live with her and Mitchell when they get their own place. The other three boys can stay at the house with her dad. She says they can look after themselves, but Carter is too little. Claire's new baby with Mitchell is a girl.

She wants to name her Lucille Massey Wright. Massey was Claire's mother's last name before she got married to Cecil Broderick.

Tina Callahan over at the stables told me Cecil's been in jail a dozen times for stealing and getting in fights. It's such a funny name—Cecil. I've only ever seen him that one time when he came to the house with Claire for dinner. He looks really young and has long, greasy hair. He works for the hose factory in Clampton. He barely said a word the whole time he was at the house except please and thank you. Claire acted like she didn't hardly know him. When he left, my mother said he was a drug addict, that's the reason for how he looks. I hope Mitchell doesn't become a drug addict because of Claire and that family. My father keeps saying that young children are a real pain in the butt, and here Mitchell's going to have two of them to look after by the time he's nineteen. Claire's not going back to school after the baby comes. She's going to work at the factory with her dad. She told my mom she's going to get her degree from the night school in Planters.

My mother's always trying to ask Claire questions in this really innocent way, like how about this? Or what do you think of that? Claire just stares at her and gives one-word answers. My dad says he doesn't even think the baby is Mitchell's. I've seen Claire with J.P. Callahan at school a couple of times. He shows up at lunch and talks to Claire under the overhang. I told Mitchell but he didn't seem to care. All he said was maybe they're friends.

14

Larson Gamble told me he could get me the phone numbers for Natalie Wright and Alaina Watson/Hopewell if I thought I had the nerve to talk to them. He said I probably shouldn't bother Mitchell's parents unless I had something really crucial. The Wrights had never gotten over what happened. "Kind of recluses," he said. He thought Lucy—Lucille—had gone off to college somewhere. He couldn't remember much about her. The family had really kept to themselves after Mitchell died. They didn't live in Faber for much longer.

"Oh." I said, distracted by the sudden coming on of a vision of Captain Gamble dancing to "Pour Some Sugar on Me" next to the coffee table. I guess I had seen him but tried to block it out. "I don't remember them at all."

"You were probably too young."

There were also quite a few references to Natalie Wright's

journal in the files, but I hadn't come across it yet. Duke Pendley's notes were everywhere. He wrote with a hard hand, and the paper was weakened by the force of his pressing.

Mitchell Wright's sister claimed he was with her not long before the coroner-determined time-of-death (roughly 7 PM). NOT in Deck River.

Claire Broderick says she fell asleep at her house in Deck River when the boys went missing. Cecil Broderick came home from work expecting them to be at his place, but they weren't.

Mitchell Wright was with his sister, Natalie, at this time. Natalie has confirmed his alibi for the entire afternoon and evening.

Later in the investigation, Alaina's name and handwriting started to appear.

Phone records from Cecil Broderick's house show he called the Wrights at 7 PM (approximate time of death) the night the boys were killed. Confirms he was looking for them. No phone at Claire and Mitchell's house. No way to confirm Claire was home.

She went out looking for the boys around eight that night. She said she was worried they were not home yet.

Apparently Mitchell and Claire had the same lawyer at first—a woman appointed by the state named Rita Leaf. I laughed out loud when I read that, but then immediately threw a hand over my mouth, feeling insensitive and immature. I didn't do God's work representing the poor and accused like this Leaf woman. I had stupid dinner parties where no one had fun and where there were too many olives and meringues. Ms. Leaf represented the couple at first, but then Mitchell got another attorney, someone his parents paid for. His name was Chess Bacon. I didn't laugh at that and kept my cool even when one of the lab technicians who'd tested the rags found in the boys' mouths was named Jason Raspberry. None of this was for my amusement. I was a real wicked woman if I could laugh in the face of tags on toes.

I found that I felt sorry for Claire because she was a girl and blamed Mitchell because he was a boy, but when I looked at his photo, this boy of nineteen with a bleached expression and lost stare, I knew I should feel sorry for him too.

Natalie's diary

Natalie's journal

Natalie's notebook

There were at least a half a dozen references, especially in Alaina Watson's handwriting, all over every page in the file once she became involved. I figured she should be the first person I talk to. Alaina Hopewell now. I'd never liked Stan Watson, however much attention I'd paid to him. I thought maybe I could remember his wife, but no one came to mind. Tommy suggested he'd been married a couple of times.

I'd also seen a couple of scribbled notes in various margins—in Duke Pendley's forceful, angry penmanship—about "removed pages." I thought maybe he was talking about the diary; it was something I figured I could ask Alaina when I talked to her.

It took me a few tries to actually get through dialing the number

I pulled up in the phone book. Ronna kept both the Yellow and the White Pages by her desk and had a ruler and magnifying glass handy for easier scrolling. "The ruler'll help you keep it straight," she said very seriously.

"I understand. Thank you." I was miffed about her no-showing at the party and couldn't hide it. I went back downstairs with Alaina Hopewell's number written on a Post-it and without further discourse with Ronna.

"Hello," a certain voice answered after a couple of rings.

"Alaina?" I said. There'd been a phone on my desk the entire time I worked at the police station, but it never rang, and I'd never had an occasion to use it. There was a small flap to the left of the receiver noting the extension. 769.

"Yes."

"This is Arlene Black Ridell."

She was silent. I'm not sure what reaction I was waiting for. She didn't know me, and why I was using my maiden name was another mystery.

"Hi, Arlene Black Ridell."

"I'm calling about the Mitchell Wright case."

"Oh." Her tone changed immediately. "Is there still a case?"

"I'm Arlene Ridell," I repeated.

"Yes, I got that part."

"I'm working with the Faber Police Department," I said trying to sound steady. "Cold Case Division."

"Isn't that something? When I was there, they could barely afford toilet paper."

"Yes!" I said, sounding a little like Tommy when he was talking to his boss. "We have toilet paper here now. But—"

"I'm not a cop," Alaina began to explain. "I only joined up for a few years, because the whole thing was such a joke, how they handled that case. It really blew my mind. And they'll take anybody…"

"Yes, like Ronna," I said—not sure where I was going with that.

"Oh, she's still there?"

"Goddamn, she acted like she had no idea what I was talking about," I said. "I mean about this case." I steadied my nerves and tried to sound very serious, capable.

"Oh, she knows about the case, all right," Alaina said disdainfully. "She started working at the station not long after it happened. She was just out of high school. She's always played dumb so she can count her paper clips in peace, but make no mistake—Ronna Rhodes knows about a lot more than she lets on. 'Cluding the Brodericks. Please."

I exhaled loudly, not really in agreement but resignation. "I'm kind of the anybody they'll take," I said about the low standards for getting hired at the Faber PD. "I had a miscarriage and nothing to do. They hired me to sit in the basement and tag evidence. I got to reading the old case files. I'm convinced I can solve this one. I can feel it in my bones."

"Yeah, I know that tune. I was convinced too, but…well, nothing came of it. Too many dead ends."

"Wanna take another crack at it?" I said, surprising myself. I wasn't usually this straightforward unless I was giving Tommy a hard time. "With me? I mean—I can't pay you or anything. I make nine dollars an hour; we could split it. I don't really need the money, so you can have all nine dollars if you want it. But I only work part-time. I've been taking some of the files home with me and reading them in my spare time." I knew I was rambling but didn't want to stop. "So I don't get paid for the time I'm doing that. Just four hours a day, five days a week. Eight to noon. I eat lunch with Ronna."

"Well I am not eating lunch with Ronna. And I don't need any money. I'll work for free."

"So you'll do it?" I said, shocked. I felt connected to her on so many levels, the most important of which was that neither of us had anything better to do than to investigate a nearly twenty-year-old crime and didn't need to be paid for it.

"Sure. I'm not doing anything else. We can just be two old broads taking on a murder investigation."

"I'm not old," I said. I was clenched tightly, sitting on the edge of my chair with nervous sweat pooling in my armpits; my thighs trembled with excitement and trepidation. Alaina had been a real cop. "I'm twenty-four."

"Oh hell," Alaina said. "Then one old broad and one baby."

"I don't have any babies," I corrected her. "Been trying for almost five years."

"Stop trying. It's not up to you."

We agreed to meet the following afternoon at Fogle's in McAllister County. Alaina explained she lived in Dolvin, which was pretty far west. Fogle's was about forty-five minutes away, definitely a little closer to where Alaina lived than Faber. I figured I'd be making a lot of concessions like this given she was the senior investigator. When I got home from work that day—after a particularly strained lunch with Ronna—I designed some stationery on the computer, using a program Tommy had shown me.

Ridell Hopewell Detective Agency I typed in large, swirling font. I pursed my lips and changed it to *Hopewell Ridell Detective Agency*.

"We're not an agency though," I said to myself. "Yet." I was excited for Tommy to get home so I could tell him of the development.

15

Tommy was in his boxers and without a shirt, sitting across from me at the dinner table while I tried to feel important and like a very serious person, a very serious crime-solving person.

"Is this really necessary?" I asked, pointing at his near nudity.

"Sorry," he said, looking down. "My pants are all so tight. Hard to eat dinner in 'em. I can hardly get my lunch down I'm so uncomfortable, and then I'm just starving when I get home. I need room to breathe."

"Where is this appetite coming from?" I said. He really had been piling the food on his plate at dinner lately. I'd asked if he was eating lunch; he said yes.

"I don't know. I'm trying to drink less." He smiled sheepishly and put a forkful of spaghetti in his mouth.

"I'm going to meet with Alaina Watson tomorrow," I said, hoping to change the subject. "We're going to solve the case."

"Can you just…go and solve cases with old ladies?" Tommy asked. He had spaghetti sauce on his chin.

"She's not old," I said. "I mean—not that old. I don't know how old she is, but I don't see why that matters. She was on the police force back then. Not back then. It's not like ancient history." I'd put my own fork down, completely turned off the food by shirtless Tommy slurping his way through his overfull plate. "Anyway I have to clear that part with Larson."

"Larson?"

"Captain Gamble."

"I think that guy's got a thing for you," Tommy said. I noticed he was sitting cross-legged like a small child on the floor in music class.

"I doubt it. I'm meeting—"

"He stared at you all night when they were over here," Tommy interrupted. "I tried talking to him, but he just looked over my head. You were wearing that formfitting dress, and he couldn't take his eyes off your rear end, then when Def Leppard came on, he was doing a thrusting dance hoping you'd see."

"What?" I was trying not to listen.

"He got low!" Tommy bellowed. "And it was for your benefit. He went front-to-back and side-to-side."

"Tommy, please don't interrupt me. I know you're not used

to me being the one with a career, but I am serious about this. This is important to me. And this food is nearly inedible," I said, pushing my plate back. "I can't even season a meatball, I'm so taken with this."

"I'm not having any trouble eating it!" Tommy laughed jovially, revealing a wad of chewed beef and sausage (I always use both when making meatballs—always) lodged in the left side of his mouth.

"Are you sweating?" I asked, seeing a line of moisture trickle from a crease in his neck.

"I don't know," he said. "Listen, Arlene. I'm excited for you about the case. I just didn't know two regular people could become police and solve cases in their spare time."

"We're not 'becoming' police. We're doing this pro bono. Larson said I could have free rein over the files, and I'm excited about it. And anyway, I do work for the Faber County police force—a fact you seem to keep forgetting." I placed my hands on the table. I'd starched and ironed a white tablecloth the previous week but didn't put it out for the party, thinking it would become irreparably stained what with all the merrymaking. I frowned—I hadn't been too merry at the party or any time recently that I could think of.

"Why are you upset?" Tommy asked, putting down his fork.

"I'm not." I shook my head. "I'm not sure really. I feel upset a lot. I think it's the baby."

"Yeah." He put his fork down decisively.

"This won't fill the void," I said.

"No, you can't eat your feelings." Tommy nodded solemnly.

"I meant solving this crime, not dinner." I pushed myself back from the table. We were in the formal dining room again. We'd been doing that a lot lately. I was tired of the kitchen; it seemed I was tired of a lot of things. I was really hoping I wasn't getting tired of Tommy.

"I'm all for it," Tommy said, smiling. He had a bit of oregano on his front tooth. I tried not to grimace.

Later, we had a college football game on television while I sat in my chair with the files on my lap. I'd taken to wearing reading glasses on the very tip of my nose so when I looked down I had some magnification. I picked them up at the grocery store to help with all the reading I was doing. It was a lot of fine print, scribbled comments in margins, and faded documents that strained my eyes.

"Larson Gamble does not have a crush on me," I said rather loudly, putting my pen down. I'd been making notes on a legal pad. I planned to present an outline to Alaina Watson the following day. "Why do you have to think that just because he's giving me a chance to do something interesting? You didn't think that when I got hired to sit in the basement with a box of Ziploc baggies did you? That work wasn't beneath my station, was it?"

"No, 'cause it's at the police station, but I did think that," Tommy said as he pushed himself up on his forearms. He'd made himself a drink after dinner. "I think he liked the idea of you working there because you're nice on the eyes. I can't blame him."

"That's not what I mean by station," I said. "And just stop. A woman can be nice on the brain too." I was really on one now that I had a partner in my investigation.

"Yes, they can," Tommy agreed, still shirtless. I frowned at his bare chest, then corrected course by saying a small prayer of thanks that I had Tommy even with all his flaws, because Lord knows I had mine. I'd used to like looking at him with his clothes off. I really couldn't say what had come over me. I pushed the glasses up the bridge of my nose a little and got back to it.

"It sounds like you're really interested in these people, Arlene. I think it's great." He looked at me directly and smiled. I did always think that if we'd had a baby, I would have turned out differently. I wouldn't have been so hard on him. He certainly was trying. He had only two cocktails that night and didn't slur a bit.

"It's so sad," was all I could think to say. "I can't wait to talk to the Wrights. If we get to talk to them. Who knows. My mother still won't talk about Bobby. Maybe the Wrights won't talk about Mitchell. That's the way it goes sometimes. I hope Alaina is still friends with them." I had assumed she was the key when I called her, but now I wondered. Maybe she wasn't such a good addition to my detective agency. I'd find out tomorrow.

I was up all night, wondering about Mitchell and then of course whether or not Larson Gamble had a crush on me. Both lines of thinking left me feeling anxious and ill. I went to work the following morning, wearing a long, loose dress and loafers that I usually saved for gardening and not a drop of makeup on my face.

"Are you okay?" Ronna asked me when I walked in.

I'd told her after our last strained meal that I didn't like sitting outside for lunch anymore. "Skin cancer," I had said. She raised an eyebrow but did not respond. I began to think of her as my nemesis. I vowed never to forgive her for all of the leftovers.

Captain Gamble almost immediately came down the basement stairs when I arrived. He'd come to tell me that if I spent time on the case outside of my work hours that I could be compensated—he had room in the budget—five dollars an hour for that work. He made sure to note that he didn't want to encourage me to do so, because five dollars an hour was below minimum wage, and if I had too many "extra" hours on my time card, the station would be flagged, and then we'd have to stop our "secret operation." He said "secret" and then winked. I thought about what Tommy said the night before and was uncomfortable. I did not wink back and shifted stiffly in my chair. He then said he liked the way I looked without makeup.

"Well, if I really looked good, then you wouldn't have noticed I wasn't wearing any." I knew I should have just said "thanks," but Tommy had really planted a seed.

"My wife wears too much makeup," he said. "I wish she wouldn't."

"Well…" I said, "a lot of people think it improves things. Makeup…" I trailed off nervously. "I guess I'll get back to it." I placed my hands in my lap and tried to appear focused.

There wasn't anything to tag, so I had more time with the files. There were four boxes that I hadn't yet touched. I continued to overlook all of the references to Natalie Wright's journal, although Alaina had appeared to think it was very important; she mentioned it every couple of pages. I wanted to make some copies before I met Alaina that afternoon. I couldn't give her any of the paperwork—the originals had to remain in my hands or at the station per Captain Gamble's orders, but I did want her to be able to look at some notes, most of which were her own.

I walked upstairs to where Ronna sat and told her that I needed to use the copy machine.

"You need a code for that. I do the new codes every Thursday, so you'll have to wait."

"But I need it now," I said rather stridently.

"Yes, but Thursday is the day I create new codes and log-ins."

"How many new codes and log-ins do you have to make that you would have a specific day for it?" I said. "There are…like… four people working here."

"And all four of those people got their copier code on a Thursday." She pressed her lips together. I thought she might have called me a bitch under her breath.

"I need to make copies now," I said again.

She'd abandoned actually facing me and was using a highlighter to color some lines in her notebook. I could almost swear she was looking at recipes and not official police business, but she moved her hand over her work before I could get a better look and say something. "You don't have a code," she said after a long, menacing pause passed between us.

"Then can you make them for me?" I leaned a little more aggressively over the top of her desk that served as a long circular barrier separating Ronna from me and anyone else who dared to confront her.

"I'm afraid not. I am only permitted to make copies that pertain to my work."

I was fuming, and so was Ronna. The iciness between us was like a pick at this point and could easily be used to tear the other one's face off. I was afraid I might say something unforgivably nasty. "Isn't that something?" I finally muttered before turning on my heel and walking back to the stairs that led down to the evidence room.

"I'm really sorry we didn't come to your party, Arlene, but I don't think that's any reason for you to be mean to me," Ronna told me in a quiet, practiced voice after I'd turned the corner. "I think you're being really silly. It was just a dinner party. I'm sure you have stuff like that all the time…"

"You had to get that last part in there, didn't you?" I clipped, having walked back to her desk with a vengeance. "You were about to say that I had a lot of dinner parties because my husband is a bigwig or, what is it? A mogul? You and everybody else who thinks I've got nothing to offer. I don't have dinner parties all the time, and I invited you, because I thought we were friends and that you'd come, but you didn't show up and had a bunch of lame excuses, so you hurt my feelings. I thought you were my friend. So there." I was talking louder than I should have been and hoped none of the officers could hear me. Their desks were just around the corner and down a short hall.

"Well, I don't have a lot of friends," Ronna said. "So I guess I don't know how to act."

"You know what, Ronna," I said, still sounding angry. "I don't have a lot of friends either. I thought I did, but I don't, so I guess I was counting on you."

"Then I'm sorry I let you down. I've never even thought I had a lot of friends," she said, trying to garner more sympathy. She needed to be the one of us who had the least friends. "Platt's my only friend and has been since high school. You definitely have a lot more friends than I do."

"Well, let's not argue about who thinks they have more than they do or…whatever. I just really wanted you to come. I wanted to meet Platt." I was trying to sound a touch more kind to match the way that I was feeling. It seemed to me we'd overcome a hurdle in the relationship and that now Ronna and I were going to have something tying us together and down, like large balloons with sturdy strings to the ground, for life. This was our first fight—the one to seal our bond.

"Gosh, he's not all that exciting," she said. "He's like me. We're two crayons from the same box." I smiled. It was a nice thing to say. "I can give you a copy code," she said. "Donna Blessing made that rule up a while back…about the codes on Thursdays. It is pretty silly." The copier was in a small room behind where Ronna sat. "I remember her, you know?" Ronna said over my shoulder.

"Who?"

"Natalie. I remember Mitchell too. I went to high school with them."

"No!" I widened my eyes and let my mouth hang open, acting like I didn't already know this. Alaina had told me Ronna was around when all of this went down, but it was nice to hear it from Ronna.

"Natalie was in my grade. I knew her brother too. They lived in the neighborhood near where I grew up. In Faber," she added decisively.

"Well, I'd really like to talk to you about it…about what you know." Now I was sincere. I hadn't seen Ronna's name in any of the files, but it was possible she knew something. Maybe no one had thought to question her because of her combative demeanor and razor-like focus on staplers and copy-code Thursdays.

She scratched her head with a bright-green-painted fingernail. "It was all anybody could talk about back then, but no, I never talked to the police or anything. I wasn't working here yet—I mean,

obviously. I was still in high school. I took this job after graduation," she said proudly. "I was hired right out of school."

"The Faber PD sure knows a smart woman when they see one,"
I said, pleased to compliment her—and myself.

"I knew Claire too. She went to school with us." Ronna looked
down at her desk, appeared to have trouble swallowing, then
resumed.

"What was Claire like?" I leaned in, eager for insight. I heard
the copier beep. It had completed my stack.

"She was a good girl. The Brodericks were poor though. Real
poor. But Claire was a good girl… She had to grow up fast, because
of the kids and her mama and all that. She was really beautiful."
Ronna tilted her head to the side as if lost in reverie. "I wasn't
surprised that Mitchell Wright liked her so much."

"I'm meeting with Alaina Watson later today," I said. "She
knew the Wrights and—"

"Oh yes, Alaina." Ronna scooted herself forward and put her
attention back to her computer screen. She pressed a few keys and
exhaled sharply. "That will be nice." She wouldn't look at me.

"We're starting our own detective agency," I said. I fully realized
how ridiculous I sounded—and also that this was not true. I wasn't
a detective; neither was Alaina—not anymore at least—and we
were definitely not an agency of any kind, but I was so excited about
the prospect of being useful that I couldn't stop saying it. I'd told
the gentleman at the dry cleaners just that morning that I had "a

board of directors meeting" later that day. He asked for what kind of business, looking my mumu up and down with piqued interest.

"Crime," I said. "Investigation. We're detectives."

"Really? Well, I'll be damned." He'd looked at my mumu again and nodded in approval.

"You should join us," I suggested to Ronna.

"No," Ronna said quickly. "No, thank you. Alaina was still here when I started. I know her just about as much as I want to." She made a check mark on a notebook, sitting catty-corner to her elbow, with irritated intensity.

"Suit yourself, but we're gonna solve this thing, and you have intimate knowledge of the case. I think you would be an asset to our team." I'd heard Tommy use similar language after a two-martini lunch.

"No, no," Ronna insisted. "I'm not a detective."

"I'm not either," I said, stating the obvious. "But we could do it." I pushed a strand of hair behind my ear. I'd thought of wearing my glasses to work that day to accentuate my dowdiness, but Tommy growled very sexually when he saw me in them that morning. I figured they were only adding to my appeal.

"Alaina is a real jerk, you know," Ronna said. "I'd stay away from her if I were you."

"Oh." I was surprised to hear that though I couldn't say why. Ronna had nothing if not hundreds of strong opinions.

"I have to get back to work now," Ronna said. She tapped

several keys on her Dijon-mustard-colored computer. "It's almost time for lunch," she nodded at the small clock that sat on her desk. It was almost eleven. We had another hour, but I could tell Ronna was counting the seconds.

"Okay. I'm really glad we cleared the air, Ronna," I said.

"Me too." She smiled at her screen before lifting her eyes to me. "And I'm sorry we didn't come to the party."

"It really wasn't all that fun," I said.

"I'm sure that's not true."

We both grinned in satisfaction as I descended the steps, the photocopies in hand.

A CONDEMNED MAN

WE WERE RUNNING THAT PLACE pretty good for a while. I wasn't
bored or distracted. It was a lot of work. I had girls here and there,
and sometimes I'd get going with a guy just so I could be an asshole.
I've never liked guys but they're so much easier to fuck with. Girls
listen a lot closer, and they want you to talk. Jorge said I should stay
away from people because of the badness in me, but then he left.
He stayed away from me, which I guess was better for him.

Anyway, I didn't think I was gonna get myself into trouble. I
liked Claire. I did. She was pretty and small. She didn't say much
but liked listening to music and messing around. She didn't really
want much from me but money and just some place to go that
wasn't with her dad and those kids. I don't know—I didn't really
think about it. She was over at Ram's a lot waitressing or whatever
but she would get out of there fast if you asked her. She had to
work all the time 'cause her dad couldn't support them none. He

was such trash, a total junkie. He made her take care of his kids, like he'd put it on her if anything happened to them. I don't know why she cared what he said. I guess she felt bad for the kids or for her mom, 'cause they were her dead mom's kids. I woulda ditched all that a long time ago. I did like Claire. She would have been fine I think if it weren't for what happened.

It was easy to do. I'm not sure why God makes stuff so easy if he doesn't want you to do it. It's like I was in a battle or something and the only way I could survive was to let my bad half have a turn. That makes it sound like it was some hard thing—the battle was with myself. Killing those kids was easy. I think I wanted to see if I could make some part of myself go away by killin' 'em, but I was still there when it was done. I saw Jorge after it happened; he came up to visit his cousin. He said the line was on one side now. I said so the bad side shrank? He said—no, it grew.

I finally went over to Mitchell and Claire's house. She's due any day now, but up to this point, Mitchell hasn't let me come see his place. He keeps making excuses about not being home or there being a leak in the bathroom or something. My mom says it's because he's embarrassed, but I went over there today—embarrassed or not. My mom and I drove by once before, but Claire was out front with the boys, so we didn't stop. My mom said we shouldn't be snooping. Claire saw us. She's about ready to burst, she's so big. I think she looks less and less happy every time I see her.

The house is awful. There's a washer in the middle of it that doesn't have a real top. They put this plastic tarp thing over it when it's running. It was on the spin cycle when I got there, and there was water shooting out of it like a sprinkler. Mitchell says Claire puts towels on the ground to soak it up. She wasn't home while I was there. She's been working with Cecil at the factory, doing some sort of thing with a giant machine that puts little lines in metal. Mitchell talks about it like she's splitting the atom there, which really annoys my dad. Mitchell used to want to be a lawyer and now he thinks the hose factory is where it's at. Claire has one more week until she gets paid time off for the baby. Mitchell was saying he hopes the baby doesn't come before that, because it's going to be hard when she can't work.

Really all Mitchell talks about anymore is work and being tired and money. He was drinking a beer when I got to their house even though it was only noon. He said he didn't get any time to relax later, because he's doing his pizza route at night now—every day, even Sunday. That's his whole life—working and feeling sorry for himself because he has to. But it's also like he feels good about having it so rough. It's like all he's ever wanted is to be someone people looked down on because he's poor.

The sink in their bathroom doesn't work, so all of their tooth-brushes are in the kitchen. I couldn't figure out why there were so many. I didn't know the other kids were living with them. Carter's been there the whole time, but Mitchell said now the other boys are staying with them too. It's actually a little hard for me to believe they brush their teeth at all.

Mitchell smokes now too. He's been doing that for a while, but now he does it in front of my parents. I think it makes my dad miss basketball and how Mitchell was so good. I know my dad thinks the reason all of this happened is because of basketball. When I see Coach Randolph at school I always turn away from him. I think he hurt my family. I know my dad thinks that, but there's nothing he can do anymore. Mitchell's not even in school; none of that matters, but my dad is convinced that if Mitchell played ball none of this would have happened. That part makes me really sad and it changes the way I look at Mitchell. I used to think it was cool when he was rebellious or whatever, but now it makes him look like a loser. Anyway, my Youth Group never thought it was cool to smoke and drink. No one at church wants to do that stuff; we think it's bad to pollute your body and mind.

The other thing is that people at school are saying Carter is Claire's baby and not her dead mother's. That really bothers me. I've been going to ask Mitchell about it a hundred times, but when he comes home to eat with us or visit, he really won't talk about Claire. It's like sitting in an oven when we have dinner as a family. My mom talks too much and too fast. She gets the whole table nervous with her worrying over everyone. My dad goes back and forth between being really nice to Mitchell and completely ignoring him. I don't think he can make up his mind about what he's supposed to do. He can't fix it. I don't think Mitchell thinks there is anything to fix—that's the biggest problem.

I heard my mom and Alaina talking before I went over to Mitchell's house. I guess Alaina had a bunch of furniture and stuff in her storage unit. She told Mitchell and Claire they could take some things for their place. Claire came over with her dad's truck and took everything—down to the old towels Alaina had her lamps wrapped in. She said she would pay Alaina for the stuff, but Alaina said no way. When I was at Mitchell's house, I looked for Alaina's furniture, but I didn't see a lot of it. Someone at school told me Claire sold it all at the Bankhead Flea Market. I don't know if my mom heard that too. She hasn't said anything.

It's Tina Callahan from the stables who's starting all the rumors about Claire and that baby. I guess Carter isn't really even a baby anymore. He does look like Claire, but they all do. All those kids look the same. They got Cecil Broderick's black hair and freckled skin. Cecil Broderick's ponytail is down to his belt loop. I caught my mother staring at it when he was at our house. My dad has never approved of long hair on men. He says clean cut is the way to go. The Brodericks are not clean cut. Mitchell used to be, but now he's starting to look like one of them. I think Claire wanted to be with him so she could be like us and not the other way around.

I wish Tina Callahan would stop talking about it. She's too old to be worried about what a bunch of high school kids are doing. She should have moved on and gotten farther away from Deck River. She's like Claire though—from a poor family. I guess maybe she thinks she did go far, because she's running the stables. She doesn't say anything to me, but I keep hearing about the stuff she says from other people. That didn't really make me feel better. And anyway, Tina shouldn't be starting rumors about anyone; I think maybe she does it because it makes people stop talking about J.P. for a second. Her boyfriend is a real piece of work. He's after every girl in town apparently. My mom even told me to avoid him at the stables. I talked to my friends at church about it and they said to pray for Tina and other gossips.

I got up the nerve tonight though to ask my mom if she thought Carter was Claire's baby. Aunt Alaina was over and they were sitting on the porch talking. They think I can't hear them or that I don't know what they're talking about, which kind of makes me feel like they think I'm a little kid. I went out there and told my mom what Tina had been saying. Alaina clucked her tongue, which I could tell bugged my mom. My mom just said people love a good story. That was it. I know she thinks Claire's had another baby though. She says that to Alaina all the time when she doesn't think I'm listening. Sometimes I think maybe Carter looks like J.P. Callahan, but he doesn't really. I don't know why I think that. It's just me thinking the worst of Claire like everybody else.

16

L acey, it's Arlene." I called Tommy's sister when I got home after lunch and before I was to leave to meet Alaina. I was all business and liked the new size of my big girl clothes. No more tiptoeing around like Tommy Ridell's wife. He was going to be Arlene Black Ridell's husband by the time I was done. "I want to talk to you about Mitchell Wright and Claire Broderick."

"Oh that…okay. Tommy said you might want to pick my brain again. I'm not sure I can really help you, Arlene. You have the police file. I'm not going to be able to tell you anything that isn't in there. I wasn't on the police force or anything; I just remember it happening is all."

"Yes, I know that," I said a little impatiently. I'd made—with Ronna's help—forty-two copies to share with Alaina. "But I'm about to meet with Alaina Hopewell—who was Alaina Watson— and I'd like to be expertly prepared." I'd started talking like I thought a very sophisticated detective would, even though most of the TV shows we watched about police had people smashing down doors, grabbing their crotches, and yelling obscenities at people. I changed my tune and told myself I was talking like an investigative reporter. I vowed that I would read the *Faber Daily* every day to increase my vocabulary and to explore other career options, like that of a journalist.

"Okay, let me think..." She sighed audibly. "I remember Alaina Watson. She was real tight with the Wrights—the kid's family. Why are you meeting her?"

"I'm reopening the case."

"Oh wow. Okay. How do you do that?"

"I...it doesn't matter at this point. I'm planning to write an article for the paper about it. Maybe. Or do the investigation and then the article." I didn't sound as sure of myself as I wanted to. I needed to figure out what my story would be for future conversations. I'd already asked Ronna to be in my detectives' club, and now I was telling Lacey I was a reporter. "I'm not exactly sure," I said more calmly, "but I have permission from Captain Gamble to look into the case. It's a cold case, which means it's unsolved."

"Yes, I know what that means. You're like Alaina, joining the police to try to solve the case. She kind of reminds me of you..."

"No," I said. I'd heard stories about how Stanton Watson ran around on Alaina for years. Tommy sure knew a lot on that topic. "No, she's nothing like me. That's not like me. You can be part of the agency," I said—still stammering aimlessly around the conversation.

"What agency? And I only mean that her husband was money-bags too. Like Tommy. I know she got a whole boatload of cash when she kicked him to the curb."

"Tommy is not moneybags," I said angrily. Lacey and every-one else were a little jealous of Tommy's success. It was all very un-Faber of him to have excelled so quickly and so ably. I couldn't shake the feeling that people were surprised he wasn't still working at the QuikTrip. "Never mind. So about the Brodericks." I didn't want to talk to Lacey or anyone else about cheating husbands and taking a philanderer to the cleaners after a divorce. I was here for justice.

"Okay…and this is just gossip, Arlene. I barely remember and I don't know—I can't, like, confirm this or anything. Claire and Mitchell were older than me, so…"

"Wait, do you know Ronna?" I said.

"Ronna?"

"Ronna Rhodes."

"Oh, Ronna Rolfe? Yeah, I knew Ronna."

"She works at the precinct with me."

"Okay."

"I want her to join the team too, but she's shy, and I think Platt is a little controlling."

"Platt Rhodes? Is that who she married? I'll be damned."

"Anyway," I said.

"Right, so this isn't oak or anything. I'll just tell you what I remember. Claire Broderick got caught messing around. That's what happened to set this whole thing off, and that's probably not in the file, because Mitchell's family didn't want people to think the baby wasn't Mitchell's."

"Okay," I said encouragingly.

"It was all over town, you know how people talk. She was—Claire that is—was apparently messing around with some cowboy named J.P. Callahan, and Mitchell caught her. He was taking care of the kids, and she ran around on him, so he lost his wad, then all of a sudden the boys end up dead near their house, so everyone said Mitchell must have done it. But they arrested Claire too. There was something funny about all of it that I didn't really understand. I wasn't really old enough at the time to get all the details, if you know what I mean, but she had a boy on the side. He owns the stables over off Post Lane. Him and his wife."

"Okay," I said. "Callahan?"

"Yeah. He was older and hung around the school all the time. Kind of creepy, really. Why's this twenty-five-year-old guy coming around the high school? But Claire had boys coming around all the time before that. I'd see her in his truck going around town, and other guys before him."

"Mmmm," I said, trying to sound official. I knew the stable

Lacey was talking about. I hadn't ridden horses as a girl. I didn't do much of anything. Kids now were in all sorts of clubs and teams. I'd just walked around our yard and hoped someday I'd get married and have lots of babies.

"So that's pretty much what I remember," Lacey said. "And Arlene…I don't think you can fully appreciate how bad it was in Deck River when they were all living over there. Those kids were so gross. Claire was okay but she was still real trash, just trying to get out. The little boys were like ragamuffins. I know family services was there day and night. They stole food from the grocery store, but nobody would arrest them, because they were so poor. Claire carried that little toddler boy around with her all the time like he was a rag doll—her little brother. She left him in the car in the school parking lot a few times when she had her dad's truck. She just laid him on the floor with a bottle and left the window cracked. I don't know why he was her responsibility, but he was. Then she had her own baby. That was all anybody talked about for a long time, but it was a long time ago now."

"I guess I was too young to be paying attention," I said.

"Yeah," Lacey agreed. "Anyway, I need to get to my step class. Jodi's a stickler about starting on time."

"Okay, Lace," I said. "Thanks for the dirt. I can't wait to talk to Alaina." I was wearing my reading glasses and feeling very satisfied by the conversation. I heard a clap of distant thunder that flipped my stomach. I hated driving in bad weather. There was a large dark spot to the north; it looked like spilled batter, bubbling at the edges on a hot plate.

"I never cared for Alaina Watson or whatever her name is now," Lacey said. "Just be careful."

"Why does everyone keep saying that?"

"I feel like talking to Mitchell's parents or Natalie would be better, but I don't know what became of her. I'm sure she left Faber. I know I would have after all that."

"Yeah," I said. "I'll keep you posted."

"You know what, Arlene? Sorry—I do need to go to the gym…"

"I know," I said. "Step."

"Right, but you said something about Ronna Rolfe?"

"Yeah."

"She's from Deck River too."

"She is?" I said.

"Yeah, she was real tight with Claire Broderick when we were little. They lived right next to them."

"She did? She acted like she was from Faber."

"Oh no, she grew up right next door to Claire. She was more like a Broderick than a Wright, mind you. Her mom's the one who had the funeral reception for the kids. No one else knew what to do. Mom went. I remember her crying about it after."

"Oh," I said. My glasses slipped down the bridge of my nose. I reached to adjust them and nearly smacked myself. "Oh dear," I said again as if I'd just discovered something horrible at the bottom of my coffee mug after I'd drank a full cup. "She didn't tell me that."

"People didn't like to admit they were from Deck River, Arlene. That's not somethin' she's gonna share over pie, not without a fight."

"Oh my God," I said upon realizing that the Nadine Davies I'd read about—the one who held the funeral reception for the boys—was Ronna's mother.

"Oh, no God didn't live in Deck River," Lacey said. "Not then. Not ever."

Lucy's here. I'm calling her Lucy even though Claire says it's Lucille. She's cute as a button, but she had trouble breathing at first. She had to stay in the hospital for a few days right after she was born. My parents had to watch Carter and the other Broderick boys—I've finally got all their names straight after them staying with us for a week. Their dad works all day and is too messed up at night to take care of them or get them to school—not even with Claire stuck in bed from the labor. Mitchell asked my parents if they could take care of everybody so he could be in the hospital with Lucy. My mom said sure, but then she got in a huge fight with my dad right after that. He doesn't want those kids here—period.

My friend Anna Laurel came over while they were staying with us but then said she's not allowed to come back to my house now. She kind of announced it at the lunch table at school, like everyone's parents would think the same thing. She said her parents didn't know those kids were staying with us. All they did was watch TV the whole time she was over anyway. Anna used to ride horses with me over at the stable, but now she does baton. Her mom didn't like how messy the horses were.

My dad threatened to move out if those kids came to stay with us again. My mom was so upset. She was crying and went over to Alaina's house. My dad doesn't like that either. Every time my mom gets upset, she runs to Alaina. Mitchell says that's weird too. He says Dad should be Mom's best friend. But the thing is Alaina doesn't threaten to leave and throw stuff against the wall all the time the way Dad does now.

Anyway, now Lucy's home with Mitchell and Claire. Claire had to stay in the hospital a few extra days too. I guess she didn't really want to hold Lucy and kept asking for Carter. My mom's very worried about them being alone at the house. She keeps finding reasons to go over there and check on the baby. Mitchell still has to work all the time, so it's Claire and all those kids there by themselves. I guess her dad's going over to sleep sometimes; he has a leak in his roof and can't stay at his place in some weather. I feel so sorry for Mitchell when I think about it.

Tina told me her and J.P. are gonna get married. She was really forceful about it, like I care. Tina seems mad at me all the time now. Maybe she thinks I want to get with J.P. too. She seems to think everyone does. I think he looks like a Slinky, and he's got this really slimy way about him. And from what I can tell, he's all over

Claire whenever he's not with Tina, and that's just gross to me. I
guess that's why Tina was always talking bad about Claire. I wish
everyone would just leave, or get a new life. We were so happy here
before all this. At least I thought we were. I thought Mitchell was
happy too. I don't understand what made him want to grow up
so fast and run off with someone like Claire. I do like her. There's
nothing not to like. My mom always tells Alaina that Claire is as
quiet as a mouse. And she is, but she's got a plan. That's the thing
about her—for some poor girl from Deck River, she sure seems to
know what's going on.

17

When Lacey and I hung up, so she could grunt and grind on fake steps at Porky's Gym, I patted my stomach, thinking maybe it was time I started doing some crunches—but that would have to wait. I had to meet Alaina Watson in an hour. I went to the mirror in the bathroom and ran a comb through my hair, reapplied lipstick, tried to pee one more time, and took off in my Mercedes with the windows down.

I had a wad of hair stuck in my lipstick less than two miles from home, and it started raining. I rolled everything up and felt uneasy. The sky looked like it was coming down on us in an elevator. I was a little small for my giant car and always felt like I was reaching up to the steering wheel. I pressed the gas, hoping I could make it to Fogle's before it really started pouring.

I pulled into the Fogle's parking lot in unison with a crack of thunder that had me jumping in my leather seat. "Whoa Nelly!" I said. It was something Tommy and I would have said together with a laugh. I blinked, realizing I was alone. I'd never ventured farther than a few miles from Tommy—not in the ten years since I met him. I'd never wanted to be far from him. I didn't want to now, but I had a fire in my feet, and he couldn't put it out. This was something I'd have to do without Tommy, or in front of him.

I'd seen only two older photos of Alaina Watson/Hopewell. Her official police photo was in one of the files. There was also a shot of her with Mitchell and Natalie Wright in evidence. Alaina had her arm around a scowling Mitchell's shoulder while Natalie stood next to them, looking a little like an afterthought. I hadn't seen a picture of Mitchell smiling yet. He was a severe young man as far as I could tell. There were a few pictures of him in the files—some from his days on the high school basketball team—but in all of them, he was furiously stoic. Boys who are trying to become men always think they have to do it so meanly. I thought about Tommy again—his big laugh and wide smile. I shook my head a little, trying to rid myself of this sudden longing. Tommy had two meetings this afternoon. He was going to be home late too. We were a working couple.

I scanned the parking lot but didn't see anyone I thought could be Alaina. It was mostly older men—curiously so. There were throngs of the upper-seventies crowd exiting every manner of sedan, with ball caps pulled low over their faces, adjusting pants that had become too loose in the rear. "Oh my," I said.

There was but one woman sitting in the restaurant when I walked in. She noticed me looking at her and stood up. Elegant, long-limbed with light wavy hair. "A rose among the thorns," she said, bowing slightly. "I'm Alaina." She extended her hand. "Please tell me you're Arlene."

"That's me!" I smiled cheerfully. It was as though I'd forgotten we were here to talk about four dead people. "Nice to meet you." I was shaking with nervousness, bug-eyed and vibrating. "Where should we sit?" I asked. It was a stupid question; Alaina already had a booth.

"Oh," she looked around. "Would you prefer something else?"

"No, sorry." I sat down hurriedly, having to force my large bags: one my purse, a ridiculously oversized satchel shaped like a crescent moon with stiff handles that wouldn't give with the force of my body weight against the table, and the other, my bag of documents to go over and share. Once on the bench, I realized I'd sat in front of Alaina's water glass—half-consumed with a straw sticking out. "Oh," I said, starting to rise and gather my things again.

"No, no. Don't be silly. Stay there." Alaina grabbed her water and moved to the other side of the table. "I don't even carry a purse anymore," she said. "Easier to get around."

"Right." I smiled. "I'm prepared for an invasion." I pointed to my pile of things.

"So." Alaina looked at me expectantly. "You work for the Faber Police Department."

"I do, but really, I'm nothing more than a bagger and tagger. I read the files when there's nothing else to do, and I'm tired of catalog shopping. So this file really got my attention. I mean—I haven't even read all of it yet, but it's riveting."

"Okay." Alaina was almost laughing at me. "Okay there, young buck."

"What?" I sat back, trying not to act offended. I wasn't. I did feel young though; she was right about that.

"No, I just...I don't know what I was expecting, but not...well, not you!" She smiled easily. I relaxed a little. "I was kind of the same. I don't know what they've told you over there, but I was also roped into this mess a little out of left field. I mean—I was, well..." she paused. "What do you know? Why don't you start?"

"I know you were Mitchell Wright's family friend."

The waiter approached and placed a glass of ice water in front of me. "What can I do for you ladies?" She had an earring in her eyebrow. I touched my own brow in solidarity.

"Nothing yet," Alaina said dismissively before the girl walked away.

"I know you were a family friend and then you worked on the case."

"Yes, well. Duke Pendley—he's retired now, but anyway—he was the lead guy on this, and he did an awful job. Just awful. They were going to put Mitchell away for the rest of his life—mostly because of budget cuts and incompetence, so I did this ramrod police training course and went official. I didn't take a salary or anything. I was trying to help. I stayed on for a while, but as soon as I figured out nothing was going to be done to clear Mitchell's name, I left. It took me a while. I held out hope for a long time, but you can't fix stupid."

"And he killed himself," I said as if she didn't know.

"Yeah." She looked down. "But you know, that happened almost immediately. Wasn't even two weeks after they found those kids."

It was raucous in the restaurant. There was clearly some sort of meeting or convention for these flat-bottomed men and their windbreakers. They were all at a long table together on the side of Fogle's, jeering and cavorting.

"Tractor convention," Alaina said with a smirk.

"Must be."

"But he didn't kill those kids," she said, scooting up on the booth. She pressed her elbows into the lacquered table and gave me a half stare, half squint. "I couldn't live with them saying he killed those kids. It made me sick to my stomach—night and day—and it was just laziness. Pendley was a lazy son of a bitch."

"Who did kill the kids?" I asked, leaning in too.

"Claire and J.P. Callahan." She said it like of course I would know.

"Shut the front door," I said.

The waiter showed up at the table again, interrupting my concentration. Alaina raised a hand to turn her away. I thought I would like to be the kind of person who could dismiss someone so eternally.

"I want to solve the case," I said. "I wanna get these people. I thought we could become a detectives' agency. That or journalists. I guess we'd have to start our own newspaper because the Faber paper isn't hiring. I checked."

"Boy, you are fired up, aren't you?" Alaina laughed. "I'll tell you everything I know but I don't think I want to work for the paper."

"I know it sounds stupid," I said.

"It doesn't. I was the same way. I mean—he was my best friend's son, but I get it. It doesn't sit right. Some people can ignore things that don't sit right. I can't. You can't either." She leaned back. "But I did end up ignoring it. You'll see the further you get into this that there is no evidence. None. Literally none whatsoever. As I said, Duke Pendley was an idiot, and it was Deck River." She was oddly dismissive.

"Yeah." I nodded uncomfortably.

"No—you don't understand that part, Arlene. You're not old enough to understand that...and you're clearly not from there." She motioned at my beaded lanyard necklace complete with daggerlike moonstone at the end. "Deck River didn't exist. Those people were phantoms. We might as well have been fishing in a sand dune. From one day to the next, there was less and less to go on. No one would talk to us. And they didn't care. They didn't care about those kids—if they'd've cared about them, they wouldn't have been growing up the way they were, and nobody from Deck River gave a shit about Mitchell Wright. He was some pretty boy from a rich family."

"Ronna's from Deck River," I said. I was about to suggest that we invite her to our next detectives' club meeting.

"Oh Lord, Ronna!" Alaina let out a roar of laughter.

"I know she's got her own style," I said. "But she is my friend, and I..."

"You'll never get Ronna Rolfe to admit she's from Deck River. Not in a million years. She's been trying to shed that skin her whole life. She came on at the station right before I left, and she'd straight-out lie to my face when I tried to talk to her about the Brodericks. She acted like she had no idea who any of those people were, and here her mother was the one who had the funeral service! She's an expert at playing dumb."

"Yes, but I think she knew Claire and..."

"You bet your ass she knew Claire. But she's never going to tell you about any of that. She married Platt Rhodes and got right with the community."

"Oh," I said confused. "What do you mean?"

"She used to turn tricks over there at Ram's. That's what Claire was doing too. Ronna'd rather lick a hot coal than admit any of that. She was a Deck River girl through and through."

The waiter showed up again, twiddling the post in her eyebrow. "Y'all want anything or you just gonna sit there?"

A CONDEMNED MAN

It wasn't the first time I ever saw those kids playing in the river half-naked. They was always doing it. It was freezing that night too, but they'd go out there in shorts and their pajamas and be over in the spillway. You're not supposed to swim that far down, 'cause they let the dam up. People've drowned in there, but if Claire's not watching those kids, then no one is. She wasn't over there. She was at Ram's. I saw her out back smoking a cigarette earlier. I wasn't into her anymore anyway. She had a baby and got all serious with that Wright kid. He was a spoiled brat from in town. I knew she was gonna get out of there sooner than later. She figured out I wasn't going anywhere, and I wasn't. I married another gal though. I just went along. She was kind of the fuel to my fire, and I liked having a wife. I did always want to be like Jorge, and he was married. A real family man.

I saw the oldest one holding a stick on the bank. The other ones were lying in the mud. They were like brain dead or something. I always did think something was wrong with those kids, not like just bein' from a bad family, but just plain dumb.

It rained all day. I remember that. I was getting stuck in mud over at Ram's. I was spinning all over the lot. I went into Faber, then came back out. I had a mind what I was gonna do. I think the one half was pushing hard against the other when I saw that kid with the stick. It was like he was going to fight me. I just took it so personal, like I was gonna get him before he got me. He was standing there with that stick and no shirt on out in the cold, and I wanted to win. It really didn't have anything to do with Claire. I just wanted to get him and the other ones. They were sitting on the ground kinda rotting away in life. It made me despise them. I don't know; I thought about the Charleys and how they beat up on me. My mama just let 'em. I think now it's 'cause she was seeing their old man at night, like getting real drunk and letting him have his way with her, 'cause she liked getting had. Chrissy couldn't stand it. Maybe I did it for Chrissy. I think they reminded me of the Charleys. I think that's it. The kid with that stick looked just like Charley when he was young. I beat Charley so bad once he went deaf in his left ear for a while. My mama moved out after that. She said she picked Charley's dad over me after what I did. She came home though. He didn't even want her for long.

18

Alaina invited me over to her house. "I had to get a look at you first," she said. "I live alone now. A woman can't be too careful."

"Oh, I understand," I said as we walked out of Fogle's.

"Nice ride," Alaina said upon seeing my Mercedes, which we were going to leave in the parking lot.

"My husband's in real estate. He's trying to compensate," I said as we got into Alaina's Wagoneer. I felt small, reckless, irresponsible, and thrilled as I buckled myself in. "We don't have kids, and he knows that upsets me."

"Well sweet Jesus does that sound familiar. We didn't have kids either," she said, starting the car.

"Oh, I want them. I had a miscarriage." She backed out of her spot with a jolt and made a sharp turn out of the parking lot. It was raining and gray but the thunder and lightning had passed to another valley. The distant mountains were shrouded in soggy, thin clouds. I shivered a little. The Jeep's seats were cold on my damp skin.

"I'm sorry to hear that. Hopefully you'll get another chance. Here—I'll put the heater on. This thing's so dirty, it's gonna fog up the windows like we're getting busy in here, but it'll clear. I could drive home blindfolded."

We were in Dolvin—a place I'd always liked. They had a handful of antique shops and a small downtown that looked like a gnome village. It was set at the base of a string of the Appalachians with Lake Millican right there in the middle. We just had Deck River in Faber. It didn't compare.

Alaina's house was an ornate Victorian sitting about two hundred feet back from the road. "There she is," Alaina said of the home as we pulled into the driveway. "I wanted to move up here when I was still with Stan, but he wouldn't leave Faber. Making too much money. We used to come up here to go antiquing—or I did while Stan complained he was bored and looked at other women. I always told him one day I'd live in this house. So here we are, and now it's mine."

There was colder air coming in; I could tell by the layer of mist collapsing into the valley to our right. The hills took a sharp turn, and that with the fog served as the wool over my eyes. Later, I would think of this as the moment—the very important moment that I missed. I was too busy being impressed with the house and all its gables. Such finery seemed unattainable in Coral Acres where Tommy and I lived, as did coral for that matter.

"It's lovely," I said. I thought of my and Tommy's split-level. It had about an eighteenth the character of this place. There was a large, flourishing garden to the right of the driveway. Even in October with the plunging temperatures, things appeared to be growing. "That's so nice," I said, staring enviously. "Tommy wants to live on Lake Patton in the lap of luxury. Maybe that is what we should do." I sounded wistful and lost. "He's always suggesting I do things like iron curtains or organize the pantry, like maybe I'd like doing that stuff if we lived in a fancier house. I don't really like moving cereal boxes around or..." I wasn't sure what I was trying to say. I was a stranger in my own body; it was the first time I could remember thinking Tommy was dead wrong about something important—me.

"Hmmm," Alaina said, trying to keep up. "Best-laid plans, right."

"Right." I was about to tell her to take me back to my car at Fogle's so I could drive home and forget all about the Brodericks. I didn't know what had come over me. I wasn't even going to be home to make Tommy dinner or hear about his day. We hadn't gone fishing in a year at least, and we'd never gone antiquing. I didn't even know that was a thing...or a word. "I do think a garden would be nice," I said quietly.

"It's a lot of work," Alaina said. "Too much sometimes, but what else do I have to do?" She put the Wagoneer in park and turned off the engine. "I'm sixty-five years old and I'm still trying to figure out what I want to do with my life. I wasted a lot of time. The wrong man will do that to you—the wrong man really knows how to waste a woman's time." Alaina continued to grip the steering wheel before nodding her head decisively and opening her door. "Let's go."

I wanted to correct her and tell her that Tommy wasn't the wrong man, but these waves of doubt that had been coming over me ever since I took my job in the basement crippled my ability to defend him like I used to. I'd made every excuse in the book about his drinking over the years. Now that the comments were about me, I wasn't as quick to set the record straight. Him being the wrong man meant I might have made a mistake. The mere suggestion of it gave me a shock of quiet sorrow.

Once inside, Alaina immediately went to a small bar in her kitchen and made us Manhattans. Every wall inside was covered in framed artwork. Every tabletop filled with stylish knickknacks, and every floorboard adorned with a small, ornate rug. It was dark inside because of the overcast skies. Alaina went about turning on tiny table lamps in intimate corners of the main rooms. It was instantly comfortable and inviting amid the warm glow.

"Okay, so now that you know about Ronna. Let me tell you some other stuff that you probably didn't see in the file." She handed me an oversized drink in a towering martini glass and sat down on a pert little sofa with small circular cushions. "Please—have a seat." She motioned toward a pair of easy chairs to her left. We were in a small room next to the kitchen. "This house has dozens of little rooms, all separated by awnings and eaves. It's one secret after another. I call this one the parlor." She smiled.

"I don't have a parlor," I said.

"You will some day. So, here we go. The baby—Lucille—that's not Mitchell's baby. That was the end of my friendship with the Wrights, and that's fine. I understood. I still understand, and anyway Dan Wright never wanted me around as much anyway. I was kind of in the way, but that's neither here nor there. Marianne Wright was my very best friend. We went to Hobbes College in Valing together. We married two very different men though. She had the family, and I had Stan. So—anyway. Sorry, the case. I'm alone out here a lot, if you can't tell." She raised an eyebrow.

"I'm alone a lot too." I sipped my drink. "Boy, you're speaking Tommy's language with these." I puckered my lips. "Tommy's my husband. He likes the sauce."

"Yeah, we'll just have one. I have to get you back to your car. Okay—so...here we go. That wasn't Mitchell's kid. Marianne wouldn't allow a DNA test, and Claire never pushed for it. Marianne and Dan took Lucy when Mitchell died. They raised her; she's lived with them her whole life. They cut ties with me a long time ago. Dan never liked that I was working with the police; you know how it goes—he thought it was my fault, everything that happened. They lost Mitchell of course, and then I tried to help, and the way Dan saw it, I made everything worse. Mitchell's name was never cleared; the case is still considered unsolved; they could never really show their faces in Faber again. We had some other disagreements..." She waved her hand in front of her face, dismissively—just like she'd done at the restaurant to the girl with the eyebrow ring.

"I take full responsibility for all of it," she went on. "I really do. They are very good people, Arlene. Salt of the earth. Mitchell got derailed, but so do a lot of people. It didn't have to be this bad. That's what really killed me. He could have gotten her pregnant, lived like trash over in Deck River, and just been a bit of a disappointment, and I'll say this—" She sat back, placing her drink on the small end table to her right. She was further along than I was. It might have been that I was hungry, but the booze was going straight to my head. I felt foggy and even a little suspicious. Maybe she'd drugged me. I'd done some stupid things in my life, but driving off to the middle of nowhere with someone I'd just met at Fogle's to drink spirits and talk about a murder case was definitely one of the dumbest. "I'll say this—Mitchell was not the rising star his father thought he was, and I may have said a few things I shouldn't have."

"Oh." Now I sat back in the small navy chair where I'd been awkwardly placed since we came in the room.

She sighed. "Yes, I told Dan Wright that he pushed Mitchell away—pushed him into the situation with Claire with all of the demands. He wouldn't let the kid just be. There were some sports letdowns, and Mitchell wasn't ready for college. He just didn't want to leave Faber. His father couldn't understand that. He was supposed to go to university and be a badass, and he didn't want to be. He wanted to stay home, near his family, near his sister especially—I think. And I do think he was in love with Claire. It was definitely the first-time-getting-some kind of love, but he cared for her. He did."

Distant thunder smacked the ground outside. I could hear a breeze and a small sheet of rain come over the house. It went darker again; the brief spires of sun that looked like they had been shooting up from the wet ground rather than down were gone. Everything around us was a muddled gray.

"There are always expectations when it comes to parents though, and Mitchell wasn't delivering. That set this thing in motion, but that's a common story, and it didn't have to go this badly. Anyway—enough of that. I messed up my relationship with the Wrights; I tried to fix it by helping with the case, which I really did think I would be able to solve...or if not solve, significantly better the chances that Duke and the rest of the yokels at the Faber PD would figure it out, but I didn't. I also wouldn't give it up about the baby. That wasn't Mitchell's baby, but...well, now I don't have contact with any of them. Marianne chose Dan over me—as she should have. But all of that's neither here nor there. The kid was not Mitchell's. I stand by that. And there were some other rumors, but anyway...I think it was all his idea—J.P. Callahan's, that is—to get rid of everybody. I'm pretty sure he thought he and Claire would get to run off together into the sunset. That didn't happen. She never got over the brothers dying, even though I always thought she had a hand in it. She never recovered. Ended up marrying some trucker from Forsyth. I think they still live over there. She never once came back for the baby—Lucy. Never once. The Wrights had Carter for a while too, but Claire got custody of him once her father died, but not Lucy. She didn't pursue it. She never came back for J.P. either."

"You don't believe Mitchell killed himself either, do you?" I asked. I had an urge to check the time. All I could think about was how Tommy would worry.

"I didn't at the time, but is that me, the guilty overinvolved friend, or me the logical bystander? As you can see…I'm assuming you've spent some time with the files—a lot happened in a short period of time. A lot of very disturbing things that local law enforcement just wasn't equipped to handle. Mitchell's death was the last in a long line of matters that Duke Pendley, Larson Gamble was around then too, and Roger Green—he retired a while ago and was never really…well, never really anything. Kind of a beat cop his whole career. And in Faber! Good grief. Anyway, they couldn't get on top of it. They never got out from under any of that. Duke Pendley didn't stay on much longer after the case was shelved. Three kids is a lot to lose…well, four. Mitchell was still a kid. Four kids is a lot to lose in a small town like Faber."

"But doesn't J.P. still live in Faber?" I said. "And we went house hunting over at Lake Patton. Duke Pendley's place was a mansion, if you ask me. A Tudor mansion." I nodded knowingly, pleased to be using this word in front of someone who clearly knew about home design. "Was his wife rich or something?"

"No, I don't think so," Alaina said. "There are no mansions in Faber," she said crossly. I felt stupid for mentioning it. "And yes, J.P. Callahan lives in Faber. Still. Completely unencumbered." She closed her eyes dramatically. "Without issue."

"What did you mean about there were some rumors? Who else did they think was Lucy's dad or..."

"Never mind that. That's the liquor." She laughed forcefully and made like she was going to get up.

"Why do you think he did it? J.P. Why do you think it was him?"

"Horse tranquilizers. That's what they think was on the rags. There wasn't enough residue to make a good determination. That and the fact that the guy who removed the cloths from their throats didn't know how to preserve evidence. At all. He was like a mechanic or something working for the coroner. They ended up bringing in some people from the Georgia Bureau of Investigation down in Atlanta, but it was too little too late. All the really important stuff was already beyond repair, but there was no question— even after all the bungling—that there was a common equine sedative on those rags."

"Is he dangerous?" I said. "J.P.?"

"What do you think? He killed three kids. But—" She paused.

"Listen, Arlene, Claire helped. I know she helped, and she couldn't live with it. We had one eyewitness, one, and he was an old drunk from the river. He said there were two people over on the bank. Two. So if I'm right, and J.P. Callahan did it, and I am right—then there was somebody else there with him."

"It sounds like Mitchell was the one who couldn't live with it." I gulped the last of my drink, suddenly committed to this new way of life. Me, Alaina, a stiff drink, and the truth. I was about to mention the female detective agency again, but held back. At this point, I didn't have anything to offer. I could be Alaina's secretary, not her peer.

"I don't know," Alaina said. "The urgency of that has faded for me. I was so sure then. I'm not so sure now." Her eyes jumped to the window. "I should get you back to your car. I think it's gonna get nasty again. Or you could stay. Who knows—maybe I'm sending you out into it."

"I can drive in the rain," I said, hoping to prove my worth.

"I'd like to help," Alaina said, standing. "I don't know about having a business or whatever you were saying before, but you know—this is the thing that sticks with me. Everything with me and Stan kind of..." She flicked her fingers in the air in front of her face. "I'm okay with all of that now, but I never got over this. I made some mistakes. I should have done a lot differently, but...well. I'd like to help. I've always wanted to make this right, you know—get that asshole."

"Me too," I said stupidly. Really I'd just found out about these atrocities a few weeks earlier and had never, not once in my life prior to that, even considered getting this asshole, or any other for that matter. "I brought some files," I said. We hadn't addressed my bulging bags—the ones I'd been lugging around all afternoon but had now left lying in a heap on the kitchen floor along with my purse.

"Oh, you've got the files with you?" Alaina's face changed.

"I brought some stuff for you to review."

"Okay." She sounded a little unsure.

"Is that all right?" I was confused. The mood in the room had done a belly flop.

"Yes, it's fine. It's fine."

"If you don't want to relive it…or…" I stood up too.

"I can relive it. I can."

"I'm going to try and see if I can get Ronna to help us too."

"Good luck with that." Alaina closed her eyes and stifled a laugh. "I'm not sure why, but okay."

"Right." I wasn't sure why I kept bringing Ronna up—everywhere I went. I'd mentioned her while filling up at the gas station the other day. "Ronna has a Taurus," I'd said to an uninterested patron at the pump next to me. The person did not respond but looked around like they might need help should I continue telling them about this mysterious Ronna.

"Are these the original documents?" Alaina asked.

"I made copies," I said. "With Ronna." I shook my head a little, annoyed with myself. "So they're copies of the originals. I didn't bring any of the journal though. I saw..."

"Oh no, you can ignore that." She'd been so eager to talk about all of this just seconds earlier; her mood was suddenly edgy and distracted. "That was a waste of time. Complete."

"Oh," I said. "There were a lot of notes about it in..."

"No, I was wrong. There was nothing there," she said hurriedly. "Oh my, this is a trip down memory lane, isn't it? Too bad I don't really want to revisit the Alaina of that time," she said after a breath. "But I will." She smiled as if she'd clarified all she needed to. "I should have done a lot differently, but that's okay... that's life, right?"

"I think that every day," I said. "I was just thinking that I wished I would stop bringing Ronna up everywhere I go. I don't know why I do that."

"I'm not sure why you're doing that either," Alaina laughed, "but this is a little different. I affected a lot of people's lives. I shouldn't have." She was sincere; the edge had turned to sober reflection.

"Let's get this guy," I said. "J.P. Callahan. Let's get him." I sounded squeaky and childlike. I could drink all the whiskey in the world, and I would probably never achieve Alaina's husk.

"We'd have to get Claire too," Alaina said, snapping out of whatever trance she'd been in at the thought of reading through her notes, remembering that Alaina. "I always felt sorry for her," she said. "I did, but I know she was in on it. I know it like I know you're standing there in my living room. Those boys went completely willingly with whoever shoved those rags down their throats. They trusted the person. They wouldn't have sat there and let J.P. Callahan stick horse tranquilizer in their mouths. She was there, and it's why she left. She couldn't stand it. She didn't go to their funeral—nothing."

"I saw that," I said. Cecil Broderick hadn't gone either. The file mentioned a complete lack of family at the service, which had mostly been attended by law enforcement and gawkers, and apparently Ronna's mother.

"She took the littlest brother eventually, but she left the rest. In the dirt...well, and with the Wrights."

"Have you ever seen her again?"

"Oh, I've seen her. That's the part of it—We'll get to that. I chased her down, I went after her. Marianne never forgave me for that."

We looked at one another. My respect was deepening. I'd never gone after anyone, except Tommy so I could marry him and have lots of babies. I gave Alaina's parlor another once-over and thought maybe I could decorate the front room at Coral Acres this way—or maybe I could properly reopen a murder investigation which, if I was honest, sounded like a hell of a lot more fun.

NATALIE WRIGHT'S JOURNAL
November 15, 1983

There's something really wrong with Mitchell and Claire. **He**
won't tell me what's going on, but ever since the baby came home
from the hospital, Claire is gone all the time. She takes Cecil's
car and just leaves. She leaves all the kids with Mitchell, and he
has a job. He has two jobs! He's still working at Flannigan's and
delivering pizzas, but I guess for the last week, he's taken all the
kids with him when he went on his route. He got in trouble,
because the baby was crying really loud, and Carter had a dirty
diaper. A customer saw Mitchell changing him in the driveway
and complained because how could he wash his hands before he
touched the food? My mom said he could bring the kids to our
house before his shift, but my dad put his foot down. He just
kept saying they have a dad. They do have a dad, but I guess he's
been really sick, like bad sick. My mom told Alaina he's not sick;
it's drugs. I don't know what kind of drugs. His hands shook the

whole time he was over, so whatever the drug is it makes your hands shake.

Mitchell actually started crying to my mom one night when he came by. He told my mom Claire is depressed and has to run off all the time because she tells him she wants to kill herself. My mom said she has postpartum depression and that there are medications for it. Alaina is really good friends with her own lady doctor and said she would get Claire a bottle of pills. My mom also said she would pay for Claire to go to the doctor. I guess she went to the free clinic for all the stuff with the baby. Alaina said the free clinic will give her depression medication too, but Alaina doesn't believe a word of it. She says Claire isn't depressed, she's just trying to get out of it.

They talk about it in front of me all the time now, especially my mom and Alaina. My dad doesn't really say much about anything anymore. He's very quiet and sits in the back at church, all by himself. He gets up and leaves before anyone has a chance to say hi to him. I guess a lot of people are saying he and my mom are going to get a divorce. I wasn't really embarrassed about any of it until my dad started refusing to sit with us in church anymore. Everyone in Youth Group puts their hands on me and prays for me even though they think Mitchell has abandoned God. My friend Anna says that doesn't mean I abandoned God. I'm glad to hear that.

The other thing is that I've been working at the stables a little bit. My dad got me my truck but he says he won't pay for gas. My mom gives me money behind his back, but not a lot. Tina and J.P.—who she calls MY HUSBAND every chance she gets—put up signs in the barn asking for people to help. I'm working nine hours a week, and it's hard! I am so tired when I'm done that I feel like I'm going to pass out. It's so cold and wet out right now too; that makes it worse. I wish it would just snow up here. It would be nicer if it would snow instead of all of this freezing rain.

My mom bought the Broderick kids a ton of stuff for Christmas. All new clothes and lunch boxes. She got Claire a new dress and some fluffy slippers. The boys have been wearing shorts to school even though it's cold out, and I guess the principal called my mom and told her they needed boots. That's the first time I've heard my mom actually mad about any of this. She kind of yelled at Mrs. Mitnick—that's the principal—and said she wasn't in charge of clothing and feeding those kids just because her son had a baby with their sister. My mom called Alaina right after they got off the phone and said she wanted Mitchell to move back home with Lucy and that she and my dad would offer to take care of the baby. Right after that is when she went and got all the Christmas presents from the mall. I know she's feeling guilty, guilty but mad too. I told her I'd go shopping with her, but she said she wanted to be alone. Both of my parents want to be alone all the time now, which basically means I'm alone all the time.

Mitchell comes over sometimes with Lucy, but usually it's when I'm at the stables. J.P. is always asking me questions and talking to me now. I can tell it bothers Tina, but I am definitely not his type. I know he used to date Claire, and Tina was always real grown-up-looking too with big boobs and tight clothes. I don't think J.P.'s interested in me the way he's interested in Claire and Tina. Anyway they're married now; Tina made sure of that. They got married and went to the beach last month. Her family went too; I guess it was warmer in Florida, because she was super tan when they got back. J.P. acts exactly the same as before, and I know he still tries to get Claire to hang out with him, because of stuff Mitchell tells my mom. Mitchell says it like Claire is so great and beautiful and that's why J.P. wants her. It makes her more of a prize to him I guess.

I never really talk to him, but I did ask J.P. if he liked being married when we were giving Portia a rinse, and he just laughed saying he has to keep Tina happy or something. Every time he's hanging around me too much, I want to say I saw him with Claire at school, but I guess that was a long time ago now. It would be weird of me to say it. He makes me uncomfortable. I can't shake it.

19

Tommy, I'm going to be a real detective!" I was effusive when I arrived home. I came in through the garage and threw my bags on the ground, raising my fists in victory. He was three drinks in and in front of the television, eating warmed leftovers—lasagna.

"I was getting worried," he said without moving a muscle.

"Yeah, it took a while to get back from Dolvin. There was a tractor trailer tipped over outside Chimney Rock, but nobody was hurt. Did it storm here too?"

"No, I'm not hurt," he said.

"I was talking about the storm, but yeah, so Alaina went after them real hard, like vigilante-style justice. They cautioned her at the station, said they'd have to arrest her if she didn't back down, but she wouldn't. She was a real hard ass. She told me all about it. I was at her house in Dolvin.

You get such better views over that way. You can see up into Tennessee way better."

"It's North Carolina over there."

"Anyway—are you even listening to me?" I raised my voice and stomped my foot. "Hey, asshole! I'm talkin' to ya!" I'd never called Tommy a name, and certainly not an expletive; not in all these years. "I'm sorry about that, but you're like a bump on a log and I'm telling you a whole mess of extremely interesting stuff, and you're lying there. You got sauce on the couch, by the way." I put my hands on my hips. "I don't mean to be a jerk wife or something, but you are a real mess, and this is very important."

"Jerk wife?"

"I don't like treating you poorly, but you shouldn't like treating me poorly neither. This is crucial information, and this Alaina Hopewell woman is one tough cookie. We're gonna get this creep."

"Gonna get who?" Tommy was on his stomach now, propped up on his elbows, looking weak and directionless. Meanwhile I'd never had so much direction. I was nearly floating off the floor from all the direction.

"J.P. Callahan. He's the one."

"The cowboy guy? I'll be damned. Married to Tina—she's always been prime real estate around here."

"What?" I scowled. "Let's not talk about women like chattel," I said.

"I just mean she used to be the big catch, you know?"

"No, I don't. Why are you eating shirtless again?" I rubbed my eye and came back with a bit of mascara on my finger. I hadn't used the bathroom in several hours; I was uncomfortable but continued to hold it, fearing I'd miss something important while sitting on the toilet. I didn't, however, consider that I looked a mess. I'd been all over two counties that afternoon in stormy, aggressive weather. I walked to the bathroom and looked at myself in the mirror. I was disheveled with smears of various powders and glosses on my face. I was glad it had been dark at Alaina's. I didn't look like a professional detective—or a professional anything.

"You okay?" Tommy called after me. He still hadn't moved from the couch.

"I'm fine. I have to pee!" I shut the door. I was jittery from the liquor, the excitement, from driving white-knuckled on the pass to get home. I was also hungry and wanting to feel lovingly toward Tommy. It was dawning on me that I might not be able to be a successful detective and a good wife at the same time. I was going to be disappointed in myself if I couldn't manage to stay good natured while accomplishing something. It was a real racket that women were supposed to keep out of life so they could be nice.

I came out of the bathroom and grabbed a bag of chips from the pantry. Tommy had managed to pull himself off the couch and walk in to join me in front of the opened door. "Oh, I didn't know we had moon pies," he said enthusiastically.

"They were on sale. I don't even like those. I don't know why I bought them. Just spending money to save money, I guess. I need to call Ronna," I said, putting a large ruffled potato chip in my mouth.

"Hello," a hearty male voice said into the phone after I'd dialed. I'd never called Ronna at home. We exchanged numbers but hadn't yet used them.

"Hey, Platt, is Ronna there?"

"Who's calling?" He was throaty and loud.

"Arlene from the office."

"Oh." He sounded disappointed. "One second. She's in the yard."

I looked out the kitchen window at the back of the house. It was pitch-black out. I tried to figure out what Ronna would be doing outside in the dark. It was nearing eight at night. I was normally in my pajamas and my reading glasses by this time.

"Hello." Ronna sounded winded.

"Hey, it's Arlene."

"I know. Platt told me."

"What are you doing?"

"Runnin' suicides," she said.

"No shit."

"No," she said. "But we don't use profanity."

"So you're working out?"

"I do it every night. I have an obstacle course back there." She continued gasping and blowing into the receiver.

"But it stormed earlier," I said as if this was the biggest

surprise in the exchange, that it had stormed and now it wasn't storming anymore.

"I can do my workout in all weather," Ronna said sturdily.

"How come you didn't tell me you're from Deck River and that you grew up next to Claire? I want you to be a part of my detective agency, but I need you to be truthful."

"You didn't ask if I grew up next to Claire or where exactly I was from. Anyway, I don't know anything about any of that. I don't know about the murders, and I already said I can't be in the detective club."

"You told me you grew up behind the Wrights."

"Deck River was behind their neighborhood," Ronna said with as much bite as I was dishing out.

"Yeah, like five miles behind. Listen," I said, trying to quell my agitation at the semantics battle we were having next to Tommy and his moon pie. "I know there's bad blood between you and Alaina, but she has regrets too." I honestly had no idea what I was talking about. I ate another chip and wondered if maybe I needed to go and set up an obstacle course in our backyard too. Tommy and I were prime candidates for running suicides. My only exercise before had been bowling league, and Tommy just bought a new power mower. We hadn't burned a calorie between us in months.

"I don't have any regrets," Ronna said. "I have to get back out there. I'm really sorry I don't want to be in the detective agency. I hate letting you down all the time, but you are kind of demanding,

Arlene. I like having lunch together and talking about vacation, but I don't want to change my life to be friends with you."

"I don't want you to change your life," I said. "I want to be a part of your life."

Tommy had been watching me closely with his mouth open, looking woefully confused. "What?" he said. I put my hand up in dismissal. It was a lot like Alaina had done. I was going to have an entire new personality by the end of this—Alaina's grit and Ronna's straightforwardness were mine to seize, and I wanted them. I looked at Tommy again, racked with guilt that I honestly believed I was leaving him behind. I wondered if he felt that way when he started to make all the money and got a fancy job title to go with it. Maybe I seemed like something that was out of fashion in light of his new circumstances.

"I like my life though. I'm not trying to change anything," Ronna said, frustrated. "Everything you want to do is stuff I don't want to do."

"I eat meatloaf," I argued.

"We can do that together."

"So you're saying we can only be friends if we do the stuff you want to do?"

"I guess so." Now she sounded mad. It was our second big fight. I never went at it like this with friends. Ronna was really bringing a fire out in me.

"Tell me about Claire." I was trying to change the tenor of our conversation.

"I can't right now. I'm working out. I'll see you tomorrow, Arlene." She hung up abruptly.

"Come on," I said to Tommy.

"What?" He had moon pie filling on his left cheek.

"We're goin' out back. We're gonna run some suicides."

20

The next morning at the office was tense. I got the impression Ronna had complained to Captain Gamble about me. He came down almost as soon as I got there and said that if I needed copies made, I should ask him. I thought we'd cleared the air about that, but it might have been my late night phone call that restarted the engine of our discord.

"Well, then," I responded coolly. "I met with Alaina Hopewell yesterday."

"Is that her new name?"

"Her old one. She went back to it."

"All right." Now he was a little icy.

"She told me she left on bad terms."

"Oh…well, that was a long time ago."

"She said she attacked Duke Pendley with a stapler?" Alaina had gotten a little bolder in her storytelling as the drink set in. By the time I left, she had herself sounding like Zorro, using office supplies to slash her name onto her defeated enemies. I went along with it; it was much more fun to think of her as hell-bent on justice than as some old woman living in a giant antique store posing as a house in Dolvin.

"Is that what happened? I don't really remember."

"Is anybody in this building going to talk straight with me?" I asked angrily. "Ronna practically grew up with these people and didn't tell me about it." I almost mentioned Ram's bar and turning tricks for a twenty, but I didn't want to believe that about Ronna, much less say it out loud. "Alaina Watson put a rain of fire down on this place, but no one said a word of that to me when I reopened this case!" I'd raised my voice from where I sat behind my small pea-soup-covered metal desk. "I don't even have a copy code." This was my final, most decisive point.

"We can get you a copy code. And Arlene," Captain Gable sighed. "You have not reopened the case. I feel I've been very accommodating, generous even. You have no license to conduct an investigation. I'm allowing you some freedom with your spare time here and was able to budget discretionary funds for your work in the afternoons, but all of this is out of…" He paused so he could wave his hands around hysterically. "Out of…just being nice. I like you. I don't want you to be bored here. I know there's not much to do most days. I'm allowing you to mess with the files, but I don't want you to—I don't want you to think you're…like in charge of anything. You're certainly not in charge of Ronna. She's worked here for over fifteen years."

"Oh, I know I'm not in charge of her," I said. I was in cream trousers—daring for this time of year and an office setting—and a pale blue blouse with large hoop earrings. I had my hair up on the crown of my head in a tight bun. I'd dressed for the job I wanted that morning—lead investigator. Or journalist. Lead investigative journalist. "No one's in charge of Ronna Rolfe Rhodes. Not me or God himself."

"If there's a personality conflict, I'm afraid…"

"There's no conflict," I said. "But I'd like her help. She knew these people…intimately." I picked up my pen and made like I needed to get back to something more important than this conversation.

"Right, but Arlene, this is just a hobby."

"No." I put the pen down angrily. "It is not a hobby. I am trying to bring justice to Faber. Justice that has eluded this town, this family, for near twenty years."

"Boy, you and Alaina are cut from the same cloth, aren't you?"

"I don't know. She gave up, but I won't. Tommy's a mogul so I don't need money. I can hunt perps for free."

Captain Gamble chuckled a little. "I'm not going to stand in your way. I just don't want you disrupting anything here at the department. And I still need you to do your job. We still have evidence."

"I can do it all. I'm a woman." I pounded my chest with my small fist. I'd taken to acting out in every way possible. It was the first day of the rest of my life as far as I was concerned.

"However you see it, I'm fine with that. It's really very attractive—your determination." He smiled a little loopily.

"Huh?" I sneered. "Tommy said you were getting a little hot on me. I don't care for it. I'm a married woman with a mission for justice."

Captain Gamble flushed bright red. His mouth puckered like he was about to say something but didn't. He walked to the stairs in small, mincing steps without looking back. I'd humiliated him—my boss. The person who'd allowed me this opportunity, the opportunity to feel so confident. I shrank in my seat, knowing I was getting too big for my britches. One day of real responsibilities and I was already a jerk.

It was quiet in my basement cell after Gamble left—too quiet. I had the files arranged in front of me but did nothing but stare at the folders for a long time. The phone rang, which is what startled me out of my trance.

"Hello," I said meekly.

"It's Alaina. I'm about to head to Faber. You ready for me?"

"Oh." I caught my breath. "Yes. I'm afraid I've just kind of made a fool of myself, but yes, I think I'm ready."

"You can't make a fool of yourself at the Faber Police, sister. Not in that crowd."

"No." I wasn't sure if I was agreeing or disagreeing with her. "I am ready for you. I can get a little further into the files while I'm waiting."

"You better warn Ronna and Gamble I'm coming. I'm persona non grata over there."

"I don't know what that means," I said.

"It doesn't matter. They don't care about me. I'm blowing smoke up my own ass."

"Sounds difficult," I said distantly. I was uncomfortable with myself and wondered if it was my brief meeting with Alaina yesterday that had completely changed my personality.

"See you soon." Alaina was undeterred by the effect my journey of self-discovery was having on me. She hung up.

I opened one of the files I'd not yet tackled in front of me and set to reading. These pages seemed to be mostly about interviews with Natalie Wright. I hadn't done a whole lot with Natalie; I hadn't even been interested. There was—in this folder—a huge chunk of her diary that apparently had been submitted into evidence as part of the case against Mitchell being responsible for the Broderick boys' deaths. Alaina had been dismissive, but not at first, at least not what I could see from the earlier files when she kept referencing it.

I picked up the journal, still a little lukewarm on Natalie generally, but I had at least an hour to kill before I figured Alaina would be in Faber. I didn't remember us deciding she was coming to the station, which I blamed on the drink and the storm and her house, which had me a little tilted with its moody decor—her mood, not mine. Mine had been one of awe. I didn't think anyone could live on their own in such style. For a split second I'd wondered if any of the choices I'd made so far were the right ones.

Natalie Wright insisted she was with Mitchell during the time of the boys' murders. He had a pizza route—on this evening he did the late shift, which meant from seven to ten, but he called in sick. This had been a damning piece of evidence against him. He called into work, so he must have killed the kids. The manager said he'd never called in sick before—not in the nine months he'd worked there. Natalie said he called in sick because he had bronchitis.

There was no mention of Alaina in this part of the investigation. She would not become an officer until well after Mitchell killed himself. Instead it was all Natalie and photos of the land on Deck River where the kids were found, like looking at a bunch of wet dirt and dead leaves pressed into the ground was going to give us a clue as to who shoved rags down three kids' throats at dinnertime.

I was deeply engrossed when Alaina showed up. It sounded almost like there was a fight, or at the very least a good old-fashioned tussle, at the top of the steps before I heard the door open then slam. It was Ronna coming to announce my visitor; she galloped down the stairs like a horse at the rodeo.

"I announce guests at the station," she said, flushed and

sweating. "I told Alaina to wait in the lobby because that's what guests do. My job is to announce guests." Her fists were clenched, her eyes bugged out and twitching. I'd lost sight of her upper lip completely. Her hair had extra volume, and I admired her commitment to its height. She sure knew a lot about hair spray.

"Thank you for announcing my visitors," I said respectfully. "I'd like it if you stayed for the meeting."

She glowered, then hurled herself back up the stairs quite athletically. The suicides were paying off. She wasn't even winded on the last step. I knew because she yelled out "Arlene will see you now!" without missing a beat.

"Excuse me, Ronna," I could hear Alaina say. "If you could please get out of my way. You're like the Berlin Wall here."

"You shouldn't be rude. You don't work here anymore," Ronna said, leering. I got up from my desk. I could hear the two women but couldn't see them. I got to the bottom of the steps and looked up. They were pressed against one another in the doorway, their faces very close with chins jutted forward.

"Girls," I said. "Cool it now."

They said nothing but continued staring, their eyes narrowed slightly. Ronna was clearly holding in her stomach. She took a large breath and pressed lanky Alaina more aggressively into the frame with her midsection—which from this angle and with the new information about her exercise regimen, I could tell was quite taut. Ronna Rhodes was all muscle.

"She's not the boss of this place," Ronna said under her breath.

"You're not either," Alaina said back.

"None of us is the boss!" I said up the stairs. "Or are the boss." I was unsure of my grammar. "But let's not fight. Let's work together!" The two women breathed heavily in each other's faces and stared with malice. "Let's use this passion for justice!" I shouted.

Alaina rolled her eyes and turned to me. "Arlene, I know you're ready to take on the world here, but—"

"You leave Arlene alone," Ronna said.

"Excuse me, ladies." Captain Gamble had approached and somehow managed to lodge himself on the small landing with Alaina and Ronna. "Mrs. Watson," he said. "It's lovely to see you."

"It's not Mrs. anything anymore, Larson."

"Nevertheless." He was blushing again. He'd had a bit of an exceptional morning. "I need you to keep it down in here, please, and Ronna, I need you back at your desk. The phone is ringing off the hook. Tyler had to run up and answer it a couple of times already."

Everyone stood stock-still and waited for the other to flinch, myself included. "My only concern here is the Broderick kids," I said softly. "And Mitchell Wright. Can we leave our egos at the door?"

"Absolutely," Captain Gamble said.

"Oh shove it, Larson," Alaina answered. I looked down, trying not to gasp.

"If you're going to be coming around here, Alaina," he said, "helping Arlene, I expect you to treat me with the proper respect. I am the captain of the Faber Police Department, and you will address me as such."

"Understood," Alaina said, smirking. She turned away from all of the puffed-up torsos in her midst and headed down the stairs. "Let's get to work."

"Captain Gamble," Ronna said quietly. "Can Tyler cover the phone today? I want to help with the case."

Gamble sighed while watching Alaina's rear end descend the stairs. "Yes, that's fine, but just for today. There's not a lot going on anyway."

"There's about to be." I nodded at the group. "Let's do this thing."

November 29, 1983

The worst thing ever has happened. I can hardly write this.
My hands have been shaking for days. Somebody killed the boys.
Cedar, Colton, and Chase—all of them except Carter. My mom
says I have to call them by their names now. We have to have some
respect. They all suffocated. The police think it was a poison. They
closed school, and all sorts of people are keeping their kids locked
up in their houses. Somebody found the boys out by Deck River
a couple nights ago, lying there by the road. Nobody knows what
happened to them, but Mitchell got picked up. Claire too. They
had to go to jail, but they let them out after a few hours. I guess
Claire said she wanted to talk to a different person than was talking
to Mitchell, which my dad says is really bad, like she's being sneaky
or something. My dad's already calling her a liar, and I don't even
know if she's said anything to anybody. He has always hated Claire.
It's even worse now though.

Mr. Pendley is the detective, and he's the one who talked to Mitchell but not Claire. He's one of my dad's friends, because of his pool. My dad's been his pool guy for years. My dad keeps saying that, like if Mr. Pendley would just realize that my dad is his pool guy, everything would be okay.

It's like a hurricane in our house, because no one can figure out what's going on, and the phone keeps ringing over and over again. There have been so many people over acting like they want to help, but people don't really care about those kids, they just care about gossip. Alaina has been staying with us, but my dad said she needed to go. We just had Thanksgiving; we were eating leftovers when Mitchell called us to say what happened. He was at our house that night, the night the boys were killed. With me. I wish he'd just stayed at our house. I don't know why he always thinks he needs to go back to Claire. She's never home anyway.

They took him and Claire in not long after that. It was the middle of the night. My parents didn't sleep; they just sat up in the living room, staring at each other. My mom went to get Lucy when Mitchell said the police were taking them in. Lucy was asleep when they got back to our house. My mom left her in her car seat.

Claire brought Carter with her to the police station. I swear he's attached, like a backpack that got sewn on to her. Lucy she leaves everywhere; Lucy is definitely not sewn on.

My mom keeps crying; she says it's because of the kids, but I know it's because of Mitchell. She told Alaina the other day that

Claire ruined his life. "Ruined it!" she kept saying. I'm like a ghost in the house. No one even knows I'm there. I could definitely be one of those bad kids who does drugs and smokes out the bathroom window, but I don't want to be. I'm my parents' only chance now at having a normal kid or even a normal life, so I have to try really hard now. No more messing up.

The police have been over to the house at least ten times. They're very polite and feel sorry for my parents. I heard the one detective guy say that. "I feel really sorry for you." My dad thought that was the worst and hasn't stopped talking about it. He says he doesn't want people to feel sorry for him, or Mitchell. He says Mitchell isn't the kind of kid you feel sorry for. We aren't that kind of family. Claire is. That's what my mom says. Claire is the one they feel sorry for. My dad says they're not even married, and the kid probably isn't even Mitchell's. It's constant arguing. They can't talk about anything. My mom cries when she makes toast. She cries when she has her cookies and iced tea. She cries when she's folding laundry. My dad won't comfort her. He's too mad, and I'm pretty sure he thinks it's her fault. He said she indulged Mitchell.

But anyway I can't figure out what any of this has to do with Mitchell. He didn't kill anybody. I guess I became his alibi, because I said he was with me the night it happened. He was. He told me he was sick and couldn't do the pizza route, so he came over to our house. He was coughing a little for sure. He had Lucy and Carter with him. He ALWAYS has Lucy with him, but it was kind of weird that Carter was here without Claire.

My parents were out to eat when Mitchell got here, and he left before they got back. He was in a hurry the whole time, looking out the window. He said he didn't want to see Mom and Dad. I think it's because he's drinking a lot more and always smells like smoke. My mom told him he could get pulled over for drinking and driving especially in his old car, because one of the taillights goes out all the time. My dad's never drove drunk a day in his life. He keeps reminding us. I did think Mitchell was acting weird, but he's been acting weird for a year now, so I barely noticed.

I don't even know what I think or feel about those little boys getting killed. Sometimes, and it makes me feel awful to say it, but sometimes I think maybe whoever did it did them a favor. Nobody wanted those boys, didn't want to take care of them, and they weren't going to amount to shit. They'd be just like their dad. I pray every time I think that. My mom starts crying and saying over and over, "They were just little boys. They were just little boys." I know they were.

Everyone is scared. They only canceled school for one day, but a lot of kids haven't gone back yet. Their parents are too scared. I think about half the people around think Mitchell had nothing to do with it and that there's a killer on the loose, and the other half think Mitchell and Claire killed Cedar, Colton, and Chase, because it was too hard to take care of them. It was hard to take care of them. I could see it on Mitchell's face. It was hard. I didn't even really like being around them when they were all together. I hate thinking that; it makes me feel sick, like I'm not sad that they died. And they were murdered. I'm so worried about Mitchell that it's like I'm forgetting they were murdered. We should all be talking about that all the time—how sad it is—but instead we're just worried. I don't understand why anyone thinks Mitchell had anything to do with it. I keep telling them he was home with me.

21

laina joined us outside for lunch. The weather was wet, chilly, and gray. Ronna had commented on the damp weather and then announced she was eating at the picnic tables almost as a challenge.

"I am always comfortable in nature," she said. "If God wants me to be wet, he makes it rain."

I said I would go too, so Alaina agreeably tagged along. Ronna was quiet and seething while she ate her stroganoff from a small thermos under the maple where we always sat. Alaina was rattling on about her contacts and her pharmacist with the three-legged dog and a small comment here and there about the case. I couldn't tell if she was uncomfortable with silence or if she really did want to share all of this extraneous information with us while trying to stay dry.

Alaina was in the middle of explaining how she'd had to have her mailbox recemented into the ground last year when Ronna put the lid back on her thermos, wiped her mouth, turned to Alaina, and said, "You'll treat me with the respect I deserve, as a sixteen-year veteran of the force, Alaina." She was leaning forward with her elbows on the table and sneering.

Alaina rolled her eyes as if she'd been waiting for this interruption. "You're not a cop, Ronna. You never were. I did not have to get your permission to print those witness statements."

"You need my permission to make copies," Ronna said with a finger pointed at Alaina's chest. It was now fully raining. We all had a thin, damp layer on our faces. Both Ronna and I were wearing heavy foundation—as was the style of the time—and would need to blot upon heading back inside. Alaina was as fresh and clean as a new fawn. She wore dangling earrings with turquoise beads and had a purple scarf around her neck. Everything about her was effortless, while Ronna had the demeanor of a big rig truck trying to make it up a steep incline. I figured I was their in-between.

"Let's go in," I suggested, hoping to squelch the discomfort.

"No. Let's settle this once and for all," Ronna roared. "You cannot make copies or use the fax machine without asking me."

"Fine, Ronna," Alaina said bitterly. "I will not press any of the buttons within fifteen feet of your desk without first getting your permission." The wind picked up a little. I could hear heavy drops that had been resting on the trees fall on the tops of the cars in the parking lot next to where we stood. It sounded like rats on tin.

"She won't need to make copies anyway," I said while impatiently collecting the remnants of my barely eaten lunch. "I can make the copies, okay? Let's go in and get to work on the case!" I made a fist and dipped my arm enthusiastically. "Ronna, you have to tell us what you know."

"She won't." Alaina walked in front of us. "She wouldn't then; she sure as hell ain't going to now."

I really didn't want to start the antagonistic back-and-forth again. "Can we please just go inside and start looking through everything?"

"Yes," Alaina said. "I'm famished. Are we ordering?"

"We just ate!" Ronna said furiously. "We bring our food from home. I don't have a rich husband!" Ronna picked up her pace as if to demonstrate how fast people without rich husbands could walk. I tried to keep up, always trying to prove that I was more like her than she wanted me to be.

"Yeah, we just ate," I said. "And Tommy's only medium rich!"

"I don't have a rich husband," Alaina called out from behind us. "I have a rich ex-husband."

"No one is rich!" I yelled. "And I have an extra sandwich today—you can have it, Alaina. Just please stop the bickering. Tommy was half in the bag last night when he got home. I gave him hell for driving like that, so he was trying to get back in my good graces. He made my lunch for me. I don't even like ham."

They were both quiet for a second. "Sorry, Arlene," Ronna

said. She looked at Alaina, who didn't know of Tommy's trouble. "We'll stop arguing."

"You can eat in the basement," I said to Alaina. "The onions'll stink it up down there, but I don't care. It's only me who has to put up with it. Let's move." I skip-stepped up the front stairs of the precinct with the two women behind me.

We spent the afternoon organizing the material. I was hoping Ronna would take the edge off and admit to knowing a lot more about Claire and the Brodericks than she'd initially let on, but she was quiet and meticulous. She went through the papers quickly, precisely, stacking, restacking, clipping, stapling, moving piles from one side of the table to another then back again. She got through three boxes in the time I'd arranged two piles of papers on my side of the desk. Alaina went over to the other table and cleared away boxes so she could sort there.

"I don't like the idea of putting some of this in the 'ignore' pile," I said. "Don't we need to look at all of it?"

"Haven't you been looking at it for months?" Ronna asked. She slammed another box on the table and tossed the lid to the side.

"No," I said. "Only very seriously for about a month. And I'm not even a third of the way through. I haven't even looked at Natalie's diary."

Alaina's head jerked in my direction, but she didn't say anything at first. "There's nothing in there," she finally offered while we were all looking at her. "I told you that."

"See? She won't tell you anything about the Wrights," Ronna said. "She won't say a word about them. Not to anybody."

"What is the beef between you two?" I asked, dropping my pen on the table with a clatter. "Is it the copy codes? Because that I would kind of understand…is it Mitchell Wright? I mean, I get that everyone else thought he was the bad guy, but…"

"She came in here and got to be a cop because she was rich and bored. Kind of like you." Ronna pointed at me. One of the overhead lights, hanging on rusty chains, swung, frame and all. It was Ronna's passion that stirred the mildew-ridden basement air. "Some of us have to have a job. A real job. We can't pretend to be police officers when our friend's kid kills someone. Or because our husband's a drunkard. Or when we're bored up in Dolvin. I work that desk day in and day out and I'm damn proud of it. I do a good job here. I don't get to be a bored childless housewife who needs some excitement." She was breathing heavy and hard. "Sorry if that's ugly, but first it's dinner parties and now it's murder investigations for fun. I'd love to have all that time on my hands. I have to schedule my grocery trips and when I'm going to make the meatloaf every week or I won't have time between my physical fitness and Platt and my job and the laundry. I'm not putting anything in the discard pile. Not one scrap of paper. You won't control the investigation this time, Alaina. We may be on solid ground, but it's not going down like it did last time."

"Well then, I think if you're going to call the shots in between doing laundry and making Platt his four-course meals, you should tell us what you know about the Brodericks. You protected them, Ronna Rolfe!" Alaina had raised her voice again.

I was still steaming a little from the comment about bored childless housewives and dinner parties. So I had a few hobbies. I'd always thought it was a good thing to have hobbies. I was about to let my mind be known when the seriousness of what we were doing washed over me. This was not a hobby. I was really trying to do something very important here. And anyway, Ronna cooked too.

"Those kids had it so bad!" Ronna erupted. "So bad. Y'all ain't from Deck River. You wouldn't understand. I never wanted to tell a buncha rich housewives and that asshole Duke Pendley what it was like on the river. What it was like for Claire and those boys. You don't get it. You'll never get it. All you cared about was keeping the Wrights out of trouble, and now they won't even speak to you. Not a one of 'em."

"I want to get it, Ronna," I said calmly. It was as though my voice sucked the anger out of the room, and we were left standing together under the dangling light fixture with the sound of clomping footsteps above us. "I really want to get it. I'm not from Deck River, you're right, but that's exactly why I'm doing this. Because I want to understand." I was about to say something about Alaina protecting the Wright family—only natural given their close relationship—but was interrupted.

"And I did get it," Alaina started up again. I almost told her to shut up, because we were about to get Ronna talking about Claire, about the river. "I saw what was going on over there. Mitchell was like a son to me. I saw how they were living."

"Yeah, but that's the thing." Ronna looked up at the ceiling. It sounded like someone was Irish dancing in the square of floor right above our heads. Ronna flicked her eyes at the racket and refocused back on me mostly, with Alaina on the periphery of her concern. "Mitchell was grown. Those kids were little. Real little kids. Cecil had mental problems and drug problems and all that. The mom was a nice girl—Becky." She stopped talking for a second. "But she had problems before she died. She was sick or something for a long time. No one knew what was wrong with her, but she got real skinny and yellow looking. Claire was more like her sister than her kid. And Claire kept those boys alive for all those years. They'd have been dead a long time before if it weren't for Claire, so I don't want to hear another time that she killed those kids. She didn't. She's the only reason they lived long enough to graduate the crib. She took care of 'em like they was her own. Y'all couldn't wait to drag her through the mud, but it didn't work, did it? She was born in the mud. Lived her whole life there. Knee-deep, bitches!"

Ronna was certainly talking like she was back on Deck River. Her vernacular had completely changed; I wondered what it was like to try to pretend to be someone else just so you could get a job somewhere respectable and be in charge of the copy codes.

"That's what's wrong with this whole thing!" Ronna had raised her voice even more. "You were after Claire from the second you got here." She pointed at Alaina angrily. "You only did this so you could put Claire away. Did you ever stop to think it was that 'son' of yours?"

"I did," Alaina said. "And a few times I was pretty sure he did it, but I wasn't sure enough."

"So can we get to it?" I threw my hands up. "Tyler's on the phones, you live alone and as far as I can tell have no responsibilities whatsoever." Now I was the one pointing at Alaina. "And I don't have any kids, so we can do this thing. Let's do it."

I heard the door at the top of the stairs open and Captain Gamble's voice bellow. "Ladies, I made everyone tea!"

"Not now, Gamble!" Alaina bellowed back.

I nodded my head in her direction.

"I hate tea," Ronna said.

"I know." Alaina picked up her pen and with that we got down to business.

A CONDEMNED MAN

WE'D HAVE TO PUT HORSES down sometimes, not like kill 'em but if there was something wrong and they needed to be still, kind of like they were dead. We'd just lay 'em down with the stuff. Once I used too much... It was kind of on purpose. I hated that hag Jessamine. She was gagging and foaming at the mouth but not until a little after her heart stopped beating. She came back around, but I got hard just watching her twitch like that. She bit me a couple of times when I went in to clean her stall. I should've killed her when I had the chance, but Tina treats the horses like they're her children or something. She woulda known I did it on purpose. She gets power from having all these dumb beasts needing her all the time. She's good with the business though. If I'm honest with myself, I wouldn't have nowhere to work if it wasn't for Tina. I can't be good all the time, but Tina'll put up with it. She's the one who found Jorge. She hired him soon as she met him, 'cause she could tell he was so good. He was the best with the horses. I told Tina that, and she just got mad and said she was, but she's not and she knew it when Jorge was around. She learned from a bunch of dumb hicks how to ride. Jorge was born knowing. I do miss him when I think about it. I think I might have been a better man if he stuck around.

Anyway, we keep the tranquilizers at the stables. Anyone who has horses keeps some around. I know junkies who use it to get high, but it'll kill you if you're not careful. I hadn't even planned on it or thought about it. It was just an urge. I've had urges before, and I've had 'em again. It was an urge. I grabbed the rags from the storage room and a bottle of tranq and got in my truck. I had to rip one of the rags in two, because I only took a couple, but that was fine. The kids were small. They all looked alike anyway—the only way I could tell 'em apart was their size. They all looked just like Claire.

22

The afternoon went by very quickly. I called Tommy's office from the phone on my basement desk and told him I would be home "super late." He acted confused. "This is Arlene," I said.

"Right!" He'd been playing golf with Rick Waring earlier that day. I frowned, knowing what that meant.

"Please get a ride home. Call Max or someone."

"You got it. What's for dinner?"

I hung up.

"So according to Natalie Wright's statement, Mitchell was with her at their parents' house during the time this happened. The coroner's report states time of death approximately seven thirty." I was wearing my reading glasses and was painfully focused.

"Yes, but…" Alaina paused like she was trying to remember her lines. "There's always been a problem with that. Her statements were inconsistent. She says it was raining when he was over, but it rained in the afternoon. It wasn't raining that evening, so that led a lot of us to believe she was lying. Or she was confused." Alaina nodded. "She was barely sixteen. She wasn't paying attention to the time; what sixteen-year-old knows what time it is?"

"I think that's a strange assumption," Ronna said. "I knew what time it was when I was sixteen."

I closed my eyes firmly. "Okay. I think you both have a point, but let's not dwell on that detail." We were doing so well up to this point, sort of. I'd argue we were actually getting along and surprisingly easygoing about a lot of things we hadn't completely met eye to eye on—like whether to use staples or paper clips for the small stacks we were making. Ronna said paper clips while Alaina said staples. She didn't care about leaving small holes in the corner of the papers. Ronna did, but we met in the middle and stapled some things while paper clipping others. That had been a nice compromise. Very encouraging, uplifting even.

"It's kind of an important detail," Ronna said to me. "We can't really skip over that part."

"I just mean let's skip over whether or not we knew what time it was when we were sixteen. The real question is would she be savvy enough to lie?" I said. "I think I knew what time it was when I was sixteen, but I don't know if I would have known how to lie in a murder investigation—not so effectively that I'd keep my brother out of jail."

"Natalie Wright wasn't savvy," Ronna said, rolling her eyes. "She was a goody-two-shoes who went to church group."

"I went to church group when I was in school," I said defensively before admitting to myself that I'd quit church group so I had more time to drink and make out with Tommy. "For a while," I added humbly.

"No," Alaina said to no one in particular. She looked around the room like she was giving a presentation to a bunch of elderly people on how to use an automatic soap dispenser. The look on her face was saccharine and pleading. "She was not a sophisticated kid. She told us what she remembered, how she remembered it. She wasn't trying to do anything, just answering questions. None of those people had ever seen anything like this before. They didn't know what to do. None of them thought Mitchell had anything to do with it though. His family didn't think they needed to lie. It wouldn't have crossed their minds. Yes. Mmmhmmm." Alaina appeared to have finished her speech and stood very still waiting for her wisdom to sink in.

"Says the mom's best friend." Ronna raised her eyes.

"Boy, you've really come out of your shell," I said to her a little flatly. "You never used to talk. Now that Alaina's here, you're a real spitfire."

"When it matters, I talk." Ronna looked at me very directly. I could almost hear her saying "leftovers." She used the exact same tone of voice.

"It's fine," Alaina said. "I like when people talk. I live alone."

"So do I, practically." I gave a half smile and picked up the photocopies of Natalie Wright's journal. "So this was kind of a waste of time?" I showed Alaina.

"Completely. I mean—there's a lot in there about Claire and Mitchell, but we never found anything we could use."

I put the papers down on the table. "This is already stapled, Ronna," I said.

"Good." She nodded in approval.

"Should we go talk to Natalie Wright?" I asked. "I mean—she's around apparently. Not here, but in Georgia at least. Would be easy to get to her." Alaina looked up very abruptly, dropping the small box of paper clips she'd begrudgingly clenched in her hand.

"No, I don't think so," Alaina said. "And I can't talk to Dan and Marianne either. I don't think we need to talk to the Wrights. That's all been said. Said and done."

"I want to talk to Natalie," I said. "If she was the key witness in preventing Mitchell from being charged, then we need to talk to her. Where does she live?" I hadn't yet mentioned J.P. Callahan, because Alaina hadn't. He was on the tip of my tongue, but I had a strange sense that maybe Alaina didn't want Ronna to know that was her theory. Of course it was also her theory that Claire had helped J.P., and we already knew Ronna wasn't having any of that. We seemed to still be in the organizing phase of things, a phase in which I felt trapped. There was so much paper. I didn't seem to be able to read or organize it enough to actually make progress. I wiggled a little in discomfort. We needed to get past the stapler.

"Atlanta," Alaina said. "Natalie lives in Atlanta."

"I have to get home." Ronna stood up from her seat at my desk. "Platt likes to eat at six. And tomorrow is Thursday. Thursday is my busy day. I won't be able to help much."

Alaina said she needed to go as well; she went up the stairs right after Ronna, acting distracted and occupied. I was surprised when I soon heard her talking to Larson Gamble in the parking lot, which sat just outside the transom windows in the basement's corner. I saw their feet—close together—and then heard their cars start at the same time. "I'll be damned," I said to myself, unwilling to admit what I really thought had just happened.

I stayed late into the evening. I read an entire two boxes of files, mostly about Mitchell. There were transcripts of all of his interviews and then lengthy medical discourse on his death, how the body was found, what determinations were made as to cause of death, time of death, events leading up to his death. He had tied a rope to one of the rafters in his parents' garage. My first thought was, where did he get a rope? I'd never owned a rope a day in my life.

Mitchell had stayed at his family's home with Lucy after he was questioned. Apparently things were amicable with Claire at the time despite appearances and what later came out after he died. From what I could tell, no one was yet accusing Claire of running around on him or of abandoning the baby, and it was only the police who had suggested she had anything to do with what happened to her brothers. All of that would come later. And it seemed to me, after looking at the documents so many times, that Alaina was the one who had introduced that theory. That Claire had betrayed Mitchell. That she was bad people. Someone capable of doing horrible things. Claire.

Mitchell's family hired an attorney for him while Claire had a public defender appointed. That seemed to be the first rift; they had their own attorneys, and they weren't living together anymore. Alaina had put a note in the margin of one of the interviews. *He's had it with Claire's cheating.* I read back through the interview. There was nothing in there about Claire having boyfriends. Alaina added that part. I thought it seemed like maybe Mitchell was afraid of Claire; he said a couple of things about really not knowing where she was that evening. I couldn't tell if he was trying to get Duke Pendley to bite on that line or if he was just being nineteen and honest.

"I don't know where she was. I'd be lying if I said I did."

Mitchell seemed to be in some sort of retreat, at least from what I could tell, even though he was careful how he talked about Claire in the interviews. There were actually recordings in envelopes attached to many of his files. I listened reluctantly. In order to do so, I'd had to go upstairs to find a tape machine. Tyler was still at the precinct, as was the evening dispatch girl—Maddy.

She was never without gum and had a curly ponytail that she was inclined to touch every six seconds. She worked the evenings until around two a.m., then another woman came in—Debbie. She was old as dirt and the source of a lot of complaints because she couldn't hear very well.

"The tape recorders are in the cabinet behind the desk," Maddy said when I asked. "But Ronna's like super freaky about people touching stuff in there, so…" Maddy popped her gum and touched her hair.

"Yes, I know. Thanks." I walked to the cabinet and began rummaging through the shelves. Ronna had everything labeled, sorted, put at perfect angles, and stacked in order of increasing size. There were two old-fashioned tape recorders on the bottom shelf of the cabinet, one of which I took with me back downstairs.

Mitchell's voice was heavy but youthful. He wasn't a country boy but maybe trying to sound like one. He was clearly emotional during the recordings and kept clearing his throat. I had a hard time listening, thinking that he was but a ghost now, a recollection only.

"I went over to my parents' house because I didn't feel good. I had Lucy and Carter with me. The other kids were with her dad."

"Where was Claire?"

"I don't know."

"Cecil Broderick says the kids were at your house—the one you shared with Claire." This was Duke Pendley's voice. He'd introduced himself at the beginning of the interview. Most of the recordings contained identical information, identical answers, the same back-and-forth over and over. Again and again.

"Well, they weren't. When I left, no one was home."

"Who was at your parents' house when you got there?"

"My sister, Natalie." He sounded tired. The same repeated line of questioning was meant to wear people down, lead them to make mistakes. Mitchell answered the questions exactly the same every time.

"What time was it?"

"I don't really know. I got there around five, I think."

"Your sister said it was raining when you arrived. It stopped raining before four that day."

"So what?" Mitchell didn't sound angry, just tired. He would take his own life four days after this interview.

"Both you and your sister claim you were together for a maximum of two hours, which would mean you left your parents' house before six. The boys were killed around seven that evening. You were not at your parents' house at that time."

"I was."

"Then it was not raining when you arrived."

"I don't know if it was raining when I got there. Natalie's the one who said that."

"You drove to your parents' home. Did you not notice whether it was raining? Did you have to use your windshield wipers?"

"I don't remember. Why would I remember that?"

"Because something very significant happened that day. Where was Claire?"

"I don't know. I said that. I said it twenty times."

"Why did you have Lucy and Carter with you?"

"I didn't feel good. I think the house is making us sick," Mitchell said impatiently. "There's really bad mold there. Any time I could get Lucy out of there I did, and I wasn't so sick I couldn't drive, I just didn't feel good is all."

"But you called in to work."

Mitchell sighed. "Yes, I called in to work." He paused for a long time. I could hear movement in the background.

"Mr. Wright?" Duke Pendley said.

"Claire and I had a fight," Mitchell said. "I didn't feel good, and we had a fight, so I left. I took Lucy and Carter with me. Claire didn't tell me where she was going or what she was doing. She just wanted to be alone. None of my friends talk to me anymore, so I didn't really have anywhere to go. Natalie was home, or at least I assumed she was, because it was raining out." He stopped talking for a second. "I mean, she rides horses, so they don't go out there when it's really wet. It'd been raining that day. I do remember that it rained that day."

"Why were you and Claire fighting?"

"Because she's never home. She got real bad depression after Lucy came, and she kind of just runs off all the time now. I don't know—boyfriend and girlfriend stuff. It wasn't like…ugly or anything."

"Does she have another guy?" Duke Pendley asked like he shared a secret friendship with Mitchell that he'd been trying to hide up to this point in the conversation.

"No. Come on. Whatever, man," Mitchell said.

"What about Ram's?" Pendley said.

"What about it?"

"There are rumors that…"

"I know what people say, but she's a waitress there sometimes. That's all. We have to work!" He sounded angry. All I'd heard about Mitchell so far—other than the obvious topics of his accusation and then suicide—was that he was from a good family, not like Claire. He was not of the same ilk as the Brodericks. He must have wanted to prove something to himself, that he didn't have to be like his father, straitlaced and buttoned up, stuffy and narrow, anal. He wasn't going to follow in Dan Mitchell's footsteps, some Johnny-six-pack slaving away for the man so he could wear golf shirts and look down his nose at the hourly-wage worker and anyone else behind on their credit card bills. No, Mitchell seemed to insist on his blue-collar status. Several times during the interview, he made mention of "people who have to work" as if Pendley didn't know; whether Mitchell wanted to admit it or not, Pendley was at work too. I thought about Tommy in his fancy car and with his even fancier paperwork. Mitchell would have considered us part of the problem, the problem with everyone who can pretend it's not as hard as it is just to get by—no matter which level you're getting by on.

My stomach growled, which caused me to look up at the clock. It was nearing eight. Tommy had the number for my desk at the station, but I hadn't heard from him. "Probably passed out at the office again," I said to myself. I decided I would go home. I had strange feelings bubbling inside of me—anguish, suspicion, and loss. It was like terrible news that made you think you'd never be able to see the world the same way again. Terrible news I hadn't heard yet.

When I got home, the house was dark and empty. I was nervous there alone. I went to the phone and called Tommy's office line, but no one answered. I thought maybe I should drive over there to see if he was okay, but I called Max Payton first.

"Have you talked to Tommy today?" I said as soon as he picked up. Max lived alone and always answered his phone on the first ring. Tommy and I made jokes about it—he must have been so desperate for someone to talk to that he literally stood by the phone—but now it made me sad. It was this film over my eyes from the day's research. I would see things in a sad light now. Sad and fearful. It wasn't funny at all that he was so lonely.

"No," Max said flatly. "Why? What's wrong? Another doo-ey?"

"No, not that. He's not home."

"Oh." Now Max sounded more genuine. "How late is it? Oh yeah, it's late. Did he have appointments or something?"

"Not at night. I mean—not that I know of. I may drive over to the office. You know they golfed today. Sometimes that means…" I trailed off.

"I know. Do you want me to go over there? I'm closer."

"Okay. Thank you. I really mean it. I'm nervous here tonight for some reason. I hope nothing happened."

"I'm sure nothing happened. You'd know by now if it did. I'll call you as soon as I get to the office. If it's locked up, I can't get in though."

"Right, I understand. I can't either. I mean…I mean, what could I do?"

"Don't worry, Arlene."

"Too late," I said meekly.

I made my way around the house like someone who's been advised to stay there in case of emergency—pending, looming, foretold, emergent circumstances. I was uncomfortable and too on edge to sit down or do anything remotely productive. I'd brought only a few things home with me but was too off to focus. I heated some leftover rice in the microwave and ate a few carrot sticks while staring out the back window.

I nearly jumped out of my skin when I heard a car in the driveway. The garage door had not opened; it was loud enough to wake an army when it went up and down. I scurried to the front and looked out the skinny windows on either side of the door. Tommy stumbled out of a long black car, nearly toppling over as he slammed the door shut. He was in his suit with his tie pulled loose away from his neck. His hair was tousled, standing on end—it was too long anyway, which only served to make him look altogether messier. I opened the front door, feeling very unsure of myself. The front light was on, but the glass fixture was dirty and smeared with what looked like soot. I was momentarily distracted by my house-keeping but was able to refocus my attention.

"Honey, I'm home!" Tommy shouted as he made his way to the steps and reached for the iron railing—missing the first time but able to get a decent grip with the second try. "My darling!"

"My prince," I said with my eyes in a forced squint meant to suggest my mood—one of cross inquiry. "Who is that?" I pointed at the car, which had not moved.

"Lawrence of Arabia," Tommy said loudly.

"Who?"

He was still at the bottom of the stairs, urging himself to make the climb up. He didn't appear able to hoist his leg the height of the first step. "It's a movie, Arlene."

"Who's driving the car? And why aren't they leaving?"

"Carrie. She's probably making sure I actually make it into the house."

"Who's Carrie?"

"A lovely young maiden from yonder over in those hills there."

"Okay, Tommy." I reached my hand down to help him up the steps.

"Arlene, I'll kill you," Tommy said jovially.

"What?" My stomach dropped. I'd been on edge the whole afternoon, what with Alaina and Ronna's power struggle and being alone at the station with Maddy, and Tommy gone when I got home. I could hear the phone ringing in the house. "Oh…it's Max!"

"I mean, if you try to pull me up the steps, you'll end up dead. I'm a heavy son of a bitch these days." Tommy leaned on the railing; his eyes were darting, unable to position themselves parallel to one another.

"Hold on." I turned around, pulling my hand away and allowing Tommy to stumble backward. The railing lurched with his weight as he nearly plopped to the ground. I ran to the kitchen and pulled the receiver off the wall. "Max? He's here. So sorry to have bothered you."

"It's Ronna."

"Oh. Sorry. Max is my husband's friend, and…"

"There's something I haven't told you, and Platt says I need to."

"Oh." I heard the call waiting beeping in. "Okay. Can you hold on…"

"Cecil Broderick wasn't Claire's dad."

The call waiting beeped again. "What?" I said. I was distracted, stressed, and annoyed with Tommy, who I could hear vomiting in the front yard. I'd heard Ronna perfectly, but I was trying to figure out what she meant.

"So you know what I mean?" she said.

"No, no I don't. Ronna, hold on, please." I clicked over to the other line, but Max—or whoever it was—had already hung up. "Damnit!" I yelled into the phone as I switched back over. "Sorry," I said.

"The other kids are his, make no mistake," Ronna said cautiously but quickly. "But Claire was around before Cecil came along. I don't even know if Becky knew who Claire's dad was, but it wasn't Cecil. Arlene—" She paused. "He used to rape Claire. I knew about it when we were little, but I've never told anyone. Ever. She was afraid of him, and she never wanted nobody to know." Ronna's voice sounded small, frightened, pitiful. There was the sense that she was trying to purge this information, much like Tommy was purging himself in the front yard. "I swore on her mother's grave I'd never tell a soul. Platt knows though. I don't consider telling your husband something like telling anyone anything at all."

"Right," I said. I then heard Tommy throw up again. We weren't due for rain. I was going to have to go out and hose that down later. He sounded closer; I figured he'd made it up the steps and was now on the small front porch—brick with a lot of divots and crevices for vomit to nestle in.

"So what does that mean?" I said.

"I just..." Ronna paused. I thought she might have been crying. "I know Claire wouldn't have hurt anybody, because she knew what it was like to get hurt. I always thought that J.P. Callahan was the one."

"You did?" I'd raised my voice to a near-frantic holler. "That's what Alaina thinks too!"

"Yeah, well, we think it for different reasons. Alaina just didn't want her precious Mitchell in trouble, and I knew what Claire was going through, how bad she wanted out of there. I think J.P. did it…in his own weird way to help her."

"But what about Mitchell?" I said. I meant did Mitchell kill himself. It always came across like I was asking if someone thought Mitchell killed the boys. I'd already decided that I didn't think Mitchell had anything to do with it—not that.

"I don't know about Mitchell, and I don't really care," Ronna said.

"But I do care. He killed himself, Ronna."

"People do that every day."

"Right, but not because they were accused of murdering three little boys."

"You don't know why he killed himself," Ronna said somberly. I could imagine her in sweats with a bandanna tying her buoyant bangs back.

"Are you working out?" I asked.

"It's after ten. I'm about to go to bed. Platt said he couldn't sleep unless I told somebody about what happened to Claire when we were young. He said if I'm going to help y'all, I have to be honest."

"Do you still talk to her? Claire?"

"No, not really." She hesitated. "We weren't as close when we got to high school. She kinda had one foot out the door, was just trying to get out of Cecil's house."

"Where is she now?" I said. Captain Gamble said he had an address on file, but he wasn't sure if it was accurate anymore.

"A way's from here. Jodupur. She's married, but like I said—I don't talk to her. I work at the police. She probably thought that meant I was against her or something, I don't know."

I had a feeling Ronna had spoken to Claire Broderick recently, but decided not to push it.

"She was never comfortable with what I knew about her," Ronna said unprompted. "Not with how she was trying to change her life. She just wanted to get away from all of that. Just didn't want to be a Deck River girl anymore."

"Why do you think she left the baby—Lucy—behind?" I said.

"'Cause that was Cecil's baby, and she couldn't stand the sight of it. I think the whole reason she got with Mitchell was just so the baby would have someplace nice to go when she finally got out of there."

"Do you think Mitchell knew that?" My teeth were chattering with nervous excitement.

"I think that's why he offed his'elf."

"Sweet Jesus," I said.

"Please don't take the Lord's name in vain," Ronna scolded as I heard Tommy hurl again.

December 17, 1983

Mitchell killed himself. It happened a few days ago. My dad found him in the garage. I don't have anything to say about it, but I couldn't leave it out. It'll never be the same. I'm so sorry.

23

I hadn't been able to fall asleep after Tommy passed out on the living room couch in one sock and his pants—unbuttoned. We'd had a short, incoherent argument about drinking and riding around with mysterious women. He couldn't answer me straight about where he'd been or who with. I finally gave up trying to make sense of the evening, what with him slurring and hiccuping. "We're getting nowhere. Go to bed," I scolded. He was already drooling on one of my decorative cushions.

Ronna's phone call was the real culprit in my evening jitters. After I'd used Comet and the hose with a small scrub brush on the front steps—I killed my hydrangeas that night, though I wouldn't know it until later the following spring—I tried unsuccessfully to fall asleep. I thought maybe it was the stench of vomit or the cleaner that was keeping me up, but it was what Ronna had told me. This was all done; every last bit of the Broderick tragedy was signed, sealed, and delivered, but still—somehow—I thought my concern over it was going to change something. I hadn't felt as sorry for Claire as I had for Mitchell, but now I did, and everything about the way I'd been thinking about the case changed. I lay in bed, bug-eyed, and finally bug-eyed in front of a Us Weekly before I eventually fell into a fitful, agitated sleep filled with dreams, during which Claire asked me, as she slid into a pit of dark water, her pert, pink face disappearing as if into motor oil, to please forgive her. I'd already forgiven her, even if I wasn't sure for what.

Tommy brought me flowers and donuts the following morning. He was up with the birds, making strong coffee and taking an extra long shower.

"I barely ate dinner" was the first thing he said to me when he came lumbering into the bedroom with a bouquet from Kroger and a chocolate-frosted donut with pink sprinkles. I'd heard him moving around the house. Apparently he'd roused himself from the couch at some point and slept in the guest room, trying not to disturb me. "Had almost nothing in my stomach when I drank that half glass of wine."

"Half glass?" I said doubtfully.

"Yeah, and I'm not used to wine," he continued, mostly convincing himself.

"Where were you?" I asked. I hadn't rolled over to look at him yet. I glanced at the alarm clock. It was seven forty. I was going to be late. I threw off the covers and slammed my feet down on the plush mauve carpeting. "Never mind. We'll have to talk about this later. I have to get to work!" I certainly didn't remember messing with my alarm the night before. I was always up at seven.

"Oh sorry," Tommy said. "I turned your alarm off so you could sleep in."

"Why? I have work."

"I thought maybe I could take you to breakfast."

I looked at the donut, placed haphazardly on one of my good plates. "After I had a donut?"

"It's an appetizer."

"Please get out of my way. I have to get to work. Why don't you go and take Vivian or whatever her name is to breakfast—the one who drove you home last night after all the wine?"

"Carrie," Tommy said uncertainly.

"That's worse. Way worse than Vivian." I turned away from him.

"Arlene, you've never been jealous a day in your life."

"I don't think I'm jealous, just tired. I was up cleaning barf off the front steps for half the night."

"I ate some bad shrimp. I had a salad!" It had not looked a bit like salad what came up on the stoop in the moonlight.

I still wouldn't look at him. "I have to get going."

I was ready in a hot second and drove to the station, late, flustered, but determined. I couldn't remember if I'd brushed my teeth after I begrudgingly ate Tommy's donut. He had stood on the front porch with his coffee, wearing an apron, and waved at me as I pulled out of the driveway. He said he was getting a late start; he wanted to mop the garage. His desperation was thick.

"You okay?" Ronna said as I walked in the front door.

"Yeah, just tired. And this weather—" I turned to point at the vibrant blue sky.

"Oh yeah," Ronna said, confused.

"Ronna," I said, casting my eyes about to make sure we were really alone. "Thank you for trusting me…with that…"

"Right," she said quickly. "Platt wanted me to."

"Well, thanks to Platt. Do you want to tell Alaina? I think this is a crucial piece of evidence."

"It's not." She wouldn't really look at me, which is what Ronna did when she was uncomfortable—she became frantically busy tidying things on her desk and pressing one key at a time on her computer. I imagined she was typing a single letter, then deleting it, then doing it again. Anything to make her look too occupied for a serious conversation. "It doesn't have anything to do with the boys getting killed."

"Well—" I paused. "It might. It's certainly crucial."

"Yes, you said that." She looked up at me impatiently. "I only told you so you'd leave Claire out of it. It's J.P. He's the murderer."

"Well, that's what Alaina thinks too!" I hissed. "So this could help us all get on the same page."

"Alaina and I will never be on the same page," Ronna said coolly.

"But you are."

She shook her head slightly, adjusted her glasses, sat up straight in her chair after rolling her shoulders back, and again tapped a single key with enthusiastic knifelike precision. "Platt wanted me to tell you. I'm glad I did, because you'll understand that Claire had nothing to do with what happened to those boys. But that does not mean Alaina is blameless."

"I don't understand you," I said.

"I have nothing to do with it."

"Ronna," I pressed in frustration.

"I have to get some things done," she said without looking at me again.

I went to the basement door—fairly certain that for every crumb of herself Ronna gave me, she took back a whole slice. She was going to let me into that head and heart of hers but only if I brought a chisel. "Is Tyler covering for you today?" I asked meekly. Somehow I'd offended her by caring about what she'd said. Or by wanting more.

"No. I'll be up here. If you need me, just come up."

"I think Alaina has a bad hip," I said as I began my descent.

"I don't," Alaina said, coming up the steps. She kept on, pushing past me aggressively before turning around on the landing and heading straight back down. "I can do this all day. I don't have a bad anything. You smell like vomit, by the way."

"Thank you. Thank you for that." I grabbed the handrail and scooted on down the stairs.

We were all a little agitated—Ronna upstairs behind her desk, hunting and pecking her way around her feelings, and me and Alaina in the basement with our necks bent in combative concentration. There was a frustration in the air that matched my mood perfectly. Captain Gamble had not come down to check on us, and by eleven I found this peculiar. Alaina was humming rather loudly, with her eyes darting to the stairs every few minutes. I shook my head; did I really want to know?

I was immersed in a rough patch in the files. The notes were filled with dozens of references to Claire turning tricks at Ram's bar. Alaina had already told me as much, only she'd included Ronna in the scandal. I hadn't revisited any of that. Ronna just didn't strike me as the hooker type. But then again, did I really know anything about her? She was definitely a bottomless pit of surprises so far.

And regardless, I hadn't brought Ronna's complicity in this behavior up to Alaina since we slugged Manhattans at her house in Dolvin. Alaina was highly preoccupied at the station, very concerned with the footsteps above us and with Ronna—who I had to admit was fastidious, and maybe a little annoying with her militant organizational techniques, which included yelling "HALT!" when something was headed to the wrong pile with a sheet of paper in hand. Ronna had even slapped documents out of mine and Alaina's grips a few times. "Put that down!" she'd bellowed.

Tyler had a meeting and Ronna was on front desk duty until he was free. Tyler had complained that he'd been demoted, to which Ronna took offense. Larson Gamble had to settle their grievance by offering them each a ten-dollar credit for the snack machine. That seemed to solve things, and Ronna was going to be able to head back downstairs—something she hadn't really wanted to do earlier as far as I could tell—after Tyler met with a forensic analyst on a drunk driving manslaughter charge he'd filed against a local barber. His name was Lief. I knew nothing about him, but felt the fact that he killed his girlfriend when he slammed his car into a sweet gum on Lassiter was an omen that Tommy was next—or rather, I was next. Lief had escaped without a scratch. I'd be the one to go seven feet under if Tommy tried to drive me home after bingo night at Rooster's.

"So Ronna," I said to Alaina.

"She's upstairs," Alaina answered absently.

"I know that. I'm asking you…"

"What? What are you asking me?" Alaina said.

"You said she was a hooker."

"I didn't say she was a hooker. I said she used to hang out over at Ram's with Claire. Claire got money there—who knows for what. It might have even been drugs or something. Cecil was on everything. Maybe she stole his stuff and sold it. People just used to say she was turning tricks for money. Anyway, what does that matter?"

It was true; some of this didn't matter. I was about to tell her that Ronna thought J.P. was behind all of this too, but she spoke first.

"I called her, y'know."

"What?" I turned to look at Alaina, who was absorbed in the spiral notebook she had in front of her. She looked like a detective the way she bent her chin down and squinted wisely. I was wearing a headscarf—I'd ordered it from Spiegel in the hopes it would make me appear more serious. Instead of commenting on my commitment to the case and exotic headwear, Ronna had asked me if I had cancer.

"I called Claire. I found her number—wasn't hard to find," Alaina said.

"What did she say?"

"Not much. I told her we were reopening the case into her brothers' deaths. She said she thought that was good. I asked her if she had any new information, and she said no. That was basically it."

"How old is she now?" I said.

"Oh, I'd say between thirty and forty? Gosh, is that how old Mitchell would have been?" Alaina grimaced slightly. "Time flies."

"Have you seen her?"

"No. Not in a long time. I asked her if she would meet me, but she said her son is sick...or her husband. Someone—it didn't sound like she was even sure who was sick."

"I'd like to see her."

"I have a feeling there's nothing to see," Alaina said. "She's never going to admit it if she helped or if she knew what was going to happen to those kids."

"Did you ask her about J.P. Callahan?"

"I asked her before. She said she barely knew him."

"You know," I said, looking furtively at the stairs. "Ronna told me the baby—Lucy—was Cecil's." My hand flew to my mouth. First Ronna had betrayed Claire's trust, and now I'd betrayed Ronna's. But I honestly didn't know how we'd solve the case if I didn't share all pertinent information with the entire investigative team. "I shouldn't have told you that, but Ronna said Cecil used to rape Claire. He's not her real dad." Alaina stared at me, saying nothing. I adjusted my headscarf and then removed it. "Not sure why I wore this," I said.

"I'm sure you'll figure it out," Alaina said. "All I know is that a lot of people thought that baby might have been Cecil's. Makes me ashamed to say it, because if we all thought he was raping Claire, why didn't we do something? But I guess, no one really cared what the Brodericks were doing—other than to talk trash about them—until those kids died."

"Goddamn," I said.

"He OD'd. There was talk—well, our boy Larson Gamble was one of the first to say he was sure of it—that he offed himself out of guilt. Not guilt over the boys but because he was raping Claire or more because he thought he was going to get caught if there was a paternity test on the baby. He used all sorts of pills that he bought from other ruffians in the area. Just took too many in the end—at least that's what we thought. He had a heart attack, but there were drugs involved."

"Don't tell Ronna I told you about Cecil." I nervously pressed my fingers on my lip. I'd been a nail-biter as a kid; the shadow was long cast, and every time I got a little uncomfortable, I nearly went back to chewing.

Alaina sighed heavily. "Listen, Arlene." She shook her head almost imperceptibly. "I don't mean to burst your bubble, but there's nothing you can tell me about Ronna Rolfe or any of these people that I don't already know. No, Cecil was not her real dad. We don't know who her real dad was, and there were definitely a lot of rumors about the baby. Lucy. Hell, there were rumors about Carter before that."

"What do you make of the inconsistencies in Mitchell's statements though? He called in sick to work, and they never really got the time right—you know when he was at the house."

"I think he was following her—Claire. He just said he was sick so he could get out of work and tail her. I think he knew what happened. He suspected she was messing around on him, or worse, he suspected Lucy wasn't his. See—that's the thing, Mitchell felt sorry for Claire. His family saw this like black-widow-white-trash vixen thing, and he saw something soft, vulnerable, mistreated. He wanted to take care of her. Badly. You couldn't tell him anything about her, not at first. I think he figured it out though, or he was starting to. That might be why—" Alaina stopped talking abruptly. Ronna was standing on the bottom step. I hadn't heard her come down, and neither apparently had Alaina.

I gulped, certain Ronna had heard me spill the beans on Cecil and Claire. I wasn't to be trusted. She'd probably want to quit the detectives' club and never speak to me again.

"I can help now," Ronna said coolly.

Alaina looked up at Ronna, then back at me. We all watched one another carefully, our mouths twitching in unison.

"Why aren't we talking to J.P. Callahan?" I asked, both trying to clear the air and move forward to the obvious next move. "We can sit around here and regurgitate all the sad stuff you girls have already fought about twenty times twenty years ago, or we can go after this guy. You both think he did it! Can we at least agree that we agree on who killed those kids?!"

"Arlene, you can't just show up and start yelling at him," Alaina snapped. "What? Are you going to bring cuffs and a Taser? We have to have evidence. That's what detectives do—they dig." She jutted her chin out for effect. "But there's no chance in hell we'll really solve this thing if people who know what happened won't tell us." She looked at Ronna again. I could feel a crack of anger and something else—like regret—pulse through the space between us.

"Ladies!" Larson Gamble's voice was the next thing to pulse through the room.

Alaina closed her eyes and appeared to take a calming breath. "He really should stop doing that." She turned her attention to the stairs. "Yes, Larson!"

"I have Natalie Wright's info!"

We all looked at one another. "Well, shit," Alaina said. "I haven't talked to that kid in ten years."

NATALIE WRIGHT'S JOURNAL
February 4, 1984

I know it's been a long time since I've written, and I'm not
going to pretend you have a personality or a soul or something and
that you care, but I want to put down everything in here. That's
why I started this, to keep track of my life so I could go back and
read about it when I'm older. I guess this is mostly stuff I won't
want to read about. I don't want to think about it ever again—any
of it—but I think I should put it here.

   We are going to move. My parents say it every day. My mom
keeps getting mad at Alaina, so I guess she thinks it would be okay
to get away from her now. They were like soul sisters for so long, but
Alaina keeps upsetting my dad. She comes by unannounced—like
she always did—but now it's like she's barging in and saying crazy
stuff. She is doing cop school, or boot camp or whatever it's called
so she can be a detective. She says Duke Pendley is an idiot and is
messing everything up. She doesn't want him running the case. My

dad says she needs to mind her own business and stop bothering us. He told her to get her own life the other day. It was the first time he said something like that, and my mom didn't tell him to cool it.

Claire basically dumped Lucy at our house and took off. That's why my mom is so upset. She can't understand leaving your child like that. Carter has been with us too—off and on. Claire wants him though. When she left Lucy, my mom said that was final. She said she won't come back for her. My mom said Lucy won't even remember Claire or Mitchell. She says we're Lucy's family now.

Claire is still under investigation, but she acts like she isn't worried about anything. She went off to live with her cousin in Hopper and left all of her and Mitchell's stuff at the house. She left all the boys' things there too. The guy who owned the place called my parents and told them the house needed to be cleared out so he could rent it to somebody else, so my dad went over and got Mitchell's stuff. I guess Cecil never came to get any of the other kids' things, because all of that was still there when my dad went. He left it, and the owner complained to my parents. My dad says he thinks Cecil stole some of Mitchell's things. His nice stuff—like his leather jacket and his high-tops and all that—was gone.

My mom tries to talk to Claire. She calls the cousin's apartment all the time to check on her and Carter. She says she doesn't want to lose touch with her, because of Lucy. My dad just can't understand this. He thinks Claire should be in jail and that Lucy isn't even Mitchell's kid. He won't admit this to Alaina though. He HATES when Alaina says that, but when she leaves, he says the same thing. Lucy's not Mitchell's. I look at her all the time, trying to find Mitchell in there. All I see is Claire. It's like she made her herself.

I haven't told my parents, but I went to the stable for the first time since Mitchell died, and Tina Callahan told me to stay away from J.P. It was the first thing she said to me, not even that she was sorry about Mitchell or any of it. She just said to stay away from her husband. I started crying, but no one knew why. I didn't see J.P. there anyway. I heard someone say he hadn't been at the stable in a while. It sounded to me like he was hiding out or something. Tina is extra bitchy when he's not there, because it's so busy, and even though she's a horse girl, she's gotten used to not having to do some of the dirty work. She bosses all of us around so she can keep her nails looking good. When I got home the other day, I wondered if I would ever go back there. If it weren't for the horses, I probably wouldn't. Everyone acted so strange around me. I was only out of school for about a week, and I guess it's because the teachers are more mature or something, but I didn't feel as weird going back to school. Everyone at the stables was kind of lurking around me like they didn't want to talk to me, or maybe it's just me feeling weird about Tina, but I guess they all want her to like them. She doesn't like me anymore. It's obvious. They are taking her side. Anyway, I guess it doesn't matter since we're moving away. I'll find a new stable. A lot of the horses at Tina's have rain rot. I probably should find a new stable anyway.

24

I told Alaina and Ronna I would drive us to Frampton, the town about twenty minutes outside Atlanta where Natalie Wright lived. Larson Gamble had run down the basement stairs with a small slip of paper in his hand. Natalie's details were scribbled in red ink. "I've got it!" he'd shouted, wide-eyed and looking for approbation.

"Stop yelling," Alaina said, snatching the paper from Gamble's hand. He blushed momentarily—the moment their skin touched. "It couldn't have been that hard to find, Larson. It's not like the Golden Ticket or something. She's in the phone book."

"No, she's not." He was gravely serious.

"Fine, then. Thank you. Natalie W. Jensen," she read. "Hmmm, don't know a Jensen."

Ronna quickly said she needed to pack and made a break for the bottom step, her stiff frock circling her ankles like a large tin bucket. She always wore sneakers with her dresses. Sneakers and heavy white socks. I figured she wanted to be ready to sprint at any given moment.

"We'll be back by the end of the day," I said. "We don't need to pack."

"I don't like gas station food," she answered.

"We don't have to eat at the gas station." It was beginning to dawn on me, really dawn on me, that Ronna was argumentative. It was as though I had only just met her and made this very pertinent observation as to her temperament.

She turned around to look at me directly, her lips tightly pressed in frustration. We faced off in the midday fall sun peering through the small basement window at us, like a busybody wanting to be involved in our town drama. "Fine," she said. I was about to tell her she always packed her lunch anyway but decided I wanted to stop talking about food and get on the road. It would take us almost two hours to get to Frampton.

"I'll sit bitch," Alaina announced. "Let's go."

Ronna complained the entire drive down that the heater was on too high and that my seat was too far from the steering wheel.

"You're too short to have it that far back."

"I'm perfectly comfortable."

"You can't make a hard stop if necessary. You're having to point your toe to the brake. Your foot should lay flat on the brake pedal."

This had gone on for the better part of six miles before I told

Ronna to shut up and eat her meatloaf. The entire car went silent for the next six miles. Alaina broke the rock-hard and ever-growing resentment by asking if we could stop at Burger King so she could use the bathroom.

"I tried calling Natalie, but no answer," Alaina said as I pulled the car over.

"That was almost two hours ago," Ronna snapped.

Alaina jumped out and trotted to the Burger King entrance. "She could be home by now!" Ronna hollered after Alaina. "She just don't want us talkin' to a Wright," she turned and said to me. Ronna's arm was up on the door panel, baking in the fall sun. Her entire forearm was scorched red and blotchy. I was briefly reminded of something distant—Tommy and the truck. Me on a summer night in Faber. There'd been nowhere else I wanted to be. I should have taken advantage of that innocence more, I thought. The imperma nence of things always hit me a little after the fact, when it was a little too late to do anything about it. A moment is nothing more than a recollection in exactly the amount of time it takes it to pass.

Alaina sauntered back to the car, clearly feeling much better, and got in. We took off for Frampton, some four exits away.

We arrived at Natalie's house roughly nine minutes later. She lived in a tidy two-story brick house on a quiet street filled with other tidy two-story brick houses all exactly the same distance away from the road with blankets of grass draped between their first brick and the cement curb.

"I mean—is she home?" I said.

The garage door was open, so we could see a minivan parked in one of the exposed spaces. I got out of the car, realizing I'd blocked Natalie—or whoever this person was—in with my unnecessarily large Mercedes. "It's rude to park in the driveway," I said, reopening my door to get back in. Ronna was still fixing her makeup, which included heavy rouge and another thick swipe of her mascara wand. She'd had to remove her glasses to apply; it was the first time I'd seen her without glasses. She looked younger, more vulnerable, uncomfortable.

"No, don't move the car." Alaina waved her hand at me like she was tired of telling me to clean my room. "Come on." She was clearly impatient and unintimidated.

"She's not the boss of me," Ronna said, getting out of the car with her freshly lacquered lips pursed in concentration.

Each of these women exhibited characteristics I deeply admired. I hoped to someday be like them both, and then absolutely nothing like either of them too. We walked to the front door of the house side by side. Alaina pressed the doorbell, and we waited.

"Fresh mulch," Ronna noticed.

"Yeah, but these shrubs look dreadful," Alaina scoffed. "Looks like they were trimmed with kitchen scissors."

"Quiet," I said. I could hear someone approaching.

It was Natalie Wright. I knew, because she looked like Mitchell. I'd stared at his photos for too long, too many times. I'd seen a few pictures of Natalie too, but it was Mitchell who I saw when a thin, unassuming woman approached the door, peeking through the frosted pane of the front door window.

"Yes," she said.

"It's me," Alaina said, stepping forward. "Aunt Alaina."

"Oh!" Natalie said, surprised but not altogether upset to see her. She fiddled with the door and yanked. "Hi," she said, scanning us, still a little reserved. She had bland features and plain clothing, not a drop of makeup on her face. Her hair was tied back in a loose ponytail.

"You look like Mitchell," I said before I could stop myself. Her eyes narrowed slightly but she didn't say anything.

Alaina sighed, clearly hoping to convey her irritation with my unprofessionalism. "We're reopening the case," she said. She shrugged like she couldn't help it. "We have to talk to you. These are my colleagues, Ronna Rhodes and Arlene Ridell."

"Arlene Black Ridell," I corrected her. "Arlene B. Ridell," I said even more confidently. I'd been impressed by the "W" Natalie had in her name.

"Hey, Ronna," Natalie said.

"Yes," Ronna said as if she'd been asked a question.

"Nice to meet you," she said to me.

"Charmed," I said. I may have even curtsied. I couldn't act naturally to save my life, such was the excitement I felt.

It was warmer in Frampton than at home. I figured it was the elevation—they were lacking. There wasn't a mountain in sight, just houses and stoplights. I swore we'd passed sixty-two strip malls since we left the freeway. The sun was more oppressive and seemed to have wiped away all personality from the place. I felt called to defend Faber and other small mountain towns like it. We had depth. We had valleys. People lived in places like Frampton because they wanted to be close to the city, which had a different depth, between the buildings and in people's souls because of depression, crime, and drugs—if you asked me...and my mother.

"Why are you reopening it? Have you talked to my parents?" Alaina and Natalie were having their own conversation. I'm sure Natalie could tell just how superfluous Ronna and I were. Ronna hadn't said a word but was breathing heavily next to me. She adjusted her glasses every few seconds and stood with her legs wide, like she was preparing for an ambush that would involve ramming and headbutting.

"No, and we're not going to," Alaina said. "But we do want to talk to you. Arlene here"—Alaina pointed at Ronna instead, who glared incredulously—"started reading the files and can't let it go. You know it's still considered unsolved."

"Of course it is." Natalie folded her arms over her chest.

"I'm Ronna," Ronna said to Alaina. No one responded.

"I'm Arlene B. Ridell."

Alaina glared at me and Ronna. "So I'm game to figure this thing out once and for all. You know I always thought it was J.P.

THE NIGHT THE RIVER WEPT

Callahan," she said a little too casually. I was surprised at the tone of the conversation. It was friendly, relaxed, familiar. It had been a long time, but I had to suppose Alaina and Natalie were like family at one point. I could tell Natalie liked Alaina, whether she wanted to or not.

"Yes, but nothing ever came of that, so..." Natalie shrugged and looked away stiffly.

"We just want to talk to you," I said loudly.

"Can we come in or should—"

"I'm kind of in the middle of something, but—yes, it's fine." Natalie moved out of the way with a reluctant jerk of her head, so we could enter the house. It smelled like Pine-Sol and cookies. I heard the television in the background, a cartoon, based on the high-pitched voices and cheery music.

"Boy, you keep a clean house," I said. It was as if I had spoken to the wall such was the disinterest in what I was saying.

Ronna seemed to be having trouble breathing and now was huffing with her mouth open wide. Her lips were turning blue.

"I don't want the kids to hear," Natalie said, her attention darting around first the hallway and then the kitchen. "We can sit in my office." She pulled back a sliding door, which led to a small room with a desk in one corner and a wicker chair and end table in another. It was more cluttered than the rest of the house had been, decorated in mint green and pale yellow. "I do a lot of my work from home, when I'm not meeting clients."

"You still working for the county?" Alaina asked.

"Family and Child Services," Natalie confirmed.

"That's noble work," I said. Again, no one seemed to care that I was contributing. Ronna cleared her throat loudly.

"Sorry, there's nowhere really to sit in here. Let me get a chair. I just want to close the door, because the kids don't really know about this." Natalie walked to the closet door in the corner.

"Can I use your bathroom?" Ronna bellowed into the tiny space, completely enclosed now that the door had been pulled shut with some effort.

Natalie directed her where to go after wrestling with the door again. She also arranged a couple of folding chairs, retrieved from the room's closet, in a semicircle so Alaina and I could sit down.

"I don't know anything new," Natalie said. "Especially not about J.P. Callahan."

"I know that, but it's good to reconnect with a crucial witness. A lot could have been missed. We were in the heart of the investigation at the time, emotions were running hot. You were Mitchell's sister; something could have gotten away from us." Alaina paused. She sounded like she was reading from a script. "And you knew J.P. too. I never really talked to you about that, but you knew him." It was all business, friendly but in a business sort of way—planned, calculating. I'd heard Tommy use the same tone, like he wanted to both watch the game with a fella while picking his pocket at the same time.

"Barely," Natalie said. She again seemed bothered by the mention of Callahan's name.

"That's a real nice stable," I said. Natalie looked at me blankly.

"I used to ride there when I was younger," she said after a long pause.

"So do you think he and Claire were gonna run off together? After the boys..." I asked.

"Arlene," Alaina scolded.

"They were seeing each other," Natalie said. "I saw them together, but not like...in love or something. I don't really know."

"Did you think that baby was Mitchell's?" My chair made a loud, guttural noise that had everyone looking down uncomfortably.

Ronna reentered the room loudly as I spoke. After nearly tearing the door off its frame, she slammed it shut and collapsed on the padded wicker in the corner. "Sorry," she said to no one in particular.

"I don't know," Natalie said, shaking her head slightly. "Lucy's... she's not a baby anymore. I mean, she's in college now. It doesn't matter anymore, does it?"

"What Arlene is trying to say..." Alaina moved her hands around in front of her chest, conveying her superiority and expertise by the elegant way she was able to flick her fingers while talking. I raised my hands and moved my wrists in imitation, though I had nothing to add. "Is that I was never able to establish a motive for why J.P. would have killed those kids. It always seemed to everyone that Mitchell had a better reason, especially since Claire did not run off with J.P. after it happened. My theory was always shot down on that account, and I couldn't get J.P. to admit that he'd had anything to do with Claire other than an old flirtation, and he wouldn't even admit to that really—she was underaged, and he was newly married. Everyone thought Mitchell had the motive to kill the kids. I think…" Alaina glanced at me warily, "I think we're trying to jog your memory. Is there anything else you saw between Claire and J.P., or between Claire and Mitchell, or did you ever see Mitchell and J.P. together? Is there anything you might have left out?" Alaina rested her hands in her lap. There had been something I was about to think, notice, contemplate. It was Alaina—her attitude of directed self-assurance, but my train of thought was derailed by Ronna's heavy breathing.

Natalie lowered her eyes like she was deciding whether or not to share something. She turned her attention to the window, facing the backyard, which had clearly been recently cut in perfectly straight lines. There was a small swing set and a couple of errant balls lying in one corner, but otherwise the scene was serene on this crisp fall day.

"You can't get a flat backyard in Faber," I said into the silence. "This is nice."

"No," Natalie said after another long pause. "There's nothing." One of her children appeared around the corner of the bulky slider.

"Mom, can I have a cookie?"

I looked at Alaina, who seemed strangely relieved. She nodded, clasped her hands, and said, "Well, that oughta do it." I couldn't shake the sense of having checked a box off Alaina's list. "Ladies," Alaina said. I didn't move for a moment; it was during this moment that I lost my nerve, and a moment once again became another part of the past.

A CONDEMNED MAN

NAW YOU CAN'T RIDE IN the rain, not rain like that. It was like a monsoon that day. It quit around four or so. I was rollin' around at Ram's for a minute before I went back in town. I didn't even really go in Ram's. Never did. It's a weird place. You can get a vibe just from who's smoking by the dumpster. Claire was there with that pal of hers. That chick'll kill anybody's mood, but Claire's loyal like that. She was always looking after the boys even if she didn't want to. I have a lot of duty in me too. I stuck around with my mama 'til she died. I wasn't gonna leave her neither. We do right by our family here. It's just the way.

I went back over to Deck. It was in my head what I was gonna do. I didn't tell nobody, but I could feel it. My one half pushing the line. Naw I wasn't alone. I don't like to be by myself. Never have. He came with me.

Natalie Wright's Journal (removed pages)
March 24, 1984

I know I shouldn't have done it. I'm up all night thinking about it most of the time, just thinking and sick over it. I feel like Mitchell must have when he started to do all the bad stuff. I'm not really even comfortable at church or Youth Group anymore. All they ever talk about is sinning and getting saved and all the stuff you shouldn't do. At first people were talking about praying for my family and being extra nice to me, but now it's the same old stuff, and I don't fit in anymore, or I don't even want to fit in there anymore. I think that's what Mitchell thought after a while. He started to have sex with Claire and it was like all of that seemed stupid.

I don't why I started doing it. J.P. used to give me the creeps, but I'd never even really kissed a boy before, not with tongue. I know it's scummy, and I wish I could say I didn't even want to or like he forced me, but he didn't. It just felt so good to be like those girls who get all the attention. I don't look like Claire or Tina, but maybe I do. He said I just hadn't come into my own yet. He said a lot of stuff that made me feel really good when he wanted me to.

I had sex with J.P. Callahan, a bunch. It was a long time ago, well not that long, but long enough. It was before all of this—before the boys, before Mitchell died. I hate myself for it, because it was just a lot of bad decisions. I haven't told anyone, but I think Tina knows. Claire started looking at me funny for a while, but she looks at everyone funny—even before all this happened. I feel like Claire hasn't said Mitchell's name once since he died. Not once. They aren't going to charge her with anything. My mom said she's leaving. She can go for all I care. I really never see her anymore. It's like she just disappeared when Mitchell died. I don't like what everyone says or how they make it all crazy about what happened, like that wasn't crazy enough. I feel like when Claire is finally, really gone from here we can go on with our lives.

I don't love J.P. or anything. I wish I hadn't done any of it. I thought maybe he was going to leave Tina for me or... I don't even know, like that would make me really cool. It's funny, it was raining both days—the first time it happened and then when everything else... Every time it rains now, I think I'm going to do something bad again. And I didn't really know. I haven't lied about that. I didn't know what he was doing.

25

We went to Applebee's after we left Natalie Wright's house. Ronna asked the server if they had applesauce. He said he had to check and never came back to our table. The manager waited on us from then on.

"She didn't tell us shit," Alaina said enthusiastically. She was drinking an extra-large beer. The mug looked like a bucket.

"Maybe she doesn't have anything to tell us," I said. I had liked Natalie. I liked her house, her kids, her tidiness and plain appearance. I'd only looked at her teenage journal a few times, thinking most of it was pretty useless and boring. I regretted that now. I had suddenly decided that I liked boring people. Who wanted to be surrounded by scandal all the time? I paused—realizing that I had situated myself right smack-dab in the middle of a scandal. Perhaps an expired one, but a scandal nonetheless. And here I was with my detective agency at an Applebee's nearly two hours from home. I grimaced in shame; just when I could have been happy with my inconsequential life, I had to shake things up and unearth an old, unsolved murder. I didn't seem to be able to get the timing right on anything.

"I'm not so sure," Ronna said. She was having an apple juice in lieu of applesauce—her first choice for a beverage. "There was something she wanted to say."

"Yeah, I got that too," Alaina said. "But I always thought that. I always thought she was just about to tell me something really important. But she never did!" Alaina smiled broadly.

"I feel sorry for her. It must have been really difficult to live with all of that." I dipped a fry in the small cream-colored ramekin of ketchup. The restaurant was busy and loud. We were sitting right beneath a television that was on high volume broadcasting a sporting event where everyone involved seemed to be screaming at the top of their lungs.

"Yes, but she's lying," Ronna said. "Through her teeth."

"Oh," I said, caught off guard.

"It's just that—" Ronna paused, clearly deliberating over something heavy.

"You aren't miss truth-teller extraordinaire either," I said defensively. "What about Ram's, missy?"

"What about Ram's?" Ronna said.

"You and Claire…" I began.

"Do you ladies want dessert?" Alaina shouted at the same time an expletive, followed immediately by a long high-pitched beep, erupted from the television above us.

"No," Ronna said. "I'm watching what I eat."

"She trains," I said.

"Yes, I do. We need to get back soon so I can complete my workout."

"Good for you, Ronna. I've always admired people who took their physical fitness seriously." Alaina attempted to smile widely again, but it was forced. She raised her eyebrows too high and blinked rapidly while exposing almost all of her top teeth. She looked menacing and devious.

"Oh my God, come on!" I shouted over a man screeching about a three-point shot and the free throw line. "Can we have a real conversation here? Please! Ronna, were you turning tricks with Claire at Ram's? What do you think Natalie is lying about? What do you know about Claire that you won't say? And Alaina, stop smiling like that! You look like the Joker."

Ronna picked up her fork and pointed the tines at my face. "You ain't from Deck River, so you won't ever understand what the hell it was like out there, and you," she said bitterly to Alaina. "You better stop spreading nasty rumors about me unless you want me to tell our little friend here about you and Gamble. And Duke Pendley for that matter."

The manager showed up at the table with a greasy menu and told us they were out of the Oreo pie.

"Thank you, but all we need is the check," Alaina said in her officious manner.

"I worked at Ram's," Ronna said. "I served drinks. Claire did some things there that she shouldn't have, but that was before she met Mitchell, and I certainly never sold my body or anybody else's."

"No one's accusing you of being a pimp, Ronna," Alaina said.

"Is that why you're not on the force anymore? Because of Captain Gamble?" I said, trying to get the focus off Ronna, who was sweating profusely with her hands in fists on the table and her lips twitching in rage. "And what do you mean, Duke Pendley?" I looked around like someone at a neighboring table might be able to shed some light on the situation.

"I can't believe you haven't noticed yet, but Gamble is a total panty pirate," Alaina said. "If you pay attention to him, he's gonna go after you, full throttle."

"So I take it you paid attention to him?" I said. "Did you pay attention to Duke Pendley too?"

"And why the hell did you tell her I was a hooker?" Ronna stood up, knocking her high-back stool over with her large, but firm-as-granite rear end. "You've got real issues with pissing people off, Alaina Watson. They didn't call you The Bridge Burner for nothing. I got real tired of you then, and I'm real tired of you now. If I didn't think this was for a good cause, I'd be outta here."

"You and your apple juice," Alaina said provocatively.

Not sixty seconds later, Alaina and Ronna were in a

bare-knuckle brawl on the sidewalk outside Applebee's. Ronna got a few good grabs of Alaina's hair while Alaina had some powerful shots to the abdomen with her pointed boots. A male patron who'd been enjoying a cigarette by the handicapped parking spaces ultimately stepped in and tore the two women apart. Another, smaller gentleman had tried to intervene by using his cane to separate Alaina and Ronna but had been unsuccessful. When his cane snapped in two after Ronna did a body slam that knocked Alaina to the ground, he removed himself from the fray and went inside the restaurant. When the altercation had finally ended, and we had returned to our table by the bar, I saw the man with the broken cane enjoying a veggie burger at a corner table. He was accompanied by a much younger woman in large hoop earrings.

"I was never a whore," Ronna said when we sat back down. She and Alaina were bloodied and both visibly shaken by the incident.

The police had been called, but after Alaina talked to the restaurant manager for a few minutes, he agreed that he would tell the police the matter had been resolved. Officers arrived shortly thereafter and quickly left with an order of wings in tow. One had to come back in for extra blue cheese. We knew this, because the bartenders shouted "get the blue cheese!" over the raucous dinner crowd.

"I was only repeating what I'd been told," Alaina said. "And yes"—she looked at me—"I've had an on-again, off-again thing with Larson Gamble for years now. It has nothing to do with why I quit the case and the police and all that. He and I talk all the time. If I didn't want to deal with him, I wouldn't. I quit because it was a dead end. It's still a dead end. I admire you for thinking you can change that, but there's just not much you can do about it. When Mitchell died, we just didn't have that much to go on. I stuck around for almost two years after that; I guess I wouldn't call that giving up.

"Natalie always claimed she didn't know anything other than that Mitchell was with her the night it happened. That saved him, but…you know—it didn't save him, not his reputation. And Claire, well, there was just no pinning it on her. No witnesses, very little physical evidence, in a practically deserted place. There was just nothing there. If you really want to solve this thing, you'd have to get somebody to confess, and you're not going to get anybody to confess."

"What about Duke Pendley?" I said. "What's Ronna talking about?"

"Nothing," Alaina answered. "He was always barking up the wrong tree."

"The right tree, get it?" Ronna said, leaning forward. "Wright? Like the name?"

I was confused. "Well, what about J.P.?" I said. I assumed my role would be to continually ask what-about-everyone-involved-in-the-case? I was fine with that. At least I was contributing.

"He's not going to tell you anything. As far as he's concerned, he got away with this scot-free. Why would he say something now? It's been seventeen years."

"What about his wife? Tina."

"What would she get out of it? And anyway, I don't think she knew. She stuck with him. They're still married. Maybe she doesn't know what happened, or she helped him. It's a dead end, Arlene. I wish it wasn't, but it is. I got the same feeling I used to get when we talked to Natalie today. There's no one out there who really knows what happened. Not anymore. I think Mitchell knew, but..." She shook her head in defeat and trailed off somewhat artificially, seeming to feel she had given us all the closure we required.

"Well, Ronna?" I leaned in Ronna's direction. She had been silent this entire time. I thought I heard her call Alaina a butt-face under her breath at one point, but I couldn't be sure. "What do you know about J.P. or Tina or..."

"I don't know a damn thing about J.P. Callahan other than that he's scum," Ronna fumed. "But you should ask Natalie Wright about that."

"What?" I couldn't hear over the television and the people at the table behind us who were trying to restrain their toddler. He kept careening down the side of the barstool where he'd been made to sit and then climbing up the side of it again.

"What did you say, Ronna? What about Natalie Wright? And if there was something we should have asked her, then maybe you should have said something earlier. We were just at her house, for God's sake!" I sounded accusing and enraged. I think I was. It had been a long day, and now Alaina was saying we should drop the whole thing, and here was Ronna with more "secret" information that she'd just barely let us nibble at before tucking it back in the waistline of her panties. I wasn't ready to give up; I might never be, and I wanted Ronna to be honest. I was tired of getting crumbs; I wanted the loaf.

"Nothing." Ronna removed her purse from the back of the chair and stood up. "I need to use the ladies' room, and then I would like to go home. Platt doesn't like to be home in the evenings by himself and I have to work out."

"It's after eight," I said. "We won't be home 'til ten at least."

She walked to the bathroom without acknowledging that I'd spoken.

"Yeah, so..." Alaina's eyes darted as if the family with the unrestrained toddler might be interested in what she was about to say. As far as I could tell, they were fighting for their survival and couldn't have cared less what we were talking about. "That's the thing—"

"What thing?"

The toddler threw a french fry that ricocheted off the lamp hanging over our table, causing it to lightly sway. I was reminded of the basement in the Faber precinct. I felt oddly homesick and forlorn. What was I doing here? With these oddball women?

In some random Atlanta suburb with slimy, uncontrollable children? If I had my own children, I thought, they would never sit on a barstool at Applebee's next to grown women who just got into a bare-knuckle brawl in the parking lot. We'd be reading Beatrix Potter under a handmade quilt and eating butter cookies off my grandmother's china. I frowned heavily.

"I don't know..." Alaina put her head in her hands. "I hate to even say this, because it was...how do I say? Just a bad bit of gossip. Anyway."

"Anyway what?" I said, frustrated and tired of the ruckus behind us. I turned in my seat finally. "I'm sorry, but isn't it a little late for him to be out?" The child picked up a piece of broccoli from his plate and dropped it in his mother's iced tea.

"Sorry," she said as though he had done this to me.

"Sorry," I said too—knowing she had enough to deal with. She had problems I wanted but couldn't make happen. Her husband was having a beer. Maybe the tea was because she was pregnant again. "Sorry," I said more vaguely. I was sorry.

"Natalie might have been having a thing with J.P. too." Alaina looked uncomfortable telling me this. "It's bound to come out. I have to tell you."

"What?" I said, disbelieving.

"I don't know. I guess someone at the stables said they saw her with him. He's a real piece of work. Scum and always running around after young girls."

"I thought he was married," I said. We'd been about to accuse him of murdering three children. His marital status had never been an excuse before, but right now it was what I had to offer. He'd made vows to this Tina woman. "Come to think of it, Gamble's married, Alaina!" I said.

"So!" Alaina said. "Stanton was married too. Didn't stop him from chasing tail."

"No. Yes," I said like I was agreeing with her justification, or disagreeing with myself.

"There were murmurs. I talked to a bunch of the kids at the stables when I decided I thought it was J.P. I went over there— kind of unofficially—and tried to get the girls to spill. They mostly said J.P. was Tina's husband and kind of quiet, just ordering people around, running the show at the stable. They'd all heard about him with Claire and others. A couple of the younger girls pulled me aside and told me that Natalie got busy with J.P. too. They said it like they knew she would be humiliated if I knew."

"Well, duh!" I said. I was thrilled, queasy, determined, disappointed in Natalie, who I'd thought was a dud. "I'm having like a real existential crisis here," I said.

"I know," Alaina agreed. "But take some advice from an old woman—don't get too attached to your impressions of people."

"But you know them, or you knew them. You had more than an impression."

"Yeah, but all sorts of really random people have wild sexual affairs while I'm doing the laundry. It never ceases to amaze me either." Alaina widened her eyes and looked toward the bathroom. I continued to get the impression—when she wasn't having her hair ripped out by Ronna or stumbling around trying to avoid a right hook—that Alaina was making fun of me, that somehow I was providing her amusement. It was fun she wanted to direct and control and yet—maybe it was Alaina who was feeding me the crumbs. I thought this might be why Ronna was so frustrated. Someone wasn't being honest, and the other person knew. I just hadn't figured out who was who yet. "Where the hell is Ronna?" Alaina said.

"Why are you giving her such a hard time?" I asked. "And you have extramarital affairs...what do you mean while you're doing the laundry?"

"I have never had an extramarital affair. Not my own marriage. And of course I do the laundry." She pointed at her shirt. It was clean; I couldn't argue with that. "Where the hell is Ronna, for God's sake? And, what is she even doing here, Arlene? I completely understand you, but she's a receptionist at the police station who's never wanted to be anything but a receptionist at the police station. Are you like a life coach or something? Are you trying to fix her?"

"I'm a bag tagger at the police station," I said flatly. "That's all I've ever been besides a waitress. I don't want to be anything in particular. I don't see why that means I shouldn't be trying to right the wrongs of the world—or just the wrongs in Faber."

"I misspoke," Alaina said. "I'm some bored old woman living in Dolvin. That's pretty much all I've ever been too. I was a bored young woman at one point, but...well, my point is that she doesn't want anything to do with this. She can't help us, and she lies. She knows stuff, but she won't tell us. She's not going to help you. Not one bit."

At that precise moment, Ronna reappeared next to the table, standing very close to me with her moist, apple-flavored breath misting my left cheek. She clutched a gnarled, matted paper towel in her hand. "Natalie Wright was with J.P. the night it happened," she said. "My mom saw them. I've never told anyone that. Mom never told neither. I think Natalie did it."

I felt something hit me on the side of the face. It was a wad of chewed broccoli spewed from the table next to us. "What?" I said in a shocked whisper. I looked up at Alaina, whose face had taken on a somber veil. The distress made her look every bit her age. It was the first I'd really noticed that she was not a young woman.

"Why are you just now telling me this, Ronna?" I said. "We were at her house earlier." Another piece of broccoli catapulted from behind Ronna's head, skimming her ear before it landed on our table next to the signed bill—Alaina had offered to pay.

"I just didn't want to say it in front of her." Ronna pointed at Alaina's drawn face.

"You just beat her up in the parking lot. Surely you could say this in front of her." I wondered if this is what having children was like—competing loyalties, a total lack of logic, fistfighting.

"She's never gonna let you go after a Wright. No matter what," Ronna said, staring very directly at Alaina.

Alaina looked back at her but didn't say a word.

I just sat in the truck. I didn't even know what he was doing. Mitchell left, and I ran out back to go with J.P., because I thought we were going to hook up, but he said he had to go back over to the river. He said he left something. I thought maybe he meant he left something at Claire's, so I was jealous and thinking I needed to prove myself or something. I could never tell anyone this. I'm really not like this at all. I don't know why I got messed up with J.P.

Anyway, I was nervous we'd run into Mitchell or that Mitchell would see me in J.P.'s truck. We weren't that far from Mitchell and Claire's house. J.P. said to get down then, so I rode in the floorboard. I thought it was so funny. It was such a stupid thing to think was funny. I stayed down there while he was out in the woods. I didn't know what he was doing. I still don't know. That's the thing—I don't know, so I'm not lying when I say that. I don't know what he was doing.

Someone told me J.P. used to kill the cats at the stable. He killed lots of stuff I guess. I know he set traps for the mice and would let them squirm in there and watch them die, but you have to kill the mice. They scare the horses and get into the food. I guess there was a cat named John Deere that he electrocuted with a live wire from one of the arena lights. I didn't see him do it, but one of the girls told me. She said he did stuff like that before, like when one of Margie's puppies had a limp, J.P. tied his back two legs together so he couldn't walk at all and ran his lighter over the dog's tail. Ellen's the one who said that stuff. Her older sister told her, so I'm not even sure it's true.

I know how it sounds, like I was this goody-two-shoes who's trying to be bad, but I'm not. I'm not bad. I was just curious and he is really nice to me, or I guess I should say he was. He's not mean to me now, but I don't talk to him anymore. I just can't. No one knows what was going on with us. I'm ashamed of it, and I do want to tell someone. I really do. I want to tell someone that I think maybe he killed those kids. They kept asking me at the police station if I knew anything, and I don't, and I just can't make myself say I was there. I can't do it. I don't want to admit it. What am I supposed to think? Like, I can't just say what I don't know. I feel like if I didn't say something in the beginning I can't say it now, and I was always so proud to be going around with him, not proud like of my accomplishments or something but proud that a guy liked me, a man. But it's not the kind of proud I want to show in front of my parents or whatever. I kept a secret before because it was so bad, but now I think I could be in trouble.

I wasn't lying when I said Mitchell was home, but when he left—that's when I met J.P. He pulls around back when he comes to get me—or when he used to. The Dockweilers are never home anymore, because their grandkids live in Florida now, so J.P. just pulls in there, and I go over the back fence. We did it like twenty times this way. I didn't think that day would be different. It really wasn't. I didn't see anything at all. I swear to God. Mitchell said he was gonna go for a drive. He didn't want to go home, because he's always fighting with Claire these days—or he was.

I don't know why I thought all of this was okay—like J.P. going out with Claire and me while he's married to Tina and us sneaking around behind everyone's back. He says Tina made him get married. He says she's really insecure and has always wanted to own him. He said a lot of stuff to me—most of it made me feel really good and pretty and grown up. I don't even recognize myself when I think about it sometimes. I'm going to change back and be the kind of person I was before. I've already started listening more at church and haven't missed Youth Group in four weeks. I don't know what I was thinking. I don't even go over to the stables much right now, because I'm scared of seeing him. Mostly scared of my feelings but also scared because I really think he might have killed those kids. Sometimes I think maybe Mitchell did see me with him—in his truck, and that's why he hung himself. I can't even say it. I can't say what happened to Mitchell. It might have been my fault. Claire sure got away from me as fast as she could. My mom and everyone else says it's because she's a bad person. I think maybe she's afraid of me.

26

I f we're going to be a real detectives' agency, I have to be able to trust you!" I was emphatic in the car on the way back to Faber. "You're both holding out on me, and I don't want to be a bitch here, but I'm the one who started the agency, so in a way I'm the president!"

"Okay, Arlene…" Alaina sounded like she was trying to be patient. "We don't have a detectives' agency. That is not what's happening. You are a minimum wage employee at the Faber Police Department who has been given the freedom to look into an old case. So I need to make sure we all understand that. That's the first thing, and yes—yes, there are things I haven't told you. I'm sure Ronna has kept some of her cards close to her chest as well…"

"We don't gamble," Ronna said abruptly. "Platt and I… It's a sin."

"Right," I said. My mother had always taught us just that.

"Fine," Alaina said. I saw her roll her eyes in the rearview mirror. Alaina was in the back seat again with Ronna riding shotgun. "Fine."

"What else aren't you telling me?" I'd raised my voice, but no one answered me.

"I told you everything now," Ronna said. "Natalie Wright was in J.P.'s truck at the river when those boys died. My mama saw it with her own two eyes."

Alaina was strangely, forcefully silent.

"Alaina?" I said.

"I don't know her mother!" Alaina churned in her seat and faced out the window, her arms folded over her chest. "I don't know what her mother saw."

"Why does Duke Pendley have a massive house on Lake Patton?" I asked with a jolt. "That's really been bothering me."

"You should ask her about that." Ronna crossed her arms over her chest now and dipped her head at an awkward angle in Alaina's direction.

"We'll get to that," I said, gripping the steering wheel with renewed vigor. I'd accelerated quite a bit and was perked up by the engine's roar. "First I want to know what this Natalie Wright business is. You realize we went to her house, right? You said nothing about this when we had the opportunity to talk to her about it. You told me at Applebee's. Both of you."

"Both of us what?" Ronna said. "I confessed about Mama... what did she say?" She pointed to Alaina in the back seat.

"I told her that there were rumors Natalie Wright was running around with J.P. too. I've been honest, Ronna."

"Honest as a drunken sinner at a church picnic!" Ronna slammed her hand down on the dash. "You know exactly what happened, and you've known for a long time! You covered it up! You let this ruin Claire's life."

"Her life was already ruined," Alaina said more somberly.

I was trying not to interrupt, or to too aggressively speed. I felt on the cusp of a breakthrough and wanted to both be quiet enough to hear it but also to remain unincarcerated once the knowledge had finally landed. I was going about twenty over at this point and we weren't anywhere near Faber. No one would call in a favor if I got locked up for reckless driving.

I glanced at Alaina in the rearview. While Ronna had grown more fierce in her position, Alaina was slinking backward, down, into a puddle. I couldn't tell if it was guilt or avoidance. Tommy did the same thing after a night of bad decision-making and regret. He melted into a running liquid so it was harder to stomp on him.

"I don't know any more than either of you." Alaina sighed in resignation.

Ronna crossed, then uncrossed, then crossed her arms one final time and sat back in the seat. "I haven't been holding out on you, Arlene," she said. "These are things I never told anybody. Nobody." She seemed pleased in thinking she had corrected herself. "I didn't get the job with the Faber PD because of Claire and all this, but I did think we could do some good when you got going on it. I really did. It never sat right with me that they just dropped it. I know they were country kids, not really cared for or much to look at or talk to, but they were little boys and somebody should have cared that they got kil't like that. It's like me—if I got kil't."

I wanted to correct the way she was saying killed, but per usual, Ronna had me on my knees with the way she could tell me something simple that made all sorts of other complicated things make sense.

"If I got kil't when I was a kid, nobody would have cared 'cept maybe my mama, but Claire and them didn't have a mother, not no more. Nobody woulda kept a case going for years trying to figure out who kil't me. Those kids were the same—just more poor kids from Deck River. Who cares about them? No one. That's why when you said you were going to open this back up, I wanted to help. I've told you what I know now. Those are things I never told nobody," Ronna said.

"Anybody," I said quietly, and then shoved my fingertips in my mouth, silently berating myself for this constant, pressing need to correct Ronna's grammar.

Alaina hadn't made a peep. I was trying to focus on the road while maintaining a responsible speed and caught a glimpse of Alaina in the rearview. She had that desolate, frail look I'd noticed in the Applebee's after Ronna beat her up, someone with shame that was pulling down on her face and everything beneath it. The weight of bad decisions, things done that didn't sit well, that made the blood thicker, heavier, harder to push through the veins.

"No," Alaina said quietly. Neither of us had asked a question.

"She knows something," Ronna said over her shoulder. "I thought she'd come back to tell the truth this time. She knows what happened." Ronna shook her head in dismay. "I get so mad when she acts like she used to—you know, real cocky but not speaking truth."

Alaina rolled her eyes. Her moment of self-awareness passed or was ejected from the car along with Ronna's grammar.

"I can't tell you what I don't know," Alaina said.

But this time—I really didn't believe it. Her expression was like that of a jilted clown.

27

W here the hell have you been?!" Tommy was standing in the yard when I finally arrived home. It was close to midnight. I'd been clear when I left that morning that I would be back very late, but he was apparently terrified as to what might have befallen me. "I've been standing out here all night!"

"I was in Atlanta," I said. "Or Frampton—wherever that is. Near Atlanta. I told you that."

"I was worried sick!" He was in his boxers and a stained T-shirt with a hole in the armpit.

"So you stood outside and howled at the moon?" I said.

"I was waiting for you to get home!" The thing about Tommy was he was never a nasty drunk. I'd never once seen him be mean to anyone—drunk or sober. Tonight he seemed different; he was on edge, like he was about to lash out at me.

"Sorry," I said. "I told you what I was doing though." I couldn't bring myself to comfort him. I might have even sneered a little. It was a whole new me, a tiny bird emerging from a delicate shell where I'd been housed the entire time he knew me. Little Arlene Black from Cove Street. "I don't know why you have to give me a hard time about having a life of my own." I walked inside, knowing I'd been nastier than I needed to be.

"Arlene, you're not the woman I married!" he said in a bellowing slur. "I don't even know what to say to you anymore. You're off with those girls all the time; I'm starting to wonder if you're a lesbian!"

"Can you not shout 'lesbian' in the middle of the night on this of all streets?" I hissed back from atop the front steps. I'd parked in the driveway, forgoing the garage when I saw Tommy out front in his unmentionables. "You know how weird Luanne is about her daughter!"

"I'm not talking about Luanne or her daughter!" Tommy yelled even louder. Luanne Phillips's daughter, Stacy, had run off with another woman some years before. She was the homecoming queen at Faber High before she married a power-company lineman and then cheated on him with a hairdresser from Coraville. They were living somewhere in North Carolina now. Luanne never got over the humiliation of her daughter leaving a lineman. Glen Campbell was her favorite singer, and it was like Stacy had no respect.

"Tommy, please come inside. This on top of me cleaning vomit off the steps last night is too much. We'll be banished from the neighborhood."

"I hate this neighborhood," he said, and for the first time in a while, I thought he sounded honest.

"You do?"

"I wanna live like kings, you know? Someplace fancy with fancy neighbors and a pool and all that. I want the country-club life."

"Oh, like in Lake Patton?" I crossed my arms over my chest but softened. "Sorry." I uncrossed them and took a step down and toward Tommy. "I do like to swim, but it's October."

"I want to move on…outta here, Arlene."

"Like out of Faber?" I said, incredulous. That was the thing—me and Tommy, we were always going to stay in Faber. We'd said it on our wedding day. Faber was home and always would be.

"No, just onto the next level." Now he was slurring something serious. He closed his eyes for a long second, then reopened them in an attempt to better focus.

"Me too," I said. "But I'm trying to do it with my professional life. I'm trying to make a name for myself as a detective, and all you care about is dinner parties with the right people on Lake Patton."

He drew his brows together, miffed but certain. "You're putting words in my mouth made from the thoughts in your head. It's almost like I have nothing to do with it. Any of it." He walked into the house through the garage, choosing not to have to bypass me on the stairs. I stood outside for a few minutes longer, looking— but far from howling—at the moon.

A CONDEMNED MAN

I DON'T REGRET IT. I can't even really understand that word. Regret.
There are useless feelings that I don't get. Part of my badness. I
started messing around with another girl from the stables, but she
was trouble for me. She told her mom she was seeing me, and the
mom called the police. Maybe that was regret, 'cause it got the light
shining on me, but that's the thing—there's no light in Deck River.
As soon as it happened, it was over. That Wright kid killed himself
and it's like because he did that they solved the case. I never even
worried about getting caught. It didn't cross my mind. There was
nobody there; nobody saw us. Maybe 'cause of the rain or 'cause
there was never anybody but Claire who worried about those boys.
I didn't think anyone would care, and they kinda didn't. It's funny
to talk like this—all serious like it was the end of the world. It was
a long time ago, and nobody never did a thing about it. Not even
Claire, and I think she always knew. I held 'em down one at a time.

They let me. The last little guy I had to chase, 'cause he figured it out, but before that, they just laid there. I found a stick next to where they were lying, and broke it in two. I put a piece of it in the big kid's pocket. I kept a little of it for myself to remind me of what I done—and maybe so I could be connected to him. I never felt more connected to anything than after I killed 'em. And they let me do it. They weren't scared or nothing, just calm. Even when the little one ran he wasn't yelling or nothing. He didn't make a sound—he was barefoot on mud. It calmed me how quiet it was, such a hard thing with no noise. I guess it was the rain; everything was wet and heavy. No noise. That's what I'll always remember. There wasn't any noise. Nobody screamed. Maybe if somebody had screamed I'd have some regret. He didn't scream neither. He didn't even tell me to stop.

28

The mood was tense at the station the following morning. Ronna was back at her desk in the front and greeted me very formally when I came in. "Mrs. Ridell," she said upon seeing me. "You don't have any mail or messages."

"Thank you," I said, dipping my head slightly.

I went down the stairs slowly, half-expecting Ronna to ask me to stay so we could talk about the previous evening's revelations, but she said nothing. It was her way to build her walls even higher after a weakness had been detected—or she'd revealed there was a way in after all.

Alaina had said the night before that she would not be in. She was exhausted and going back to Dolvin. I would spend the morning alone in my hole. I'd all but run everyone off with my passion for the case, my passion for the split-level house, my passion for the truth, my passion for making people who hated one another spend a lot of time together in close quarters. I took a few breaths to calm the flood of self-realization that was deeply unflattering. I wondered if I'd been asleep for most of my life and was now awake or if it was the opposite. I used to be awake and was now in some altered state, sleepwalking and unable to fully rouse myself into consciousness.

I walked over to the table where we'd so expertly sorted the files and stood, feeling strangely hopeless in spite of all of yesterday's significance. People were saying important things, but I couldn't do anything about it. I walked quickly past my desk, barely noticing that there was a small stack of evidence bags that needed my attention. It wouldn't take me more than twenty minutes based on the size of the pile.

I was resigned to bagging and tagging and then waiting on lunch with Ronna all morning when I noticed an errant folder, its edges worn and rubbed to softness, lying on the edge of the table. *Natalie Wright's Journal.* It was the copy of her notebook. Someone had clearly been looking at it, because it wasn't out when we left the precinct the night before. Alaina, Ronna, and I had come inside to use the bathroom and make sure all the basement lights were off before getting into our respective cars and heading home. I'd gone downstairs to check that everything was in order; the folder had not been on the table. It now sat where I'd left my coat. I hadn't brought it with me to Frampton. A last-minute bout of insecurity had me thinking a mink stole was inappropriate for witness interrogation. I retrieved it before leaving. There was nothing else on the table.

Ronna was the only one of us who had a key to the station. She used it proudly, flamboyantly even. I thought to run upstairs and accuse her of tampering with evidence but decided against it. To hell with Ronna, I said to myself. I would do this my way.

I sat down quietly, hoping not to be disturbed. If Natalie really had been spotted in Deck River that night—as Ronna and her mother claimed—then the journal was significant. Boring but significant. To add fuel to the fire, Natalie may have been messing around with J.P. Callahan. Maybe they'd been doing the nasty in his truck before the boys were killed. I scolded myself for my thoughts. Who was I to chastise someone for doing the nasty in a truck?

Included in the file were photos of the cover of her diary—purple with a floral border. It was more like something an elderly woman would write her grocery list in than a teenage girl's longings and daydreams. Along with photocopies of the cover were copies of places where Duke Pendley must have thought pages were removed. He copied the torn sheets as proof that she'd taken things out. *Removed—DP* he'd written on each photocopy of the missing chunks. He always marked his territory in the files, probably hoping that if he was right about something, he'd get the credit he deserved, wanted.

The journal was a bound notebook, therefore it was easy to see that yes, indeed, some pages had been torn out. There was many a rough edge, jagged shards where pages had once been. I'd kept a diary for a while in middle school. All I wrote about in it was what kind of wedding I wanted to have and how many kids and what kind of house decorations. I had used to look at catalogs my mother got in the mail; how any of these stores found her, I'd never know. We were down a long, barely inhabited road, deep in mountain farm country without a spare nickel and no nice clothes or home furnishings to speak of. My mother ignored the offerings while I pored over them. I even cut pictures of my favorite bedspreads out and pasted them in my journal. I remembered looking at it when Tommy and I bought the split-level and thinking how silly I'd been. I didn't care what kind of bedspread I had if I had Tommy. I shook my head in spite of myself, this constant confusion over what I was feeling and what I thought I should be feeling was in the way. I couldn't stop deriding myself while at the same time patting myself on the back and then wondering what I was doing. The confusion was like a thick syrup that I just couldn't wash out of my hair. It had been a long few weeks.

Natalie Wright's journal had no pictures of furniture or pillow shams inside. She did have a lot of rudimentary drawings of horses and silly devotions to one horse in particular, Feather. I'd tried to read the journal before, but couldn't get through a few pages without giving up. She had about as much personality as I did at that age—a different personality but in similar quantities, very little. I had to give it to myself though—at least I hadn't spent the better part of my teen years mooning over a hoofed animal. A vision of Tommy in his boxers with partially digested food littering his chest hair came to mind. Maybe it wasn't all that different after all.

A lot had happened the day before, weighty events that hadn't yet dissolved into my understanding. I'd never interrogated anyone before nor shown up at someone's home to reopen a murder investigation. I'd never seen two grown women—one in a long, matronly skirt—get into a fight in a parking lot. Also Ronna dropping these bombs left and right—pertinent information that she seemed to projectile-vomit at me after going to the bathroom. The night she'd called to tell me Cecil was Lucy's father (or at least she was pretty damned sure of it, given his history with Claire), she'd told me she was in the bathroom when Platt said she needed to be honest with me. Toilets flushing seemed to provoke Ronna's truth. I'd never been so moved by the press of a handle. Alaina's sultry, overconfident demeanor, which had been so appealing before, now seemed spooky, like she was trying to manipulate me. I might have got some good ruminating done when I got home from such an important day if Tommy hadn't been standing out in the yard, accusing me of cheating on him with the women in my detectives' club.

Instead I had the journal in my hands, a continued, stifling sense that I was being misled, and an overwhelming urge to either tattoo Ronna's name on my bicep or try to choke her to death with a brick of day-old meatloaf. Alaina did not rouse the same zeal in me; what had started as intrigue had turned to suspicion, mistrust, dubiousness on par with being told that nice young man over there is giving away cotton candy and free rides in his minivan.

I was flipping through a few pages of Natalie's notes and doodles when the room went sideways. I gripped the desk, feeling off kilter, dizzy, faint. It was Alaina, I thought. She wasn't protecting Mitchell. She was protecting Natalie. There'd been word that two people were out on the bank near where the kids were killed. Everyone had thought it was Claire and Mitchell, but maybe it was J.P. and Natalie? I had a wave of nausea come over me that was accompanied by a flashback to Tommy's wave of vomit on the porch, chunky and forceful. I was almost certain I would need the trash can. The wobbly feeling passed and in its place came a rush of unfettered rage.

I walked to my desk and yanked the phone out of its cradle. I had Alaina's number written on an index card Scotch taped to the desk. She answered after a few rings, sounding groggy but like she knew it was going to be me on the other end of the line. "Good morning."

"It's Arlene."

"I might have known."

"If you don't tell me what you know, what you really know, I'm going to blame you for Mitchell's death. I'm going to come out and say that was your fault, because if you knew he didn't kill those kids, but you were too worried about Natalie to tell the truth, then he hung himself because of you."

"Arlene?" It was Ronna. She'd made it halfway down the steps undetected. "Tommy's here."

"Hold on." I slammed the phone down on the table and looked up at Ronna. She appeared sorry and meek. "I'm in the middle of a breakthrough!" I said.

"I know, but Tommy…"

Tommy was standing in the lobby in a suit and carrying a bouquet of flowers. "I thought I'd take you to lunch," he said, smiling a little too widely, like he was trying to keep from crying.

"I just got here," I said. "It's eight in the morning."

"I mean breakfast!" He was talking very loudly. Ronna cleared her throat to express her disapproval. Ronna did not take kindly to raucous interruptions in her domain. She'd excused a copy paper salesman a few weeks back for his loud voice and the way he dropped his satchel of paper samples on the floor with a thud. To add insult to injury, he'd moved one of her perfectly placed chairs in the waiting area so he could elevate his booted feet.

"I'm on the clock from eight to noon. You know that," I said to Tommy. I hadn't said much to him before I left that morning. He'd gone to bed in a huff the night before, sleeping in the guest room with the door firmly shut.

It was another crisp autumn day. Had it not been for recent developments, I would have been planning a chili tasting for me and Tommy or perusing the Pier 1 Imports in Davison. In the past I'd made pine cone bird feeders with peanut butter and seed. I'd fashioned my own wind chimes out of antique horseshoes I bought at the flea market on Provost Street. I'd gone around the house, making sure every couch and chair had a blanket neatly folded and thrown over its corner. I'd lived this way for years; it was no wonder Tommy asked me if I ironed the curtains. Maybe I'd seemed like the type to do that—or worse, enjoy it. But here I was annoyed at Tommy for trying to take me out, annoyed with myself for my internal conflicts, yelling at Alaina for something I suspected she'd done nearly twenty years ago, thinking Ronna looked extra frumpy in her apron-style dress with its intentionally mismatched buttons.

"Okay, sorry," Tommy said. "I know." He put the flowers—carnations that he clearly picked up at the 7-Eleven—on the counter. "I'm just tryin'."

It was silent in the lobby, save from the ticking of the wall clock. "They must have made six million of those things," I said, pointing to the wall. "That same clock has been in every classroom, every office building, every doctor's office I've ever been to."

No one responded. There were other things to say. "I guess I'll get going." Tommy turned on his heel.

"You could come down with me and see what this thing is all about," I said. Ronna raised an eyebrow, then looked away. There was probably a rule against civilians going into the evidence locker—which wasn't a locker but an open room where I, another civilian, sat day in and day out.

"Don't tell Gamble, okay?" I said to Ronna. She pretended to type with her hands perfectly placed like we learned in keyboarding class, but did not respond. "And I'm gonna need to talk to your mother today," I said with a little jut of my chin. "In light of recent developments."

"She's in a wheelchair," Ronna replied.

"Okay," I said, not sure how this would prevent me from speaking to her. "Does she have a phone?"

"It's upstairs," Ronna said before going back to her precise typing.

"So," I said to Tommy as we got downstairs. "This is where the magic happens." I pointed at my desk.

"At least you have a window," Tommy said. "The secretaries in our office don't even have windows. They just sit in these little box things. They decorate 'em, and it's kind of sad or…I don't know, it makes me depressed sometimes."

"Cubicles," I said. "At least they have a job." I shrugged. Whenever Tommy showed dimension, I was taken aback. That's the trouble with being the life of the party; no one expects you to get past the surface, not even your wife.

"So," I said. I placed my hands together like I was praying. I was dressed very smartly on this day, feeling after the previous day's events that I had much to prove—mostly to myself about what I was doing reopening this case, poking at a fire that had long gone out with only a few embers even left to spark. I was meddling. That was something old women did when they ran out of responsibilities of their own. But it was too late to let sleeping dogs lie. I had all sorts of information that had never made it into those case files. I had a mind to try and get in touch with Duke Pendley to give him an update. I'd wanted to tell Gamble too, but the way he licked his lips every time I mentioned my research had me on my heels.

"We went to interview Natalie Wright yesterday. She's married with kids now. This happened almost twenty years ago, mind you. Her brother, Mitchell Wright, is dead—suicide. He killed himself after they found Claire Broderick's three brothers dead by Deck River."

"I know all this, Arlene," Tommy said. "I've been listening."

"Coulda fooled me!" I said. He sagged a little. His suit was sharp, freshly pressed and sitting nicely on his broad shoulders.

"Sorry, Tommy. I'm in a state these days. I really am." I paused. It was Duke Pendley making his way to the front of my head—him and his house on Lake Patton. I frowned.

"Sorry? Or in a state?" Tommy asked.

"I'd say both. Listen—"

"I am!" He paused. "I don't mean to be impatient," he said.

"Well, the thing is—" I really did want to talk about the case. I had his attention and was excited about it. "I'm really starting to think that Alaina was right—it's J.P. Callahan who did this, and I'm sorry to say that I do think Mitchell Wright took his own life—may he rest in peace—but I don't think it was Claire with J.P. when it went down. I think it was Natalie. I mean—that's what Ronna said. Her mother saw them, but let me ask you—"

"Okay," Tommy said. We were both standing by my desk, so I motioned to the chair and sat down myself. I leaned forward on my elbows, resting my chin pensively on my knuckles.

"How much money would you say Stan Watson has?"

"Boondoggles," Tommy answered.

"Speak English, please."

"A lot. I think I meant 'beaucoups.'"

"And Alaina hung him out to dry in the divorce?"

"Don't all women?"

"Don't tempt me," I said, and then smiled lightly. Tommy did too. It was warming between us; the edges of our liquid had a little sizzle, some small bubbles of hope.

"Could she have bought Duke Pendley that big fancy house?"

"Who?"

"Duke Pendley. The house we looked at on Lake Patton."

"The Tudor?"

"Yes, the Tudor." The sizzle was gone. We were back to square one. There was something about that word that could really cool me off.

"Why would she buy him a house?"

"I mean—could that be how he got that place?" I was talking

more to myself than to Tommy, who was leaning forward, elbows on knees, trying to look both thoughtful and concerned while clearly having absolutely no idea what I was talking about. "What I'm thinking," I went on, "is that maybe Pendley was onto this Natalie Wright thing and Alaina paid him off to just go away. He quit not long after this case. And he was the one who deemed it unsolved—or closed it rather. Said it was a dead end."

"Isn't it?" Tommy leaned back.

"I don't think so. Ronna told me last night that her mother saw Natalie Wright with J.P. Callahan the night of the murders."

"The horse guy? Married to Tina?" Tommy perked up.

"Yes, Tina."

"But…"

"Quiet," I said, lifting my hand. "Tina's butt has nothing to do with this."

"Right."

"Ronna said she kept that a secret her whole life, but then I went and looked in Natalie's journal, and there are pages missing left and right. Duke Pendley noticed it. He was hot on it—marking them and making copies. Maybe once Alaina figured out what happened, she gave him the money for the dream house to get him to walk away. Can you find out when he bought that house? You're the property guy."

"Commercial real estate," Tommy corrected me.

"I don't know what that means, but fine."

"Yeah, I can look it up." He nodded. "If it would help you, Arlene. You sound like you've really got this thing figured out."

"I need to talk to Ronna and Alaina," I said, starting to get up from my chair. "Separately. It was a mistake to ask them both to be on the detective squad, but how could I have known?"

"If Alaina was the bad witch here—you know…" Tommy moved his hands around grandly, demonstrating both his competence and concern about what I'd said. "Paying people off and trying to frame this other broad, why would she have agreed to get involved?"

"I don't know," I said. I thought of Claire's pert, determined face. In all the photos of her, she had a small, surly upturn at the corner of her mouth—like her cheek got caught on a fishing line. Her eyes were scolding and impatient—tired of explaining what no one was going to understand. "I don't think she tried to frame—" I stopped myself. "Maybe she didn't really know what happened, but she was still trying to protect those kids. It's confusing," I said, mostly because I felt sorry for Claire and then suddenly Alaina too. Maybe she was trying to do the right thing. I couldn't decide which salad dressing to buy half the time; I wasn't sure what I'd do if I ever had to make a real tough decision.

"What do you do if nothing is the right thing?" I asked Tommy.

He looked surprised. "Well, that's just life," he said. His contribution to the analysis had obviously been quite satisfying.

"That's a pretty big revelation, my friend," I told him.

"I can't figure out what I'm supposed to do half the time, and

I sell warehouses," Tommy said again, tossing his hands around in front of him. "I don't know what I'd do if it was life or death, or... whatever—jail."

"I was just thinking the same thing about salad!" I said enthusiastically.

"Yeah, salad's tough. Anyway, my grandpa used to tell us there are four kinds of people in the world—"

"Pappy?" I said. I'd known Tommy's grandfather for just a minute when we were still in school. He'd been an ambling, lanky bag of bones with enough wrinkles on his face to make a maze. His voice was gravelly but kind. He played solitaire and liked Oprah and refused to skim the fat off pea soup. I could remember several an argument over whether Tommy's grandmother should stir it in or spoon it off. Pappy was a stir-it-in kind of fella. He said what good is ham if you can't have the fat?

"So the four kind of people in the world..." I prompted Tommy, who looked like he was trying to figure out what he was going to say.

"So, let's say you're eating something really messy...like ribs." He leaned forward, in a better position to explain.

"I'm with you."

"So, one person eats some ribs and wipes their hands on their pants, the second person gnaws a bone and uses a napkin to get cleaned up. The third person won't eat a rib, because they don't want to get their hands dirty."

I waited. "You said four kinds. I use a napkin," I added. "You're the pants guy. But usually it's your shirt." I demonstrated, rubbing a hand on the side of my shirt.

"Right, I'm a love handle guy," Tommy said with a decisive head dip.

"So what's the fourth?"

"The person who doesn't want you to think they ate one and gets clean somehow without anyone knowing."

I squinted. "What are you saying?"

"You gotta figure out which one of these gals—this Claire or Natalie—ate a rib and hid the mess."

"As I live and breathe, Tommy," I said. "You come outta nowhere sometimes, don't ya?"

"Or maybe it was this Alaina who hid the mess, 'cause she didn't know who did it and didn't want one of these young girls to go down, you know—if it really was this Callahan guy."

"Right," I said. "Oh shit!" I jumped from my chair. "I was on the phone with Alaina!" I walked around my desk; I'd been sitting in a chair in front of it, facing Tommy. The receiver was still off the cradle. "Alaina?" I said into the mouthpiece. "Are you still there?"

"Yes," she said. "I'll come in."

"Do we talk loud, Tommy?" I said as I put the phone back down. "Do you think she coulda heard us?"

"I've always been loud as a John Deere," Tommy said ruefully.

THE NIGHT THE RIVER WEPT

"Okay." I walked to the stairs. "Ronna!" I scrunched my mouth into a jagged line before continuing. "Tell someone to get the phone for your mother. We gotta talk to her." I was picking at my finger-nails with my teeth again—only a breath away from nine years old even at twenty-four. I don't think people ever really grow up. We're just pretending to keep from embarrassing ourselves.

29

She doesn't even have an upstairs," Ronna said. She was halfway down with her head hung low. I hadn't heard her coming.

"Huh?" I said.

"Mama. It's a ranch. She can get to the phone."

"Okay."

"That's great news!" Tommy said loudly. He was right—he did sound like a tractor half the time. "Great news, Ronna!"

"Okay, Tommy," I said, hoping to temper his excitement. Tommy's enthusiasm was often misplaced, like turning a light on in the wrong room where no one would be while the rest of the house was full—and dark.

"And anyway, I talked to her," Ronna said. "She said she'd be willing to testify or whatever it is. She saw Natalie Wright and J.P. Callahan in Deck River that night. Natalie was in J.P.'s truck over by

Ram's. She didn't see J.P. do nothin' though. He was walking. That was it. Natalie was waiting for him."

"Why was your mother at Ram's?" I asked, then blushed. "Not…I just mean—so we can say…"

"She was lookin' for me," Ronna said. "Me and Claire."

"Was Claire at Ram's too?" I said.

We were all standing, including Tommy, who rose like a giant stalk between Ronna and me. He looked back and forth between us, grunting as he put his hands in his pockets, then removed them, then adjusted his belt, then reput his hands in his pockets, then scooted his tie knot down, then up again, then to the left while putting one hand in his pocket and then back to the right with the other.

"No," Ronna said. "She wasn't there that night." I could tell this was a hard thing for Ronna to admit.

"Ronna." I paused dramatically with my hand outstretched like I might begin a moving modern-dance routine, or a mime performance.

"No, Arlene. Don't." She was flushed and perspiring—the usual. Her hair had less volume this day, which I attributed to her sadness. How could her bangs fly free with all of this weight on her broad, toned shoulders? She sagged a little before speaking again. "I was a kid then too. I was as scared as the rest of 'em, and then Mitchell Wright killed himself over it. I couldn't say what I knew. My mama neither. Don't judge her. That's how we get through most of the time—keep our heads down and try to make rent."

303

"Truer words," Tommy said, putting his hand on Ronna's shoulder in solidarity, which she clearly found uncomfortable. She tried to shrug him off but was too defeated.

"I thought you and Platt owned your house," I said abruptly.

"Arlene—" Tommy looked at me bug-eyed.

"Fine—make our mortgage," Ronna said. "Doesn't have the same ring to it."

"Sorry," I said—feeling like the only person in the room with a bucket on my head. It had become a familiar sensation, to be so ridiculous and out of sync. "I didn't mean…"

"I'll call Phil to see when Pendley's house sold," Tommy said robustly.

"Oh yeah! Ronna, do you think Pendley had some ill-gotten gains that he bought his house with?"

Her face widened, then sank. "What's a illgot?"

Tommy began to explain with more hand gestures before I interrupted him. "What I'm saying is—Duke Pendley sure was living high on the hog for a police officer. That's bugged me since we toured that house. How'd he afford that? His wife didn't do diddly-squat. I remember her from the pool, growing up. She just worked on her suntan and drank margaritas. Then they have a giant Tudor on Lake Patton?"

"What's a Tudor?" Ronna asked.

"Precisely!" I said, stomping my foot for effect. "I think he got paid off. He was onto something. Did you ever hear that there were missing pages from Natalie Wright's diary? 'Cause there are." I walked over to the table where I'd set the journal file. "Pendley's handwriting is all over this sucker. He's got copies of all these places where pages are torn out. I'm wondering if Alaina ripped this thing to shreds to protect Natalie."

"I don't know nothin' about the diary missing any pages," Ronna said. Now she was chalk white. Her facial perspiration had gone from looking like someone after an exhilarating long-distance run to someone about to vomit. "All's I know is that people were saying J.P. got around that stable, including Natalie, if you know what I mean."

"And your mother said Natalie was with him the night it happened."

"But how do you know J.P. did it?" Tommy asked urgently. It was the most important question that had been at both the front and back of our investigation—but always spoken about as a foregone conclusion. Both Alaina and Ronna thought he did it, and I'd been thus convinced, but there was no evidence. I silently applauded myself for thinking in such professional terms. I sounded like a real detective—if only from within the confines of my own mind.

"We've got to get your mother's statement on the record."

"She said she would swear to it—or whatever." Ronna had stepped forward. It was her breath that smelled of hot dogs; at least that mystery was solved. "I'm pretty sure Claire knows too. I think she knew what happened. That's why she left."

"But why'd J.P. kill those kids?" It was Tommy. "Why'd he do that?"

"Maybe he was in love with Claire," I said.

"I wouldn't kill nobody for love," Ronna said.

"No, maybe not." I looked at Tommy, who smiled back. Ours was some sort of innocent love—simple and soft. I couldn't imagine Claire Broderick had ever had anyone smile at her innocently. Maybe the little boys. I'll bet they smiled at her.

30

I said I was going to go to Claire's house. "I have to," I told a tightly wound Ronna, whose mother was going to do a sworn statement. Larson Gamble had come downstairs with a box of petits fours to share. "My wife's taking a baking class!" he announced to our stricken faces. "The pink ones are the best... something strawberry." He was beaming.

I quickly explained the latest developments while Ronna stood listening, her expression much like that of a person trying very hard to avoid passing gas.

"Oh," he said, disappointed that his wife's pastries weren't going to be the highlight. "Well, yes, we need to talk to Mrs. Rolfe. I can go get a statement."

"Davies," Ronna corrected. "She ain't married to my daddy no more."

"Of course."

Tommy stood conspicuously among us like a young child listening closely to his parents' conversation. It dawned on me that Larson Gamble's last encounter with Tommy had been his arrest, or was it when Gamble did the shimmy to Def Leppard at our house? Either way, I was compelled to wonder why life had to be so humiliating.

I had Claire's address. I'd had it a while but kept it close. I was messing around in old mud, but I didn't want to get everyone else dirty too. I hadn't had the nerve to confront her, mostly because in the beginning I was scared to; I thought she was in on it, but that changed. My fear turned to pity, which was actually more difficult for me to confront. How could I talk to her, dredge up her past with my rusty rake, then leave to go back to my split-level and my drunkard of a husband who made lots of money and who was mostly pleasant to be around? I'd be a real jerk if I left all of this mess on Claire's doorstep again, just when she thought she'd finally got her shoes clean. And let's be honest, I didn't think Alaina or Ronna would agree to it, and I didn't seem to be able to do anything without them.

But on this day, I was able to go it alone—or at least with Tommy. He and I left the precinct together in his car. It was filthy, cluttered from stem to stern with wrappers, receipts, empty plastic bags, and the occasional beer can or empty booze bottle. I tried not to act disgusted. I never went near Tommy's car—he had a Mercedes too. It was required that the sales team at Hall Street look successful.

"You take people out in this?" I said after biting my tongue for the first few minutes that we rode together.

"Oh, yeah. Everybody loves Betty."

"Her name is Betty?"

He grinned; I even thought I caught a wink.

"Hey, you," I said like I used to. "So who's gonna do the talking? Me?"

"Of course you. This is your thing. I'm just transport."

"Or Betty is. What if she isn't even home?"

"Then we'll wait. I don't have any appointments today. I'm a free agent."

"I don't think we can just sit in front of her house all day. Somebody'll call the cops."

"Then we'll move every couple of hours."

That was the way the journey went. It was about forty minutes to Revel where Claire now lived. She wasn't Claire Broderick anymore. Claire Hammond; it definitely didn't have the same ring to it. I pondered what she'd look like as we slid past the rolling landscape. Nothing but dips and crests all covered in green. There were massive, sprawling trees conspicuously planted. In the summer, a person would see cows or horses beneath their cover, hunting for shade. It was brisk today, windy and beaming. I loved days like this. Fall could take your breath away up north. I never tired of the way things mellowed, then popped when the color of the earth's freckles started changing. Tommy and I had used to talk about that—what were trees? He said moles; I said freckles. "Maybe they're hair," I'd offered.

"Hmm?" Tommy asked.

"Just thinking about all these trees."

"Like a beard, huh."

We got to Claire's neighborhood after a couple of wrong turns in central Revel. Every street was a one-way, and Tommy couldn't find his ass from his elbow when it came to going north on Ladder Avenue.

"This is cute," I said of the main drag.

"S'fine. They don't do a lotta business over here. Just like pizza and stuff." He pointed at a coffee shop.

"I like it. I don't think I've ever even been to Revel," I said.

"No reason to come."

Claire's street was quaint, as was the rest of it. The houses were small but well-tended. Claire's yard was a weed quilt, but she had flowers planted by the mailbox and a small sign stuck next to fading, crusty gardenias that said COME ON FALL! There was a wooden H hanging from the front door—Hammond. From what I could gather, Claire had a few kids but they would have been older now. There were no bicycles in the driveway—just an older Ford Mustang with a dent in the passenger side door.

Tommy pulled all the way up the driveway. "Gettin' a little close, aren't we?" His car was nearly touching the Mustang.

"I don't want anybody to try and hightail it outta here."

"Let's not set ourselves up for a confrontation. I want to talk to her, not get into a fight." I'd regaled Tommy with the story of Alaina and Ronna's tussle in the parking lot. He said he'd have paid good money to have seen it.

Tommy had barely shut off the engine when the front door opened. The house was similar to where Natalie Wright lived in Frampton, but the mood was something else entirely. Things were faded, on the edge of disrepair, in need of grace. The girl who stepped out onto the front stoop—missing a couple of bricks, and a safety hazard from my vantage point in Tommy's car—was young, late teens as far as I could tell. She looked a lot like Claire, but ganglier, longer, leaner. She had that mean look of kids who grow up knowing they can't compete with a certain class of people. They'll never be real estate moguls or college professors. Half the flock in Faber was the same way, but I'll be damned if my mother was going to let me have an edge like that. I was raised in the bubble. That was another thing Tommy and I talked a lot about. We hadn't been allowed to touch the underbelly of the foothills. I'd been kept close and special. My mother never complained. I think that's what sets it all in motion—the anger that it all turned out this way and probably will for another hundred years, at least for the infected bloodline. My mother said I was lucky and good. I guess it was all I needed to hear. I didn't ever feel any different from that. We weren't dirt-poor though. Poor but not like dirt. I could never make a face like this girl in front of us on the steps.

She was just about to have a fit about something. It was on the tip of her tongue.

"Who'r y'all?" she said angrily, mostly to Tommy. He'd rolled down his window. I started to get out of the car with my hands up like I was in the process of being arrested and searched—for something I definitely did.

"I'm here to see your mother," I said sheepishly.

"You are?" she said.

"Yes. Is she home?"

"Claire!" the girl yelled into the still-opened door. "There's business people here askin' about you!"

Her drawl was thick and milky. It washed over us, heavy and clinging.

"Why ya call yer mom Claire?!" I yelled at her in my best imitation of her voice.

"'Cause I want to," the girl said back.

"Why are you talking like that?" Tommy asked me.

"Shut it, big boy!" I said, still pretending I was on the level.

A couple of seconds later, Claire Broderick came to the door. I knew it was her immediately. Her face was exactly the same shape and shade of light pink. Her eyes were glassy; I thought for a second maybe she'd been crying. "What?" she said, looking directly at me. It was like the carriage of an old-fashioned typewriter slid hard to the right when our eyes met. The jarring clink was unmistakable.

"I'm Arlene!" I shouted.

The sound of another car came crashing over my voice before I could further introduce myself from where I stood—still in the driveway. I hadn't moved any closer to the house. It would have been difficult to get any closer given where Tommy parked. I turned to see Ronna barreling up behind us in her light gray Ford Taurus. She kicked up some dust as she made the sharp turn, slamming on her brakes just in time to avoid hitting Tommy's car. Her hair's volume—due to driving with her windows down in the sharp early November air—had made a full recovery from the morning and was standing at unprecedented levels. Her face was as the color and sheen of a ripe apple.

"Ronna?" I said, disbelieving.

Tommy opened his door and got out, perhaps concerned that Ronna would go for my face. "Arlene!" he shouted while rounding the front of the car, sliding the last corner on his left butt cheek. "Get down!"

"Claire!" Ronna shouted. She also seemed like she'd been crying or was about to.

"Hey, Ronna," Claire said. She was frumpier, heavier throughout, older and visibly wearier. That happened to women especially. I was to come upon it myself in some years.

"They're lookin' into all that again. She's not a real cop." Ronna pointed at me apologetically.

"No, I'm not a cop," I said like I was giving a seminar on not being a police officer. "But I do want to ask you some questions about the case—your brothers. Mitchell."

Claire looked to Ronna. "They died," she said.

"They died 'fore I was born," the daughter said, sneering.

Claire flinched slightly, her face passed under a shadow of old uncertainty, her long-neglected defense swept under the rug, trampled and forgotten. She'd told the same story two hundred times, and she didn't want to tell it anymore. Her lips pulled to the side, tightly pressed while she scratched her forehead with nubby nails. She hadn't planned on having to answer for this today.

"I know they died—they were murdered!" I announced somewhere between a bellow and a shriek. I was surprised by the seriousness in my voice. I'd been floundering, bouncing around between two sturdier women, ricocheting off their superior knowledge and body mass index, but I was standing on my own in Claire's driveway. I was the one who'd started this ball rolling. "I can't sleep another night on this planet not knowing what happened to them." I was talking to the daughter. I suppose it was easier to address her. I'd never seen her mug shot before. I'd never heard her voice pressed onto the wrinkled strip of an ancient cassette tape. "They were murdered."

"Yeah," Claire said. She might have just figured out I wasn't going to accuse her of anything.

"By J.P. Callahan," I said.

"Let's all stop yelling!" Tommy hollered at the top of his lungs. He was standing next to me in his button-down and tie looking painfully out of place.

"Quiet no one's yelling anymore," I said, both grateful and annoyed by his presence.

"Claire, I told 'em you didn't have nothin' to do with it. I told her to leave you alone." It was Ronna.

Claire was quiet, stoic even. She looked dazed. Ronna dipped into the Taurus and cut the engine, which had been rattling in our midst. The silence enveloped us. Tommy cleared his throat like he was about to shout again, but I spoke before he could. "I just want to know what happened to your brothers. And to Mitchell," I said. "I don't know why I care so much, but I do."

Claire stared at me hard. She was blank, unfeeling, bleary. "I didn't do it," she said. It was as though she was admitting it for the first time. To herself.

"I know," I told her, as if it was my validation she was seeking. It was absurd that I should claim this kind of kinship with a person, a tragedy, an ugly piece of history that had been so neglected by time and everyone who should have cared, but I claimed it. I even thought of myself as Claire's friend. I'd forged an alliance with a perfect stranger. I would probably need to seek therapy after we closed the case—which I was certain we would do, but in this particular moment, I was just as certain of myself. A townie with a wardrobe fit for tacky royalty who worked in the basement of the police station and who couldn't keep her mess of a husband on a short leash, I was a lot of things—many of them unfortunate, but I was certain.

"I know you didn't." I started to walk toward her. "I know you didn't do it."

Tommy abruptly moved his substantial frame in front of me and put his hands on his hips, facing Claire defiantly. "She's trying to help you!" he said.

"Is that Shelby?" Ronna asked. She sounded different—meek and sorry, like a child who's used to being reprimanded, pleading and on the edge of sadness. "She's so grown."

When Claire turned her head to the side, I saw flecks of gray in her dark hair. Her face was pulled down with the weight of age and perennial distress. She didn't speak again, apparently so caught off guard by my sudden, passionate appearance in her driveway that she was rendered mute. She looked around, perhaps trying to figure out what to do to make us all disappear, like her brothers, like Mitchell. I was a shovel digging away her finally level plot. Claire shook her head very slightly and looked down before walking inside the house. Shelby followed closely behind her; the edge had worn off. They were tired people, not up for a fight, just tired.

"Arlene," Tommy said seriously. "I think this might be a bad idea. I think we should leave." I walked around Tommy's lumbering girth; his butt was still on the hood of the car. "Arlene," he said. "This is a bad deal."

I walked to the front door of Claire's house, which she'd left open, and went on inside, completely ignoring Tommy and Ronna.

I shut the door behind me. "You can tell me," I said to her. She was standing in the small hallway that separated the front door from what appeared to be the kitchen. Seeing her so clearly, after all these months staring at the photos, imagining what she would be like, how she talked, how she walked, how she moved her hands. She was unsurprising in everything but her delicateness. She had been distraught and calculating for most of her life, tethered to people and places that were only making it worse, and yet she still held some preciousness in her. It was hope or endurance, which are really the same.

"I just want to know what happened," I said. "I know you don't owe me. I have no right to know. I'm a nobody. I had a dinner party, and only seven people came. No one cares what I think or say. Ronna doesn't even want to be friends with me. I just can't get it out of my head—what happened to those kids. What happened to Mitchell." I was about to mention Lucy but thought better of it. I wanted to tell her I knew Lucy wasn't Mitchell's kid. That I would have left her too. That Claire did the right thing by making sure she went to a good family. "We talked to Natalie," I said, taking a risk. "I know she was seeing J.P. We know she was there that night."

Claire didn't move. Her face remained unchanged. I was a fool. She'd maintained her story for almost twenty years. She wasn't going to tell me anything in the small parquet foyer of her house with its square inlay and chipped walls, half-painted in gray, half-untouched.

"I don't think I'm important. I'm just trying to talk to you—woman to woman. I know I don't understand. Ronna says I can't understand what it was like for you, living in Deck River with Cecil." I pressed on while her face twitched. I could tell it was some effort to swallow. In every photograph I'd ever seen of her, she had her loose curls pulled back in a little knot on top of her head. It was the same today. "Claire, I know what happened to you," I said stupidly. No, I didn't.

That did it. Whatever chance she'd been giving me, she stopped. She turned around and walked toward the kitchen. I could hear a ruckus developing outside; there were shouts and scuffling. I opened the door expectantly.

"You stay out of it, you son of a gun!" It was Ronna, ferocious and yelling. She had Tommy in a headlock.

"Don't mess with her!" I shouted at Tommy. "She's tough as nails!"

Ronna let go of Tommy, and I heard a small hiccup of laughter behind me. Claire was smiling. "Sorry," she said. "Ronna's just always been such a hard-ass."

I gave a small laugh too, feeling like I was breaking through a brick wall with a dull knife. I was making progress, but slowly and vulnerably. "She cares about you a lot," I said. "I do too." I'd probably gone too far again. "She's the best friend you've ever had," I said to Claire. I was pointing at Ronna, who was still panting. I'd almost forgotten about Tommy. It seemed everyone had. He was also panting and standing by the car, massaging his neck, scowling in discomfort.

No one said anything for a long minute. "Can't you just tell us what happened?" I asked. "Tell us the truth."

Claire looked at me from the depths of her suffocated recollection. "I don't know what happened," she said. "But don't blame Natalie. He had a way about him, 'specially with sixteen-year-old girls. We were easy to fool."

Natalie Wright's Journal (removed pages)
July 10, 1984

I know you don't have feelings and you don't care, but I'm probably not going to write in here much anymore. I think it gets me in trouble—all of this thinking about everything. I went back through and just…I don't know, I was really embarrassed, like how could I let myself get caught up in this. And it keeps hitting me that Mitchell is dead. He's really gone. I don't know what I was expecting, like we'd wake up and he'd be there. Back. Like none of it happened.

It's hitting my dad the hardest. I know he thinks it's his fault, because of the way he treated Mitchell in the end. I think my mom thinks it's his fault too. She looks at him different now, either like she's done or like she's holding on to something. It's either-or—she's completely full or completely empty. We were her life. My dad had the business and his family, but for my mom we were everything. She liked the way things were with two kids and Alaina around—drinking iced tea and hanging out on the porch. I don't think she had any really big plans for us, not like my dad did. She probably didn't care if Mitchell went to college or what he did so long as he was happy and nearby. It wasn't the same for her when he quit basketball and said he wasn't going to University of Georgia. She didn't think it was the end of his life or something the way my dad did. I know she didn't like Claire and was worried about that, but it was just a baby. People have them every day. My dad had to make such a big deal out of everything, make everyone think they were doing something wrong—really wrong. I wonder what he'd do if he found out I was seeing J.P. See this is the awful part, sometimes I get a real kick out of thinking that I was so bad or something, like I wanted to be some hot stuff around town like Tina or Claire. I know they're not hot stuff, but that's just the impression. People look at them different than they look at me, and I liked thinking I was their style or something. I can't make sense of it; I just felt better, older, more of everything when J.P. first went after me. When I started to give into it, it was like I was a grown-up and sexy. I mean—I liked it at first, but now I hate it. I hate that I liked it if that even makes sense. It makes me feel powerful but awful about myself all at the same time. It's the guilt. I think I'll always have a lot of guilt. I hate that, especially when I think about everything that happened. I still don't think it was my fault, not about Mitchell at least. I think he might have done that anyway. My mom says now she can see how depressed he was—for a long time. I still won't ask J.P. about the boys. I won't even talk to him, but that's okay, because he won't talk to me either. It's the guilt.

3 1

Ronna's mother gave her statement from her home. By the time we got back to the station, Alaina was there along with Larson Gamble. We all met in the basement even though the lobby or Gamble's office would have been a perfectly suitable place. The basement had a hold on us—collectively. The best thinking was done in such uninspiring environs.

Gamble adjusted the zipper on his pants several times while telling us that Mrs. Davies said she had seen J.P. Callahan's truck parked on Blythe Pass the night the boys were found and that when she circled back by—about a half hour after originally seeing him—he was getting into his truck. There was a passenger inside who Mrs. Davies identified as Natalie Wright from the kids' school. *I thought it was strange, but I didn't put it together. I still can't say I saw anything other than that, but I never saw J.P. over in Deck River before except once when he was picking Claire Broderick up from Ram's.*

I looked at Ronna closely after reading the statement. She was worried about something, stuck in some soft earth that was giving way too readily. "If your mama…" I started to say. "This woulda helped Claire." I was talking too softly to be heard. There was commotion all around and Tommy breathing like a freight train next to me. I couldn't figure out why he was still there, so injected into what we were doing like with a turkey baster.

"What?" Tommy said to me—the only one listening, but I blinked my questions away. It was like I'd seen something that wasn't there, or if it was—I couldn't find it again.

"Do we have permission to bring J.P. Callahan in?" Alaina asked hurriedly. She hadn't greeted a single one of us; her focus remained entirely on Larson Gamble, who was distracted by his pants and seemingly unable to make a next move.

"We can go pick him up?" Gamble answered, still messing with his fly and his attention darting from face to face, empty space to empty space, from desk to chair to filing cabinet. "But I can't charge him. I mean—this isn't enough to charge him with murder."

"What if we get Natalie Wright to talk?" It was Alaina again. I watched her closely. I'd been convinced she didn't want Natalie Wright involved, had done everything in her power to keep her out of it.

"But that's not enough," Gamble scolded. "It's not enough that he was there—in Deck River. There were a few hundred people in Deck River that day. It's not enough."

"But what if she saw him with something? The tranquilizer or rags or…" My voice sounded like it was bouncing off the rim of a hollow log. I cleared my throat, wondering if this would help me get my footing. "No one ever talked to her about anything except where was Mitchell when it happened. And even then, she didn't know. I think it's pretty clear with the way Pendley did the timeline that Mitchell wasn't actually with Natalie when those kids were killed. He was with her that day, but it was never a real alibi."

"I guess," Gamble said uncertainly. "But that was Mitchell's alibi, 'til the end. It was why he couldn't be posthumously charged. He had an alibi."

"It was hers too." It was Ronna, who for some reason was standing behind Alaina with her umbrella in her hand. "That was Natalie's alibi too, and then Mitchell died. So no one could ever challenge her on it."

"You're not saying—" Tommy put his hand over his mouth in fearful, shocked realization. He looked as though he might cry. When he spoke, it was as though everyone realized what I already had—that he had no place among us and was a terrible intrusion. He'd driven me back to the station, but I'd overlooked that he came inside with us. Inside and down the stairs. I hadn't asked him to accompany me, but he was determined to be by my side. He was working through his guilt about Carrie, or Vivian—whatever her name had been—the vomit, and standing in the yard yelling at me the night before. Tommy always did fight guilt by applying himself heavily to whatever part of me he could get his hands on. "Oh my God!" He raised his voice.

"Hold your wad there, Tommy," I said. "I'm not saying that."

"No," Alaina slapped her hand down on my desk. "No. That's going too far. See, that's the problem—I never wanted anyone to know about this, because I knew this would happen! It's not enough that she might have gotten roped into a bad deal with Callahan, now she has to be evil. Now she has to be a murderer. Natalie's not a murderer. Mitchell wasn't either. People get pulled down by the circumstances, their surroundings, they end up in the wrong place at the wrong time with the wrong people. That doesn't mean she murdered someone." Alaina was emphatic. "That's not fair to her or those boys, because that's not what happened. A Wright didn't do this!"

"See, that's..." Ronna began.

"I know, Ronna. I got it." I raised my hand high above my head. Everyone looked at it, possibly expecting that I had planned to demonstrate something with this very hand. I didn't. I just stood there. Still and waiting. "We know that you think she was just trying to get them out of trouble. We know that. Or at least I do. You've told me that."

"I was trying to get them out of trouble!" Alaina yelled. Her eyes were gleaming, full and trying not to dump her rage all over her face. "I was! That's exactly what I was trying to do. Who wouldn't have done that? They were like family to me. I fucked it all up in the end, because I didn't clear anybody's name, and the whole world still thinks Mitchell had something to do with it. I didn't help anybody. I didn't do anything, so why does it matter?"

"It matters because you might have impeded a police investigation," Larson Gamble said studiously.

"Oh please, Mr. Can't-Keep-It-in-His-Pants!" Alaina said. "We've had a lot of fun over the years, Larson, but don't take that tone with me. I know what's up!"

"Ladies, ladies," Tommy said, trying to calm the room down by calling Larson Gamble a woman. "Let's everyone take a breath here."

"So Alaina?" I pressed. "Was Natalie Wright with J.P. when it happened?"

She didn't say anything at first. She was fuming—maybe because she'd both been caught "impeding a police investigation" and also messing around with Mr. Can't-Keep-It-in-His-Pants. It seemed two admissions had been issued, simultaneously.

"No one read the journal. Not at first," Alaina said. "I don't even know who asked her for it, but she handed it over. Everything was in there—about her going with him that night."

"Would anyone like tea?" A jovial voice sounded down the stairs. It was Tyler.

"No!" Ronna shouted back. "Don't leave the desk! It's Thursday!"

"She really is committed to her job," Tommy said approvingly.

"You're goddamn right," Ronna said with a nod.

"Quiet!" I raised my hand in salute again. Again, I was able

326

to silence everyone while doing nothing more than extending a limb.

"So I read it," Alaina said of Natalie's journal. "I read every page. And although she never says she saw anything—because she didn't, she really didn't—I tore some of it out," Alaina said as if she were convincing herself that this is what anyone would have done. "There were already pages missing. A lot of pages missing!" She'd again adopted that false enthusiasm—not too dissimilar from Tommy doing business but with a more manic edge, like if she didn't pretend everything was okay, she was going to take off all her clothes and run through a campfire, shouting *Geronimo!* It was the face of a woman on the edge. I looked at Ronna, who was holding her upper body like she was carrying a refrigerator. She had a slight knee bend, ready to pounce. I hoped we wouldn't have another violent altercation.

"And after I read it—and mind you, this was a while after all this happened," Alaina said. "We'd lost Mitchell, the investigation was stalled. I read it, took out the pages, and shoved it deep in the stack. Then Duke Pendley read it and told me we needed to get the missing pages. He was convinced Natalie knew something about what happened. He still thought it was Claire and Mitchell—mind you. I was the only one who thought...no—" She paused. "I knew it was J.P. I was the only one who was thinking that. J.P. Callahan's name had never even come up, but when I read about Natalie running around with him, I just...I just knew." She looked away, lost in a distant thought that she couldn't quite get her head around. Something fluttering just out of recollection's reach on a breeze she didn't feel anymore. "No…no one even said his name, not before I figured it out."

"Well, if you're so great, then how come you kept him outta jail all this time?" Ronna said. "That didn't do right by anyone. You let him off the hook, so your fake kids wouldn't have to take the fall. That ain't right."

"No," Alaina said, but she didn't offer any other explanation.

"Alaina," Larson Gamble said somberly. "This is a rather serious…"

"I don't have them anymore," she said to the middle of the room. We'd been standing in a circle like a summer camp about to let out, a group of friends who were headed to different parts of the state and who would no longer have anything in common. The bulb dangled above us like a spider from a precariously placed web, swaying on an undetectable current of air sliding by our faces, none of us sure what to do or say.

"That's the first time I've seen Natalie in at least ten years," Alaina went on. "She's a stranger to me. We lost Mitchell, then I lost them all. I lost them all anyway."

"Why?" I said. "Why did they stop talking to you?"

"Because their son died, and they thought I was going to do something about it. Someone took something from them, and they needed a place to put the blame. I stepped in—like a fool—and offered myself right up. This isn't a game." She looked at me sternly. "This isn't for fun. I didn't get involved because I was bored. I was trying to fix something. I was trying to get it right. For my family."

"They ain't your family," Ronna said.

"And Claire isn't yours." Alaina leaned forward with her chest out. Ronna leaned right back, her much larger chest nearly touching Alaina's peasant blouse.

"No," I said. "It's not fun, is it?"

"People's tragedies are not for shits and giggles, that's for sure," Tommy said with an inappropriate lightness, which he quickly followed up with a belly laugh. "HaHA!"

I had been rather enjoying myself though, as uncomfortable as it was to admit it. I thought maybe I liked being frustrated; I liked yelling at Tommy; I had a good time watching grown women fistfight.

"Quiet, Tommy," I said. He stopped making noise, but his mouth remained open. "But Alaina, you can't fix this. You didn't fix it. It was broken long before—"

"You know what, Arlene?" Alaina interrupted me. I thought she was about to really give it to me, really lay into me about my outfits and my spending all this time up on my high horse, but she didn't. "Maybe you would be a good detective. I did give Duke Pendley a big chunk of change to walk away. He was hell-bent on Natalie's diary, and I convinced him to let it go with a little help from my friend, if you know what I mean." She raised an eyebrow.

"Stop talking like a mobster," Ronna said in frustration.

"That was wrong, Alaina," I said.

"Yes, it was." Larson Gamble dipped his head, perhaps slowly coming to the realization that he might have to arrest his girlfriend. I blanched at the thought of them rubbing pelvises. I'd seen Gamble dance. The man could get low, but it wasn't pretty.

"Well, there you have it," Alaina said. "I came clean." She took a deep breath. "I'll do what I have to now; I did what I had to then."

"But you didn't," I said. "If Natalie Wright didn't know…or didn't do anything, then why lie about it?"

No one spoke. I'd answered my own question.

"We're going to have to bring her in," Gamble finally said. "We don't have a choice." A piece of litter slammed against the transom window, obscuring our vision of the trimmed grass and parking lot. It was silent in the basement while everyone looked at the Snickers wrapper stuck to the outside of the building.

"Why can't people clean up after themselves?" Ronna said. It was like it was the only thing left to say. I didn't have the feeling of profound satisfaction I'd been hoping for. I felt even emptier when I really thought about it. It wasn't a relief. It still happened. My mind went to the photo of the boys on the riverbank. That didn't go away, no matter what we knew about Duke Pendley's Tudor house.

A CONDEMNED MAN

I LEFT 'EM THERE. I wasn't going to take anybody with me. I really didn't know what I was going to do 'til I did it. I had this urge, kind of like when I want to see a girl. It presses on me. I get real focused to make something happen. I've taken a lot of chances with girls, some boys too. I don't care who starts my urges. Like with Claire and a lot of those types of girls, it was kind of like who cares. No one's really paying attention to them. Tina always overlooked that stuff, because she didn't want to be alone. She's always worried about saving face. I know that about her. Once you know something about a person, you can work around it. I don't want to be alone neither but I'd overlook other things. Tina don't run around on me. She's too focused on keeping me captured. That's how she gets her rocks off. She thinks she's got me in a cage or something.

But I did start to get different pressure. I wanted to be with different kinds of girls, like real different. I wanted to fight those kids and kill 'em off and get with like…the good girls. I'd done all the bad girls and got them all wound up but I hadn't really ruined anybody. Someone like Claire Broderick is already ruined. I wanted to get someone good and condemn 'em. I feel like the Charleys did that to me. Like my line was right where it was supposed to be—'cause everyone's got good and bad in them. That was why Jorge prayed all the time. He said he'd want to do bad stuff, but Jesus would lay a calming hand on him. The Charleys beat me up so good all the time that Jesus didn't try to lay any hand on me. I got so mean from it. I think my mama told God not to help me, because she liked screwing the Charleys' dad. It's always been like that in my family—the urges get in the way. It's a lot of pressure with so many urges. I really wanted to condemn someone like me. I like the feeling I get when the line is gone. I just wanted to see if I could push it away for someone else. I think she liked it too. She liked letting me tell her what we were going to do, and when it was done, she seemed happy. She changed some. I think it was happiness because she got to see another side of life. There are so many sides of things. People really do get set in one way, but there are others. I showed her.

3 2

We all got in Tommy's car this time to drive to Natalie's. I was uncomfortable with how Claire had become an afterthought. We'd barged in on her, made her defend herself, then left. Now Alaina had told us what she'd done, and it seemed pretty definitive. I thought we should have called Claire or released a statement that she had nothing to do with it. I thought we should have done something.

No one else mentioned her. I could see a deep-set wrinkle in Ronna's forehead release and her eyebrows glide up her face a centimeter or two. She was lightened—Alaina had been made a villain and no one was talking about Claire anymore.

Then Tommy made the mistake of asking if we should go to Ram's first.

"Why?" I said. "So you can get a good look at some river tail?" I was back to yelling at him, mostly because I hadn't eaten, and there he was tagging along with us like he didn't have anything better to do. I hadn't asked for his assistance, and I didn't like him trying to infiltrate my detectives' club—even if one of the detectives was now being detained, soon to be the center of her own criminal investigation. Tommy did, however, have the largest car, and I think Ronna secretly enjoyed riding in a Mercedes. She'd first suggested I drive, then gave in willingly when I said I was low on gas, and maybe we should take Tommy's car.

"I'll drive!" Tommy shouted passionately. There was a bag of barbecue peanuts on the front seat. I hadn't noticed them before and wondered if I'd been sitting on them all the way to and from Claire's.

"It's not open anymore," Ronna corrected me about Ram's. "And no, I'd never go back there. I worked as a shoeshine girl there for some time. I don't have the fondest memories."

"Shoeshine girl?" I said.

"Yes, Arlene." She glared at me. "I was a shoeshine girl." Her gaze was unflinching, even while settling herself into the back seat of Tommy's car. I thought maybe I should offer her the front, being that she was a guest, but I really did love to sit shotgun while Tommy was behind the wheel. I couldn't imagine looking at the back of his head. I'd spent the better part of my life reaching over with my left hand to give him a squeeze or a tickle. A wave of soft sadness grazed my face as I buckled in. Like a long piece of silk being dragged over my face, I had the fleeting sensation of being precious, touched by a tenderness and innocence that was only available to the sublimely inexperienced. It was a reminder that nothing would ever be the same; this flick of a feather along the side of my memory I had barely had and would not again be able to properly recall. Just like Tommy's red truck, it was gone.

"You okay, Arlene?" Tommy asked.

"Yes, sorry," I said. "I was thinking of the past...or something."

"That'll do it," he said, smiling at me. My only friend in the world. Even when I was yelling at him.

Tommy started the car while we all settled in. "What are we even going to say? I can't arrest her. I'm not a cop," I said.

"I'll arrest her," Ronna said. She clasped her hands and flipped them inside out, giving herself a good stretch while she straightened her arms. "I can bring her in with one arm tied behind my back."

"No," I said. Tommy had pulled out of the parking lot; we were making our way up Douglas Street at a steady clip. Larson Gamble was staying at the station; he needed to decide what to do about Alaina. He'd called her a flight risk before being reminded that the nearest airport was two hours away in any given direction. "No. We shouldn't go. This is up to real law enforcement, not a bunch of local idiots," I said.

"Speak for yourself," Ronna said. "I am not an idiot."

"I know," I sighed. "Sorry, Ronna."

"Thanks," Tommy said lightly.

"That's not what I mean. Stop the car, Tommy."

He pulled over and looked at me. His face was doughy and willing. I thought of the first time I flew on an airplane. I was with my family and going to see my grandmother in Texas. We'd driven there before, but my mother put her foot down and said she wouldn't do thirteen hours behind the wheel again. I was around thirteen at the time. There was a young boy on the plane—unaccompanied. He got to wear a special pin on his shirt and was given extra attention and pretzels by the flight attendants. I thought he must have been ten years old. I couldn't believe he was brave enough to go on the plane by himself. I was glued to my mother's side, always looking up to her or my father for direction, reaction, some sort of clue as to what I should do, how I should act. I even needed help with my seat belt, thinking it somehow different than in the car. My mother had to tell the flight attendant that I wanted cranberry juice, because I was too intimidated to order it myself. I'd always looked to Tommy for the same. I required him. I was not the little boy on the airplane, able to go it alone. This was one of the most significant moments of my life, sitting in Tommy's filth-ridden Mercedes about to go harass a witness from a long-ago, mostly forgotten case—and I was with Tommy. I still couldn't do anything by myself.

"I'll go on my own," I said.

"Oh no you won't." Ronna unbuckled even while the car was still in motion. "I'm not letting her get away with this!"

"Ronna, sit back and gettahold of yerself!" I hollered. "You didn't want anything to do with this a month ago, and now you're like a sweater I can't take off. I started this thing. I'm lead investigator in the agency, and I..."

"Hold on," Tommy said, raising his hand. He then carefully put the car in park and turned to me. "You girls go. I'm not a part of this. Take my car. I'll walk back to the station and wait for you. They have peanut butter Twix in the vending machine."

"That is your favorite," I said seriously.

I reached for the door handle, thinking of how to tell Ronna I wanted to do this on my own. I paused my movement while Tommy got out of his own side of the car. Ronna's flushed face and eager sweating softened my resolve. I thought about the burden of her knowledge.

Her mother didn't want to tell anyone she saw J.P. and Natalie, because she was looking for Ronna at Ram's bar. That was what I decided. It was to protect Ronna from embarrassment, but it didn't seem like enough. In her statement to Gamble, she'd said she was inviting trouble if she told anyone she was over there looking for her daughter. Gamble apparently had made a comment along the lines of: surely it was more important to aid in a murder investigation, especially where there were children involved, to which Ronna's mother merely said, "Nobody really seemed to care about those kids. They'd-a-cared about 'em if they thought they were turnin' tricks at Ram's, but not if they just got dumped somewhere. They'd been dumped somewhere their whole life."

Ronna was one of those kids, no matter how hard she tried to shake it. She was a Deck River girl, part of the sad scenery of a place that would be pretty if only the people weren't such trash. The leaves are the same on the trees in Deck River, but nobody thinks to admire their sheen in a spring sun. The people are like the abandoned houses and trash on the side of the road too, just one of a thousand reasons that's nowhere to be from, not even for a leaf.

"Ronna, I'd be honored if you'd join me," I said. "I know this has weighed heavily on you over the years."

"You don't know nothin'," she said, but it didn't hurt my feelings. I just thought she sounded sincere.

"Was there anybody else there?" I said as Tommy began his trek back to the station and I settled into the driver's seat. I'm not sure why I asked. Alaina had given me some confidence in my instincts, and I was going to exercise it. I'd had a bug in my ear all day about why Ronna and her mother kept seeing Natalie and J.P. a secret all this time. I was as surprised as Ronna to hear myself ask.

"Huh?" Ronna said, adjusting the waist of her skirt and smoothing the fabric over her knees.

"Did your mama see someone else with J.P.?"

"No," she snapped back at me. "No!" Apparently it was a denial worth repeating.

August 1, 1984

I'm not going back to school in Faber. My parents found a house in Jesper, so we're going to move over that way. School starts in a couple of weeks, and I guess I'm going to be late. I don't really think anyone knows about what happened outside Faber. It's not like national news or something. People here still think Mitchell did it. We get looked at funny at the store, at the gas station, wherever. We haven't been out to eat since Mitchell died. It's too small here; everyone knows but they don't know what to say. If they thought it wasn't his fault, and the police messed up, then they'd be over with brownies. Instead, they turn away and pretend they don't know my mother.

Even Alaina isn't really coming around anymore. My dad kind of told her to go screw herself, like he really said that. She got all chummy with the police and is like all of their best friend. My dad says it's her fault that the case went off the rails. They kind of just dropped it—the police. Like, everyone was doing all this research and interviewing people, then they stopped. It's over. No one even talked to J.P. about it. I was thinking I could write an anonymous letter or something to the station to say that I think something weird was going on that night. Claire's gone. She never even looked back, and I don't think she ever talked to J.P. again. Sometimes he looks at me at the stable, like stares me down. I feel like I must be so attractive that he can't help it, but that's just such a bad way to think about things that it literally makes me want to kill myself. I don't know what's wrong with me anymore. Things were better but now they're bad again. I let everyone down. I'm going to send a letter to the police. Or I guess I could just tell Alaina. She works for them now. I'll make her swear not to say I was there. I can just tell her and let her figure out how to handle it. I know she doesn't want me to get in trouble, and she says it's her mission to make sure Mitchell's name is cleared. She swore to my mother she was going to solve the case, which is probably pretty stupid because she's not a real detective. I mean—I guess she is now. If I tell her, she might get them at least to look at J.P., or start spreading rumors that it was him. It would feel good to get back at him. I definitely think he ditched me. I heard he was hanging out with Dana Foster now. She's even younger than I am. She's got a belly-button ring and goes to the tanning bed all the time. I think I'll tell Alaina that J.P. and I went out there that night. I really think I will. She'll know what to do. I mean—I didn't see anything, but he did something bad.

I just can't pretend anymore. I feel like everyone can see that I'm not good anymore, and that's why my parents really want to move. They don't think we're good people. They think they messed up or something. They're trying to start over. I hope Lucy's a better kid than me and Mitchell were.

33

We were almost to Natalie's house—actually in her neighborhood—when I heard honking behind me. I'd been deep in revelatory thought while Ronna slept in the passenger seat. She'd brought her small, tightly furled umbrella with us in spite of near-perfect weather and spent the first part of the long drive to Frampton rapping it on her left palm, as if in anticipation of giving someone a hard beating. She quickly thereafter fell asleep, her mouth opened wide and lopsided while small gasping sounds escaped her throat. The umbrella, however, remained clinched tightly in her hand, a death grip of sorts.

"Oh my God," I said as I was nearly overtaken by Alaina in the Wagoneer. She was flashing her brights, honking, and swerving wildly. All I could think was either she'd killed Gamble, escaped, and come now to kill me, or he'd released her thinking her hardly dangerous or likely to flee. I hoped to God the latter was the reason she was bearing down on me like a man with a broken leg on a crutch.

I pulled the car over, nearly decapitating a mailbox. Alaina pulled up next to me with her windows rolled down. "Let me talk to her," she said rather calmly. "Let me talk to her."

"You already talked to her!" Ronna was awake and screeching over me.

"She'll tell you the truth if you let me talk to her first. Please. Please." Alaina's face was stricken, remorseful, haggard. Deep lines had revealed themselves, cut into the surface of her skin with regret's chisel and guilt's relentless pounding. She squeezed her eyes shut, then reopened them. "I won't let you down."

———

Ronna and I sat in the car, idling in Natalie's driveway, for the better part of half an hour before Alaina and Natalie emerged. They were holding hands, Natalie's face blotchy from crying while Alaina remained stoic, decisive, pinched.

"Let's go back to Faber," Alaina said through my open window. I had Genesis in the tape deck and had been on a bit of an emotional journey while listening. Phil Collins really knew how to get under my skin. "She's going to come in and make a statement."

"About twenty years too late!" Ronna bellowed. She'd drifted in and out of consciousness while we'd sat in the car, falling asleep then reawaking angry and confused, limbs flailing while she tried to hide the drool that repeatedly escaped from her mouth while she dozed. The left lapel of her navy print dress was soaked and filmy.

"But it's never too late to make something right," Alaina said like a greeting card.

"No," I said either in agreement or dismay. I couldn't be sure.

"She rides with us," Ronna said, slamming the umbrella against her palm once more.

"Fine," Natalie said. "That's fine. I'll get in back."

It was a long drive back to Faber. A tractor trailer overturned on 75 North that shut down four lanes. We sat for a full fifteen minutes without moving, before being directed to drive on the shoulder, one car at a time. No one spoke, except to mutter dismay at the wreckage and delay. I'd been concerned Ronna would be red-hot and firing away at Natalie for the full seventy miles, but she said nothing. No one did. We watched different patches of the side of the road slide by us in chunks. Pine after pine after pine— it was one long tunnel. Different from the mountain roads where the trees grabbed each other from either side. This was like being a ware in a factory, making your way from one stage of the appara- tus to the next. Claire had worked in the hose factory. That closed down some years earlier—production moved elsewhere. Now, if you worked local it was at the marble plant. I wasn't sure what they did there, something to do with marble, but they didn't make anything like at the hose factory. I chuckled a little thinking about Tommy and his pancake factory.

"Where did he get that from?" I said to myself.

"What?" Ronna said. I was instantly grateful for Tommy—I couldn't laugh with other people the way I could laugh with him, even if I mostly yelled at him lately. I had definitely yelled at him about the pancake factory.

Larson Gamble and Duke Pendley—who I had to be told was Duke Pendley—were waiting outside the station when we finally arrived. Pendley was an old man, hanging from his skeleton like torn rags. His face, sagging and hollow, looked at us forlornly as we exited our cars. I knew shame when I saw it. It was true that those boys hadn't mattered all that much. That was the real shame of it all. No one felt they were owed anything. No stepping forward on their behalf.

"Hey," Alaina said as she walked up to the two men. "Why are you out here?"

"Tyler cooked broccoli in the microwave," Larson Gamble said. "Cleared the place out."

"Oh," Alaina said, eyeing Pendley. I had to imagine it had been a long time since they'd last seen each other.

"Unbearable," Pendley said. "He used Velveeta too." I could tell Pendley had been a good-looking younger man, but his later years had not been kind.

I heard Natalie take a deep breath from the back seat. "Okay, then," she said as she opened her door.

I was not allowed to sit in on the interview. Apparently, the fact that I had been sent to retrieve a potential suspect was way beyond the bounds of professionalism and could get Gamble in trouble should we ever be audited. I figured most of what we were doing was forbidden by the police code, but this was the first I'd heard of anyone caring.

"I suppose you could be an independent contractor," Gamble mumbled under his breath.

"Yes, in my husband's car," I said. "Wait a minute—where's Tommy?"

"He walked home," Gamble said. "The machine was out of Twix. The guy is coming to refill it next week."

"Poor Tommy," I said. Gamble was eyeing me. I realized fully that I'd been given such breadth because he was hoping to have a little below-board fun with me at some time during my employ. What I might have mistaken as faith in me, confidence in my gumption, was now just a guy dancing to Def Leppard next to an olive bowl, hoping I'd notice the rhythmic thrust of his hips. I was disgusted but remained committed to my cause.

Alaina and Natalie were interviewed separately, then together. They combined their stories and confirmed that Natalie went to Deck River with J.P. the evening of the murders. She did not see what happened but said he had brought tranq and rags with him and made no secret of it. She said he was away, and not visible from her vantage point in the truck, for about twenty minutes and did not tell her what he was doing. She did not see the Broderick boys and claimed to have no idea what she and J.P. were doing there. She said J.P. claimed he was "cleaning up a mess." She didn't elaborate on what they did after they left Deck River. She said that was kind of the end of their dalliance. Somehow it had been a demarcation— one she apparently did not challenge.

"I could tell something was wrong," she said. "He kind of went into himself after that. And I had...I don't know, the creeps. When we drove away from the river that night, I turned around to look behind us. I could see something on the ground. Or someone. I think I knew right then. It was on the news later, and Mitchell had to go talk to the police, but I didn't... I don't know what I was thinking. I was sure but then I wasn't, because why would he do that? I was sixteen. I don't know..."

I listened to the tapes after Natalie had left. Alaina drove her home. Alaina was going to face criminal repercussions for withholding crucial investigative information, but Natalie would not. There was no use in it. Duke Pendley was also going to face charges for taking bribes as a public official. He and Alaina might go to jail. Larson Gamble seemed reluctant for any of this to happen and just as reluctant to share the details of it with me. I was suddenly Arlene in the basement with my fancy outfits and my Sharpie again—a bag tagger who didn't really belong, playing at something, trying at significance. The afternoon was a transformation, or a reversion.

Ronna went back to her desk and sat down with her little black headset propped on her head, the earpiece resting on her left ear and the mouthpiece perched in front of her lips. She had not resorted to violence at any point after beating herself with the umbrella in the car. As soon as Natalie and Alaina came out of their respective interview rooms—one being the custodial closet, because the Faber Police Station didn't have two interview rooms—Ronna appeared deeply satisfied. My admiration for her grew. She had really only wanted Natalie and Alaina to tell the truth. That was what all the bull-in-a-china-shop act was about. I'd been the catalyst, but the bird finally got the worm. I couldn't help but think I owed Ronna a debt of gratitude, and maybe she me, but we'd have to get to that.

I drove home after state authorities arrived at the station. One of them was an attractive woman who Gamble immediately sidled up to. He did a shoulder shimmy when he offered her a seat at his desk. I caught him sticking his chest out when they were talking by the front desk and thought I smelled fresh cologne when he returned from "grabbing something" from his car.

Tommy was in the backyard, watering the weeds—at least he tried. He didn't know which part of the yard actually needed watering. He had skipped over my dying vegetable garden—none of the fall planting had been successful—and gone straight for the mulch pile and the weeds along the back fence.

"Hello, super detective extraordinaire!" he said upon seeing me. He was wearing my gardening gloves and had a large chocolate stain on the belly of his shirt.

"It's so good to see you, Tommy Ridell," I said. I was smiling. Really smiling.

"Did you get him?" Tommy hollered over the whir of the hose, now just spraying a steady stream right at the house's siding.

"Oh," I said, startled. "No. I can't...get anyone really. They sent a state trooper over to his house. They're bringing him into the county police station in Feld."

"So you won't get to lay the hammer down?" Tommy asked.

"No," I said, suddenly annoyed. "No, I was never going to lay anything down."

"Right." He walked over to turn the hose off.

"I think we're supposed to get rain tonight," I said, further agitated by this waste and misunderstanding. "I wasn't going to get to like prosecute J.P. Callahan or something."

"Well, if he did it," Tommy said.

"What do you mean, if?"

"Isn't it innocent until proven guilty?"

"Right, but that's in court," I said. "He did it. Natalie and Alaina told us he did it."

"Okay!" Tommy threw his hands up. My gardening gloves were stretched to their breaking point and made it only about halfway down Tommy's hand. "Sorry. I was just saying, you've got this Alaina lady on record saying she paid the old dog a buncha money to get lost, and then you've got the girl saying she was out there with the cowboy...J.P....but nobody saw anything."

349

"So what," I said. "He'll confess now. We've got his balls in a vise!"

"Got it." He smiled disbelievingly. I was totally thrown off, offended even at his casual attitude.

"We solved the case, Tommy."

"Okay! Okay. Just as far as I can tell, the fat lady hasn't sung yet."

"She'll sing when he's behind bars for good!"

"Good," Tommy said, still not fully committed. "That's good."

My mood—whatever it had been—had changed. "You know, Tommy," I said more calmly, less combatively. "Ronna's mother kept that secret for a long, damn time. I just don't buy that it was 'cause Ronna was over shining shoes at Ram's. I just don't buy that."

"Maybe she was doing worse?" Tommy raised an eyebrow suggestively.

"No, I don't think that's it," I said. "I really don't think that's it."

A CONDEMNED MAN

I ONLY MET HIM THE once before. He came to the stables with Natalie. One of those dads who don't come around much but when they do they think they're in charge of everything. I remembered him. He didn't know nothing was going on with me and Nat, but he was nosy anyway. He called me up the next day, just outta the blue like that. He called during the day when none of the kids were around. School time. That's how all this got going. He said he wanted me to help get ridda his problems. He was meanin' more like Claire, get her to go away or…I don't know what he meant, but he got my wheels going. He said he could give me some money to make Claire get lost.

I told Natalie to stay in the car that night 'cause he was there. It was like this added pressure to make sure she didn't see him. Or him her, 'cause he woulda killed me! If he saw I was with Natalie—you know, like that. There was more pressure on me. It made me even more into it, you know. The feeling got deeper.

He was kinda arguin' with me when I held 'em down and showed him what to do. He asked me if I'd ever done it before, and I was like—of course not, man, not on a person. I can remember the way those kids were looking at us, like they trusted us but they knew what was gonna happen. He fought with me more'n they did. He started to figure it out and got scared like he was gonna have to stop it, but he couldn't. "The writing's on the wall, my friend," I told him. "This is done. I'm over the line—I'm there." He didn't know what I was talking about. He was thinking he was a fool. And he was. Some people are just fools when it comes to their kids. I don't have kids. Never wanted 'em. Just seems like another thing to make your line move all the time. Jorge said his kids made him a better man, but I don't see that often. Jorge was a true believer. I'd be ashamed for him to know what I done. He's the only person. Not Natalie's dad. I did whatever I wanted in front of him, and it didn't bother me to see he was so upset about it. It would've bothered me to see Jorge. Jorge has kids. Little kids like Claire's brothers.

It was Dan's idea. The whole thing. I just helped. I don't know why really. He said he wanted my help but when I showed up with the tranq he said it wasn't what he was talking about.

I don't know what he thought we were gonna do. I told him to meet me over in Deck River that night, so he said he would. I knew what I was gonna do. He shoulda figured we weren't gonna like write Claire a mean letter or something.

I had some time with Nat first, you know—but after that night, I didn't really see her anymore. I couldn't after what we did.

She didn't see anything. She didn't see him. I know she didn't. I'd've been able to tell if she saw him. I woulda known. I can tell stuff like that. She woulda run or somethin'. She was just sitting real tight down on the floor of the truck when I got back. She was upset 'cause I left her there for so long, but not 'cause she thought something went down or that her dad was there.

It was hard to see her after that. I guess I felt bad, not for what we did, but for how it ended up for her. Natalie. Yeah, that was bad what happened to them. He wasn't a man like me at all. He got too wound up, tight like. That was his pressure. His pressure came from wanting to make it right for his son, just get rid of the thing that was poisoning him. Like a weed killer. You ever watch it after you spray? They just shrivel up and die; they rot right there on the spot. He was tryin' to do that to something—tryin' to fix it, get rid of it, get it to shrivel up and die. I just don't think he knew what that means. I seen all sorts of animals die. I knew what it would look like. He said he didn't mean to hurt nobody. After. He got mad at me, shoved me around, but he was scared. Simple kinda fella—just thinks everybody is the way he is. Doesn't think there's badness or that anybody's gonna do anything wrong. That's why he was so mad at his son like that. He didn't get why his son would go off with Claire and make the family name bad, but people do that. He just wasn't the kind of guy to do it. He wasn't the kind of guy to kill those kids either. He asked me to help him. I kinda think it's 'cause he knew I was the kinda guy who could.

But I don't know, maybe he really did just want me to push Claire around or something so she'd go. He kept saying that—"I told you to scare her!" All I could think was that I did. I did scare her. And she left.

34

G amble called me the next morning first thing. I'd planned to go to work. Nothing was said the day before about whether or not I was still needed at the station, so I assumed I would resume my role as normal. I was up, dressed in a flannel shirt and jeans with my hair tied back in a bandanna. I looked like Rosie the Riveter. I wasn't sure what I was trying to prove, but I ate three hard-boiled eggs for breakfast and did a couple of squats by the refrigerator, feeling strong and capable. Tommy had left very early. He needed to catch up after taking the day off the day before.

"We've got J.P. at the station. We're going to interview him," Gamble said.

"In the closet or the interview room?"

"The room," Gamble said. "Ormond spilled bleach all over the closet floor last night. It's being fumigated right now. No one can go in there."

"Has he confessed?"

"No. They had him in county lockup all night, but he didn't say anything. The officer who brought him in said he didn't seem surprised to be picked up. Said he just went with them. His wife was making a big fuss, but he didn't say a thing."

"Okay," I said. "Is there any evidence for me?"

"Yeah, there was a house fire off Madden last night, so there are a few things. I just wanted you to be prepared that he's going to be there."

"Yes. I'm prepared." I paused. "Are there houses off Madden?"

"Just the one. But I guess not anymore."

"Shame."

"Not really. It was a dump."

We were both quiet for some time, breathing into the receiver. I thought I might grow so uncomfortable I'd tell him that a lot of ladies around the precinct—and even a couple of the men—were calling him Chester the Molester behind his back.

"Arlene," Gamble said quietly. "Listen."

"I don't call you that," I said, forgetting that I hadn't actually said the part about him being a sexual deviant out loud.

"What?"

"Nothing. Sorry. I'm listening."

"He's agreed to give us a confession."

"Oh my God."

"Right, but…he says he wasn't alone."

"I thought you said he wasn't talking. And anyway—we know he wasn't alone. Natalie Wright was with him. In the truck. We know this! She admitted it last night. Alaina too." I was strident.

"He's not talking. His lawyer said he'd talk to us, said he was willing to fess up, but that he wasn't alone. He said he'd confess if we brought the other guy in."

"Wait, what?"

"The other guy…he say's he'll…"

"No, I heard you. Who? Who's the other guy?"

"Mitchell's father. Dan Wright. He says Claire was there too. Says she didn't have anything to do with it, but she found him with the kids. He says she's known all along."

All I could think was that that was why Ronna's mother never told anyone. She saw Claire too.

"Okay," I said quietly after a long pause. "Okay." Those Deck River folks sure stuck together.

A CONDEMNED MAN

His son woulda done the same thing to himself if it'd been Claire dead with a rag in her mouth. He didn't kill'm'self 'cause of the boys. And anyway I'da liked to have done that to her. Just sometimes I'da like to have shoved something down her throat. They's already dead when she showed up. I saw her coming when we was still there, but she didn't say nothin'. She saw Dan. She just didn't say nothing; she just showed up. She was lookin' for those kids, 'cause she always took good care of 'em even if she didn't know how. I told you what happened. I did it, but he was there. He wanted me to do somethin'. I's never gonna do anythin' to Claire. Dan mighta. It was Claire he's so mad at anyway. That's why he's lyin'. Claire just showed up. Don't let him tell you she was in on it. It was just me 'n' him. It was his idea. We just had different ideas about it. I can still see the look on her face, you know. She didn't even cry; she just stood there, staring at me. She knew it was me who done it. She probably thought I's gonna do it a long time before that. I kinda felt sorry for her standing there starin't at me. She never did seem to be able to do anything about her life.

35

I wept for a week straight after I found out about Claire. I kept saying to Tommy, "She knew! She knew! Why didn't she say something? Didn't she care?" He'd calm me down here and there, trying to say the right thing but mostly failing.

"There, there, Arlene."

"We can't possibly understand what goes through other people's heads and hearts."

"Here, have a cookie."

"You sound tired."

"No, I wouldn't have done that either."

"Want a back rub?"

I found I would shake uncontrollably when I got to really ruminating on it. They'd interviewed Claire. I heard those tapes too. She sounded far away and empty when she talked.

"I couldn't find them nowhere. Cecil didn't know where they

were neither. He told me to go out and look. Mitch had the babies. I was just real low then. I'd get tired and fall asleep everywhere. Just the way it was after the baby came. Real low. I went over to where they'd play sometimes, cause there's boards nailed to a tree there, so they could climb. I don't know who did it, but it's like a ladder. Been that way forever. They'd climb up on the tree and just sit there. It rained that afternoon, but they didn't really care about rain. I saw J.P. standing there. I couldn't figure it. Mitch's dad was there too. He was crying. They saw me but they didn't say nothing. I turned around and walked away. I didn't want to get Mitch's dad in trouble, 'cause he was already so upset all the time, and I knew it was J.P. who did it. There was no doubt in my mind."

"She didn't want to get Mitchell's dad in trouble, because she was planning all along to leave the baby with the Wrights," I told Tommy over breakfast. I was usually feisty in the morning, then weepy and disconsolate as the day wore on. What started as fury turned to waterworks and melancholy by dinner. I was doing a lot of eggs—scrambled in the morning, fried at night. Tommy asked if we were pinching pennies; I told him no. I was having trouble looking at bloody flesh at the moment.

"I know it in my bones, Tommy. If it'd just been J.P Callahan standing there, Claire'da run straight to the police, but she had a plan. That was Cecil's baby, and she was gonna leave it with a good family. A family from the right side of town. She had it all worked out. When she saw him standing there with J.P. Callahan, she just didn't know what to do. I bet she was kinda relieved in a way. She could really walk away. They were all gone, and Lucy had somewhere nice to go."

"Except Lucy didn't." Tommy always interjected when I got going on this. "She knew it wasn't a nice place to go. Mitchell's dad helped J.P. Callahan kill her brothers."

"I don't think he helped," I said furiously. "Pass the Lawry's." I was moody all the time now. Moody and furious at the state of things.

For a while, Tommy didn't let me go into work. There was a trial in town. Dan Wright and J.P. Callahan, not together but back-to-back. There was a lot of local press around, filming outside the station. Ronna wore a balaclava to and from the car so as to avoid scrutiny. I'd called her at the station a few times just to check in and chat, but she always had an excuse to quickly get off the phone with me. There was a toilet overflowing, Tyler had sprained his ankle, someone stepped in gum in the lobby. I knew she just didn't want to talk. I understood her completely, however much it bothered me. The feeling was gone, and we were never going to be able to get it back. We knew too much—mostly about each other.

Ronna and I had one honest conversation before she started rattling off excuses every time I called or came by. I think it was because she laid herself so bare that she couldn't stand to talk to me anymore. I'd gone in to tag some evidence, before Tommy said I needed a break. The superfluousness of my job there had never been clearer. I told Gamble I couldn't come in for a while, and he said "okey dokey." I think the mean way I was holding my face had turned him off a little. "Pour Some Sugar on Me" was playing in the lobby on Ronna's small radio that she kept on her desk, always tuned to Comfort 101.9. He didn't move a muscle, and I know he heard it. He would shake his hips for me no more.

"Your mama saw Claire, didn't she?" I asked Ronna my last morning at the precinct. I'd done my bangs in her style—using a half bottle of Aussie spritz and my curling iron. I'd been hoping she'd feel the connection we once shared. I even put some leftover meatloaf in my purse in a not-entirely-sealed Ziploc baggie. Smells are the most powerful when trying to conjure nostalgia. At least that's what Lacey said; she'd read a book on it while on the StairMaster and made sure to tell me.

"Shush now, Arlene," Ronna said pleadingly. "We got the guy now. And you did that. You can feel good about that. Okay? He's going down." It was almost Christmas. I'd assumed the onset of the holidays was going to make me feel better, but it didn't. I'd lied and told my family I'd become a vegetarian at Thanksgiving and didn't eat a bite of food while we were at my parents' house, not even the vegetables.

"I don't want to feel good, Ronna. I wanna know what happened," I said. It was blustery and gray out. The holiday decorations on the precinct's front railing and doors looked cheap and like they'd been hung out there a few seasons too many, in dire need of a refresh, or a trash can. It wasn't cheerful to see Santa's face on a scallop of shiny garland hanging from Ronna's desk. It actually made me feel sad and more alone than ever.

"What happened is this, Arlene. And I'll never repeat it. He raped her a hundred times. He waited 'til after her mom died, but he was awful to her. Made her life awful. I really do think she loved Mitchell. I think she wanted to marry him and run away together, but Cecil got her pregnant. Okay? She was Mitchell's first girl…you know, in that way, and he didn't know to even think she'd be doing it with anybody else. It never even occurred to him. She loved Mitchell. She got the idea in her head that he was a way out. When she saw his dad out there with J.P., it just stunned her. She didn't want to tell Mitchell. That's why she didn't tell anybody. Because of how it would hurt Mitchell—and Lucy. The plan all along was that Lucy would go with Mitchell and his good family. That was the plan. She didn't want to hurt nobody else." Ronna inexplicably had a pack of bologna next to her keyboard. I glanced at it before she hurriedly pushed it into her lap and scooted forward so I couldn't see it anymore.

"If she was trying to help Mitchell, she sure did a shitty job of it," I said. "He killed himself. He got accused of the murders, Ronna. What you're sayin' to me doesn't make sense."

"She didn't know he was gonna do that, Arlene! She got accused too. She was trying to figure out what to do, and then he went and hung himself." Ronna's eyes were wet. I'd never seen her show any emotion but anger, more specifically anger at Alaina. She reached behind the left lens of her glasses to wipe a tear that was fighting with her resolve to hang tough in front of me. "You don't even know," she said. "You don't even know. She was worried about that baby. She didn't know he was gonna do that."

"Did you know Mitchell, Ronna?"

"He was a good boy," Ronna said, sniffling. She adjusted her glasses, removed the bologna from her lap, and used her index finger to fluff her bangs. "I like your hair today," she said to me. "Looks real nice."

"Thanks," I said. I reached into my purse, thinking I could present the leftover meatloaf, but Ronna spoke first.

"And Arlene," she said. "My mama wudn't never gonna tell on Claire. We just don't do that."

36

The mayor held a vigil for the boys, Mitchell included but in an awkward way that still seemed to insinuate that he was to blame for what happened. We were to also feel sorry for Mitchell Wright, but not really sorry. People came and cried and lit candles. There were some photos of the kids and stuffed animals. The whole thing left a bad taste in my mouth. Most of the people crying in their raincoats were old enough to have done something for the Broderick children while they were still alive. All I'd heard was how bad it was for them, and then all the grannies showed up with their trembling lips, twenty years after the fact.

"They bought them stuffed animals now?" I told Tommy before we abruptly left the ceremony. "They don't need stuffies now." Tommy silently agreed, which is what he did about everything that had to do with the case. He agreed with me without offering a syllable in commentary.

His only advice had been that I should stay away from the station, take a leave of absence, allow Tyler and Ronna to pick up the slack. "Oh, there's no slack," I'd said. "I didn't do anything there. You were right. I was eye candy for Gamble." Tommy didn't comment.

I was already looking in the classifieds for something else. I decided I liked working and wanted to do more of it, but not necessarily in the criminal law field or in a basement.

I'd never been so unsettled as I was knowing what actually happened to those boys. It was a quiet kind of unsettled. The truth cast a gloom, a sinister shading to everything around me. Suddenly Faber seemed like an awful place to live. It was like something out of a horror film or a ghost story where everyone is miserable with sallow skin and wearing gray all the time. I had a wad of remorse caught in my throat, for the kids but also for the Wright family, mostly because they were casualties of their own vanity. And Claire. Her vacant stare in the photos of her at the time haunted me. I was never going to understand why she didn't say anything then, when she had a chance to help Mitchell. Truth was, she wasn't saying anything now. She didn't come to the vigil and had remained scarce. Gamble told me it was like pulling teeth getting her to talk. Ronna sat in the room with her along with a state-appointed attorney. Apparently the only thing she really said was that she didn't want to think about it anymore.

Dan didn't admit to killing anyone, or even touching a hair

on the boys' heads, but he said it was his idea to "do something." Those were his words. "Do something." J.P. told his whole story, much like he was proud of it.

In the end, I was treated almost as if it had been my relation who'd done it, my kin. I was contagious what with my thirst for knowledge. I really don't think people want to know what happened if it at all makes them feel complicit. How do three little boys get murdered in the middle of the evening right after Thanksgiving and then nothing is done about it for nearly two decades? Faber prided itself on its sense of community. There was a collective community responsibility that went completely ignored. I think I reminded people of that—especially people at the police station who'd made it their life's work to dish out responsibility in precise amounts. I wasn't charming enough for "The Charming Place" anymore.

Alaina was not being held in jail but had posted bail and was looking to make some sort of arrangement with the prosecutor's office—the events in question having happened so long ago. Ronna circulated a memo citing that Nazi war criminals were still facing punishment for the atrocities committed during the war, some sixty years earlier. She put a picture of Alaina on the flyer with the words *Nazis Must Pay* in bold, striking font. Larson Gamble collected the handouts and had a talk with Ronna about her personal investment in the outcome of Alaina's "situation," as we were calling it. Duke Pendley had offered to pay back in full all of the money he'd been given by way of a donation to the Faber Public Library which was already a brand-new, county-funded building where nary an expense had been spared. It was decided that because Faber was such a small town and did not need another brand-new library, the money would go to making improvements at the police station instead. Pendley said he wasn't a frequent library user and hadn't known the local branch had so recently been rebuilt. He tore up his check to the library fund and wrote a new one to the Faber PD.

Ronna wanted both Pendley and Alaina jailed. She even suggested a Soviet work camp she heard was operating in Alabama. She said all these things in my presence but not to me. Maybe her reluctance to continue our friendship had been because I had somehow let her down, disappointed her with this outcome. Claire had not been entirely absolved. That was the only reason Ronna cooperated with me in the first place; she'd wanted Claire cleared.

Claire had also withheld pertinent investigative information, impeded police procedure, lied to authorities. For Ronna, it was a failure unless Claire was canonized by the local Catholic church, who Ronna seemed to think determined a person's worth even though she was not Catholic and—I think—had Catholics confused with another denomination. She told me Catholics were strict vegetarians one day when trying to make a case for Alaina's public execution. I wasn't sure, so I didn't argue. Ronna showed me the sainthood application she was filing on Claire's behalf. "Claire's Christian but I know she wants to be a saint too," Ronna explained.

She would talk to me in this way—as long as nothing personal was shared between us, we could talk about other people. When I asked her how her workouts were going, she pretended not to hear me and said she needed a Tums.

It was as though I'd put a lid on myself; it quieted me. I didn't have the strong, pulsing ambition I'd once had. Now I was thinking about getting my library sciences degree so I could spend more time reading, and also because librarians seemed very well-dressed in Faber. Draping clothing with a lot of heavy jewelry ruled the day at the Faber Public Library. I only noticed because Duke Pendley's gesture had been in vain, and we were all made aware of the millions that had recently been spent on the new facility. I made a point of going over and checking it out. I was duly impressed with the women who worked there. I thought these were my kind of people. And I had to admit I'd been more fulfilled reading and researching the crimes against the Broderick boys than I was when we started to untangle the knot. There was a quiet letdown in the discovery. No one was as fascinating as I'd hoped, no one as complicated. It was the dregs of the earth, tearing up through the soil like starved worms, who did this. There wasn't a single interesting thing about J.P. Callahan. I laid eyes on him a few times while they were bringing him in and out of the station. He was always handcuffed and looking down. I don't know what I expected to feel; I felt nothing. I decided I would become more interested in the Broderick kids and Mitchell Wright and that I would stop thinking about J.P. Callahan entirely. Dan Wright was a different story, because he fought his bad rap with all the determination he could muster, and then some. He wouldn't let it go—that he didn't intend for what happened to happen. According to Gamble, that would be up to the attorneys and the judge to sort out. I was apathetic.

"What the hell did he think was going to happen?" I'd asked Tommy of Dan Wright. "You lie down with pigs, you get up smelling like shit." We talked about the case in fits and starts. Tommy was trying to redirect my attention like a child who'd been told she couldn't have a toy at the supermarket. Look, Arlene! Shampoo! I wouldn't be redirected. "I don't know how he can think we'd believe he just stood there idly by while J.P. Callahan was dosing those kids. What? Did I just emerge from under a rock yesterday?"

"Maybe he didn't know what Callahan was doing," Tommy offered. We'd go out to eat to ease the tensions at home but find more tension in the restaurant.

"The waitress hates me," I'd declare when the wrong dressing accompanied my Cobb salad. "She thinks I dragged that family through the mud. No sirree, they dragged themselves." I'd slammed my palm down on more than a few tables in central Faber.

Tommy said we should go on a vacation. "You wanted to go to North Carolina," he said. "We could rent a cabin or stay in a lodge."

"Or Ohio," I suggested.

"Huh?" Tommy was now equally afraid of the waitstaff. They'd brought him the veggie plate instead of the burger and shoestring fries he'd ordered. "She does have a real mean look in her eye," he said of our server. "Do you think she knows I hate squash?"

"She don't know nothin'," I said. I felt like Ronna for a second, but only when her guard was down. It comforted me at the same time it rolled a wave of heavy sadness over my head, forcing me under.

"We can go to a lodge," Tommy said again.

"Yeah, I guess."

The time at home was sour, empty, barren. I got to thinking about having children again. Tommy and I had never stopped trying. That train just kept rolling down the tracks, barreling along, never even braking for a station. I hadn't even had a scare. Just one month after another of regularity, steadiness, dependability.

I decided to go and sit in on one day of Dan Wright's trial. I wouldn't allow myself to dignify J.P. Callahan with an appearance. I thought I might spit on him if I got too close. I'd made myself listen to the tapes of J.P.'s interviews. He was a hollow man, nothing but bone and skin. All the soft stuff on a person was air on him. He was filled with nothingness. The way he talked was like a regular person with normal concerns like the price of gas or man-the-grass-isn't-growing-this-year. He had no mood at all. I was like a barometer with people usually. If I wasn't really tightly wound in my own knot, I could get a read on people pretty good just from the way their face either did or didn't match their mouth. Listening to J.P. Callahan, even though I wasn't watching him, all I heard was someone who had no idea. He just didn't see it the way I did. He didn't see himself at all. I wondered if he showed up in the mirror. I couldn't bear the sight of him, so I stayed away, but I did let myself go and sit for Dan Wright. I had a fool's pity for the man. I had a fool's pity for all of them. It was like it was a pity I couldn't better understand them, and that was foolish of me.

Dan Wright was an old man, whether or not he meant to be or he could even get the senior discount at the movie theater. He had frost-white hair, in between silver and gray, translucent almost. His eyes were dark and his mouth turned up on one side, down on the other. He was hunched and trying to make himself invisible. All I'd heard was that his defense team was going to try to pin more of the blame on Claire, try to make it seem as though she was there long enough to have stopped it, that Dan wasn't the assailant; it had been J.P. while the boys went along with it because Claire was there—their sister.

Callahan wouldn't budge though and said Claire only showed up at the end, was stricken, and more or less ran away. He wouldn't throw Claire under the bus, no matter how little it affected his case. He also wouldn't let Dan Wright off the hook.

Dan was not going to testify. Alaina was also in the courtroom, as was Natalie and who I assumed must be Mrs. Wright. They were people hardened, polished to a shine so tight one false move would shatter it. I heard the prosecutor's opening statement and felt, once again, that this was all my fault. He called Dan Wright vain and prejudiced, so disgusted by his son's relationship with a "townie" that he was willing to try to kill her and her family. The prosecutor said it was but by the grace of God that Claire didn't end up dead too. Alaina shook her head during much of his speech. Natalie and his wife were expressionless. I looked for who might be Lucy, but I saw no one who would match her age with the Wrights. I'd been told Carter Broderick went to J.P. Callahan's trial. Carter was my age and living in Tennessee; he'd grown up in Jodupur, then Revel with Claire. He was her one true love, and she never let him suffer a day, it was said. Apparently Carter was going to give a statement to the court at the sentencing.

Dan Wright's lawyer spoke more plainly, gruffly even. He said Dan made an offhand, casual comment to a violent, habitual offender and sociopath, and that when the two men met, Dan was as surprised to see the children there as he was to see J.P. with rags and tranquilizer. He claimed there had never been a plan, never an agreement as to what was going to happen, only Dan saying he wished something could be done about the Brodericks, because—as he saw it and as the lawyer said—"they were ruining his son's life."

J.P. Callahan had a rap sheet a couple of pages long—sex with a minor a few times, solicitation, snatch and grab at the Sears. He'd been in some bar fights and hung out around people's houses, giving them the creeps and compelling them to call the cops just to get him to leave them alone. Dan Wright was an empty slate. His lawyer made sure to reiterate that several times.

"A man completely knocked off-balance said the wrong thing to the wrong person at the wrong time and ended up witnessing a triple homicide in Deck River. He should have reported it. He should have turned himself in, should have offered himself as a witness. He didn't, because he was scared. His son was arrested not four hours after it happened and was dead less than two weeks later. There wasn't an opportunity to set the record straight."

I stood up and left at that part. This was my beef with Claire too. They should have said something, reported it immediately, shot J.P. Callahan in the head for all I cared, but to stay silent was a sin against God's most holy covenant. You'd never convince me otherwise, and I wasn't even sure I believed in God anymore. Not after this.

Alaina followed me out of the dingy courtroom. I'd never once set foot in the county courthouse and was stunningly unimpressed when I finally did. A relic from the early seventies all done up in mustard and pale brown, it sat at the back of an enormous parking lot with nary a tree in sight. The benches squeaked with every twitch of a body, and the ceilings were low and made up of stained fiberglass panels. I hoped to never enter the building again.

"Arlene!" Alaina called after me. She could tell I'd seen her and wasn't waiting up. "Arlene! Wait!"

"What?" I said, turning around to face her, galled by her insistence on talking to me. "What do you want?"

"I didn't know." She was breathless, which I found inexplicably irritating.

"You know Ronna'd like to see you hanged?" I said.

"What?" Alaina ran her hand through her hair. "Are we still hanging people in Faber?"

"You've all got another thing coming. I'm glad I'm not in charge of the hereafter. I'm not sure I could be kind." I turned on my heel and walked out the door. She trailed after me for a bit but gave up. The sliding doors opened for me—almost as though commanded by God as he'd been on my mind—then banged shut in the middle of one of Alaina's calls for me to slow down.

I walked to my car, got in, slammed the door, and waited. It was late winter; we were past the holidays, having taken breaks from prosecuting violent criminals and liars so people could make a roast and buy gifts for their grandkids. I'd picked out a new suit for Tommy, then apologized when he opened it. "That's so ugly," I said as he pulled it from the packaging with a wide, expectant smile on his face. He got me a new pair of diamond earrings, which I still hadn't worn.

I started to cry, but it was a frustrated, abrasive kind of crying, and I found the more I got into it, the more it took on a life of its own.

"Is there a dog in that car?" I heard someone say behind my Mercedes's rear window. "I hear barking."

After about twenty minutes of gasping for air and trying to remain conscious, I drove home. Tommy was there. He'd started coming home for lunch so he could make a salad and "avoid the booze." No more trips to Morrison's Cafeteria by his lonesome. That's apparently what he'd been doing as of late: hitting the buffet by himself, then grabbing a to-go cup of Coke and dumping Jack Daniel's in it when he got in the car. He admitted this to me like I would think it was funny. I didn't. Now he was eating at home— raw vegetables and seltzer water.

"How's the salad?" I asked upon entering. He made a good salad; I had to give him that. He used odd vegetables that most people skip over, like radishes and raw green beans cut into tiny pieces. He was looking healthier with a nice sheen to his face that made me think he was getting all his nutrients. A lot of his pants that had spent the better part of six months bracing for impact with his rear end were starting to sag again.

"S'good." He smiled. There was a bit of spinach stuck to his left incisor.

"I'm gonna get us some foster kids," I said. "Let's face it, you can't put any gas in my tank, or my engine's no good—one or the other. I want to help some kids like those Brodericks. I'm near sick to my stomach about their short lives, the apathy—the sheer apathy."

"Sure." Tommy shrugged.

"I think if I was a foster kid, I'd like living with us," I said.

"Me too!" Tommy was cheerful and encouraging. "Thank God we got the bigger car. You'll need the room."

"Yes," I said.

My last official day at the precinct had included donuts,

tea, and a lot of strange sighing and weak hugs. Ronna stayed at her desk, claiming she'd broken her ankle on the way to work that morning and could not join us. When Gamble said we could move the farewell to the lobby, she said she was in too much pain.

———

When I was a teenager, long after my brother Bobby died, I put a picture of him on the dashboard of my car, right next to the mileage ticker. I made an oval with masking tape and pressed it there, so Bobby could watch me drive. I always thought it was the greatest honor to ride in the front of someone's car, like a prized trinket hanging from a rearview, or the favorite child, or a spouse. I didn't move Bobby's picture to my new car after I got married. I kept it, but I didn't tape it to the dash. He must have thought I forgot about him. He died the same year as the Broderick boys, even if I didn't know it at the time.

I'd swiped Cedar's, Colton's, and Chase's school photos from the file and kept them in the drawer on my nightstand. No one noticed they were missing, which was no surprise. One day, after the trials, I grabbed the pictures, ran down the stairs and out to my car where I arranged them in front of my fuel gauge and speedometer. I promised I would not forget them, and I swear their cheery, innocent, untarnished smiles got wider right there before my very eyes. I put Bobby's picture right next to theirs, and then Mitchell's basketball photo, which I'd also taken from the precinct. It was about a year after that that we moved into the stucco house on Lake Patton. I dumped my coffee in the grass every morning. It did wonders for its luster.

LOOKING FOR MORE
LO PATRICK?
KEEP READING FOR
AN EXCERPT FROM
HER DEBUT NOVEL,
THE FLOATING GIRLS.

CHAPTER 1

We moved into the house on Hack Road when I was a baby. I don't remember anything about being a baby or moving to Hack Road, but it's where I lived my whole life. My father built the place with his own two hands and "no help from anyone else!" It wasn't even true—he had lots of help, but this was the Whitaker way. I laid claim to good deeds or impressive projects that took no sweat from my brow too. I once took credit for cutting steel for the Walton Waterway Bridge that led to denser land across the bay. I wasn't even born when it went up.

My family didn't live close to the road, but addresses were hard to come by in Bledsoe, so we said we were on the road anyway. We chose our own address: 1234 Hack Road. All options were available. Imagination was also hard to come by here.

We were a ways back, hiding under a large oak tree that my mother called a Spanish moss. A fragile woman, she was not so eagerly corrected. *It's an oak*, no one seemed willing to tell her. *Live oak*. We kept quiet when she was wrong; she might shatter.

We were a solitary type of family without a lot of people around to tell us the right names of trees or other useful things. My mother was the quietest woman my father knew; he used to say it all the time. "Sue-Bess, you're the quietest woman I know." She would nod silently, hoping to keep her title.

People don't really give their children names like Sue-Bess anymore. Those were simpler times meant to be complicated by hyphens and awkward combinations. Now, we're one-named people, except for my sister, Sarah-Anne, who got extra because of her hair. Blond hair has always made a favorable impression on my mother. One name was not enough for hair like that. My name is Kay—mouse hair gets only three letters.

My brothers are Peter and Freddy. My sister who died was Elizabeth. I was almost two years old when it happened. Sarah-Anne was coming up on four. Elizabeth died from being born too early. I came the day I was supposed to. If only I had known what would happen if Elizabeth tried to pop out before her time, I would have told her to stay put. Elizabeth was my parents' last, best chance. There were to be no more Whitakers after we went to her funeral in the yard outside our house. Under the oak. Under the Spanish moss.

We lived in Bledsoe, Georgia. It's a place and a culprit. I know there were seasons, but all I can remember is heat and rot and people sitting, just sitting. Inside, outside, under a tree, in a tree, with cold drinks sweating in their hands, wet cloths on their sweating heads, their feet in a bucket of ice water (my father's favorite), or just lying half-dead-like, roasting like a pig on a spike. Begging God for a cloud.

Grown-ups love to talk about weather, but in Bledsoe, the kids joined in too. The heat gave us a whole new vocabulary and a lot of passion to use it. When I heard the grown-ups go on about it being warm and needing rain, or "we're flooded," or "the trees'll fall over," or "the roots'll dry up," or "the dust'll choke us to death," or this and that, I was compelled to join in: "Woe is me! Hotter than the dickens!" "I'm on fire out here!" "Soles of my shoes turning to butter today!" "More sweat than sense, I'll say!" I did say it was "hot as shit" once, but I got popped for that. I could feel it in my jaw for a long time after. It kept me honest. Honestly quiet. My daddy did the popping while my mother set the good examples.

It took a solid six minutes to run from Hack Road to our house. I timed myself once with a stopwatch that my oldest brother, Peter, got for Christmas. For a while there, he timed everything—even how long it took him to go to the bathroom, both ways—but my father put a stop to that and wiped the watch down with a wet cloth. I was eight years old when he got the watch, ten when I timed myself running from Hack Road to our house, and twelve when I timed myself running from our house to the house I never knew was there, which was exactly nineteen minutes from Hack Road and thirteen minutes from my house.

"I'm just gonna see how far I can run without stopping!" I called out to Peter one afternoon.

"Suit yourself, but don't die of heat exhaustion."

It was August. This is when things got a little dire. Typically you made it through July by pretending to like the heat and wading in salty marsh water with its slimy bottom. "This is nice!" I'd say to no one in particular. "How refreshing! Heat's good for the soul!" Sometimes you just sat down in the creek that went all the way to Dune River and let water run over your privates, which are definitely the hottest part of the body besides the head. By August, none of that did any good. You were as hot as a firecracker, and even the night didn't cool you off. We lived on miles of shoreline, but there were no beaches—just dirt vanishing into liquid. There was no white sand in Bledsoe, and no one came there for vacation. The ocean was for fishing and isolation only.

Freddy was a year and a half older than me, so we were a little too close in age to like each other much. Peter was almost four years older and always a good influence. Sarah-Anne was in the middle of the boys. My parents must have been busy for a time. We were very close in age and proximity, and we didn't have a lot to occupy us in such barren lands. There was a good deal of rabble-rousing. Whenever we got going, my father told us to cool our jets and sent us outside, so that we wouldn't disturb my mother, who was in a near-constant delicate state. Sarah-Anne wasn't included in group punishments—probably because of her hair.

"I'm goin' out for track next year," I said as I did some warm-up stretches before my timed run.

"Middle school track is a joke," Peter said. He played basketball at school, which was not a joke. We watched *Hoosiers* at least four times a week. Peter had said he wanted to walk down the aisle at his wedding to the theme song.

"But the dad's a drunk!" I had argued.

"Lotsa people are drunks, Kay," Freddy had said. Freddy liked to read more than most people and, because of this and other character flaws, was a know-it-all. He knew how to either rile you up or calm you down with his knowledge. No, you couldn't die from holding in your pee; yes, many people have a fear of being kicked by a horse; no, an overbite wasn't a serious medical condition; yes, alcohol could kill you if you drank it like a pig at the trough; no, Sarah Anne wasn't a mute.

Fear and loathing of alcoholism was a common topic in our home. My mother grew up in a house with a "buncha drunks," so we heard a lot about what the bottle can do to people with the few words she spoke to us. I was so convinced that booze was at the root of all problems, I even got to telling people that the neighbor's dog was a drunk. "Dog's drunk!" I would holler when that obnoxious mutt got going full throttle at six o'clock in the morning.

My father had ordered me to keep my voice down. The neighbors lived almost a mile away, but their dog liked peeing in our weeds. He was over a lot with his leg lifted and his mouth open like he was choking on something. Even if he was a total pain in our ass, my father didn't want me yelling at the neighbors' dog. One of the brothers next door had an AK. My father said he heard it banging when they thought we weren't home.

"I'm never gonna get drunk," I had promised often and loudly. My mother wore a pleased expression along with her sundress whenever we made promises to avoid evils.

I took off at the sound of the small beep that came from the stopwatch. Peter said "Go!" and watched with fierce concentration.

I ran quickly but not at full speed. I knew to pace myself as I planned to go for at least a half hour. Bledsoe is as flat as a table. It goes and goes and goes, but there's no view. The most a person can see is the low-lying brush in front of them. Most of our land had sand for dirt. There was a spot to the left of our house that had good soil, peach-and-blueberry-growing dirt. The farther you went behind our place, the closer you got to the marsh lands. That's where the running got a little tricky. A boy in my third-grade class, Martin Brown, had a waterbed that we used to take turns rolling around on while at his house. He'd invite all the kids over and give us frozen Butterfingers from his parents' fridge like he was paying for our time. When we were done licking our hands, and there weren't any more Butterfingers to give away, we'd play on his bed. I had a hell of a time getting up from that thing; no matter how much I pushed, I just sank deeper. That's how it felt running in the marsh. Your foot would take forever to find something solid to press down on, but the deeper you went meant it was harder to get your foot back out and onto the next step. I had a feeling quicksand was a lot like Bledsoe. I did try to run on Martin's bed once. It was like trucking it over a half-full inner tube with a tear. Damn near impossible, and I was right—it felt the exact same as the marsh behind my house.

We rarely wore shoes in the summer, mostly because of the heat, and because if you went far enough from our house, you'd end up in the water. When we were small, we were deathly afraid of alligators (common, according to Freddy—the fear of them, not gator attacks), but as we got older we knew that if we just kept running, they'd leave us alone. It's when you stop and stare awhile that you give your weakness away—our weakness being flesh and bone. And blood.

I was always in a dress, Sarah-Anne too, which was my mother's doing. She wore them as well. My mother could sew only one thing; we had dozens of dresses with an identical cut but varying fabrics. Obviously my mother's were larger than mine, but Sarah-Anne and I wore the same size. She didn't grow like a weed the way I did. She grew like a frightened potato—back into the soil with all the other potatoes, afraid to show their faces. I never could understand why we ate dirty roots. Sarah-Anne was the mole child.

I kept on running for what felt like an hour and then started to wonder how Peter was going to know to stop the watch when I got to where I couldn't go anymore. It was pure marsh under my feet. My mother and father said we shouldn't go wandering out into the swamp because of snakes, bugs as big as your hand that nobody knew the names for, and briers that could take your toe off with one wrong step—*and* because we didn't know who lived back there. They emphasized that last part. It was in their nature to think that strangers were worse than wildlife.

It was getting deep, and the bottom half of my dress was soaked. I stopped to catch my breath, figuring that a few seconds to adjust my clothes and pull my underwear out of my bottom wasn't necessarily cheating. I could hear what sounded like a broken violin being played not too far from where I was standing. I froze.

"Peter!" I yelled. The music stopped immediately, and I remained very still knowing that I'd both heard something and then not heard it anymore. "Peter!" I called again. There was some rustling and then the sound of splashing about twenty yards from where I was standing. At first, I saw nothing there but a large gathering of high seagrass. Standing in front of a thick blade was a boy about my age. He'd blended in at first, but as my breath slowed down, I was able to make out his shape. He looked at me with a shit-eating grin on his face. If I hadn't known better, I would have said he was expecting me, but his smile evaporated a little as he took me in. I hated to disappoint someone so keen on standing in the water, so I waved. He took a few steps backward and sat down on a ragged stump before reluctantly lifting one of his hands in a half-hearted greeting. He was holding a guitar in his other hand;

his feet were in the water. I waved again, not sure what else to do. He didn't look a bit familiar. We knew everyone in Bledsoe one way or another, so this was curious enough.

"What's that?" I asked, pointing at the guitar. I knew full well what a guitar was, but I felt like asking what he was doing with it out in the middle of the marsh.

"Guitar," he said, shrugging. He looked over my shoulder for a second.

"Right, but what are you doing with it way out here? Don't seem like you're playin' it right. Got a rotten sound." He looked behind me again. "I'm on my own," I said. "Nobody else comin'."

He shook his head a little, like he was setting himself straight. "Missin' some strings," he said lifting the guitar as he pointed to his left. "I live out here." I turned to see a small house on stilts, like a lady in heels, sitting right there in the middle of the reed grass. Beyond that sat a thick group of mangroves—my mother hated them fiercely. She said it was against nature for a tree to grow in the water. I usually shuddered at the sight of them, in direct imitation of my mother. She could shudder the wings off a ladybug. It didn't seem like he was going to say anything else, as was common in this weather. Words were few and far between in late August without air conditioning or a hope in the world.

READING GROUP GUIDE

May contain spoilers. We recommend not reading these questions until you've finished the book.

1. Why do you think Arlene became so obsessed with the Broderick case?

2. Pregnancy loss carries a lot of stigma in our society, and Arlene is clearly grieving the loss of her pregnancy. Why do you think there is still so much stigma when it comes to people talking about or expressing their grief in the wake of a pregnancy loss?

3. Why do you think Ronna didn't disclose to Arlene that she knew Claire and the Brodericks?

4. Why do you think Arlene was so committed to getting both Ronna and Alaina to help her with the investigation?

5. Do you think Claire was complicit in the deaths of her brothers?

6. In what ways are Arlene and Tommy perfectly suited for each other? In what ways is their relationship an absolute disaster?

7. Arlene seems to seek other people's approval in a big way, particularly at the beginning of the story with Ronna. Why do you think she cares so much about what other people think? And how does her behavior shift over time?

8. Natalie's journal entries are an important part of the story and in solving the case. Did you keep a diary when you were younger? Do you still have it? Are you surprised by some of the things you wrote about?

9. In what ways did Arlene change and grow throughout the story?

10. In the end, do you think Arlene got what she wanted?

The backwaters of Georgia hold many buried secrets.

But they won't stay buried forever.

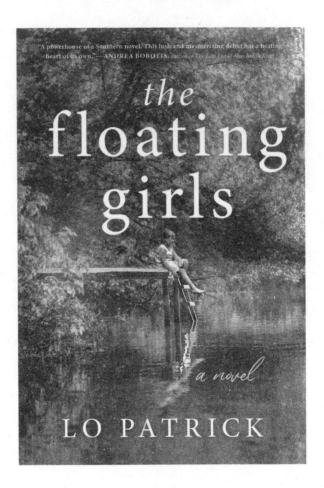

"A powerhouse of a Southern novel. This lush and mesmerizing debut has a beating heart of its own." —ANDREA BOBOTIS, author of *The Last List of Miss Judith Kratt*

the
floating girls

a novel

LO PATRICK

One hot, sticky summer in Bledsoe, Georgia, twelve-year-old Kay Whitaker stumbles across a stilt house in a neighboring marsh, and upon Andy Webber, a boy about her age. He and his father have recently moved back to Georgia from California, and rumors of the suspicious drowning death of Andy's mother years earlier have chased them there and back.

Kay is fascinated and enamored with Andy, and she doesn't listen when her father tells her to stay away from the Webbers. But when Kay's sister goes missing, the mystery of Mrs. Webber's death—and Kay's parents' potential role in it—comes to light. Kay and her brothers must navigate the layers of secrets that emerge in the course of the investigation as their family, and the world as they know it, unravels around them.

"A masterly achievement."

—*Publishers Weekly,* STARRED review

"A powerhouse of a Southern novel."

—Andrea Bobotis, author of
The Last List of Miss Judith Kratt

ABOUT THE AUTHOR

Lo Patrick's first novel, *The Floating Girls*, was a finalist for the Townsend Prize for Fiction and a *Reader's Digest* Editor's Pick. She lives in Georgia with her husband and two children.